SIGHT
UNSEEN

SIGHT UNSEEN

IRIS JOHANSEN

AND

ROY JOHANSEN

ST. MARTIN'S PRESS ❧ NEW YORK

SIGHT UNSEEN. Copyright © 2014 by Johansen Publishing
LLLP. All rights reserved. Printed in the United States of
America. For information, address St. Martin's Press, 175
Fifth Avenue, New York, N.Y. 10010.

www.stmartins.com

The Library of Congress Cataloging-in-Publication Data is
available upon request.

ISBN 978-1-250-02052-9 (hardcover)
ISBN 978-1-250-02053-6 (e-book)

St. Martin's Press books may be purchased for educational, business, or promotional use. For information on
bulk purchases, please contact Macmillan Corporate and
Premium Sales Department at 1-800-221-7945, extension
5442, or write specialmarkets@macmillan.com.

First Edition: July 2014

10 9 8 7 6 5 4 3 2 1

For Cecilia Aiko Oliveira Johansen.

Always remembered, forever loved.

SIGHT
UNSEEN

PROLOGUE

DAMN, SHE WAS GOING to kill him.

Gary Decker turned onto Market Street and gave the accelerator some extra juice. On this of all nights, he hadn't wanted to be late picking up Corrine. She had arranged dinner and drinks with friends at Nobu, an occasion she had pitched as a casual get-together. But he knew better. It was another attempt to parade him before her friends and convince them that he wasn't the jerk they all thought he was.

Screw 'em. He was marrying Corrine, not those immature losers.

He smiled. With an attitude like that, how could he not win them over?

Ah, hell. He could do this. He did the dog and pony show for his firm's obnoxious clients; he could do it for his fiancée's judgmental college pals.

He called Corrine as he pulled up to her Sabre Springs home, surprised that she hadn't already phoned to give him an earful for being so late.

His call went straight to voice mail.

He glanced up at the two-story Spanish-style house. Dark. Had she gotten pissed and left without him?

He cut the engine and walked toward the front door. He knocked. No answer. He pulled out his key and let himself inside.

Soft classical music wafted from the stereo in the living room.

Weird. Not Corrine's style at all.

He called softly, "Honey?"

No answer.

He moved into the living room. What little light there was came from a single lamp in the corner.

The classical music became softer.

Gary froze when he saw Corrine. She was seated on the sofa, dressed like an uptight business executive in her tweed jacket and skirt. Her hair was pulled back, and she wore oversized black spectacles.

Definitely not Corrine's usual style. She managed a funky La Jolla art gallery, and her attire, during work and after, often consisted of Capri slacks and a tie-dyed T-shirt.

Gary smiled. "Hey, you didn't tell me we had to wear costumes tonight. What are you supposed to be, a corporate lawyer?"

No response.

Damn, she *was* pissed.

Okay, he'd better be both humble and persuasive.

He moved closer to her. "Don't get me wrong. I kind of like those glasses. Maybe you can wear them for me later?" He sat down next to her and gently rubbed her thigh.

Cold. So cold.

He stiffened. "Honey . . . ?"

He pulled the glasses from her face. Her bloodshot eyes were wide open and stared back at him.

Only then did he notice the bruising on her neck.

Oh, God.

He jumped to his feet and stumbled backward.

Holy shit!

Corrine. Dead.

It was even harder to believe since this . . . *thing* didn't even look like her.

He fumbled for his phone, his hands shaking.

Something snapped around his neck.

Shit!

Choking . . . Must fight . . .

No air.

Must break free . . .

He felt his attacker's hot breath in his ear.

Darkness creeping over him . . .

It wasn't just breath, he realized as the darkness overtook him.

It was his killer's laughter.

CHAPTER 1

"NICE TO MEET YOU, KENDRA. Sorry I'm late. I'm Dean Halley."

Kendra Michaels stood and shook hands with the handsome man who had just dashed into the Gaslamp Bar and Restaurant. She was experiencing a sinking feeling. Halley's smile was a couple shades too white. He was also too good-looking and too well dressed. He breathed casual elegance and easy charm.

Mom, what have you gotten me into?

Halley's brows rose. "You are Kendra, right?"

"Yes." She forced a smile. "Sorry I had to cancel last week. Things got complicated."

He shrugged. "It happens. But we're here now, so that's what matters."

He was also too polite.

Oh, for God's sake, give the guy a break.

It was her mother's first attempt at arranging a blind date, and anyone but Kendra would have said that she'd done well.

Of course, the evening was still young.

Kendra had come straight from the office, where she had conducted five music-therapy sessions back-to-back. Her clients couldn't have been more different from each other, ranging in age from eight months to ninety-two years. Her techniques varied for each patient, with simple mood-soothing music for some, with more complex exercises to draw out others who were autistic and emotionally withdrawn. Not all would respond to her techniques, but she had high hopes for a few of them. Despite the presence of this charming and too-perfect man in front of her, she wanted nothing more than to go home and write up her impressions while the sessions were still fresh in her mind.

Don't let him see it. She had promised Mom. She smiled. "Yes, that's all that matters."

They took a booth in the bar and placed their drink orders. Dean drummed his fingers on the tabletop. "Your mother told me a lot about you, but I forgot almost all of it instantly."

Now that was both honest and promising. "You sure know how to flatter a girl."

"It's not because I wasn't interested. I was. But after she told me you used to be blind, I had trouble thinking about anything else."

Way to go, Mom. "She actually led with that?"

"Good salesmanship. I was intrigued."

"I don't need anyone to sell me. What you see is what you get."

"Of course you don't. Poor choice of words. I'm sure you're as leery of setups as I am. What exactly did she say to convince you to go out with me?"

"She said if I didn't, she would use her keys to scratch disparaging things about me on the hood of my car."

He smiled that charming smile again. "She didn't really say that."

"She did. And she said she would let all my plants die the next time I had to attend an overseas conference. So you see, I had little choice."

"Now it's my turn to be flattered."

"I think she was joking, at least about the car."

"This would make some interesting fodder for the next departmental dinner. Do you mind if I tell the other faculty members?"

She smiled. "I wish you would. Though from what I understand, it probably wouldn't surprise anyone. Ask around. She's made quite a reputation for herself."

He chuckled. "You're right about that."

Dean and her mother, Professor Diane Michaels, were both history professors at the University of California Campus in La Jolla. Mom had been cooking up this date practically from the time Halley had taken over the post the previous spring. But as Kendra's eyes darted over him, she went still with surprise.

How . . . interesting. Did Mom have any idea that Halley—?

"So you were born blind?" he asked.

She sipped her wine, still trying to process her observations. "Yes. And I stayed that way for the first twenty years of my life."

"Incredible. And two surgical procedures later, you now see perfectly."

"I don't know perfectly, but well enough. Probably better than you without your contact lenses."

He raised his eyebrows. "If you could see that in this lighting, then you're doing all right."

She nodded toward the bar's street window. "Car headlights helped. My mother actually deserves most of the credit for how I turned out. I never felt handicapped. I learned to use what I had."

"And you gained your sight from some kind of stem-cell procedure?"

She nodded again. "In England. They did a lot of the early work in ocular regeneration. It was an amazing time of my life, and a little overwhelming."

"I can only imagine."

No, he couldn't even begin to imagine, and Kendra didn't want to talk about it. She glanced up at a large TV over the bar. A live remote newscast was at the scene of a horrific traffic accident, and the reporter was struggling to make sense of the carnage and twisted metal strewn over the roadway.

Dean turned to see what had grabbed her attention. "Quite a pileup."

She nodded, her gaze narrowed on the screen. A helicopter shot of the scene showed that the roadway was covered with work lights, police cars, and fire trucks, and was atop a tall white bridge.

She suddenly straightened in her chair.

Then she stood up and stepped closer to the television. Dean quickly joined her at the bar.

"The Cabrillo State Bridge," she said, studying the overview that the helicopter shot offered.

"The one that goes toward the zoo?"

She nodded. "Those *idiots*. They're treating it like an accident."

He turned toward her. "Why wouldn't they?"

"Because it's not an accident."

Dean laughed, but cut it short when he realized she was serious. "Um, why do you think that?"

Kendra was still staring at the television and shook her head in disgust. "They're blowing it. I can't believe it. They're totally blowing it."

"I still don't get how—"

Kendra muttered a curse beneath her breath. "I wish we'd never seen this damn thing."

"I'm starting to wish that, too," he said dryly. "Want me to ask the bartender to change the channel?"

"No."

"Come on, let's go back and sit down. I'll tell you all about myself." He tried to take her arm, but she remained planted at the bar.

"I know quite a bit already," she said absently, her gaze still locked on the television. "I know you've been to prison."

He froze. "What?"

Her eyes narrowed on the screen when another camera angle came on the screen. "When you were younger."

He was silent. "Nobody knows that."

"You grew up in Florida, then spent some time in the Northeast. Maybe your college years? Are you an Ivy Leaguer?"

"You Googled me?"

"What? No, life's too short." She swore again. "I can't believe those damned cops don't see what's right in front of them."

"Let's get back to me for a second. Does your mother know about the prison thing? Because if this got out—"

"Don't sweat it. I didn't know until two minutes ago. I was just looking you over to see what Mom saw in you, and it popped up."

"What else 'popped' up?"

"You're a motorcycle enthusiast. That's where a lot of your time and money goes. Not just riding, but the tinkering. You have a Harley Sportster. I'm thinking you did some degreasing on it today."

"Jesus."

"I take that as a confirmation."

"Either you were spying on me, or you're psychic."

"Neither." She was still concentrating on the screen. "Fools. Not one homicide detective there. Not one. All accident investigators."

Dean smiled. "Your mother said you were very observant and not to let it rattle me. I'm just now realizing what she meant by that. And, for the record, you did rattle me."

"Sorry. Mom always tells me to wait and let things just come out in conversation. I was distracted."

"Don't be sorry. I like it. I'd always heard that blind people develop their other senses to an amazing degree. I guess you're living proof. But it must be more than that."

"I'm a little obsessive. No, a lot obsessive. I now treasure everything that I can see. And I won't let go of what I learned from my other senses when I was blind. I don't take anything for granted."

"I'll accept that answer. But you have to tell me how you knew all those things about me."

"Sure." She pointed to the television screen. "But first I need you to drive me there."

"To the accident?"

"It's not an accident, remember?"

"Now?"

"Yes."

He was silent a moment. "Don't tell me you're one of those fetishists who get off on—"

"Someone needs to talk to them before they break down the scene and destroy evidence." She turned and looked him in the eye. "I walked here. Either you're giving me a ride there, or I'm calling a cab."

"So our date is over?"

"It's only over if you don't give me a ride."

Dean looked back at the television, where the news copter was circling the platoon of emergency workers and their flashing vehicles. He shook his head. "Got to be the weirdest date of my life."

KENDRA'S CELL PHONE RANG WHEN they were on the road only ten minutes. She made a face when she glanced at the ID. "Mom. I was half expecting this."

"Really? We haven't had time for her to wonder if I'm threatening your virtue."

"It's not my virtue Mom's concerned about." She accessed the call. "Hi, Mom. I'm with Dean Halley now. I didn't no-show, and I haven't scared him off yet." She looked inquiringly at Dean. He shook his head. "No, he thinks I'm weird, but he's sticking with me."

"Brave man. I knew I could count on him. He's a fine teacher and a great guy. You have to admit I did a good job of bringing you two together. Now all you have to do is cement the relationship."

"A relationship neither one of us wanted from the beginning. Why, Mom?"

"You know the answer. Dean is steady and wonderfully normal. He's as close to the guy next door as I could find. That's what you need, Kendra. Dean could lead you away from all those police and FBI types and make you enjoy it. He's intelligent, gorgeous, and has a sense of humor. The only thing he'll want from you won't be anything more complicated than sex."

She chuckled. "I told Dean you wouldn't be concerned about my virtue."

"Screw virtue. I'm concerned about your life. I want you safe."

"I know, Mom," she said gently. "And that's the only reason I gave in about tonight. I love you and wanted to give you the chance to play Mother Teresa and save me from myself. You've done that all my life and done a great job. Tell me, are you missing it?"

"Maybe a little. You were my whole life for quite a while." She cleared her throat. "But that doesn't mean that I'm not right in this. Now, do you like Dean?"

"We haven't had time to—" She glanced at Dean. "Yes, I like him. At first, I thought that he was too pretty, but maybe he can't help that. And he doesn't try to dodge, and I think maybe he's honest."

Dean smiled, still staring out the windshield. "You do know I can hear everything you're saying, right?"

"You didn't put him through any hoops?" Diane asked.

"Not intentionally." She had just spotted blinking lights ahead. "Look, Mom, I have to go. I'm in his car and I—"

"You're going out to dinner?" Diane sounded pleased. "That's progress."

"Yes, isn't it? I'll talk to you later, Mom." She hung up.

"You're very close," Dean said quietly. "I thought so when Diane was talking about you to me. But you just confirmed it."

"I love her. She made me what I am. Both physically and mentally."

She grimaced. "Well, maybe not quite. I take full responsibility for my faults and the wild oats I've sown. She had nothing to do with them."

"Wild oats? You're a music-therapy teacher."

"Who after I began to see believed that the wine of life should be tasted to the last drop."

"Really?" He looked intrigued. "Diane never mentioned wild oats to me."

"She wouldn't. You're her idea of the wholesome guy next door. She wouldn't want to scare you away."

"I notice you didn't disillusion her . . . yet."

"No. I'll have to probe a little more." She smiled. "Guy-next-door types generally bore me. It shows a lack of courage to reach out." She held up her hand to stop him from answering. "Later. Those lights up ahead is our destination. We're going to have to run the gauntlet."

"MA'AM, YOU'LL HAVE TO GET BACK in your car and clear out. Authorized personnel only."

Kendra and Dean had driven around the two-mile-long line of stopped cars that extended from the bridge, down Laurel Boulevard and across the 1-5 freeway. A stocky, female traffic cop was holding back the curious onlookers, mostly joggers and dog walkers, angling for a glimpse of the chaotic scene.

Kendra turned back toward Dean, who had just parked his car on the side of the Prado Road that transitioned to the bridge's two-lane roadway. She motioned for him to join her.

The traffic officer glared at him and raised her walkie-talkie as she would a lethal weapon. "Sir, don't even think of leaving your car there. I have a tow truck on speed dial."

Kendra waved him over again. Dean hesitated, then climbed out of the car.

The stocky cop shouted something that was lost in the roar of the circling news'copters. Kendra surveyed the scene behind her. There *had* to be someone she knew here. She had assisted in a few police investigations in the past few years, but none of them involved the accident-investigations cops now on the bridge snapping photos and taping off the scene.

Finally, she saw a familiar face. Lieutenant Wallace Poole, a tall, gangly, bald man who seemed to be doing little other than positioning himself toward the bank of news cameras.

Poole . . .

Kendra tried to remember if she had pissed him off during the Petco Stadium case a couple years before. Not that much, apparently. He stepped closer and waved her through the police line while simultaneously quieting the walkie-talkie-wielding traffic cop. He smiled. "Why, Dr. Michaels, what brings you here?"

"The same thing that brings you. How many fatalities?"

"Four." He gestured back to the three wrecked vehicles on the bridge. "A man and woman in the convertible, a man in the pickup truck, and a woman in the minivan." Poole's eyes narrowed on her face. "I thought you only helped out on murder cases. Who called you in?"

"I'm being rude." Kendra motioned toward Halley. "This is Dean Halley. Care to walk us through it?"

Poole appeared more mystified than before, but he nodded. "Uh, sure." He led them past a fire truck and a line of road flares.

Dean shot her a "what-in-the-hell-are-we-doing" glance, but Kendra was busy scanning the scene in front of her.

The pickup truck, charred and dripping with extinguisher foam, was still smoldering alongside the bridge's right-hand railing. A gray tarp was thrown over the driver's compartment, obviously to conceal a corpse. The convertible BMW was right behind, grill first into the granite railing. The minivan was on its side a few paces behind, also surrounded by mounds of extinguisher foam.

Poole motioned toward the pickup truck. "We figure the driver of the truck lost control and plowed into the bridge. It triggered a chain reaction. The Beamer swerved and hit the stone railing. The van swerved the other way, rolled, and ended on its side."

Kendra nodded. "No one was wearing seat belts?"

"No. That's probably why none of them survived."

"And no air bags deployed?"

"No. The investigators say it's not all that uncommon unfortunately. They get stolen, or if they're deployed once, they're expensive to replace, and some people just don't do it. It's also possible that the crash sensors were faulty, or the trigger wires can get severed early in the crash sequence."

"That took four lives." Kendra leaned toward the BMW 320 coupe. It was easily the most intact of the cars, with no fire and only damaged at the crumpled front end. Two bodies were slumped in the front seat. They were a man and a woman, late twenties, both dressed in buttoned-down business attire, as if they were on their way home from a Fortune 500 board meeting. Blood ran from their heads and was splattered across the windshield. There were two impact shatter points on the glass, one in front of each victim.

"Anything about this look strange to you?" Kendra asked Poole.

"It *all* looks strange to me. What are you getting at?"

"Look at the number of windshield cracks radiating out from the impact points. The number is proportional to impact speed. With the speed that would have been necessary for those skulls to cause these kind of cracks, there should have been much more damage to this car's front end when it struck the railing. I could see that from a barroom TV on Fifth Street. That was the first thing I noticed." She leaned over the windshield and examined it more closely. "May I borrow an evidence glove?"

Poole peeled off his right glove and gave it to her. Kendra slipped it on and rubbed her fingers across the cracks, both inside the windshield and outside. She occasionally closed her eyes, letting her sense of touch guide her in a way that was seldom necessary anymore.

She finally looked up and stepped away. "And, what's more, the force of impact came from outside this windshield, not the inside."

Poole leaned down to look. "Both sides are shattered. How can you tell?"

"There are two kinds of fractures here. Radial fractures, which jut out like the spokes of a wheel, and concentric fractures, which are like a series of circles radiating outward. The concentric fractures are always on the impact side. It's difficult to see which side they're actually on, but you can feel them." She peeled off the glove and handed it to Poole. "Want to try?"

"No thanks. I'll take your word for it."

"Anyway, your forensics guys will back me up." Kendra glanced around. "I take it no one actually saw the accident?"

"No. The zoo and botanical gardens had been closed for hours. There's not a lot of traffic here after dark."

"So what were the victims doing here?"

"Don't know. We've just started notifying the next of kin." He motioned toward the still-circling news'copters." Although some may have found out already." Poole turned to Dean. "What about you? Are you with the media? Who are you again?"

Dean extended his hand. "Dean Halley. History professor. Just along for the ride."

Poole looked at Kendra.

"He doesn't have anything to do with this," she added quickly. "Blind date."

Poole glanced from one to the other. "Huh. And how's it going?"

"Pretty good, I think," Kendra said.

Dean nodded. "Except for the dead bodies. Could have done without that."

Poole stared at Kendra. "Then why in the hell are you here, Dr. Michaels?"

"I didn't want evidence compromised. I'm sure your medical

examiner will tell you this later tonight or tomorrow, but these people didn't die here."

Poole gazed at her for another long moment. "What makes you say that?"

"There would be a lot more blood if they had hit this windshield with enough force to kill them. They both have identical bruising on their necks, as if they were strangled by the same patterned belt or cord."

Poole examined the corpses in the BMW more closely. "And how did you know you would find this?"

"I didn't. But like I said, I could see this accident wasn't what it seemed to be." She pointed to the long skid mark behind the overturned minivan. "This was meant to look like it came from that van, but I don't think it did. If you skid on antilock brakes, the mark looks like a series of dashes, not an unbroken line. Another thing I spotted from the news helicopter."

Pool walked over to the unbroken skid mark and squatted to look at it.

Kendra followed him. "The van burned quickly. There was a Toluene-based accelerant used."

"Toluene?" One of the investigators, whom Kendra had just seen draw a chalk line around a severed hand next to the van, looked up at the word. "As in a solvent for paint?"

"Or for model-airplane glue."

"How do you figure that?"

Kendra grimaced. "I smell it. It's a lot like benzene."

The investigator, a slender man with short gray hair, stood up and sniffed the air. "I'm smelling a lot of things right now, but that isn't one of them."

"Trust me. Take samples and run your tests. These cars were burned intentionally."

The investigator looked at her skeptically. "Trust you? Pardon me for asking, but who the hell are you?"

"Someone you should listen to, Johnson," Poole said. He took Kendra by the arm and guided her away. "Look," he said in a low voice, "I'm going to call in Homicide. Stick around for a few, and I'll have you—"

"No."

"What?"

"I'm not sticking around. This has taken up enough of my evening already. I just wanted to give you a heads-up. Your forensics people can take it from here."

He stared at her in shock. "You can't be serious. You came out here just to—"

"Just to keep you from mistaking a murder scene for an accident. Though I guess I shouldn't blame you too much. It's probably one of the most unusual murder scenes any of you have ever seen." She glanced back. "Although, like I said, I doubt whether any of these people actually died *here*."

"And this doesn't pique your curiosity just a little bit?"

"Sure. I'll keep up with it in the newspaper. Good luck with your investigation."

Poole frowned. "I can make you stay, you know."

Kendra smiled. "On what grounds? Failure to perform police work on command?"

"What about civic duty?"

"I just did it. I told you everything I know. Good night, Poole."

Kendra turned and moved around the forensics techs crouched behind the BMW.

Dean cast another look at the scene as they walked away. "I know you were just trying to impress me back there."

"Did it work?"

"Of course, but it was totally unnecessary. You had me at 'prison.' You still owe me an explanation for that, you know."

She took a quick look over her shoulder. Poole was still glaring at her. "Later. Right now, we'd better get to your car before Poole has it towed. He isn't very happy with me at the moment."

THEY DROVE BACK TO KENDRA'S condominium complex in less than fifteen minutes.

"You were amazing," Dean said, as he walked her to the building's front door. "The cops thought so, too. You could see it on their faces."

"Trust me, those expressions can turn sour in a hurry. Especially if they think I'm making them look bad. Poole only wanted me to stick around because he knew his superiors wouldn't have believed that he'd come up with those answers."

He nodded. "I can imagine there would be problems. But why aren't you interested in following up? Seems like a pretty interesting case."

"I already have a job. It's a lot more positive and fulfilling to me than what those people are doing on that bridge tonight."

"Music therapy."

"Yes. I help people. And I conduct research and publish papers that help *others* help people." She unlocked the door. "Anyway, thanks for the ride. I'm sure this wasn't the evening you had in mind."

"It was better." He grinned. "Sure beats first-date small talk."

"Not sure what I can do to top it. You want to quit while we're ahead?"

"No way." He stepped closer to her.

She couldn't deny how likeable she found him. She was happy at that response. She smiled. "Well, you have my number."

"Whoa, whoa, whoa. I'm not saying good night until you explain a few things to me. Let's start with my bike. How did you know about that?"

"You have helmet head."

He ran his hands through his hair. "Impossible. I've washed my hair a couple times since the last time I wore a helmet."

"Not your hair. Your skin. You have a clean tan line around your neck, and an inverted "U" that frames your face. And there's a slight singe on the inside right leg of those jeans you're wearing, right about knee level. The Harley Sportster's rear exhaust pipe would hit you about there every time you have your foot off the pedal at a long stoplight."

"Just the Sportster?"

"There are others, but that's probably the most popular one. And the Harley Davidson sunglasses tucked into your shirt clinches it a bit more."

He laughed and patted the sunglasses dangling from his neckline. "Do you ride?"

"I used to run with a pretty wild crowd, and I sometimes rode with them." She raised her right pant leg and showed a small burn scar on her inside right calf. "It's never a good idea to ride a motorcycle in shorts."

"And here I was thinking you were so brilliant."

"Well, it only happened once. I'm a fast learner."

"I have no doubt."

"And I caught a whiff of Castrol Simple Green on you. That's how I knew you were doing some degreasing today."

"Actually, it was yesterday. And I've showered since then."

"Were you wearing those shoes when you were working on it?"

He looked down at his brown walking shoes. "Maybe."

"And you'd be surprised how long our skin can hold on to odors, shower or no shower. It's like a big sponge."

"Okay. And how did you know where I'm from?"

She shrugged. "Your speech. You have a Central Florida dialect, peppered with an adult New England influence."

He stared at her for a moment. "An adult New England influence?"

"If you'd moved there when you were younger, it would have a different sound. It would have had a different effect on the speech patterns you've been practicing since birth. I figured you moved there around college age."

He nodded. "You're right. But not quite Ivy League. Boston U. So you're a linguistics expert, too."

"Not really. Like you, I've met thousands of people in my life. From an early age, I got into the habit of listening and matching what I heard with what I found out about them. When you can't see, you use what you have."

He nodded, then paused. "Okay, now tell me what I really want to know."

"Prison."

"I've taken steps to make sure that period of my life won't get in the way of my future. I didn't think anyone in the city was aware of it, and I'd like to keep it that way."

She tilted her head. "I'll make you a deal. Tell me what you were in for, and I'll tell you how I knew."

"You got it."

She took his left hand and angled it into the entranceway light. "I'm sure almost no one would notice this, but there's a very faint tattoo remnant here, between your thumb and forefinger. You obviously tried to have it removed."

"You're right. Almost no one notices. And if they do, they see that it's a box filled with an X. Like a strike on a bowling score sheet. Not like any prison tattoo I've ever seen."

"And that was your intention when you tattooed over the five dots that were originally there. Five dots. One in the middle representing the prisoner, four more on each corner representing the prison. A pattern that's almost always tattooed on the hand between the thumb and forefinger. It's the placement that gives it away more than anything else."

"How do you know so much about prison tats?"

"Like I said, I used to run with a rough crowd." She looked him in the eye. "Your turn."

He jammed his hands in his pockets and glanced away from her. "Well, you're right. I had a drug problem in grad school, and I got in so deep that I supported my habit by selling some to my fellow students. Really stupid. I went away for thirty months. I got clean, got my Ph.D., and never looked back."

"Except when you look at your hand. There are probably ways to get rid of that tattoo more completely these days."

"It's okay." He held up his hand and looked at it. "Sometimes it's good to remember what an idiot I can be. You know?"

She nodded. "I know."

"So may I still call you?"

Kendra studied him. She liked Dean's forthright manner. No excuses, no tap dancing around the mistakes he had made and clearly regretted. She also appreciated that dry sense of humor and his lack of intimidation when she'd virtually ruined the possibility of a normal evening. Mom was right, he was a good guy. She smiled. "Sure. Call me."

"Great." He kissed her on the cheek, turned, and headed back down the sidewalk toward his car.

MYATT READJUSTED HIS BINOCULARS as he shifted in the tall grass. He had found a spot that offered him an excellent view of the Cabrillo State Bridge. Close enough to see what was going on, far enough away that he could watch undetected.

He panned across the bridge, taking in the scene.

The wrecked cars.

The smoldering van.

The elegantly dressed corpses.

It was beautiful.

Kendra Michaels's visit had thrown the cops into a tizzy, and the scope of the scene had abruptly changed. They already knew it was more than just an accident. He had expected them to make that discovery later that night or possibly in the morning.

No matter.

If anything, Kendra's appearance was a welcome development. Disappointing that she had left with such an apparent lack of interest, but he'd draw her back in.

The game is on, Kendra.

Even if you don't realize it yet . . .

CHAPTER
2

Seaport Village
San Diego

THE SEVEN-YEAR-OLD GIRL WAS squeezing Kendra's hand so tightly that she threatened to cut off her circulation.

Zoey Beale was a new client whom Kendra had only seen twice before. The child showed signs of agoraphobia; she was terrified of crowds and clearly uncomfortable in any environment other than her home. Zoey did, however, enjoy music, which prompted her referral from a psychologist affiliated with Rady's Children's Hospital. Kendra preferred to meet clients in her studio, but she had made an exception in Zoey's case, bringing a guitar to the girl's home to calm her and build trust over the course of the two initial sessions.

Building trust to take her out of her comfort zone.

The little girl nodded even as her hand squeezed tighter. They walked down the embarcadero and approached Seaport Village, an open-air shopping center by the bay. It was a sunny Saturday afternoon, and the place was already jammed with shoppers and lunchtime restaurant patrons.

And scores of street performers. Perfect.

Three African men stood on the sidewalk playing a soothing melody on their wood pipes. Dressed in orange-and-yellow tunics, they swayed in perfect unison to the music.

Kendra stopped fifteen feet away and glanced down at Zoey. The music had captured her attention. She was transfixed, and after a minute, her iron grip loosened. A minute after that, the crowds and unfamiliar surroundings seemed to melt away.

Kendra pointed ahead. "There are more musicians up there. Want to go see?"

Zoey nodded. As they walked together, Kendra sensed less hesitancy from the little girl.

Good. Come on, Zoey. It can be a wonderful world out here. Let me show it to you.

Two young men were using an assortment of inverted plastic industrial food containers as drums, beating them with kitchen utensils. Zoey obviously liked the rhythms and unusual sounds, and she began bopping her head to the beat. Again, her surroundings seem to fade, but faster this time.

This could work.

This could be the key that Zoey needed to—

The little girl shrieked.

A pair of mimes had jumped in front of her and were doing their usual shtick. They were pretending to be marionettes, jerking in time to the performers' drumbeats.

Kendra pulled Zoey close and shielded her from the creepy spectacle. "It's okay, honey. It's all right."

The mimes approached them, putting on cheerful faces that were probably meant to comfort the girl, but only appeared more weird and frightening.

Kendra leaned close to the mimes and pointed up the embarcadero. "Take that shit somewhere else," she hissed. "Now!"

Zoey was crying. Her mother, Danica, who had been watching behind a vendor cart, ran toward them. "It's okay, baby. It's okay." Danica held her daughter close. "Nothing to be afraid about. Everything's okay."

"I'm sorry," Kendra mouthed.

Danica nodded as she guided her daughter toward the parking lot. Kendra watched them, her fists clenching helplessly.

Dammit.

One step forward, two steps back.

She stood there until Zoey and Danica disappeared from view.

"Can you blame her?"

That voice. That all-too-familiar voice. "Adam Lynch." She turned around to face him.

It was Lynch, all right. Powerful, sexy, dynamic. And he was wearing that movie-star smile that probably melted most women's hearts but just pissed her off. "Hello, Kendra. Good to see you."

Lynch was dressed in slacks, loafers, button-down collar shirt, and a tan jacket. He stood out from the shorts-and-T-shirt crowd who currently inhabited the place. But then he always stood out wherever he was, she thought. It wasn't only the appearance but the aura of magnetism and toughness that he emitted. "Hello, Lynch. My, my, what a surprise."

"Surprise?"

"You know, this doesn't seem like the kind of place you'd go for an afternoon out."

"Really? And where would you see me?"

"Hmm. Maybe playing golf with your fellow government agents, drinking disgusting whiskey drinks, trading war stories, comparing notes on your favorite ammo clips."

He smiled again. "I'd be offended if that wasn't pretty much how I spent last Saturday. You should join us sometime."

"I work on Saturdays."

"Yes, I noticed. Things were going really well with that girl until the mimes showed up." He shrugged. "I could take 'em out for you. You know, for old times' sake."

This made her smile. "There was a time I would have thought you were serious."

"There was a time I *would* have been serious. But that was before you knew me. I've mellowed."

"Not likely." It had been almost a year since she had last seen Adam Lynch. He was a former FBI agent who lately had been working as a freelance operative of choice for a variety of officials in the U.S. Intelligence community. Lynch had recently recruited her for a case that, although overall successful, reminded her how grim and gut-wrenching that line of work could be. She had no desire for a return engagement.

Lynch leaned against a lamppost. "I heard about your show on the bridge last night."

"My show? Is that what they're calling it?"

"It's what I'm calling it. I wish I'd been there. I love watching you in action with all pistons firing."

Kendra nodded. He was wearing that infuriatingly charming smile again. It annoyed her that she could see the appeal even if she fought against it. "Why are you here, Lynch? Why in the hell are you spying on me?"

"'Spying' is such a nasty word. It implies a nefarious purpose, which couldn't be further from the truth."

"Oh, my money is definitely on nefarious. It's in your DNA."

"I wasn't spying. I was waiting for an opportunity to speak to you. I didn't want to interrupt your session. I know how important your work is to you."

"It's everything."

"I read about your study in the *New England Journal of Medicine*," he said. "Your music-therapy techniques are being adopted for autism patients."

"It's all about helping people make connections with the outside world. Whether it's autism or Alzheimer's, music is often the way to reach people and bridge those gulfs. I've been designing protocols to assess the effectiveness of various techniques. It's a young science, but we've made a lot of progress."

"But you did manage to find time to join the Eve Duncan case. I read the file. Amazing investigative work, by the way."

"I only did that because Eve is a good friend. She needed my help."

"You helped save her life. And probably a lot of other lives."

She gestured impatiently. "Why are you here, Lynch?"

"You were right. That accident scene on the bridge last night was staged."

"Tell me something I don't already know."

"The case has been kicked over to the FBI. It has the mark of a serial killer. But you already knew that, didn't you? That was remarkably similar to another case of yours, an old one."

"I don't know if I'd say remarkably similar."

"I would. Multiple murders made to look like an accident. That was Stanley Veers's M.O., was it not? He killed at least fourteen people over a three-year period in Houston and Austin."

"Veers is now on death row in Huntsville Penitentiary."

"Thanks to you. He killed people for years before anyone realized they were murders, not accidents. Serial killers usually like the attention, but not him. He created his own private thrill show. He liked the idea of committing murder right under everyone's noses. I'm sure you thought of him when you were at that crime scene last night."

"Of course I did, though it was more ambitious than anything Veers did. The investigators think the killer may have coned off one end for a few minutes and used a truck to block the other. They're still trying to identify possible staging areas. It's a staggering feat to pull off. But unlike Veers, this one wasn't all that concerned with covering his tracks. He wanted the world to know what he had done."

"But not immediately."

"Probably not. He knew the media would report the accident but that it would soon be revealed as something else. He'd get to have his cake and eat it, too."

Lynch nodded. "That's the way the FBI profilers see it."

"And since when did you become the Bureau's errand boy."

"Errand boy?"

"They sent you to talk me into working with them on this case. Am I right?"

"In a roundabout way. Senior Special Agent Griffin knew better than to contact you directly. You've made your attitude known in no uncertain terms regarding working with them again. He asked some higher-ups in D.C. to have me approach you."

"Roundabout is right. Why did he think you would be any more effective than asking me himself?"

"Because I'm so damn charming and likeable?"

"Next?"

Lynch smiled. "You're not going to make this easy, are you?"

"Of course not."

"I was tasked to talk to you because they thought we worked well together last year."

"Oh. Well, we did."

"You admit it?"

"Of course. Sometimes a sledgehammer is the best tool for the job."

He laughed. "So I'm a sledgehammer. And I guess that makes you a precision-tooled scalpel."

"Well, if you want to push the metaphor . . . yes."

"So be it. The Bureau wants a scalpel to help work this case. And not just any scalpel. They want you."

"You said that you were tasked to talk to me. But I thought you only took jobs you wanted to take. You're a freelancer."

"That's correct. I do only take jobs that interest me."

This time there was no high-wattage smile. Just sincerity and maybe a hint of warmth.

Maybe.

Lynch's nickname in the Bureau has been the Puppetmaster, given for his ability to manipulate people and circumstances to his own ends. He had been able to pull off incredible feats by that skill. Was he manipulating her now? Probably.

He stepped toward her. "Listen, to tell you the truth, I don't give a damn about working on this case. I was only intrigued with the idea of working with you again. You know I always work alone, but that time with you was different, special. I wanted to do it again. If you tell me to go to hell, I won't spend another minute on this investigation. I'm actually in the middle of something else right now."

"Cloak-and-dagger stuff?"

"In a way. But the powers that be thought this was important enough for me to try to bring you in. Aside from your, shall we say, unique skill set, you're one of the few people who've had any success dealing with a killer like this."

"Only because killers like this are so rare."

"You know that's not the only reason. Modesty doesn't become you, Kendra." Lynch paused as a pair of Goth-looking street performers walked past, playing their violins. "By the way, who was the guy?"

"What guy?"

"The guy who was tagging along with you last night. I heard something about a blind date, but I figured the cops on the scene got that part wrong. Even you aren't so socially inept as to bring a date to a murder scene."

"I needed a ride."

He clicked his tongue. "Oh, Kendra . . ."

"I think he liked it."

"Even worse. What kind of ghoul likes going to a murder scene?"

"You said you wish you could have seen me there last night."

"Because this is my job. Professional interest. What does this guy do?"

"He's a history professor."

"Definitely a whack job."

His attitude was very peculiar for Lynch, Kendra thought. "Hmm. Jealous much?"

"Jealous? That's ridiculous."

"I thought so, too, considering our relationship. I'm just going with what I see and hear. My 'unique skill set' you know."

"Then you're slipping." He laughed. "Have you seen that swimsuit ad that's been showing up on the sides of buses around town? The one with the Asian woman in the striped bikini?"

"Sure."

"I've actually been dating her."

"Bullshit."

"It's true. Her name is Ashley."

Kendra raised her brows. "Wow. She's beautiful."

"Yes."

"And are you taking her to her high-school prom?"

"She's twenty-five."

"Then she should be old enough to know better."

He tilted his head. "Jealous much?"

"Not in the slightest." This conversation had taken a very personal turn, and she had always tried to avoid that with Lynch. He was a dangerous man both professionally and personally, and she admitted that she was drawn to him. It would be terribly easy to become involved sexually with him. It was what would come after that she worried about. Better to stay clear. "But I'm afraid you're wasting your time, Lynch. I really don't have the time or the inclination to play detective."

"So you're telling me to go to hell."

She smiled. "Yes. Go to hell."

"Okay. Good enough. I can now tell them that I asked."

"Yes, you can. And . . . believe it or not, it was good to see you."

"The feeling's mutual, Kendra. There's one more thing. It may or may not make a difference to you, but there's something about this case you don't know."

"It won't make a difference to me."

"Maybe not." He reached into the side pocket of his sports jacket and pulled out the small manila envelope protruding from it. "It's all in here. Look at it, don't look at it, whatever."

Kendra took the envelope with a noncommittal shrug. "Okay."

As he started to leave, he pointed to the white-faced street performers who had found other people to annoy. "And if you need me to knock off those mimes, the offer's still open."

She smiled. "Got it."

KENDRA STROLLED THROUGH THE BUSY Gaslamp District and toward her condo building on E Street. She was trying not to let Lynch and that blasted murder investigation take over her thoughts. She had already decided not to open the envelope, but she still resisted the urge to toss it in one of the many trash cans on her way home. The FBI was smart to send Lynch as their ambassador. They had formed a strong partnership in their one case together, and he was enough of an outsider from all that bureaucracy that she trusted him.

And, she had to admit, she did find him extremely attractive. His movie-star looks hadn't captured her, but his supreme confidence—backed by smarts, aggressiveness, and steely determination—had sparked the heat that had grown between them during the course of their investigation.

Sparked the heat. What was she, a schoolgirl?

Shake it off.

Kendra entered her building but decided to take a detour on her way to her unit. She approached a door on the second floor and knocked.

Two seconds later, she heard the electronic dead bolt unlock.

"Come in!" Olivia called from inside.

Kendra opened the door. Olivia Moore was seated at her desk, typing away at her computer keyboard. It's where she was almost every time Kendra visited these days.

"Just a few more seconds. Sit down," Olivia said as she continued typing. "Gotta keep feeding the beast."

"The beast" was Olivia's blog, *Outta Sight*, which was a popular Internet destination for the vision-impaired. Her Web site, which the blind could enjoy with Screenreader and other specialized text-to-speech applications, featured interviews, travel tips, and product reviews. In less than two years, Olivia had grown her evenings-and-weekends hobby into a full-time job that generated a six-figure income.

Finally, she pushed away from the desk. "Done. I was reviewing some new gadgets. I get stuff in the mail every day now. It's amazing what's out there. We sure could have used some of this stuff back at Woodward."

Kendra smiled. She and Olivia had met as children at Woodward Academy, the school for the blind in Oceanside. Among the many emotions that greeted Kendra upon regaining her sight was the sadness and strange guilt about leaving Olivia behind in the darkness. Olivia, whose vision had been taken by a childhood traffic accident, was not a candidate for the regenerative corneal procedure that had given Kendra her sight. Olivia, for her part, had expressed nothing but support and happiness for her friend. But Kendra knew that Olivia spent a lot of time scouring the Internet for experimental procedures that might one day give her back her own vision.

Olivia tossed back her glossy dark hair, her beautiful face suddenly lit with a mischievous smile, as she picked up a palm-sized object and aimed it at Kendra. "Stay still for a second."

"So you can tase me? If I'm on the floor twitching and wetting my pants in the next ten seconds, I will be very angry with you."

"It's not a Taser. Just wait."

After a moment, a man's voice sounded from the device. "Aqua blue."

Olivia lowered the gadget. "Is that right? You're wearing an aqua top?"

Kendra looked down at her shirt. "Yes. That's impressive."

"It's for picking out clothes, sorting laundry, or maybe even to help connect audio or video cables. There are some bugs, but it works pretty well. I just uploaded my review."

"Cool. You get to keep all this stuff that the manufacturers send you?"

"Most of it. It's good exposure for them. I just don't have enough time to review it all." She stood up and moved across the room to the sectional sofa where Kendra was sitting. "But enough about that. How was your date last night?"

"Good. Mom kind of knocked it out of the park. He's smart, kind of funny, good-looking . . ."

"Uh-oh. I sense there's a 'but' coming."

"No 'but.' I had a nice time. I'll probably see him again."

"A nice time. Hmm. Tell me you didn't do your Kendra thing on him, where you disturbingly told him his entire life story?"

"Well . . ."

"I knew it."

"It just happened. He didn't mind."

"Of course he minded. That freaks guys out. Not just guys, but everybody. People like to parse themselves out to dates that they're just getting to know . . . You know, they like to wait a few dates before they discuss the STDs, the rotten credit history, the six hyperactive kids who . . ."

"Or the prison time?"

Olivia's face froze. "Seriously?"

"Yes. It was a drug thing in college. It's long behind him."

"If you say so."

She was silent a moment. "I actually have some bigger news. I saw Adam Lynch just a few hours ago."

"And there's the 'but.'"

"No, why do you keep saying that? There's no 'but.'"

"Oh, yes. The hunky government agent from your past appears, and the new guy pales in comparison. That's your 'but.'"

"If we can move past my 'but' for a second, Lynch tried to recruit me for another job."

Olivia nodded. "Of course he did. You told him to go to hell, right?"

She smiled. "I used those very words."

"Good. How many times do you have to tell them you're not interested in this stuff? I don't see how they have the nerve to—"

"Actually, I kind of inserted myself into this one."

Olivia went still. "And how, exactly, did you do that?"

Kendra told her about the Cabrillo Bridge crime scene, her observations, and her conversation with Lynch.

After she finished, Olivia didn't speak for a moment. "The envelope he gave you . . . is that what I heard you put on the coffee table?"

"Yes."

"I have a paper shredder near the desk. Go ahead and put it in."

"I'll take care of it later."

"Take care of it now."

"I—I don't know what's in it. They might need it back."

"Do you really think they took a precious, one-of-a-kind piece of evidence, dropped it into an envelope, and gave it to you without even telling you what it is? And didn't you just tell me his exact words were, 'open it, don't open it, whatever'? That doesn't sound like something they need back."

"You're right."

"So go over there and shred it."

Kendra picked up the envelope but didn't move from the couch.

Shit. She couldn't make herself do it.

Olivia's lips tightened. "You and I both know you're going to open that envelope. And I know you're going to help out on that investigation, even if you don't."

"So you're clairvoyant now?"

"I don't need to be. We've known each other most of our lives."

"But I turn down cases all the time."

"Most of them, yes. But as much as you say you're not interested in this one, you can't help yourself. It's intriguing you. Even though you know it will probably put you through the ringer. I think it's possible some of those cases—maybe even most—would have gone unsolved without you, and maybe you know that. So it could be that it would tear you up more *not* to do it. But if that's true, that's really screwed up. Is that the reason?"

"No."

"Then do you even know the reason?"

Kendra leaned back on the sofa, still clutching the manila envelope. "I love my job, dammit. There's nothing I love as much as my music-therapy work. I really do think I'm helping those people."

"Of course you are."

She waited.

"Okay. But sometimes I go weeks, months, without seeing signs of improvement in any of them. It goes with the territory, but it still makes me feel . . . powerless."

Olivia half smiled. "And taking on these FBI cases makes you feel powerful?"

"Not really. Sometimes just the opposite." She thought about it, trying to find an answer for herself as well as Olivia. It was time she stopped hiding and faced those reasons. "But those cases are finite problems with clear-cut solutions. I don't often get that in my day job."

"But your day job won't get you killed."

"I love life. I'm very careful, Olivia."

"Sometimes, that's not enough."

"I know. Believe me, I usually leave the dangerous stuff to the people with guns."

"Usually. That's not very reassuring." Olivia stood up. "Well, your psychosis will have to wait because I'm throwing you out. An Australian newspaper is calling me for an interview in a few minutes."

"Whew." Kendra grinned. "Saved by the bell."

"This conversation isn't over," Olivia said sternly.

"Warning duly noted." Kendra stood up and hugged her. So many years fighting the darkness together, so much love, so much friendship. "And I know it's only because you care."

"Damned right," she said gruffly. "You're my best friend, and I refuse to do without you." She released her and turned away. "Now get out of here."

KENDRA WALKED UP TO HER third-floor condo, let herself in, and tossed her keys onto the small foyer table. She was about to toss Lynch's envelope next to them when she stopped.

Olivia was right. No way in hell she wasn't opening it.

She tore open the envelope and unfolded the small sheaf of papers inside. After less than a minute, she froze. "Shit," she whispered.

She let the papers and photo printouts fall to the floor.

She stood there for a long moment, trying to process what she had just seen.

What in the holy hell?

After another few seconds, she picked up her mobile phone and punched a number.

Lynch answered immediately. "Hello, Kendra."

"You son of a bitch. You knew I'd look, and you knew I'd call."

"Yes. All of the above."

Kendra realized that her hands were shaking. "I need to meet Griffin and everyone else at the Bureau working on this."

"I just set up a meeting between you and the entire team. They don't want to wait until Monday. I told them I'd have you at the FBI field office at nine tomorrow. I'll pick you up at eight thirty."

Eight thirty in the morning. It could be five o'clock for all she cared. She knew she wasn't getting much sleep tonight.

"See you then." She cut the connection.

AT EIGHT THIRTY THE NEXT MORNING, she was out in front of her condo and waiting when Lynch roared up in his Ferrari. "Good God, are you still driving that ostentatious piece of junk?" she said as she got into the passenger seat. "Did it ever occur to you that most men don't require that kind of ego building?"

"I don't either, but I love great pieces of machinery, and I'm willing to pay for them." He glanced at her. "Bad night?"

"Rotten. But I'd still think this luxury cruiser was unnecessary if I'd slept like a baby."

"But you wouldn't be so rude as to tell me so." He suddenly grinned. "Correction. You probably would. What was I thinking?"

"You're right." She sighed wearily. "It was rude. It's not my business if you need bolstering."

"Now that really hurt." His gaze was searching her face. "Angry?"

"I was angry. You were playing with me yesterday. You can't resist manipulating everyone around you. I don't appreciate it."

"I thought you might need time to adjust to the idea. Wrong?"

"You were manipulating," she repeated.

"Okay, I admit it. It comes so naturally that I don't know I'm doing it sometimes."

"Not true. You always know what you're doing. You're sharp and calculating and you—" She broke off. "God, I'm dreading this meeting, Lynch."

"I know you are." He added quietly, "But if it will help, I want you to know I'll be there to watch your back."

"I don't think it will help. Not with what I'll be facing when I walk into that office . . ."

FBI Field Headquarters
San Diego

"DR. MICHAELS, GOOD TO SEE YOU AGAIN." Special Agent in Charge Michael Griffin was seated at the head of the long table in the field office's cramped conference room. He didn't stand to greet Kendra and Lynch, although the three other agents in the room did.

Bill Santini, a sandy-haired man with a large middle-aged paunch, smiled. "Hello, Kendra. Welcome back."

It was actually a genuine smile, Kendra thought. She had never been his favorite person. But Santini had become much nicer to her since she'd let him grab an outsized portion of the credit for their last case together.

A slender man in his late twenties stepped forward and adjusted his wire-rimmed glasses, which were slightly too small for his face. "Special Agent Roland Metcalf. It's a true pleasure."

Kendra shook his hand. "Thank you, Agent Metcalf."

The remaining agent, a thirtyish woman with short blond hair, approached. "Thanks for helping us, Dr. Michaels. I'm Special Agent Saffron Reade."

"Agent Reade is why you're here," Lynch said as he pulled back a conference table chair for Kendra. "She put together that packet I gave you."

"So it's *your* fault," Kendra said to Saffron, not entirely joking.

"Afraid so."

"Sit down, everybody. Let's get started." Griffin leaned back and placed his hands behind his head. His silver hair had grown whiter in the year since Kendra had last seen him though his angular face was still unlined for a man of his fifty-or-so years. "I'm sure we all appreciate Dr. Michaels's coming down here this morning."

Why the hell didn't he get down to it and stop all these pleasantries? Kendra thought as she sat down at the other end of the long table. He was being entirely too formal and polite. He always addressed her as Dr. Michaels when he was annoyed at any situation. Griffin had never liked or understood her. And none of these agents really liked her being here. She had never been shy about criticizing their methods and lack of vision, and they didn't appreciate that she was usually proved right. Patience. It had been a sleepless night as predicted, but she wasn't tired. The contents of that damned envelope had been an unpleasant jolt of pure adrenaline. She still felt sick to her stomach.

Griffin motioned to Agent Reade. "Please begin."

"Certainly." Reade pressed a button on the remote, and a projection screen lowered on the wall behind Griffin. Motorized shades closed over the window. A ceiling-mounted projector whirred to life, and a PowerPoint presentation appeared on the screen. The first image was the accident scene that Kendra had visited only two nights before.

Reade turned toward the group. "As you know, Dr. Michaels, the Cabrillo State Bridge staged-accident scene bore some hallmarks of another case of yours in Texas, the Stanley Veers killings. His victims varied in age and gender, but each was killed in a way that was made to look like an accident." Using her small remote, Reade quickly displayed shots of Veers's murder scenes. "But as you've seen in the packet we gave you, we believe this new perpetrator has killed at least two other times in the past month. On October 17, a woman in Mission Valley was garroted with piano wire, which was then coiled up and placed in her mouth." Read displayed the graphic crime-scene photos, some of which Kendra had already seen in the packet. "Then, on October 25, a man in Old Town was stabbed and the Latin phrase *Mens Rea*—guilty mind—was carved on his chest." Again, Reade showed crime-scene photos that Kendra had already seen. "San Diego PD initially worked those cases and had no reason to think they were the work of the same person. But when this office was consulted on the Cabrillo Bridge scene, things started to fall into place. We realized there is something that links these cases."

"Yes." Although Kendra had the entire night to tussle with it, hearing Reade review the cases still seemed so unreal. "The link between all these cases . . . is me."

Everyone in the room was silent, waiting for her to continue.

Kendra stood up and gazed at the last gory crime-scene photo for a long moment before speaking. "The piano wire victim was killed using the M.O. of Martin Stout, who murdered four women exactly the same way in Reno, Nevada. It was one of my first cases." Kendra looked at Reade. "Your packet didn't say what kind of piano wire. Do you have any idea—?"

Reade interrupted her. "Size 19 Roslau piano treble wire."

Kendra nodded. "Imported from Germany. Exactly what Stout always used. And the second victim was killed in the manner of the so-called Latin Killer, Lukas Hendricks, who carved Latin phrases on his victim's bodies. Another one of my cases. I assume those were hold-back facts pending the investigation?"

Reade nodded.

Griffin placed his palms flat on the table. "It appears someone is re-creating your greatest hits, Dr. Michaels."

"Delicately put as always, Griffin."

"We both know there's nothing delicate about me. Someone is taunting you, Dr. Michaels. It's no accident that they're doing it in your own backyard."

"And they're doing a damned good job of it."

"I'm sure this comes as quite a shock. But now you can understand why we needed to reach out to you."

"Of course. And you can understand why this case truly sickens me."

"It sickens all of us. Our profilers believe the killer is someone who might best be described as a fan of your investigative work."

Kendra shook her head. "That's bullshit. I don't have any fans."

"Well, that's a surprise," Griffin said, deadpan. "Dr. Michaels, we're talking about someone who may at some point have reached out to you, either directly or perhaps on a public forum. Does anyone come to mind?"

"No, I do get e-mails through my business Web site. Some are interested in my cases, but most want to know about the medical procedure that gave me my sight. They're either blind themselves or have a blind friend or relative."

"Hmm. We should zero in on those who have expressed some interest or knowledge of your investigative work. Do you still have those e-mails?"

"I do. I'll sort through and pass them along to you. As for what's being said about me on online forums, I have no idea."

"We do," Metcalf said. "I've built a file going back several years. Activity surges whenever there's mention of you in media accounts of your cases. We're using IP addresses to build a database of the people who post on discussion boards, news-story-comments pages, and the like. We've already seen that a lot of the same people pop up again and again."

"See, you do have adoring fans," Lynch said.

Griffin nodded. "One of whom might have killed six people in the last few weeks. Metcalf, do you have a copy of that database for Dr. Michaels?"

Metcalf slid a USB memory stick across the table to Kendra. "Here's what we've come up with so far. Please review it and see if anything sets off any alarm bells."

"Will do." Kendra took the stick. "Although I generally try to avoid reading things being said about me online."

"It's almost all quite complimentary," Metcalf said. "Though I was surprised there were no direct quotes from you concerning any of your investigations. None at all."

"I never talk to the media about the investigative work I do. Whenever someone asks, I shut them down immediately."

"But you obviously have no problem discussing your music-therapy work. You've been quoted in dozens of articles about that."

"Yes, and I've written dozens more myself. Plus two books so far. It's an emerging field that needs all the attention it can get." She shook her head. "Trust me, I wish it's all I had to think about right now."

Reade raised the PowerPoint remote. "Shall I continue?"

Griffin leaned forward. "Actually, how far did you and Metcalf get downstairs?"

"It's pretty much done. We were there most of the night."

"Good. We can continue down there." Griffin turned to Kendra and Lynch. "We moved some of our sections off-site, and this building's entire second floor is vacant right now. Everything's been ripped out, and it's a mess while we wait for the crews to come in and remodel. But it does give us plenty of room, which is in short supply up here."

"Room for what?" Lynch asked.

Griffin stood and grabbed his jacket from the back of the triangular-backed chair. "I'll show you."

CHAPTER
3

"I DON'T BELIEVE IT." KENDRA'S voice echoed in the large space, bouncing off the bare walls and concrete floors.

"Amazing," Lynch whispered.

They were with the FBI team on the vacant second floor, surrounded by nineteen freestanding bulletin boards. Each of the boards was packed with crime-scene photos, press clippings, and detail sheets of Kendra's cases.

"This is all of them, isn't it?" Griffin waved his arms over the boards. "Every one of your murder investigations."

Kendra couldn't answer at first. All those faces. All that death. All those places she had tried to forget. They were coming at her from every direction.

"You okay?" Lynch asked.

She nodded. Lynch was the only one who really knew her, who realized how this display might affect her. To the others, these were just her "triumphs," her "greatest hits." She finally turned toward Reade and Metcalf. "I'd forgotten I'd been involved with so many cases. I can see why you spent almost all night down here."

"It's our case data center," Griffin said. "We're calling it 'the war room.' These boards have the details of every murder you've ever investigated. You've only done five for us, but we've also included the ones you've done for other police departments and investigative units. We're working with San Diego PD to make sure that there haven't been others that match some of these."

Kendra stopped to look at the face of the twelve-year-old Steve Wallach, who had been killed the night after she joined the hunt for the Marina killer.

Steve would have been in high school now, dating, driving, maybe thinking about college. He might even—

"Kendra?" Lynch said softly.

She nodded in acknowledgment and forced herself to look away from that boy's face.

"Dr. Michaels," Reade said. "If there's any relevant information we left off any of these boards, please let us know."

"Sure."

"Exceptional job, isn't it?" Griffin was strolling among the bulletin boards, like a patron at an art gallery from hell. "Since you're going to be helping us, I thought it might be helpful for you to refresh your memory of these cases. Not to disparage Agent Saffron's PowerPoint skills, this is probably easier to take in."

Like a dagger to the heart, Kendra thought. Don't look at them right now. Don't let them see how it brought back all the nightmares.

"Doesn't matter," Kendra said. "I could never forget any of these cases. I talked to the loved ones of every victim on these boards. That's not something I could ever forget . . . as much as I would like to."

God, she wanted to get out of here.

Lynch quickly stepped between her and Griffin. "Has the medical examiner given you a preliminary report on the victims from the bridge?"

"Yes, it came in last night. Dr. Michaels was spot-on about the couple in the BMW. They were both strangled. The driver of the pickup truck appeared to suffer from blunt-force trauma, but the body was burned pretty badly. You were also right about the accelerant used. It was paint thinner, heavy on the toluene."

"What about the driver of the minivan?" Kendra asked. "She was burned, too. I didn't get a good look at her."

"She was a thirty-two-year-old female from Old Town," Griffin said. "She had multiple contusions in the chest, consistent with stab wounds. According to the M.E., her body appears to have been refrigerated."

"What?" Lynch said.

Kendra nodded. "The killer kept her on ice until he was ready to unveil her. Do we know when she disappeared?"

"Four days before the crash," Reade said. "She was an unemployed teacher. She had a roommate, but when she didn't come home, the roommate just thought she had taken off for Phoenix to visit her parents."

Look straight at Griffin. Keep your eyes off those boards. "What about the driver of the pickup truck?" Kendra asked. "Do we have a timeline on him?"

"He disappeared three days before the crash," Griffin said. "He was a family man from North Park. San Diego PD had actually been working his disappearance."

"I wouldn't be surprised if his body was also refrigerated," Kendra said. "Do we have any information on the couple in the BMW?"

Griffin nodded. "They were fresh kills. They had both been to work that day, literally just hours before. They were due to meet friends at a restaurant earlier in the evening."

"Have you identified and sealed off the locations where each of these victims were most likely taken?"

Griffin smiled sourly. "Hard as it may be for you to believe, we do possess some rudimentary law-enforcement skills."

Griffin's polite facade was beginning to slip and his antagonism to show through. It had lasted longer than she had thought it would. Screw it. Her own control was frayed and ready to break. "So that's a yes?"

"Yes."

"Okay. What I would like to do is visit the medical examiner, followed by visits to each of the suspected abduction or murder scenes."

"We can arrange that," Griffin said. "The only question is which one of us will accompany you?"

Lynch tapped his chest. "That would be me."

Griffin's brows rose. "Really? I was told in no uncertain terms that you were too busy to participate in our investigation. Once you convinced Dr. Michaels to join us, you were supposed to be on a plane to Washington."

"One of the nice things about working for myself is that I'm the one who decides what I'm supposed to do. For the time being, I'll be working this case with Kendra." He paused. "In case she needs a sledgehammer."

"What?"

"Long story."

KENDRA SMILED AS SHE AND LYNCH buckled themselves into his Ferrari and roared out of the parking garage. "Your bosses in D.C. aren't going to be happy about this."

"First of all, they aren't my bosses. They're associates."

"Associates who hire you, authorize payment, and for whom you perform work at their direction. That sounds a lot like a boss to me."

"Kind of like Griffin is your boss right now."

"You're absolutely right. Chalk this up as reason one thousand and six why I hate doing this. But at least I reserve the right to walk away at any time, a right I've exercised on more than one occasion."

"So have I. Another thing we have in common." Lynch put on his sunglasses as he sped onto the I-8 freeway. "If it eases your mind . . . Although my working this case may infuriate one 'boss,' it will make another ecstatically happy."

"Good. And I'm sure your swimsuit model will be happy. Maybe I'll even get to meet her."

"Alas, she'll be on the island of Majorca for the next week. She's on a photo shoot."

"That's convenient. Ashley is sounding more and more like a nonexistent Canadian girlfriend fabricated by the nerdy guy in high school."

Lynch half smiled. "We had one of those guys in my school."

"Of course you did. It was you."

"No."

"So you say. In any case, there's one of those guys in *every* school." In spite of their banter, she had no doubt that Lynch's Ashley was real and probably jumping into his bed at every opportunity. He was not only sexy but had that aura of power that was nearly irresistible.

He shrugged. "I guess you're right. Speaking of the lovelorn, I think young agent Metcalf was crushed that he wasn't the one joining you on this case."

"Really? I didn't get that."

"Then you're not as observant as I thought."

"Well, I'm sure our paths will cross. I was impressed with how much work he and Reade have already done. They probably know as much about my old cases as I do." Kendra pulled the USB memory stick from her pocket. "Griffin says this also includes the case files of the latest victims. Is your tablet handy?"

"Under the seat. Go ahead and transfer the contents of that stick into it. You said you want to start by visiting with the likely abduction points?"

"Actually . . . First, I'd like to go somewhere else. Let's go to Kearny Mesa."

"As you command." He stepped on the accelerator. "Why don't you lean back and close your eyes? You need to relax. Griffin put you through the wringer back there."

"Yes." She looked out the window. "And I don't think he even knew he was doing it."

"I'm not so sure." His lips tightened. "You've hurt his pride on occasion, and Griffin usually tries to get his revenge."

"Is that why I was sensing your protectiveness raising its head? I don't need it, Lynch."

"Of course not, you're one tough cookie." He smiled. "But I need to throw my jacket on mud puddles for you every now and then. It's my basic DNA."

"Save it for Ashley."

"It's not the same. Protectiveness isn't even on the radar with her."

No, it would be sex and nothing but the sex.

Maybe.

"Go ahead, close your eyes," he coaxed.

His voice was deep and velvet smooth, and his smile was lighting his face and softening the hardness. Charisma and manipulation, but maybe there was something more complicated beneath it. At any rate, she didn't mind accepting being soothed and comforted just now. She felt raw and hurting, and the faces of those victims were still there before her. She had been grateful to feel Lynch beside her in that room filled with horrible memories.

She might even be grateful now that he was demanding nothing from her but that she let him exert that protectiveness he claimed was his DNA.

Not that she would ever admit it to him.

"I am tired." She closed her eyes. "Wake me when we get there."

San Diego County
Medical Examiner's Office
Kearny Mesa

THE MEDICAL EXAMINER'S OFFICE, like the FBI field office, was a seven-day-a-week operation, but both places were obviously operating with slim Sunday skeleton crews. Kendra and Lynch had to wait two full minutes until their door buzzer was finally answered by an assistant, who escorted them upstairs to the labs. Five minutes after that, Dr. Christian Ross appeared, wearing his green scrubs. Ross was a bearded, chunky man in his sixties. Kendra had always thought he was one of the best medical examiners in the business, thorough and methodical. He also possessed the rare ability to adjust his medical explanations to the medical/scientific knowledge of whomever he was speaking with.

He grinned as he recognized them. "Ah, Kendra Michaels and Adam Lynch. Be warned, I'm a bit bleary at the moment. I've been working sixteen hours straight. This case of yours has taken on a new urgency in the last day or so." He gestured for them to join him in the hallway. "I would invite you up to my office, but the place is a damned mess. What can I do for you?"

"We won't keep you long," Kendra said. "I just wanted to ask you a couple of questions about Gary Decker and Corrine Harvey. More specifically, their clothing."

The doctor looked at her in surprise. "Their *clothing*?"

Kendra nodded. "They were the victims in the BMW, Doctor. Did you get any indication that they may have been put into those clothes after they were killed?"

Lynch was gazing at her thoughtfully but said nothing.

Dr. Ross paused for a long moment. "What makes you think that?"

"Yes or no?"

He finally nodded. "Yes, as a matter of fact. But I didn't think anyone outside of this office knew it yet. I was planning to include it in an amended report later this morning. Is there a leak in this office I need to be concerned about? Because if there is—"

"There's no leak."

"Then how—"

"You first. How did you arrive at your conclusion?"

Dr. Ross shrugged. "It wasn't difficult. The murderer made sure we wouldn't miss his handiwork. The assistant who prepped the body for autopsy noticed it right away, but the information didn't reach me until hours later."

"What information?"

"The male victim's shirt was too small. So the back was split and pinned to the coat for presentation. It's an old mortician's trick. Funeral homes are often given clothing for the public viewing that has actually become too small. So they split the back open to give it room. The killer wasn't taking chances on our powers of observation. He made sure there was no way this could be mistaken for anything else."

"Like the accident scene as a whole," Lynch said. "None of this was ultimately meant to fool anyone. This was all for your benefit, Kendra."

Dr. Ross leaned toward her. "Your turn. How did you know?"

"The other night, I noticed that both victims' fingernails had snagged fine threads from the clothing they were wearing."

"You didn't mention that before," Lynch said.

"I wasn't sure if it meant anything. But it's a bit unusual when it's the fingers on both hands of both victims."

"I noticed that," Dr. Ross said. "But I'm embarrassed to say that it didn't lead me to the answer that you found. So you think that the clothing on both corpses was changed?"

Kendra nodded. "When we put on shirts and jackets, we move our fingers in the sleeves to navigate past the fabric. The dead, of course, can't do that. Their fingers get caught at every twist and turn, and their nails snag at the threads. This couple was killed, then their clothes were changed."

Lynch grimaced. "Who the hell would do something like that?"

"Wayne Shetland," Kendra said.

"Who?"

"It's another one of my cases," Kendra said. "Up in Fresno. Check the file in your tablet. Wayne Shetland murdered his victims, then dressed them in different ways. The press dubbed them the Paper Doll Murders."

Lynch nodded. "So our copycat replicated another case from your past. He wanted to be absolutely certain that the police would see this for what it was. And he wanted it brought to your attention."

Dr. Ross sighed. "If you'll excuse me, I now have still more amendments to make in my report." He cocked his head at Kendra. "Unless you have something else for me?"

"Not right now, but it's early yet." She headed back down the hall. "Thanks, Dr. Ross. I'll keep you posted."

LYNCH'S MOBILE PHONE RANG JUST as they reached his car. He unlocked her door for her but stood outside talking while she climbed inside.

She watched him speaking into the phone, obviously growing more tense and agitated by the moment. Since gaining her sight, she had been fascinated by the visualization of human speech—the delicate interplay of lips, tongue, and teeth. But her burgeoning lip-reading skills were now handicapped by Lynch's intermittently turning his back to her as he paced. In any case, she didn't need special skills to know this call wasn't making Lynch happy.

He finally put away his phone and climbed into the car.

"Bad news?" she asked.

"Annoying news. I have to leave town."

"When?"

"In about three hours. I'm afraid I'll have to take you home."

"Ah-hah. On orders from your boss who's not really your boss?"

"Something's come up in D.C. I guess I shouldn't have cultivated the reputation of being so damn indispensable."

"Really?" she said mockingly. "How sad that it's come back to bite you in the ass." She gave him a sideways glance. "Just out of curiosity, what's come up?"

"It's classified."

"That, I figured. I also figured you would tell me anyway. I believe I've proved I can keep a secret."

He laughed. "Yes, you have."

"So spill it."

"What the hell." He threw up his hands. "Someone in one of the congressional offices has been leaking sensitive information."

"Leaking it to whom?"

"To whoever will pay the most, probably. Lobbyists, defense contractors, journalists . . . Depending on what the information is. I've been charged with finding the leak and plugging it."

"When you say 'plugging,' you're not speaking in terms of a 1930s gangster movie, are you?"

He smiled. "As in, plugging someone full of lead? I love this dangerous and romantic conception you have of me."

Actually, she could see Lynch in that tough, reckless role. The romantic concept was a harder stretch. Unless it was heavy on the sex. There was no question about Lynch's sexual abilities and inclinations. "I just knows what I sees."

"Well, no. I'm speaking purely in terms of stopping the leak. I've been planting false information during the past few weeks, and this morning it finally yielded something. Unfortunately, our suspected leaker isn't talking. They want me to come back and lead the questioning."

"Don't you mean interrogation?"

"That's probably a more accurate way of putting it. But they want him under more psychological duress than physical."

"I can see why they're desperate for your expertise. If there's something you excel at, it's driving people crazy."

"I like how you take my gifts and twist them in such a way to make them sound like insults."

"Oh, so your unique brand of manipulation is now a 'gift.'"

"What would *you* call it?"

She tilted her head, thinking about it. "A curse. A bane. A blight. A pain in the ass. Take your pick."

Lynch started the car and roared out of the parking lot. "Well, I'm afraid you'll have to do without my gift for the time being. Perhaps young Agent Metcalf will get his chance with you after all."

"I don't need a tagalong."

"Or you could just wait for me to get back. It will only be a couple days."

She looked away from him. "A couple days can be a long time. In case you haven't been paying attention, there's a sicko out there who will kill again."

"You're not the only one working this investigation. You can use the time to get up to speed on the case files."

She gazed at him in disbelief. "You've got to be kidding. You expect me to sit around waiting for you, spinning my wheels? Stay in D.C. as long as you want. I've always done very well working alone."

"I know you have." He paused. "But we both know this case is different. The killer wasn't just targeting those victims. He was targeting *you*. He has you in mind when he's planning his murders. Who knows what's next?"

She didn't answer. There wasn't anything to say. She had been thinking the same thing.

She said it anyway.

"We all have a pretty good idea what's next," she said quietly. "It's on one of those bulletin boards at the FBI field office."

They drove in silence back to her condo. Why in the hell did Lynch's imminent departure bother her? She didn't need him. She didn't need anybody.

Twenty-four hours earlier, he was the furthest thing from her mind. Now she was feeling all out of sorts because their hours-old partnership was suddenly interrupted, and he was off to intimidate some D.C. crook?

Because he was right. This case was different. And she might hate to admit it, but it felt good to have that sledgehammer by her side.

He pulled in front of her building and let the engine idle for a long moment before speaking. "You've got my number. Keep me posted, okay?"

"Sure."

"And Kendra . . ."

"Yeah?"

He leaned forward and kissed her squarely on the mouth.

She tensed. What on earth was he doing? Her first instinct was to recoil. Her second was to press closer. The second instinct won out. She was kissing him back, she realized.

Strength. Warmth. Safety.

She had subconsciously expected any touch or overture from Lynch would involve sex and passion judging what she knew of him. Not this feeling of being guarded, treasured. It confused her . . .

He finally pulled away. "Say it," he said warily.

"I'm not going to put you on the spot." She had to catch her breath and steady her heartbeat. "I know it was an impulse on your part. A gesture to express your regret that I'm going to have to go it alone. It was very . . . friendly, and completely unnecessary."

"I'm glad you've been able to analyze my mind-set and actions so thoroughly," he said with irony. "It's a shame that you can't be sure whether you're right or not. That could be very frustrating." He gave her another kiss on the tip of her nose. "Be careful," he whispered.

She quickly climbed out of the car and almost ran into her building without looking back.

"WHAT IN THE HELL?"

Kendra actually said the words aloud after she entered her condo and plopped down behind the desk. Lynch's impromptu kiss had left her bewildered and out of sorts.

And admittedly aroused.

That sexual response had come out of nowhere after she had carefully detailed the reasons why it couldn't be that kind of reaction or caress. Or perhaps it had been waiting below the surface, submerged by her surprise that Lynch had acted in a way that she considered out of character. As she had left him, she had suddenly been swept away by a physical jolt of pure lust that had sent her running. It shouldn't have startled her, she told herself. From the moment she had met him, she recognized that Lynch was a force with which to be reckoned on all levels. She had just experienced one of the more primal levels, and it made her a little dizzy. The essential maleness and sexuality of Lynch, the *feel* of him.

Probably just the reactions he was going for.

And yet it hadn't seemed calculated. Lynch's actions were generally designed to achieve a specific result, but this one seemed spontaneous, beyond the realm of any rational thought. And that last kiss on the tip of her nose had been definitely big brotherly.

To hell with him. She'd be damned if she was going to spend the next couple of days trying to figure out what it meant, when he probably didn't even know himself. Especially when bikini-model Ashley was out there waiting to jump back into his bed.

Kendra pulled the flash drive from her pocket and plugged it into her computer. She perused the document files, both for the current investigation and collections of Web forum posts devoted to her and her cases.

She knew from her e-mails just how fascinated some people were about real-life murders, but she was still amazed at the level of obsessive interest on display. There were dozens of true-crime forums, she discovered, each populated with scores of people who traded opinions and insights over the cases that were hot in the media at any given time. Their fervor was such that they might as well have been discussing favorite sports teams.

And she was one of the players.

Although she never discussed her cases with the media, that didn't stop other cops, family members, and even perps from spilling their guts to whoever would listen. The discussion boards frequently got the facts wrong, but she was surprised at the number of tiny details they actually got right. Her surprise wasn't because the details were necessarily secret but because she didn't think anyone could possibly care about each case's minutiae.

But clearly some people did care, and one of them had murdered six people.

Kendra finally turned her attention to the current investigation files, which featured photographs of each place where the Cabrillo State Bridge victims had been killed or abducted. She paged through dozens of shots of the Sabre Springs home where Corrine Harvey and Gary Decker had been taken.

Typical Southern California Spanish-style home, all stucco and clay-tile roof. The pics didn't show much. Hopefully, the cops and the FBI hadn't already traipsed all over the place and destroyed whatever value the scene could have to her.

She picked up her phone and punched Griffin's mobile number.

He answered immediately. "Griffin."

"It's Kendra."

"No kidding. You know, they invented something a few years back called caller ID . . ."

"If you're through being a smart-ass, I want to take a look at Corrine Harvey's home in Sabre Springs."

"Now?"

"Yes. As soon as possible. The scene hasn't been broken down, has it?"

"No, it's still sealed under the jurisdiction of San Diego PD. But I heard that Adam Lynch had to hightail it back to Washington."

"That's right, he did. Can you get me a key?"

"Look, it's already getting dark out. Why don't we wait until to-morrow morning? I'll have Metcalf or Reade call you and arrange—"

"That's pretty lame. I'm not afraid of the dark. And I don't need anyone to hold my hand, Griffin. Do you want my help on this inves-tigation or not?"

He cursed under his breath. "Fine. I'll call San Diego PD and have them open up the house for you. But if you get a lead on anything, I want to hear about it right away."

"Of course."

"Don't 'of course' me. I've been down this road with you before. Remember that we're working together on this case. This isn't the Ken-dra Michaels Show."

Kendra smothered her irritation. Just as she thought. Griffin wasn't nearly as concerned with helping her as he was with making sure that she kept them in the loop. "You have to admit, Griffin, it's a damned good show."

He muttered something that was probably obscene. "It's just as well that Adam Lynch has left you on your own. His damn arrogance has been rubbing off on you. The last thing we need is another Lynch around here." He hung up on her.

A POLICE CRUISER WAS PARKED in front of Corrine Harvey's house when Kendra arrived. The yellow police tape had already been pulled and rolled up on the walkway, and light poured from every window.

A young uniformed officer stepped outside before she reached the door. "May I help you?"

"I'm Kendra Michaels. I believe you're expecting me?"

"Yes, ma'am. You're why I'm here." He shook her hand. "I've been told to extend every courtesy to you."

"I appreciate that, Officer . . ." She read the nameplate above his right breast pocket. "Jillette."

He raised a small plastic basket. "I'm afraid I'll have to take any photography or recording devices before I can let you come inside."

Her brows rose. "Seriously?"

He shrugged. "Departmental procedure."

"Since when?"

"There have been photos of closed crime scenes that have found their way onto the Web and the TV news lately. If there are any shots you need, let me know, and I'll have a police photographer come here and take them for you. The department will have to sign off on any photos you request."

"I'm sure that won't be necessary." Kendra put her cell phone into the basket.

The officer stepped aside for her to enter the house.

Kendra was first struck by the unique and adventurous artwork that adorned each wall in the foyer and living room. Not a surprise, she thought, since Corrine Harvey managed an art gallery.

But the abstract paintings pulsed with rage and brutality, streaked with blood reds and bold, violent slices. If indeed the woman died a horrible death here, the surroundings couldn't have been more appropriate.

"Kinda scary, if you ask me," the officer said.

She wasn't asking, but she had to agree. She glanced around the living-room area, paying particular attention to recently shampooed carpets.

There, near the sofa, were two large indentations that didn't appear to be footprints.

Knee prints, perhaps?

Yes, that was it. Someone had been standing near the couch and was brought down to his knees. Almost assuredly a man, judging from the size.

"I think Gary Decker was strangled here," she said aloud.

The officer studied the carpet impressions. "Are you sure?"

"No, not absolutely. Too many people have walked across the carpets for me to be positive. But the footprints leading to this spot are the only set that don't match any of the prints leaving the room. I'll bet Gary Decker wore a size eleven-and-a-half, maybe a twelve."

She caught a faint whiff of pomegranate on the couch. Slightly tart. Perfume?

Not perfume, she realized. Body lotion. Jafra Royal Pomegranate. Corrine Harvey's lotion of choice?

She cast one more glance around the living room. Not much more to be gleaned here.

She turned toward the kitchen, where, as in the case-file photos, she saw a lawn mower and pressure washer. She stepped toward them.

"Weird place to keep these, huh?" Officer Jillette said.

"She didn't normally store them there." Kendra opened the kitchen door and glanced into the garage. "I'm sure they were usually out here. But the killer needed to make room for Gary Decker's BMW. That's where he loaded the corpses before taking them to the bridge. Probably not something you would do in a front driveway."

The officer nodded.

Kendra closed the garage door and turned back into the main house. "I'm going upstairs. Do you need to follow me?"

He shook his head. "No, I'll just stick around to lock up when you leave. Take your time, Dr. Michaels. I'll be waiting out front."

"Thanks."

Kendra climbed the stairs and scanned the home office and two bedrooms. Slightly messy, but nothing out of the ordinary.

She stopped in the hall.

Damn. She hated doing this.

There were few things sadder than walking through the home of a murder victim, photos of happy times never to be recaptured. Monitor screens of e-mails never to be answered. An open book never to be finished.

Just the way it was when Corrine was casually living here the last day she would ever have.

Shit.

Okay, get a grip. Kendra moved down the hall to the master bathroom, where she detected another whiff of that cloying body lotion. This was probably where Corrine rubbed it on, but the scent was still stronger than it should have been with normal use.

Strange . . .

She scanned the bathroom's blue pearl granite countertop for the lotion bottle.

There was none.

She turned around and glanced around the bedroom.

Nothing.

Of course. The bottle had been broken. Recently. Perhaps two nights before, as Corrine readied herself for a dinner date?

But had Corrine merely dropped it, or . . . ?

Kendra got down on her knees and felt around the floor of the cabinet's baseboard. There appeared to be nothing but dust.

She reached around the corner, stretching her fingers between the cabinet and bathtub.

She felt something cold and sharp.

Success!

She pulled out her hand, and with it a single piece of glass between her forefinger and middle finger. She examined the glass. Black letters were visible on its surface, just enough to let her know that she was right about the lotion brand.

Kendra turned back into the bedroom and moved toward the door to the hallway, which had been left open against the room's corner. She gripped the doorknob and swung the door open.

She inhaled sharply, her gaze looking down at the floor. "Shit."

A pair of man's shoe prints were embedded on the rug behind the door.

The impressions were deep and well-defined in the carpet. Someone had obviously been standing in place, hiding behind that open door for an extended period of time.

Not just anyone. Corrine Harvey's killer.

He'd waited for Corrine to arrive home and come upstairs, where there would be fewer avenues for escape. Kendra could almost see, feel, the malice and heady satisfaction her killer must have been experiencing as he waited. He'd probably had it all planned. He must have felt the excitement of the kill to come as he heard her come up the stairs toward him.

Corrine hadn't even known he was there.

Kendra felt sick as she imagined the woman passing by that door where her killer waited.

He must have attacked her after she'd walked through to the bathroom. Perhaps the lotion bottle had broken in the struggle.

Might she have gotten it on her clothes?

Kendra moved to a walk-in closet on the other side of the bed. As she opened the door, she was immediately struck by that fresh lotion odor again.

Kendra pushed her face close to the hanging clothes, working her way down. She finally stopped and pulled out a gray long-sleeve T-shirt.

The lotion was smeared and splattered on its front, and the fabric was slightly torn.

Corrine Harvey had been killed in this shirt.

Kendra followed the scent to the clothes folded on a shelf above. She finally found a pair of black Capri slacks, also stained with Jafra Royal Pomegranate lotion. Why would her killer have put her clothing so neatly in this closet? It was bizarre.

She drew a deep breath. The sadness was close to overwhelming as she went through that poor woman's clothes.

Get over it. Do your job.

Kendra found a plastic shopping bag on the closet floor and placed the clothes inside. If the killer had struggled with Corrine Harvey, there was a chance that he might have left skin cells—and his DNA—on the clothing. It was a long shot, but she had seen cases turn on far less.

Corrine Harvey's home phone rang on the nightstand beside her bed.

And rang.

And rang.

And rang again.

She assumed it would soon go to Corrine's voice mail or an answering machine, but after a solid minute, the ringing continued.

She slowly walked toward the bedside table and glanced at the cordless phone's caller ID display.

She froze.

My God.

The display read: MICHAELS, KENDRA.

The call was from her mobile phone. She braced herself to slowly pick up and press the talk switch. "Yes?"

"You found the clothes." A whisper, soft, hoarse. She couldn't be sure if it was male or female. "You found the clothes she was wearing that night. I knew you would."

Kendra went still. "Who is this?"

"I've been watching you, Kendra . . . What a pleasure. You never disappoint."

She turned toward the large windows overlooking the backyard. Was he watching her even now? She ducked down and crouched next to the bed.

"Who the *hell* is this?"

"You'll find out soon. I can't tell you how eager I am for us to come together." His whisper cut through her like a razor.

Her eyes flew around the room again, this time for something, anything, she could use as a weapon.

"Where's the police officer?" she asked. "He had my phone. What did you do to him?"

The man chuckled. Kendra was sure it was a male voice now. "You should be more concerned about yourself."

Think of something. Keep him talking.

"What did you do to him?"

"Why do you care?"

"He has nothing to do with this."

"Really?"

"Yes. It's all about me and you."

"I'm glad you see it that way. I wanted to make certain that was absolutely clear."

"I could hardly miss your intention." She quietly moved toward the hallway. Surely, she would have heard this psychopath if he'd come upstairs . . . "Is the officer still alive?"

"For now. Tell me about him, Kendra. Humanize him for me. Maybe if I can look at him as a real-live human being, I won't discard him like a scrap of meat."

"Like you did all those other people? Ask him yourself."

"I'm asking you."

"I—I only just met him."

"But that's not a problem for you. Do what you do, Kendra. Tell me about him. Dazzle me. But I warn you, if you hang up, I will cut this phone line immediately. Then I'll cut you and this cop. I can't have you calling for help."

Where in the hell was this sicko? Outside the house? Waiting for her at the bottom of the stairs? In the next room?

"I'm giving you a chance to save him. Tell me about this police officer."

Kendra took another step toward the hallway. She froze when the floor creaked beneath her feet. To cover it, she said quickly, "He's prob-ably a swimmer."

"Indeed?"

"Yes." She strained to hear any sound of movement in the house. "Toned arms and shoulders, pronounced back muscles, flat stomach and narrow waist. Not a weight lifter, not a runner, but a swimmer."

"Interesting."

"He used to smoke, but not anymore. He has the smoker's wrin-kles around his upper lip, but I could smell no trace of cigarette smoke on him."

"Excellent."

"He's left-handed but writes with his right hand. A parent or teacher probably made him do that as a child."

"How disturbing."

"I was tipped off by a writing callus on the side of his right-hand middle finger."

"Yes, I see it."

"I'd like to show you *my* middle finger about now."

That made him laugh, and she heard his laughter echoing off the walls downstairs. At least now she knew where he was. "I'll bet you would, Kendra. What else can you tell me?"

She tried to think, to give him anything that would delay the butchery.

"He shaves with an electric shaver. One with three round heads, which means it's probably Norelco or Braun."

"You could tell that?"

"Yes. His stubble is slightly uneven. I can also tell he shaves in a circular motion."

"What else?"

"I think he's from the South. He deliberately suppresses his accent. To do that, he unnaturally shortens his vowels and emphasizes the second consonants of his words . . ." She went still as it all came together. An icy ripple shot through her body. ". . . just like you."

He was silent for a long moment. "What are you saying, Kendra?"

She didn't answer, struggling to fight the wave of panic engulfing her.

He finally dropped that whisper. "You *know,* don't you?"

"Yes." She swallowed hard. "He's *you.* You killed that officer before I even got here."

"Bravo, Kendra."

"You somehow knew I was coming here. Dear God, I was close enough to touch you and I didn't even realize—"

"I *did* touch you, Kendra. And I'll do it again."

The threat was clear. He was going to be on the move.

She ran to the bedroom windows. It was a long way to the concrete path below.

She heard a footstep on the stairs.

Then another.

And another after that.

He was coming after her. She'd seen him, and he couldn't let her live.

She tugged on the windows. They didn't budge.

More footsteps on the stairs . . .

She had a minute, maybe less.

Kendra grabbed a vanity stool and threw it through the window. It shattered, and the glass was still falling as she hurled herself through the opening.

For an instant there was silence, as all sounds—the breaking glass, the pounding footsteps—vanished, as if part of a long-ago nightmare.

Then she struck the cold cement patio.

Pain.

Searing, stabbing pain in her legs and left wrist.

She rolled as she landed, bleeding in a dozen places from the shards of glass.

She looked up. The man was at the window, staring down at her. He abruptly turned and bolted out of view.

Shit. She had to get out of here.

She pulled herself to her feet, hoping that her legs would support her weight.

They did. For the moment.

She staggered toward the block wall that separated the yard from the next-door neighbors. She lifted herself up and over, fighting through the horrible pain in her left wrist. She hit the wet grass on the other side, then ran for the side yard. She crouched beside a tall bush.

Weapon. Find a weapon.

As her eyes grew accustomed to the darkness, she spotted a shovel leaning against the house. She gripped it with the blade extended before her.

Come and get me, asshole . . .

She held her breath. She expected to hear the sound of the sliding back door, but there was nothing.

A car started on the street.

Was that him?

It idled for a few seconds, then roared away.

She slowly stood up, still gripping the shovel.

There was only silence from Corrine Harvey's house.

He was gone.

CHAPTER
4

"THE PARAMEDICS SAID YOU were being a real pain in the ass to them," Griffin said as he walked up Corrine Harvey's driveway toward Kendra. "I told them welcome to the club."

"Thanks for your support." Kendra drew the paramedic blanket tighter around her. She couldn't seem to shake the chill. Slightly over an hour had passed since her escape from the house, and the place was now surrounded by squad cars, work lights, and evidence-collecting police officers. Kendra carefully stood up from the driveway, where she'd been sitting since dismissing the paramedics. Every muscle was stiffening more by the minute. "They wanted to take me to the hospital. I told them I didn't have the time." She raised her left arm, which was covered by a wrist wrap. "It's not broken, only a sprain. They gave me this and bandaged my cuts and treated my bruises. What more do I need?"

"An X-ray or two? Those bruises on your cheek and arm look pretty nasty. You tumbled out of a second-floor window. I sure as hell wouldn't let one of my agents back on duty until they'd been checked out by a doctor."

"Then it's a good thing I'm not one of your agents. And I didn't tumble, I dove out."

"Those paramedics have you pegged. A complete pain in the ass."

And she couldn't deal with any more well-intentioned people trying to stop her from doing what needed doing. She didn't have the strength right now. "Any news on the police officer?"

"No. Still no sign of him." Griffin jerked his thumb toward a squad car parked on the street. "That's definitely his car, but there's no sign of a struggle there or in and around the house. The officer may still be alive."

She hoped that was true, but she had a feeling that the officer hadn't been that lucky. She had examined his car herself five minutes before the paramedics arrived on the scene and been relieved that there was no body in the vehicle. "I was led to believe he was already dead. Not that the sick bastard's word means anything."

"No, it doesn't."

Kendra was fighting off a wave of nausea that she tried to believe was caused by the pain and shock of her fall. It didn't work, those vivid memories of that killer were shaking her to her core. "Unbelievable . . . That psychopath was standing right in front of me, and I had no idea."

"You're lucky to be alive," Griffin said harshly.

"He knew I was coming. He arrived here before I did. We need to figure out how he knew."

"Metcalf is already working on it. This guy was actually wearing the cop's uniform?"

"At least his badge and name tag. The uniform looked like the genuine article, and it was a good fit. It could have belonged to the officer, or this guy might have brought his own."

"Dr. Michaels . . ." Griffin hesitated for a long moment. "Kendra. This guy, this killer, knows you. He knows how you work. He knew you would be visiting this house at some point."

"What if I hadn't come alone?"

"He would have waited for you to go alone to another scene. Which you would have done. You know it, I know it, and he knows it. Your presence on this case may actually be feeding his appetites, goading him on."

"He was doing a pretty good job of it already. But if you're saying you'd rather I bow out—"

"I didn't say that," he said sourly. "I might have been thinking it, but I didn't say it. I know you're too valuable right now for me to indulge my personal feeling. I'm just pointing out that it's something of which you should be aware."

"I'm not likely to forget it. Believe me. I'm aware." She pulled the paramedic blanket closer around her. "I need to sit down with a sketch artist. Someone who really knows what he's doing."

"He's already been set up. I figured you have a pretty clear picture in your head of this guy."

"I do. Like a photograph."

"The police have an amazing old guy they use sometimes. He's retired, but he occasionally still—"

"Bill Dillingham."

"You know him?"

"Yes. He's very good. One of the best anywhere. The sooner we can get that sketch in circulation, the better."

"You're damn right." Griffin rubbed the back of his neck. "You're the only person alive who has actually seen him. That puts an awfully big target on your back."

"He was more interested in watching me work. He clearly got some perverse thrill from being so close to me without my knowing it."

"Well, that's in keeping with our profiler's workup on him. He's obviously fascinated by you. But now he has to know that tomorrow a sketch of him will be in every newspaper and TV news broadcast in the state."

A young crime-scene investigator approached them with a clear plastic evidence bag. "Excuse me, Ms. Michaels, we found this hanging in the porch." He raised the bag to show that it contained a Blackberry mobile phone.

"That's mine." She turned to Griffin. "He got me to surrender it with some bullshit story about not allowing cameras inside."

The investigator pressed a button on the phone through the plastic bag. The screen lit up. "You may be interested in this."

Kendra and Griffin leaned over to look at the screen. A memo page was on the main screen with a succinct message:

A PLEASURE TO FINALLY MEET YOU, KENDRA.
DON'T FORGET THE MOLE . . .
    YOURS TRULY
    MYATT

Griffin stared at the message. "Do you know any Myatt?"

Kendra thought for a moment. "I don't think I've even heard that name before."

"We'll search every database we can find. But what about that message? 'Don't forget the mole?' What the hell?"

Kendra turned away, revolted by the thought of that nutcase pawing at her phone, tapping out a message to her. He must have taken the time to write this before he had fled the scene. "He had a small mole just above his left nostril." She made herself look back at the message. "He obviously isn't too worried about our police sketch."

"Or he wants us to think he's not worried."

Kendra looked up at the investigator. "You said this was hanging in the porch? How exactly?"

He raised another clear evidence bag with a piece of sheer, tan-colored fabric inside. "It was in this, hanging from the doorknob."

Griffin grabbed the evidence bag and held it up toward one of the work lights. "Is this what—"

"It's woman's hosiery." She moistened her lips. "Calf high, sheer nude." She was feeling that icy chill again.

Griffin's eyes narrowed. "The bastard's referring back to another one of your cases, isn't he?" He added slowly, "I remember this."

"So do I. Griffin, pull together everything you have on the Vince Dayton case." She flung off the blanket and strode toward the unmarked police car parked next to the driveway. One of the work lights was angled toward the vehicle's front end, clearly marking it as the site's unofficial command center. Four cops had maps spread out on the hood, marked with highlighter pens of possible escape routes.

"Forget the streets and freeways," Kendra said curtly. "Map out the nearest bodies of water."

The cops just stared at her.

"Do it. Beaches, ponds, marshes . . ." She shouldered her way into the group and stared down at an unfolded map. "And it has to be someplace he can access without being easily seen."

A tall, graying officer dressed in his dress blues gazed at her from the other side of the car. "Dr. Michaels, I'm Captain Yates. Do you know something that we don't?"

She wished she didn't. "My phone was left inside a sheer stocking on the front porch. The exact same size and type of stocking used by Vince Dayton in four Central Coast killings a few years ago. It was one of my cases."

Yates brow wrinkled. "He strangled his victims with a stocking?"

"No. He injected them with a paralyzing agent and drowned them, usually in just a couple feet of water."

Yates nodded. "I remember now. Each victim was found with a stocking over her head and face."

"Exactly. A stocking like the one your investigator found around my phone. Your missing officer may be wearing one of those right now. And I'm afraid he'll soon be facedown in a nearby body of water, if he isn't already."

Yates spoke to Griffin, who had joined the group. "I know the FBI has taken the lead in this investigation, Special Agent Griffin. But if there's a chance of getting our officer back, there's no way we aren't going after this guy right now."

"Of course," Griffin said smoothly. "I wouldn't think of interfering. We're only here to provide whatever support we can."

Kendra ran her fingers over the map, tracing an east–west line to the coast. "I'd start here, with the closest and most direct route to the bay. Then work north and south to the more isolated areas. He's going to want to get his car as close to the water as possible but still do it without being seen."

Yates thoughtfully studied the map. "You sound as if you've got a real bead on this son of a bitch."

"It's what Vince Dayton would have done. And whoever this copycat is, he's shown us that he does his homework."

Yates nodded. "Good enough for me. We'll bring in the Harbor Police and get a 'copter out. If he's there, we'll find him."

Scripps Park
La Jolla

MYATT GRIPPED THE STEERING WHEEL tighter as the adrenaline surged through him. Damn, he felt *alive*.

He had been face-to-face with Kendra Michaels, and she hadn't had the slightest idea. He could have killed her right there and then, but Colby was right. It was better to delay gratification, like the jungle cat that toys with its prey before finishing it off.

He turned onto a dark side street and parked. He sat in silence for a moment, listening for breathing in the rear compartment of his Infiniti G37 SUV. At first he heard nothing. Had he botched it? Dammit. After all his preparations—

There it was. Labored, shallow breathing. The cop was still alive.

Tricky stuff, this Vecuronium. Too little, and the cop could possibly move and call for help. Too much, and his respiratory system would seize.

Myatt smiled. He'd struck that delicate balance. Not that it would matter for too much longer anyway.

He opened the door and climbed out of the SUV.

Torrey Pines State Reserve

12:15 A.M.

DAMMIT, WHY HAD THERE BEEN NO WORD? It had been hours since they'd arrived here.

Kendra's hands clenched as she paced outside the police department's mobile command vehicle, which to her looked like an RV on steroids. It was equipped with an array of microwave and satellite antennas on the roof, plus an interior wall of flat-screen monitors that reminded her of NASA mission control. The vehicle and its four identical siblings had been the subject of much controversy because of their five-hundred-thousand-dollar price tags.

The search for Officer Jillette was being coordinated from this command center, which was now parked on a beach parking lot in the Torrey Pines State Reserve, a coastal state park that offered hundreds of acres of prime hiking trails and spectacular lookout points. The search had been under way for more than three hours, and Kendra could see two helicopters in the distance with the searchlights playing over the surf.

Find him. Find him alive. Don't let that bastard have played his twisted games.

She tensed as her cell phone rang. Griffin?

No. And she didn't need this right now, dammit. She accessed the call. "Who phoned you, Lynch? You've barely had time to get to D.C."

"Evidently enough time for you to try to get yourself killed," Lynch said roughly. "And Griffin says you won't check in to a hospital. Stupid. Very stupid, Kendra."

"I don't need any more treatment. And I don't need your telling me what to do. You have business to take care of for all those bureaucratic types, and I have business here."

"At least, go home and rest. Griffin told me that you hadn't stopped since you did a swan dive out of that window."

"So he called you and told you to persuade me to do what he wanted me to do. It's not going to work." She paused. "We haven't found that police officer yet, Lynch. I saw a photo of his wife and child in his squad car when I searched it. It was warm and sweet and . . ." She stopped and cleared her throat. "He's alive for me now. I can't go home until we find him . . . one way or the other."

He was silent. "Okay, I can see that I'm not going to get anywhere. Just be careful." He added impatiently, "And Griffin didn't tell me to do anything. I'm not under his orders."

"No, but he played you. Admit it."

Another silence. "Maybe. Griffin is no fool."

"But nowhere near as manipulative as you are, Lynch. It surprises me you let him do it."

"I was upset. For some odd reason, I didn't like the idea of you one-on-one with a serial killer and having to fly out a window. Just one of my little idiosyncrasies. You could have waited for me, dammit. This wouldn't have happened if I'd been there." He paused. "I'm thinking of scratching this assignment and flying back on the next plane."

"Don't be an idiot. I didn't need you. I'm alive and well and I was face-to-face with our killer. That puts me a step ahead of where I was before."

"Toward being a target."

"Yes, but it was exactly what the bastard wanted, and I learned from it. You'd have slowed me down. Stay where you are. I'll see you when you've plugged your leak. I won't accept your help or presence before then. By the way, your assignment sounds terribly boring. I can't imagine how a black-ops agent of your supposedly lethal reputation was ever drawn into it. How the mighty have fallen." She didn't wait for an answer. "I'm hanging up now." She pressed the disconnect.

She drew a deep breath and leaned wearily back against the aluminum side of the RV. She'd been wrong to add that last taunt at Lynch. But she'd wanted to get him annoyed enough at her so that he'd stop thinking of her as a victim to rescue and go about his own business. She'd noticed that Lynch had a few protective tendencies that had to be curbed on occasion.

And, on this particular occasion, she found herself too ready to accept and embrace those tendencies. She was feeling very much alone and vulnerable. Exposing herself as a lone target had all the advantages she had told Lynch, but remembering that confrontation still shook her. It had shattered her confidence in herself, and she was having to rebuild. It would have been comforting to have Lynch here until that restructuring was complete.

But when had she ever relied on anyone else to bolster her? It was a sign of weakness and not an emotion she would have wanted to show Lynch. He was megastrong, and she wanted his respect, not his pity.

But she wasn't feeling very strong herself at this moment, she thought. She was beginning to be aware of aches and pains that she'd firmly suppressed. She had to get busy. She needed to straighten away from this vehicle, go find Griffin, and see what was happening. Surely he could—

"I prefer to work in a nice warm squad room, you know, Kendra. It's too chilly out here."

Kendra's gaze flew to Bill Dillingham, who was approaching from the other side of the parking lot. He sported a white beard and one of the thickest heads of white hair she had ever seen. Bill was in his early-to-mid eighties and walked with a stiff, unsteady gait.

"Bill, what the hell are you doing here? It's after midnight."

"And it's cold and damp. If I get sick and die of pneumonia, it's all on your head. I got tired of waiting at the police station."

"Sorry. We have a developing situation here."

"Guess what? It would have continued to develop if you had deigned to meet me at the station for an hour or so. Lucky for you, I can bring my work with me." Bill slightly raised the large pad he was carrying under his arm. "It's important we do this right away." He grimaced. "Considering the fact that you look like you've been run over by a truck, you're probably not in good shape to remember much of anything anyway. Even in normal circumstances, memories fade, your recollections get all twisted up by the conversations you have in the hours after the event . . . This shouldn't be a surprise to you, Kendra."

"It isn't. But you don't need to worry about it with me."

His faded blue eyes twinkled. "Of course not. The great and powerful Kendra Michaels is incapable of the cognitive errors that plague the rest of the mortal population . . ."

"Not fair. I'm not saying that."

"That's exactly what you're saying. Sixty years of experience tell me that the ones who claim to be infallible are the ones I need to worry most about. Next thing I know, I'm sketching someone my witness actually saw on the Carson show the night before."

Her lips twitched as she suppressed a smile. "I hate to tell you this, Bill, but I was in elementary school the last time Johnny Carson was on the air."

"Aah, your ageist barbs don't work on me. Those late-night hosts are all the same anyway. Take all the cheap shots you want. I've heard 'em already."

"That was a comment, not a cheap shot. You're the only sketch artist I wanted for this job, Bill. Of any age. This could be an unusual challenge for you."

"That sounds ominous."

"It's not. But I need someone with imagination and creativity."

"Hmm." He studied her face. "You've piqued my curiosity. Not enough to make it worth crawling out of my nice warm bed, of course, but at least now I'm curious why I've been forced to do it."

Kendra smiled even as she felt a pang as she noticed how frail Bill had become. Damn, it seemed as if he'd aged a decade in the two years since she had last seen him. Time could be so cruel.

"But I'm not staying out in this wet air." He steadied himself by placing a hand on the mobile command center. "Do they have room for us to work in this monstrosity?"

"It's a little noisy." She gestured toward her car, which was parked a few yards away. "Is there enough light to do this in there?"

He raised a flexible-neck book light clipped to his pad. "I brought my own. Let's get to it, young lady."

They climbed into her car, with Kendra taking her place behind the wheel and Bill sitting in the passenger seat.

He rested his pad on his knees. "Okay, let's start with the shape of his face. Square? Oval? Triangular? Some of each? Think. Give me a canvas, and we'll work from there."

"Sort of square . . . with high cheekbones."

"Good." He started to work, his pencil flying over the pad. "Like this?"

"No, chin more pointed."

His graphite pencil moved lightning fast, correcting. "Like this?"

"That's it."

"Now we go to the eyes. How far apart?"

The next fifteen minutes flew by as Bill used his eraser as artfully as he did his pencil. Kendra had no sooner voiced a correction than it was incorporated into the sketch. He quickly generated a reasonable likeness of the man she had seen earlier. But after still another fifteen minutes of working together to refine the sketch, it became so real, so on the mark, that it actually chilled her to look at it.

"Amazing," she finally said. "That's him, that's the man we're looking for. You're incredible, Bill."

"Yes. But this is just another day at the office. So what's with all the talk of imagination and creativity?"

She was silent. "I've been thinking. It's hard for me to believe that he would actually let me see what he really looked like. There were moments tonight when I was vulnerable. He could have killed me, but he didn't. That meant the game isn't over for him. He has something else in store for me. I believe he'd try to keep me from knowing anything that might give me an advantage." She looked down at the sketch. "I wonder . . . If he might have been wearing a disguise."

"Like a fake nose?"

"No, I think I would have spotted that. But we need to look at this sketch and think about what he might be doing to throw us off. The minute this hits the airwaves tomorrow, he knows a family member or coworker may recognize his face and call the police down on him."

Bill shrugged. "Maybe he doesn't care and is prepared to leave his old life behind."

"It's possible. But I think he does care. I think perhaps he's somehow taken steps to change his appearance. But he's done it in such a way that I wouldn't be able to immediately spot it as a disguise."

"I see what you're getting at." His pencil touched the hairline he'd drawn. "Maybe a good hairpiece, or hair coloring, possibly some false front teeth?"

"Maybe."

"You wouldn't have observed those things?"

"Not necessarily. He gives me a lot of credit, so he would have been especially careful. I can usually detect dentures from the effect it has on speech, but I didn't get that from him. With some practice or expert help, he could have fooled me."

Bill's eyes were narrowed on the sketch. "These cheekbones could have been extended and rounded off with some silicone packs placed between the upper lips and gum. It's amazing how much something like that can change the shape of the face."

"That's why I need you to show me. Can you draw different versions of this sketch, based on how you think he might look in everyday life without a disguise?" She urged, "And try to think of every single trick he might have used?"

"Hmm. But only tricks that Kendra Michaels wouldn't have detected."

"Yes."

He smiled faintly. "You're right. That's a challenge. I'll see what I can do. In the meantime, what should I do with this sketch?"

"Let the police department distribute it. I can't hold that up because I have a theory that he managed to stage a switch. That's the face I saw tonight, right down to the little mole above his left nostril. I have to stand by it. It's as if you sucked this right out of my brain and splattered it across that page."

"Not the most eloquent compliment I've ever received, but I'll take it. I'll drop this off with—"

RAP-RAP-RAP.

They were startled by the loud knock on the driver's side window.

It was Griffin.

Kendra opened the window. "Any news?"

"Yeah." He opened the driver's door. "Come on. We're going to Shell Beach."

IT WAS ONLY A SHORT RIDE in Griffin's car before Kendra had to abandon the vehicle to walk with Yates and the other police officers.

Grim faces. Tense faces.

Not a good sign, she thought as she strode after them down the concrete stairs that bridged the roadway with the small La Jolla cove known as Shell Beach.

As the name suggested, the area was well suited for collecting shells but was even better known for the sea lions that played and sunned on the rocks just offshore. Even now, Kendra could hear them braying in the darkness, voicing their displeasure at the helicopters overhead and the interlopers charging into their territory with flashlights.

Kendra and the dozen or so officers reached the beach and continued their single-file march in a wide arc that curved toward the shoreline. The area had obviously been roped off in the interest of preserving the scene, but she knew that the high tide was only hours away from erasing whatever evidence was left. You could never stop nature from taking back whatever it chose.

There was little question where they were headed since a half dozen flashlights were already trained on the spot up ahead.

The spot where Officer Gil Jillette lay dead.

He had been found facedown in one of the beach's famous tide pools, wedged into an intricate rock formation. He was now on the beach, and as Kendra stepped closer she could see that he was dressed in his uniform and that the JILLETTE name tag was in its rightful place above his right breast pocket.

And a stocking had been pulled taut over his face, flattening his features and giving him the appearance of a department-store mannequin.

Just like all the others, two years before.

She forced herself to look at the dead officer's face. Even through the stocking, she could see that his eyes were open, staring up toward the stars.

Damn. He'd done nothing to deserve this. He should be home with his wife, little girl, and that funny-looking Chihuahua/Jack Russell Terrier mix.

The memory of that family photo she had seen on the dash of his squad car was streaming back to her. She felt a wrenching sadness at what lay before that family.

One of the officers waved his hand over the corpse's grotesquely swollen neck. "What's this? He wasn't in the water that long."

Kendra leaned closer. "He had a reaction to the Vecuronium Bromide."

The cop looked at her. "What?"

"It's an anesthetic. The killer's a copycat, and Vecuronium Bromide was the drug of choice. I'm sure this man has it in his system."

Most of the officers were glancing at each other and obviously had no knowledge of the killer and his emerging pattern. Their expressions all conveyed some variant of "what is this crazy bitch talking about?"

Never mind them. She carefully scanned the corpse. Could Gil Jillette tell her anything else?

Come on, don't let that bastard get away with doing this to you. Help me. Show me.

But she couldn't tell much that was different. Just a confirmation of what she already knew. The name badge had been put on by the killer, not Jillette. The pin had missed the stitch-reinforced hole and pierced the shirt just outside the ring. The shirt was still wet, but even so, Kendra could see this was a mistake Jillette never made himself.

Anything else?

Maybe one thing. A rawness around his lips, with some hairs pulled out of his moustache . . .

Her head swiftly lifted. She said urgently to the circle of police officers, "Hurry. Go search the beach. Try to find a large adhesive bandage or maybe a strip of duct tape. If you do, bag it as evidence. It was probably placed over his mouth, then torn off. It may have the killer's DNA. Understand?"

"Go," Gates said sharply to his men. "Move it!"

The policemen scattered like leaves in the wind.

Kendra watched them for a moment but then shook her head to clear it. She was suddenly feeling weak and foggy. She'd been energized by the search for Jillette, but every ounce of her energy had now drained away. It was as if the evening's events had come rushing back to her, pummeling her emotionally and physically.

"You look like you're ready to collapse." Griffin was behind her. "Now will you go to the hospital?"

"No."

"Kendra, dammit, you're—"

"I'm going home. I need to get my head around everything that's happened tonight." She glanced at him. "And don't you ever phone Lynch and tell him that he's to interfere. That was completely ineffectual, and I won't tolerate it."

He shrugged. "I thought it was worth a shot. We still need a full statement about what happened back at the house."

"I gave a detective my statement, and Bill Dillingham has done the sketch. That's enough for now. Who has Corrine Harvey's clothes that I took from the scene?"

"Our forensics guys took it. It's already in the lab."

"Good. Listen, I'll come to your office tomorrow. Anyone else who wants to hash this out with me can join us."

"Okay. But just know I'm putting a guard outside your condo effective immediately." He raised his hand as if anticipating her objection. "You don't get a choice in the matter. There's a serial killer on the loose, and you're the only one who has seen him. That makes you extremely valuable to this case. I can't afford to lose you."

"How sentimental. I'm getting all teary-eyed here."

"I figured it's the only reason you'd go along with it," he said gruffly.

Kendra smiled wearily as she turned away from Griffin. For once, he was displaying all the signs of being a decent human being. It was as if the rough edges had, at least momentarily, been sanded away. "Actually . . . you're right. That makes perfect sense. So who's going to give me a ride back to my car?"

* * *

"IT WAS A PLEASURE TO MEET YOU, Kendra. Don't forget about the mole . . ."

She opened her eyes with a start, her heart pounding.

Dammit.

It had been another restless night. This was the third time she'd had that dream, always ending with that psycho in the police uniform turning toward her and smiling. But instead of texting her his message, he was saying it aloud, taunting her in the cruel whisper she'd heard on the phone.

She rolled over in bed and glanced at the clock—7:45 A.M.

Enough.

She swung her feet over the edge of the bed and had just started to get up when her phone rang. No ID. She picked it up from her bedside table. "Hello?"

"Ms. Michaels, this is Agent Nelson. I'm standing watch outside your unit right now, and there's a woman here who says she's your—"

"Mother, dammit."

Kendra could hear her mother's voice shouting and haranguing the poor man, both through the phone and through the two closed doors that separated her from the building hallway.

"I hear her, Agent Nelson. Sorry about that. She can come in."

Kendra got up and paused to glance at herself in the mirror as she threw on a robe.

Damn, she looked like hell. The bruises had swollen, and the cuts made it look like she'd been in a knife fight. Maybe if she threw on a long-sleeved shirt to help hide the damage . . .

Too late. Her mother had let herself into the condo with her key, and she would be charging into her bedroom in a matter of seconds.

Oh, well. Face the music.

Kendra swung open her bedroom door.

Diane Michaels stopped dead in her tracks. She was speechless for once, gaping at Kendra's cuts and bruises.

"Morning, Mom. Pancakes or waffles?"

"What the hell happened to you?"

"I had a little problem." Kendra moved past her and walked toward the kitchen. "I'm sure you know, or else you wouldn't be here."

"No, I came here because I heard about that police officer who was murdered. The news said that the killer is copying your old cases."

Kendra froze in the act of reaching for the coffee cups. "I should have known. No way this could stay a secret."

"And no way this should have ever stayed a secret from *me.*"

Kendra turned back around. She didn't like that tension in her mother's voice. She was accustomed to her mother's exasperation, but this was something else. The woman was truly frightened for her.

"Mom, I'm fine."

"Don't tell me that. I rushed over here, and the first thing I see is that . . . thug standing in front of your door. I didn't know what to think. Then I come in here and see you looking like this."

"It looks worse than it is."

"It looks pretty damned bad."

"I won't argue with that."

"So tell me what happened. *Now.*"

"I will. Calm down." She put on the coffee. "But I might as well make you breakfast while I do it. If you ran over here this early, I doubt if you had it. How about omelets?"

"I don't want a damn—" She gazed at Kendra's expression, and said, "Fine. Anything." She dropped down in a kitchen chair. "Now stop trying to soothe me and tell me who beat you up."

"No one. I did it myself." She opened the refrigerator door and started searching for the eggs. In the next few minutes, she told her mother everything, from her experience on the bridge all the way to Shell Beach early that morning. Her weak attempts to minimize the danger sounded as ludicrous to her as it probably did to her mother.

There was no way to hide it. No two ways about it, she thought. It was one hell of a scary night.

When she was finished, her mother got to her feet and stabbed her finger toward a chair. "You sit down. I'll make breakfast."

"You're forgetting something. You can't cook."

"Do you have frozen waffles in the freezer?"

"Yes."

"Then I can make breakfast. Sit down."

Kendra took the seat she'd indicated at the table while her mother rummaged around in the freezer. "I wanted to save that cop, Mom," Kendra said quietly. "But he was probably facedown in the tide pool before we even knew what was happening."

"You were lucky to save yourself." She pulled out a box of Eggo frozen waffles, tore into the packaging, and loaded them into the four-slice toaster. "By the way, Dean told me all about your adventure on the bridge the other night."

"I guess he's running for the hills about now."

"Just the opposite. You turned him on. I never thought your gifts of observation were good for anything but getting you into trouble. Apparently, they can also be an aphrodisiac."

"Trust me, they're not."

"Tell that to Dean. He can't wait to see you again. He said he'd called you but had gotten your voice mail and you hadn't returned the call. He was quizzing me about ideas for your second date. It was sweet, really."

"He's a good guy. But I really can't think about him right now. Not until this case is over."

Her mother slowly turned back toward her. "You're not seriously thinking of continuing?"

Here it comes. "I have to."

"No. The FBI has to, you don't."

"No one knows those cases better than I do. For all the Power-Point presentations and bulletin boards the FBI studies, no one else has actually lived and breathed each and every one of those cases."

"One person has, Kendra."

She stared at her mother while she grasped her meaning. "Yes, you're right. The killer has. All the more reason why I need to be a part of this."

"And what do you think he's going to do when he gets tired of playing?"

"He's not anywhere close to getting tired of it."

"How do you know?"

"Because I've dealt with killers like this before."

"Not like this."

"Close enough. He's just getting started. I've only just begun to give him the attention he's obviously craving from me. He has compulsions, sick needs, to be satisfied. I can use those against him."

"But he knows you, too, Kendra. A hell of a lot better than you know him. He knows where you live and work, and he can get to you whenever he wants to do it."

Kendra started to point toward the hallway, but her mother cut her off.

"And don't think that some FBI bodyguard can stop a high-powered rifle with a laser scope," Diane said. "If this sicko has shown us anything, it's that he's capable of killing in any number of ways. The second you step out of this building, you're vulnerable." She sat down next to her and took her hand. "Too vulnerable." She gently ran her fingers over Kendra's cut and bruised arm. "To *see* you like this, baby. It just makes it more real. I could lose you."

"You're not going to lose me. Trust me, the FBI is extremely motivated to keep me alive."

"It may not be enough."

"Then it's enough that I'm motivated to keep myself alive. This killer's chosen to make this case intensely personal. He's reaching and trying to hurt me in any way he can. And he's going to keep murdering people until he's caught. Don't you see? I have the best chance of stopping him."

Her mother was silent. "I'm having trouble seeing that you have a better chance than all the manpower and resources of the Federal Bureau of Investigation. It doesn't compute, Kendra."

"Yes, it does. In this particular case, it makes excellent sense. And I don't have a problem turning my back on the FBI. But I do have a problem turning my back on whoever he may try to kill next."

Her mother leaned back in her chair. "You know . . . In those months and years after you got your sight, your wild days, I was so afraid. You'd been given this amazing gift, and I thought it might be too much for you. You were so intent on absorbing every new experience, both good and bad, that I was afraid you might . . . self-destruct. I don't think you realize how close you came."

"I do realize." Her hand covered Diane's. "But it took me a while longer to realize how hard it must have been for you, Mom. I'm sorry for everything I put you through."

"It was hard." She paused, then said brusquely, "But we got through that, and I guess we'll get through this, too."

"We definitely will."

"Particularly since I intend to move in here with you."

Kendra's eyes widened. "What?"

"I don't trust that guard in the hall, but I trust myself. I think I should—"

"No, Mom," Kendra said firmly. "That's not going to happen."

Her mother sighed. "I didn't think you'd go for it, but I thought I'd try." She added slyly, "Well, at least call Dean back so that I can see a safe future for you on the horizon."

"Mom, you're incorrigible." She couldn't help but chuckle. "You remind me of Lynch. Pure manipulation."

"Lynch is a very dangerous man. I'm not dangerous to you. I'm only a mother trying to pave your way to a better life. Will you do it?"

She made a face. "Yes, I'll call Dean. But that's all I'll promise."

"That's enough . . . for now." She grinned. "I couldn't leave here without some vestige of victory."

"And you have it." Kendra added gravely, "But I do have some bad news."

"What?"

Kendra sniffed the air. "You really can't cook. You just burned the waffles."

CHAPTER
5

AT NOON, KENDRA MET with the FBI team and three police officers who were visibly seething from the murder of their colleague. She had seen this kind of desperation in investigators before, usually reserved for killers of fellow officers and children. Unfortunately, such raw emotion occasionally led to sloppy police work and false arrests. She had assisted in more than one case in which her most valuable contribution had been clearing innocent suspects who had been targeted by overzealous detectives.

Once again, she recounted the events of the previous evening, making sure they took note of the observations of the killer she had made, even down to the type of shaver he used.

After almost two hours of debriefing, she finally stood up to excuse herself. But Special Agent Saffron Reade still had one significant insight to share.

"I believe I know what Myatt means, Dr. Michaels," Reade said. "Remember? That was the name he signed on your mobile phone message."

Kendra stopped. "I could hardly forget. You definitely have my full attention."

"John Myatt is the name of a forger. A painter. Scotland Yard called him the biggest art fraud of the twentieth century. He's said to have sold his fakes to art galleries and auction houses all over the world. He could create uncanny copies of a wide variety of artists."

Kendra was silent, trying to put together the connection. "Our murderer must see himself in the same way. He's copying the work of people he thinks of as artists."

"Exactly," Reade said. "That's something to keep in mind. He doesn't see himself as a butcher. He thinks he's an artist, and he wants his work to be admired." She paused. "Very often, that desire can lead to a criminal's downfall."

Kendra nodded. "I can see that. Good work, Reade. Thank you." She turned to go.

"And thank you, Kendra," Griffin said as he held the door open for her. "You've been very cooperative." He added softly, "Surprisingly cooperative. I'll only keep you for a little while longer. Will you come down the hall with me for just a moment?"

"I'm done," she said bluntly. "You're not getting anything else out of me."

"No third degree." Griffin was ushering her down the hall and into a small conference room. "This won't take you more than—"

"What's this?" Kendra stopped just inside the door as she saw a gray-haired man waiting for her in the conference room. He had a large, brown leather satchel on the floor beside him.

The man smiled. "Hello, Kendra. I'm delighted to meet you."

She turned back toward Griffin. "Who is this?"

"He's your doctor. Whether you want him to be or not."

"No way. Seriously? You called a doctor here to examine me?"

"No."

"Then how in the hell—?"

The doctor opened his satchel. "I'm Dr. Paul Thompson, Dr. Michaels. I work out of the Scripps Medical Center. I'm here at the behest of Adam Lynch. He phoned me at about four this morning. He was most insistent that I examine you. I was prepared to open my office early for you, but he said you'd never go for that."

"So he found the one doctor in San Diego who makes house calls."

"Actually, I don't. Mr. Lynch is a very persuasive man."

"No one would argue that point." Kendra nodded toward his satchel. "That explains the strange doctor's bag, which isn't really a doctor's bag at all. You usually carry that to work with a laptop and ham sandwich inside. Am I right?"

Dr. Thompson smiled as he pulled a stethoscope from his bag. "Sometimes tuna."

Kendra turned toward Griffin in disbelief.

"We checked him out," Griffin said. "He's who he says he is."

Dr. Thompson pulled a folded paper examination gown from his bag. "Now, if I can have you change into this . . ."

"Are you kidding me?"

"Mr. Lynch wanted me to be very thorough. I can wait outside while you—"

"Go away. That isn't going to happen."

"My instructions are to follow you wherever you go and stand by until you consent to a full examination."

"You have nothing better to do?"

He didn't answer directly. "Mr. Lynch is compensating me exceptionally well for my time."

Kendra shook her head. Lynch was probably laughing his ass off at that very moment. Okay, she could fight and waste her time and energy, or she could submit and get through the exam in record time.

And get back at Lynch at the earliest opportunity.

She finally snatched the gown from the doctor's hand. "Fine. Both of you get out of here while I change. Only the doctor comes back in. I want to get this over with."

She looked at Griffin, whose broad smile was turning into a gleeful chuckle. "Griffin, I don't believe I've ever seen you laugh before."

He shrugged. "It's just nice to see that Adam Lynch can piss off other people as much as he does me. I'm looking forward to watching you get your revenge." He turned and walked out the door. "Enjoy your exam."

HEARD YOU'RE IN FINE SHAPE. GREAT NEWS.

Kendra's grip tightened on her phone as she stared at the text message from Lynch. She hadn't even reached the elevator when her phone vibrated with the alert. Dr. Thompson had obviously phoned Lynch the second she had left the room.

She texted in reply: ALL GOOD, EXCEPT FOR OCCASIONAL NAUSEA CAUSED BY ONE ADAM LYNCH. NO KNOWN CURE.

His response came seconds later: CONDITION MISDIAG-NOSED. OBVIOUSLY NOT GETTING ENOUGH ADAM LYNCH. WILL WORK TO RECTIFY SITUATION SOON.

She typed her reply: NO RUSH, CONDITION RAPIDLY IM-PROVING WITH EACH LYNCH-LESS DAY.

He fired back: PATIENT HAS OBVIOUSLY SUSTAINED MAS-SIVE BRAIN TRAUMA. ONLY EXPLANATION FOR LACK OF APPRECIATION FOR AMAZING ADAM LYNCH.

She replied: HAVE ARRANGED INVASIVE AND INCREDI-BLY PAINFUL RECTAL EXAM FOR YOU. COULD COME AT ANY TIME, WITHOUT WARNING. WATCH YOUR BACK.

He answered: PROMISES, PROMISES. SEE YOU SOON.

Kendra pocketed her phone.

In spite of her annoyance with Lynch's arbitrary action, she found her anger was beginning to fade. She had left the doctor thinking what a colossal waste of time the exam had been, but she couldn't help feeling a bit moved. Although several people had urged her to see a doctor, only Lynch had taken the time and trouble to actually bring one to her. Who does that?

Only Adam Lynch.

She entered the elevator, and Special Agent Roland Metcalf wedged his shoulder in just as the doors were about to close. He quickly stepped into the elevator with her. "You forgot something."

"What's that?"

"Me. I'm your guard today."

"Really? I thought that was below your pay grade."

"Actually, I'm also sort of partnering with you, assisting you, providing whatever support you may need."

"And providing your boss with updates on my progress?"

He grinned. "That was implied, yes. But if there's anything you'd rather keep confidential . . ."

She shrugged. "Tell him whatever you want."

"Good, so what's on the agenda today?"

"Well, considering that I flew out of a second-story window last night, wouldn't you think I might just want to relax?"

"Hell, no. Nobody thinks that. Come on, what are we doing?"

"You guys are beginning to know me a little too well. Kinda depressing." She studied Metcalf. If she had to have a bodyguard, at least it was one who could be of some use to her. He carried himself with an ease and jauntiness that made it clear that he didn't take himself—or anything else in the world—too seriously. A pleasant change of pace from most other FBI agents she'd met. "Okay, how much do you know about cars?"

"Cars? I know you're supposed to change the oil every three thousand miles, but it's really okay if you wait and do it every seven or eight."

"Awesome."

"Glad I passed the test. So what are we doing?"

"I'm pretty sure I heard the killer start his car and drive away last night. I can identify the make and maybe the model of the car if I hear it again."

"Now *that's* awesome." His eyes were glittering with eagerness. "Where do we start?"

"Car dealers. Not the most accommodating bunch, especially since there's no chance of a sales commission. I'll need you to flash your badge around."

"It's what I do best, ma'am."

"I certainly hope not." She smiled. "And don't call me ma'am. I'm not that much older than you."

His smile held equal parts mischief and a hint of sensuality. "Roger that, ma'am."

KENDRA CHOSE TO FOCUS THEIR ATTENTION on the Convoy Street "auto row" of car dealerships within walking distance of each other. True to his word, Metcalf was very good at flashing his badge and exuding an air of authority that made the dealership managers snap to attention and race around their lots with fistfuls of keys. They started each model in their lines, punched the accelerators, and even drove around the parking lots when Kendra requested them to do so.

After listening to thirty-five vehicles at four dealerships, Kendra was certain she'd heard a six-cylinder engine the previous evening, but she knew little else. She thanked the Honda sales manager in the parking lot and turned to Metcalf in frustration. "This is starting to feel like a fool's errand."

"I also do those very well. But we won't be complete fools until we impose on every sales manager on this street. So what do you say we—"

"Wait!" Kendra listened. "I hear it."

"Where?"

"Shh." She looked toward the road and saw a car speeding by the dealership. "There! What kind of car is that?"

"Uh, a blue one." Metcalf grabbed a nearby saleswoman and pointed to the vehicle. "Pop quiz. Name that car."

She responded immediately. "Nissan Skyline."

Metcalf turned back to Kendra. "Is that a possibility?"

She nodded. "There's a Nissan dealership one block up. Let's go."

FROM THE MOMENT THE MANAGER turned the key in a Skyline, Kendra recognized the engine's growl as the same as she had heard the night before. She heard it again in a 370Z, and several more times in the nearby dealership of Nissan's luxury division, Infiniti.

In the Infiniti showroom, Kendra compared brochures for the cars. "Look." She pointed to the engine specifications. "Each one of those vehicles has a VQ37VHR engine, the same as the Nissan Skyline and the Z."

"Does it?" Metcalf used his mobile phone to snap photos of each of the brochures. "Amazing. I'll have to take your word for it. After all the cars we've heard today, everything was sounding alike to me."

"Did they look alike to you?"

"Not really."

"As someone who grew up without being able to see, I used the sounds I heard as my single biggest way of perceiving the world. Those engine sounds are as different to me as the difference between seeing a red car and a blue one, or a sports car and a pickup truck."

"That makes sense, but it's still fascinating to witness." He paged through the photos he had taken with his phone. "I was hoping we could cross-reference ownership records with driver's licenses, and maybe put together a virtual lineup of license photos for you to look at. But we're looking at eight different models of cars here."

"I know. Even if we narrow our focus to San Diego registrations, there are probably thousands of owners."

"Still, it's another piece we can match against potential suspects.

We'll check it against auto registrations on that block and make sure you weren't hearing a neighbor's car. I'd say that's a decent afternoon's work."

"And at least now I have a pretty good working knowledge of various automobile engine sounds from the six dealerships we visited."

He gazed skeptically at her. "You'd really remember if you heard them again?"

"Most of them. A couple weren't that distinctive, but I could do pretty well with the rest."

"Interesting." Metcalf collected the brochures and walked with her out the door. It was getting dark, and the dealership street signs down the block had just started to flicker on. He gestured over his left shoulder. "I think I just heard a car pulling into the lot behind us. Are you telling me just by listening, you could—?"

"It's a Toyota FJ. Probably without the four-wheel-drive package."

They both turned and saw the distinctive, boxy form of a Toyota FJ cruiser.

Metcalf shook his head. "Incredible."

"No big deal. But if it had been from a car dealer we didn't visit today, I might have been out of luck."

"We should hit those other dealers sometime to round out your repertoire. You never know when it could come in handy."

"This isn't my day job, Metcalf. I'd actually be happier if it never came in handy."

He laughed. "Nah, I don't believe that. You have a gift. It would be like Superman deciding that journalism is his true calling, or Batman thinking that his life's work is really dating supermodels and making money."

She gazed at him in horror. "Oh, God. You're a comic-book geek."

Metcalf smiled. "So everyone who enjoys the art of graphic storytelling is a geek?"

"I knew it! I'll bet you're one of those fan boys who takes over the Gaslamp District every summer and goes to Comic-Con."

"That doesn't make me a geek."

"So you do go." Her face suddenly lit with amusement. "Whoa. I just got a mental image of you wearing a brightly colored Spandex costume with big boots, cape flowing behind you . . ."

"I don't wear a costume."

"Do the people at your office know?"

"Of course they know. I have to take off work."

"You actually take off work?"

He shrugged. "Don't want to miss anything."

"Be honest. You tell your fellow agents that you're away on an annual fishing trip with your college buddies, don't you?"

"I'm not discussing this anymore."

"Aw, come on," she urged teasingly.

"Nope. You obviously have no respect for the artistry and economy of storytelling in the modern graphic novel."

Her smile faded. "I'm only kidding, Metcalf. You have the right to your opinion and to enjoy life in any way you choose. I admire you. I respect the fact that you're reaching out for what makes you happy. I hope you keep on doing it."

"Oh, I will." His eyes were twinkling. "It keeps me young. You ought to come with me to the next Comic-Con." He paused, then added slyly, "Ma'am."

"Low blow. I might just—" She stopped as Metcalf's mobile phone rang.

"This is probably Griffin," he said as he pulled the phone from his pocket.

"You don't have John Williams's Superman theme as your ringtone?" she asked solemnly.

"Not during work hours." He strolled a few steps away and answered his phone. After less than a minute, he returned to her. "Are you up to a meeting at the FBI field office?"

"Now?"

"Yes. That was Griffin as I thought. They have an idea how the killer knew where you were going last night." He moved toward the car. "You'll probably want to be part of this."

HALF AN HOUR LATER, Kendra and Metcalf were standing in the FBI field-office conference room with Griffin, Saffron Reade, and a bearded technology specialist who had been introduced to her as Robert Windrey.

The technician was leaning over a laptop set up on the conference-room table. Griffin waved everyone over to gather around.

"Kendra, our team did an electronic sweep of your apartment, but there was no evidence of any listening devices," Griffin said.

"So you think the leak might be on your end?"

"Doubtful, but Windrey here has some thoughts on the matter."

Windrey glanced up at Kendra. "I'm going to play something for you, Dr. Michaels. Listen to this."

He pressed the space bar on his laptop keyboard, and a male voice rang from the speakers. It was Windrey's own voice, Kendra realized. He sounded stilted, overenunciating each of his words: "Testing, testing . . . Broadcasting to any and all within the sound of my voice. Testing, testing . . ."

Windrey smiled proudly, as if expecting her to be as impressed with him as he obviously was with himself.

"Okay," Kendra said. "What does that mean?"

Windrey was still smiling. "I was using your cordless phone. I was able to wirelessly intercept and record any call made to or from it. I think our killer is able to do the same thing. He intercepted your call to

Agent Griffin yesterday. He knew you were headed to Corrine Harvey's house even before the police did."

Kendra slowly sat down at the conference table. "Incredible. I thought these digital handsets were supposed to be almost impossible to hack."

"That was true once. The Digital Enhanced Cordless Telecommunications, or DECT, standards were pretty safe for years. But certain software tools used by manufacturers and security professionals to evaluate the devices have leaked onto the Web. They can be used to hack into wireless phones and other DECT devices like traffic lights in Germany and traffic-control systems in England."

"Great. Very reassuring."

"The good news is, you should be fine if you just plug in a corded handset." He qualified, "At least for the duration of this investigation."

"Absolutely. Believe me, I'll be unplugging my cordless phone the second I get home."

"No," Griffin said quickly. "We don't think you should do that quite yet."

"But he just got through telling me that—"

"We may be able to use this, Kendra," Agent Reade interrupted. "Think about it. We were discussing this earlier. We now have an advantage we didn't have last night."

Kendra's glance moved slowly from agent to agent. "I believe I know where you're heading."

"Do you?" Reade asked. "I thought you might. And is it something you would be comfortable going along with?"

"Depends. What exactly do you want me to do?"

Reade opened a leather folio, pulled out a thin sheaf of papers, and placed them in front of Kendra. "This is your script."

Kendra laughed. "My script? You aren't fooling around."

"It's only meant to be a guide," Reade said gravely. "What we have in mind is this: You'll go home with your FBI guard in tow. A few minutes later, you'll call Griffin with your cordless phone. We've crafted a scenario in which you've decided to visit the home of Kristy Ludwig, who was the victim in the minivan. We'll have agents staked out all over your area. Windrey here tells us he probably has a listening station within a block of your condo. Anyone in the area who goes on the move after your phone call will be noticed by someone on our team."

Kendra scanned the telephone script they had written for her. "You really think he's still listening to my calls, even after last night?"

"*Especially* after last night," Griffin said. "It goes back to the profile. He's obviously fascinated by you and wants to be noticed by you. It follows that after finally making contact, he'd love to hear what kind of effect he had on you and your psyche. We think he may still be listening."

She spent a few minutes going over the script. "If we do this as written, I could be setting myself up as bait."

"I won't deny it. You'll be surrounded by our best agents. We need to draw him out."

Kendra turned the sheaf of papers over. "Okay, what's next?"

"Then, after the call, our agent takes you to Kristy Ludwig's home. We'll already be staked out there, but you won't see any of us until you're inside."

"You really think he'd be brazen enough to try something again?"

"If you follow that script, we think he might at least follow you."

"Did your profilers and behaviorists tell you that?"

Griffin sighed. "I detect a bit of cynicism in your voice."

"Not at all. I have tremendous respect for the work your profilers do. I just don't want to underestimate this killer. He's taken great pains to study how I work, but I'm sure he's also studied how the FBI works."

"Possibly. But last night he took an enormous risk. We think it's worth trying to coax him into taking another one. If he does, this time we'll be ready for him. Will you help us?"

Kendra glanced around the table at the agents who were staring hopefully at her. She thought about it. The plan was risky on a number of levels besides the fact that working from a script went completely against her grain. But they were right, she realized. If this was going to work at all, the chances were better now, while he was still basking in his recent victory.

She finally nodded slowly. "Yes, let's go for it."

KENDRA PICKED UP THE CORDLESS handset and was surprised to see that her fingers were slightly trembling. Nerves or anticipation? If that soulless bastard was really listening, she wanted nothing better than to cut loose and threaten every form of bodily injury imaginable. But she couldn't show her hand, whatever the hell that was.

She punched Griffin's number. He answered on the second ring. "Michael Griffin."

"Griffin, it's Kendra Michaels."

"You just left the office. Can't get enough of us, huh?"

His attempt at natural-sounding banter sounded forced. She hoped to hell that her acting was better than his.

"Yeah, I just got in. Listen, I've been thinking. I want to visit Kristy Ludwig's house. She was the driver of the minivan on the bridge the other night. Your team thinks she was snatched at her home, right?"

"Yes. Just like Corrine Harvey. But after last night, there's no way in hell I'm letting you go there alone."

"Then have some of your biggest and best meet me there. I think our killer might have left a calling card at Corrine Harvey's house without even realizing it. If he inadvertently did the same thing again, I think we can get this son of a bitch."

"A calling card?"

"Yeah. I didn't even realize how important it could be until just now."

"Uh-huh. So are you going to clue me in?"

"I'll let you know if it pans out."

"Come on. I can't help you unless you help me."

At least he could deliver that line realistically, Kendra thought. She had given him years of practice. "We'll discuss it later. Right now, I just need to go to that house."

Silence. "I can't have anybody meet you there for at least an hour."

"Then I'll be there waiting." She hung up the phone.

Your move, Myatt.

AFTER A HALF-HOUR WAIT, Kendra's armed FBI escort drove her to Kristy Ludwig's one-story home in Old Town. She was unnerved as they walked from the car to the house's front door. Even though she knew there might have been a dozen agents watching her, she hated the idea of not being in control. The target on her back had never been bigger, and she had helped paint it there herself.

She felt her muscles relax as she stepped into the house and swung the door closed behind her.

Agents Griffin and Reade were in the living room.

"Are you okay?" Reade asked.

"Yes. Just tell me this paid off."

Griffin and Reade exchanged discouraged looks.

Kendra cursed under her breath. "Nothing at all?"

"Not so far." Griffin's gaze narrowed at his laptop s screen on the coffee table. "No unusual movement in the vicinity of your condo building. We stopped a couple of people who were leaving buildings on your block, but nobody who didn't belong there."

"And here?"

"Not yet," Reade said. "There are agents all over, and Metcalf has a bird's-eye view from the parking garage at the end of the block. He hasn't reported any suspicious activity."

"Great."

For the first time, Kendra glanced around the living room. She hadn't considered visiting the house since the victim's parents had already sent cleaning crews in and begun preparing their late daughter's home for sale.

It was immediately apparent that Kristy Ludwig worked erratic hours, ate in front of the television, and occasionally smoked pot. Kendra's visual scan abruptly stopped when she spotted a laundry hamper stuffed with baby toys. Damn. She remembered that Ludwig was a single mother who had left behind an eighteen-month-old girl. The toys and high chair brought it home in a way that a few lines in a case file could not.

Kendra stared at those toys for the better part of an hour while it became apparent that she and the FBI had utterly failed in their attempt to smoke out the killer.

"I'm calling it," Griffin said in the manner of a surgeon declaring a patient dead. "Suspend the operation."

Reade picked up her radio and notified Metcalf.

Griffin turned toward Kendra. "Thanks for your help. Looks like you're going to need that guard outside your door for a while longer."

"The condo association will be so pleased."

AS KENDRA UNLOCKED HER FRONT DOOR, she turned back to the young FBI Agent, Donald Nelson, who was acting as her guard. "If you need to use the bathroom or want something to eat or drink while you're here, you're certainly welcome."

"That won't be necessary, ma'am, but thank you."

"The guard who was here last night didn't either. They must be teaching bladder control at Quantico these days."

The agent smiled. "Can't confirm or deny. It's classified. Good night, ma'am. Just call if you need me."

Kendra entered her condo and tossed her keys on the foyer table. She'd already canceled her appointments with her clients for the next few days, but she'd told them she was available for any questions. Thank heavens, there was no one who was at a crucial point in their therapy. She checked her watch—10:35 P.M. Check to see if there were any messages. Too late to return phone calls, but perhaps she could dash off some e-mails and—

She froze. She couldn't breathe.

Holy shit.

There, scrawled on her living room wall in red paint, was a message.

NICE TRY, KENDRA. BUT YOU'RE BETTER THAN THAT.
        —MYATT

He'd been here.

In her home.

She felt violated.

Was he still here?

She went still, listening for any sign of him.

She held her breath and moved toward the door. Stay calm. All she had to do was scream, and that FBI agent would be at her side in seconds.

Or would he?

Her mind raced. What if he'd been dispatched as easily and cruelly as that young police officer?

What if Myatt himself was waiting on the other side of that door?

Shit-shit-shit.

Keep moving, don't panic . . .

Are you there, you bastard? I almost hope you are. I want to come face-to-face with you again.

She gripped the doorknob with one hand, the dead bolt with the other. She flipped the dead bolt and threw open the door.

The FBI agent stood there, safe and sound. "Ma'am? May I help you?"

She took a moment to catch her breath. "Yes, you can. Come in and take a good look around, Agent Nelson. But first, call Griffin right now and get him out here." She moistened her lips. "It seems our psychopath paid me a visit."

THE FBI EVIDENCE RECOVERY TEAM arrived before Griffin, Metcalf, and Reade, and they appeared to be gathering little from the scene besides the paint shavings scraped from her wall. Kendra watched them work for a few minutes before stepping away and leaning wearily against the wall in her building's corridor.

Metcalf joined her. "Hell of a couple days, huh?"

"Yeah, you could say that."

He looked down the hall, where Griffin and Reade had just stepped from the elevator. He lowered his voice. "You were right about this nut. He was two moves ahead of us."

"He does his homework, that's for damned sure."

Griffin approached Kendra. "I guess our little radio show didn't fool anybody."

"That's not true." Kendra shrugged. "We certainly fooled ourselves."

Metcalf laughed, but cut it short after Griffin shot him a withering glare.

"I want to know how Myatt got into my condo," Kendra said. "The locks on my doors haven't been broken, and he would have to be a master locksmith to pick them. I made sure of that when I moved in."

"Give us a little time," Griffin said. "We'll have an answer for you."

Reade broke in. "And we've already begun a door-to-door search here in the building. We've identified the traffic and security cameras in the area, and since you were gone less than two hours, it narrows our focus on how much footage we need to request and examine."

Kendra looked away. "I'm sure Myatt identified those cameras, too. He probably did it days ago. He probably mapped out a route to avoid them all, and if he couldn't do that, he disabled a camera or two." Her glance shifted back to the agents. "It's what I would have done."

Griffin looked through the open doorway at the scrawled message on her living-room wall. "Day one of Criminal Profiling 101 tells us that we shouldn't assume that the perp will think and behave as we would ourselves."

"Normally, I would agree. But not only is he incredibly detail-oriented, he considers himself an artist. Every brushstroke has to be painted just so, or it all falls apart."

"We still need to follow every angle. Everyone makes mistakes."

"And I'm sure he's already made a few," Kendra said. "We just haven't found them yet." She turned to Reade. "Where do we stand on that police sketch?"

"It made the late edition of the papers, and it's been on all the evening news shows. We've already had dozens of calls on the tip line."

"Hundreds," Griffin corrected. "Hundreds and hundreds. As usual. No matter how specific and detailed the sketch is, everyone is convinced that their coworker, college roommate, or kid's soccer coach is a serial killer."

"We'll do a preliminary check and gather photos for as many as we can," Reade said. "We'll have you come in and take a look. Maybe even tomorrow."

Kendra nodded. "Good. The sooner the better."

"You have a place to stay tonight?" Metcalf asked.

Kendra gestured toward her doorway as two more evidence specialists entered. "Sure. Right there." Before he could respond, she said, "Just joking. I have a friend who lives in the building."

"A friend who won't mind an FBI man lurking outside her door all night?"

"Actually, Olivia might be into that." She grinned. "But I'll tell her to keep her beautifully manicured paws off the poor guy."

CHAPTER
6

"DID YOU FIND EVERYTHING?" Olivia asked, as Kendra came out of the bathroom into the guest room. "You haven't stayed overnight for a long time. Not since we had a few too many cocktails after I made us that fantastic lasagna dinner last year."

"It was fantastic. You're a great cook." Kendra glanced at Olivia, who was standing in the doorway. "Has it been that long? It seems like yesterday."

"You've been busy. So have I."

"You've got that right." She pulled back the sheet and slipped into bed. "Thanks for taking me in tonight."

"Don't be stupid," Olivia said. "We're closer than sisters. Who else would you go to?"

"No one. Except Mom. And that would have opened a huge can of worms again." She punched the pillow and settled in the bed. "I'm fine, Olivia. Go back to bed."

"Shall I turn out the lights?"

"Please."

Olivia reached out and flipped the wall switch, and the room was plunged into darkness. She stood there, silhouetted against the light streaming from the hall behind her. "Kendra . . . I've always wondered something ever since you had that operation."

"Wondered what?"

She was silent, then asked, "How do you feel about . . . darkness?"

Kendra wished Olivia hadn't turned off the light. She couldn't tell by her voice what she was feeling. Olivia was too good at hiding her emotions. "Why do you want to know?"

"Darkness is home for me, it's my comfort zone. Before you gained your vision, you felt that way, too. It was something we shared. I know it can never be that way again, but I was curious. Is there an instant of panic? Or is there comfort?"

Olivia had been wonderfully generous and happy when Kendra had gained her sight, but there had been many large and small issues about adjusting their relationship to the new status. Evidently, this was one of the questions that hadn't been addressed. "How do I feel at the moment I turn out the lights and go back to the dark?" She was silent, thinking. "I guess I never analyzed it. When I first opened my eyes after the operation, I was frightened. It was all too much. Too bright. Too gloriously vivid. It took me weeks to adjust, then I gradually became accustomed to that world. Oh, not like someone who had always had their sight and took it for granted. I could never take it for granted. But I became drunk with the headiness of it. I wanted to taste every vision and sensation. I went a little off kilter trying to do it. But you know that."

"Yes, you worried me." She paused. "But I might have done the same thing if it had been me."

"I *wanted* it to be you, too. God, how I wanted it," Kendra said. "It will be you someday. We'll find a way."

"I'm exploring every avenue. Every new treatment that comes along," Olivia said. "I'll get there. We've always walked side by side. I don't want to be left behind."

"That's not going to happen. We'll always be together." That wasn't enough of an answer. Olivia's question had contained deeper meanings. "And how do I feel now about darkness? There's no panic. I could accept it if I lost my sight again. I would hate it, but we made the best of it before I was given my miracle. And, yes, there are moments when I feel a sense of comfort when I shut my eyes and let the darkness flow around me. It brings me back to the past and to you. It reminds me what we had together. That was all good."

"You're damn right it was." Olivia's voice was a little throaty. "But I didn't mean for you to give me this long, involved speech. I just asked a simple question."

"There's never anything simple about you, Olivia."

"Okay, I feel insecure every now and then." She started to turn away, then turned back. "I don't want you to go back to your place even after the FBI tells you they've plugged up the hole this rat crawled through. Why don't you plan on staying with me until that nut is caught?"

"No way."

"I thought you'd say that. Think about it."

"Okay, but not tonight." She yawned. "It's been one hell of a day. And I don't expect tomorrow to be any easier. I seem to be on a fast track and can't get off."

"And you're on it alone, dammit. When is Adam Lynch getting back?"

"I have no idea. Good night, Olivia."

"You want him back, too."

Kendra turned over on her side. "See you in the morning."

Olivia laughed. "Good night, Kendra."

She closed the door as she left, and the darkness was almost total.

As Kendra had told Olivia, the darkness held no real fear for her. She had faced that demon and knew how to live with it. But the darkness did release her mind to race in circles. She could still see that message on the wall of her living room.

How the hell had he managed to get into her condo?

Not tonight. Shut down. She was too tired to think clearly.

If Griffin didn't find out the answers tomorrow, she would go back to the apartment, and something would trigger it for her.

Go to sleep.

You want him back, too.

Maybe she did, but she'd never admit it to the arrogant bastard.

Shut down. Go to sleep . . .

SHE SLEPT LATER THAN USUAL. Her cell phone rang and woke her at 8:40 A.M. the next morning.

Mom!

Kendra had to clear her head and sound bright-eyed and bushy-tailed. She hadn't expected to have to confront her before coffee.

"Good morning." She struggled to a sitting position. "I meant to call you yesterday afternoon and tell you everything was going well, but I got busy and I—"

"Your voice sounds as if you just woke up. You never sleep past seven. Are you okay?"

"Fine. I was just up late talking to Olivia." That was at least true. "And that fall took a little toll on my stamina."

"I told you that you should have gone to the doctor."

And that was something else to put her mother's mind at ease. "Well, it turned out the doctor came to me. Lynch sent a physician to the FBI headquarters with orders to check me out."

Silence. "He did? How . . . unusual."

"Yeah, that's what I thought. But I went through with it because it was easier than fighting off the doctor who evidently had strict orders. I'm absolutely fine, Mom."

"That's good," she said absently. "But it was still an unusual move on Lynch's part. I never figured him to be that protective. Now, if it was Dean, I can see how he'd be concerned enough to rush medical help to make sure you were—"

"Don't read anything into anything Lynch does," she interrupted. "He just likes his own way. He thinks he always knows best and tries to bulldoze his way through. That examination should never have been done, and I'm still a little pissed."

"But you did it, and that's unusual, too." She abruptly dropped the subject. "I ran into Dean on my way to class this morning, and he says you didn't call him. Why not?"

"The same reason I didn't call you. I was busy. I believe you're nagging, Mom."

"Perish the thought. I never nag. I remind. And occasionally persuade. At the moment, I'm reminding you that you made me a promise. I could tell Dean was disappointed that you hadn't taken the time to call."

"Poor man. I'm sure he's just waiting around for me to touch base with him again."

"That's right, why not? You're not only a fascinating woman but you come of equally wonderful stock. I'm pretty damn fascinating myself. Who wouldn't want to have me for a mother-in-law?"

Kendra chuckled. "I can't imagine. But you're going too fast. I went on a blind date and now you have me on my honeymoon? You're scaring me, Mom."

"Turnabout is fair play. You scared me when I saw you yesterday morning. And now Adam Lynch is sending you doctors and hovering over you. Didn't you tell me they call him the Puppetmaster? I don't like mystery men. I particularly don't like mystery men who manage to convince you to do things you don't want to do. When are you going to call Dean?"

She sighed. "After I take my shower and have a cup of coffee. Talking to him should be a pleasure after having you run over me."

Silence again. "I don't want my pushing to turn you off him. He deserves a chance."

"Your pushing drives me nuts, but I still love you. It won't prejudice me from realizing that Dean is a good guy and probably deserves more than I can give him. Now let me go, so I can start my day . . . and squeeze that call to Dean into the mix."

"Okay. You'll tell me how it goes?"

"It's just a phone call."

"But one thing leads to another. I really like him, Kendra."

"And so do I. But I'm not going to report back to you all the time."

"Oh, very well." She was clearly disappointed. "I'll accept occasional—"

"Mom."

"Good-bye, Kendra. You take care of yourself." She hung up.

Kendra was shaking her head as she got out of bed and headed for the bathroom. It hadn't gone as badly as it might have. She'd been able to avoid telling Diane about the events of yesterday by throwing in Lynch's action as a distraction. And her mother was so focused on Dean that she'd allowed Kendra to get away before she bombarded her with many questions.

But there was no doubt she'd have to call Dean right away and put her mother's mind at ease. She'd made her a promise, and she'd keep it.

She stripped down and turned on the shower.

Just as soon as she checked to see if Griffin knew yet how Myatt had gotten into her condo.

AGENT DONALD NELSON WAS sitting at Olivia's kitchen table drinking a cup of coffee when Kendra walked into the room thirty minutes later. He was staring at Olivia in bemusement, and she was obviously exerting her not inconsiderable charisma.

"Hi," Kendra said. "Is there enough coffee for me, Olivia? I just talked to Mom, and I need bolstering."

Agent Nelson jumped to his feet. "Let me get you one, ma'am. I was just—"

"Sit down. Finish your coffee." She moved to the cabinet and got a cup from the shelf. "If Olivia managed to lure you away from the hall and that stern sense of duty, then you must have really needed it."

"I'm finished." He turned to Olivia. "You've been very kind, ma'am."

She smiled brilliantly. "My pleasure, Don. Anytime."

"Thank you." He turned and left the kitchen. The next moment, the front door closed behind him.

"Naughty," Kendra murmured as she poured her coffee. "You dazzled the poor lad."

"You heard him." She grinned mischievously. "I was just being kind." She shrugged. "You slept late. I was bored. I needed company."

"And you wanted to see if you could lure him away from hard-and-fast duty."

"He was closer to you in here." She sipped her coffee. "And I've never seduced an FBI man before. I wondered if all that training and indoctrination made a difference in how they responded. Not that I actually wanted to go to bed with him. I was just exploring the preliminary steps."

"To see if you could do it."

She nodded. "You know that some men are uncomfortable and repelled by interaction with a blind woman and others are fascinated and drawn. I've been working on turning the odds totally in my favor."

"He was dazzled," Kendra repeated. She sat down and lifted her cup to her lips. "Why not? You're gorgeous and full of life and—"

"Blind," Olivia said. "But as I said, I'm making headway on all fronts." She changed the subject. "Your mother was difficult?"

"No more than usual. She's concerned. She wants me safe, with a big, strong man to take care of me." She made a face. "Ridiculous when you consider how independent my mother is."

"She's a good woman and superintelligent. I've admired her all my life."

"So have I." She took a swallow of coffee. "And that's why I let her still try to manipulate me on occasion. It's all for love."

Olivia nodded. "And that's a damn good reason. You can't fault—"

Kendra's cell phone rang, and she glanced at the ID. "Griffin."

She accessed the call. "I didn't expect you to get back to me this early. It's only a little after nine. I hope that means good news. Do we have a lineup for me to look at?"

"We're working on it. But it shouldn't be too long. But we do know how he got into your condo."

"I'm not sure that qualifies as good news," she said warily. "How did he do it?"

"He has a key."

"A serial killer has a key to my condo. I can't tell you how wonderful that makes me feel."

"Take it up with your building's management office. It turns out it's probably the least secure place in your entire building. It's fronted by a sliding glass door with a flimsy-as-hell lock. There's no one there after six, and he was probably able to pop the lock with a screwdriver. Your key is missing from the peg board in the back room."

"Their security cameras?"

"Disabled. No disks."

"Great. I'd already decided to have my lock changed. I think I'll forget to give the management office my new key."

"Probably not a bad idea, at least for a while. Just a minute. Agent Reade is here." She heard him cover the phone to speak to the agent, and there was a moment of silence. Then he said to Kendra, "She's almost finished with coordinating the photos. Listen, do you want to come in around two and take a look at some photo lineups off the tips we've been getting? We've put together a few dozen pics from people who think they recognize the police sketch. I've glanced at some of them, and most aren't even in the ballpark. A few might be promising though."

"I'll take promising. See you at two." She hung up and told Olivia, "He used the key I gave to the management office. So simple."

Simply deadly. A careless mistake, and she was left open and vulnerable to Myatt.

"It shouldn't have been that easy for him," Olivia said.

"No, but often crimes would never be committed except for a single error from someone who has nothing to do with the target themselves." She grimaced. "We all depend on our precious conveniences. I gave a key to the condo superintendent, so he can let in a plumber or deliver packages. Didn't you do the same thing?"

"Yes. After all, he's bonded. I trusted that they'd keep it secure."

"And so did I. But then no one expects a raid on a condo office by a serial killer. It's outside the box. I don't know how long he's been planning his access to get to me. The security cameras . . . and then the actual intrusion." She shivered. "And I wasn't even the target. He could have attacked me anytime before all this started. But that isn't what he wanted. He wanted me to know how clever he could be. He wanted me to admire him. And he wanted me to know how vulnerable I am."

"You stay here," Olivia said firmly. "No arguments."

"And how do I know that he hasn't scoped out your place, too? He's studied me, and he has to know you're my friend. He wouldn't leave the possibility I'd turn to you out of his equations." She got to her feet. "I'll have Griffin check out the security cameras in this area, too. But I'm not going to expose you any more than I have to." She leaned over and gave Olivia a kiss on the cheek. "I've got to get going. Thanks for the port in the storm. I'll be in touch."

"You'd better be. I want you back here, Kendra."

Kendra smiled over her shoulder as she reached the door. "You just want to practice your wiles on my poor bodyguard. I have to save him from himself . . . and you."

KENDRA HESITATED AS SHE LEFT OLIVIA'S CONDO. She'd been planning on going back to her condo to have a look around and see if Myatt had left any more calling cards that were more subtle than that shocking message on the wall. But she'd made Mom a promise, and she couldn't put it off any longer. It was only a phone call, and she could make it while she was walking back to her own condo.

She quickly dialed Dean Halley. "Hi. Kendra Michaels."

"At last," he said. "I was actually expecting you to call. I thought that Diane had a glint in her eye this morning when I saw her. Did she attack with all flags flying?"

"She just reminded me what a great guy you are and what an idiot I was not to let you come into my life."

"All true," he said solemnly. "But I had no idea that I stood quite that high in her books. I admit I'm flattered."

"Don't be too flattered. Your main attraction in her eyes is the security factor. She thinks I'd be safe with you."

"Ouch. Am I that boring?" He paused. "I guess you haven't told her about my prison record?"

"Not yet. I thought that should come from you if it was pertinent to the situation."

"Very generous of you." He added softly, "I want it to be pertinent to our situation, Kendra. I want to be close enough to you that we'll be as frank as old friends . . . who might be traveling toward another crossroad. I hope you'll feel the same way given a little time."

She felt a ripple of shock. "We barely know each other, Dean."

"I'm trying to remedy that. Give me a little cooperation. I've never met another woman who sent my head spinning like you do."

"No one put you through what I did on a first date," she said dryly.

"I enjoyed every minute of it. I want more."

"You've got to be a masochist."

"I like you. Do you like me?"

"Yes." She paused. "And not because I think you're particularly safe. I like your sense of humor." She added ruefully, "And your stamina in putting up with me."

"I have a confession to make. Your mother was right. If I cared about someone, I'd work very hard to keep them safe." He added hurriedly, "But I wouldn't be boring about it. I wouldn't interfere."

She chuckled. "Yeah, sure." The difference in his attitude and Lynch's was like day and night. Lynch had no compunction about interfering in her life if he chose. Dean was civilized and intelligent, and she was finding it very refreshing. "It's a common human characteristic to want to protect the people we care about. I'd feel the same way. It's the way we respond to that instinct that's important."

"Okay, it's settled. We have a very promising beginning. We just have to cement it. When can I see you?"

She said quickly, "Not for a while. I'm involved in a very nasty case."

"All the more reason why you need light relief. I'm not going to demand that you devote any extended amount of time to me. I just want to see you occasionally to remind you that I'm here. I'm not going to let you walk away and forget me."

"I don't have time to—"

"What are you doing this morning? I only had one class, and now I'm free. What about meeting me for a cup of coffee? Give me one hour. You name the place and the time, and I'll be there."

"Dean, I'll be busy most—"

"Look, I know that you probably think I'm weird being this persistent. Hell, maybe I am. But I wouldn't have gone on that blind date if I hadn't been interested in what I'd heard about you. And I wasn't disappointed. I'm trying to grasp the moment." He added coaxingly,

"And think how happy it will make your mother. Won't it put her mind at rest?"

"Yes." It would most certainly do that, and Kendra was finding she wanted to see Dean again. What the hell. She had time before that lineup at two. "Okay. There's a Starbucks on Broadway, just east of Kettner. Noon?"

"I'll be there." He laughed. "And I'll work on being so damn charming that I won't have to use your mother to get you to meet me next time. Bye, Kendra." He hung up.

He *was* charming, Kendra thought. And she found she was looking forward to seeing him again. Dean was so wonderfully normal. It would be a break in the nonstop tension of wondering what horror Myatt would commit next.

But first she had to go back into her condo and let the evil that was Myatt possess her once again.

She braced herself and entered the hallway leading to her front door.

KENDRA'S HAND CLOSED ON THE DOORKNOB to her condo. It took her a long moment to turn it and let herself inside.

Damn. It didn't even feel like home anymore.

There was now nothing safe or comforting about this place, where just twelve hours before that monster had invaded and made it his own.

No, he needed her permission to make her feel that way, and there was no way she was going to give it.

Fight him. Block out the fear that gave him his power to change her world.

She stood in her foyer and took a deep breath.

It didn't feel like home to her now, but it would again. One day.

She glanced up at the painted message on her living-room wall:

NICE TRY, KENDRA. BUT YOU'RE BETTER THAN
THAT.

—MYATT

She turned and strode to the utility closet in the kitchen and
grabbed a gallon can of primer she'd used to paint the kitchen door six
months ago. It was half-full, and that would do the job. The forensic
team wouldn't be pleased with her for doing this before they'd officially
released the apartment. Too bad. A paint crew would be here in a couple of days, but she couldn't stand the thought of that spray-painted
scrawl in her living room for a minute longer.

She snatched a lid opener and brush from her kitchen utility drawer,
then popped the top from the primer. She stood on the couch and
slathered the primer on the wall above, covering the message one letter
at time. She was sure the Bureau had already identified the brand and
shade of the paint and was attempting to track down every can sold in
the last few weeks. It was a long shot, but there was always the hope
that Myatt might be dumb enough to get caught on a Walmart security
camera while using a credit card to pay for his purchase.

Fat chance.

She suddenly froze.

She stopped applying the primer. She studied the spray-painted
letters for another long moment. With outdoor graffiti, stray paint particles almost always told her at what vantage point the vandals were
spraying from: up, down, right, or left.

Here on her wall, the paint seemed to be hitting dead-on. Did that
mean he had stood on her couch, just as she was doing now? Or did he
stand on something else?

She glanced around the room.

The coffee table perhaps, but a dinette chair would be easier to
move. Kendra moved over to her dinette set and inspected the chairs.

Yes.

There, on the chair closest to her living room, were a few tiny white and green particles. Familiar particles. She had seen them before, but never in her condo.

She grabbed her keys, walked outside, and climbed the stairway to the rooftop pool, which was actually little more than a wading pool surrounded by a sundeck. Flower boxes and barbecue grills lined the area. There, on the building's south side, tiny green and white fertilizer pellets had blown out of the flower boxes and scattered onto the deck.

Kendra knelt and picked up a few of the particles. It was the same as what she'd seen on her dinette chair.

She brushed them from her hands as she stood and looked at the building next door. She was still staring at it as she pulled out her mobile phone and punched Griffin's number. He wasn't available, so she had the call patched through to Metcalf.

"Don't tell me," he said. "You're calling to bust my chops about Comic-Con some more."

"There's plenty of time for that later. Right now, I want to talk about fertilizer."

"Oh, if there's anything I find fascinating, it's a discussion about plant nutrients."

"I found some fertilizer particles on a chair in my condo. The same stuff they use in the flower boxes on my building's rooftop pool deck. It's all over the deck on the south side of the building, just six or seven feet from the building next door. That's how I think Myatt was able to avoid being seen by security cameras and the agents who were watching this place last night. He was in the building next door. He stole the key from the management office earlier in the evening or maybe even the previous day. He jumped from the rooftop to this one, then came down to my condo. He left the same way."

"Hmm. We've already obtained outdoor security camera videos from that neighboring building. We'll see if they have any interior cams." He chuckled. "Fertilizer, huh?"

"The particles probably got caught in his shoe treads, which then came off when he stood on a chair to spray paint his message on my living-room wall. There's a chance that Myatt might not have been quite so careful of those video cameras in that other building. Even a glimpse might help."

"We'll get right on this. In the meantime, the calls are still pouring in about that police sketch. We're looking forward to having you come in and quickly eliminate a couple hundred of them for us. It will save us some serious manpower."

"Griffin said you'll be ready for me at two. I'll do my best, Metcalf." She hung up.

She checked her watch. Time to scan this deck and her apartment before she headed for her appointment with Dean. She doubted if she'd find anything else, but you could never tell. She moved toward the deck surrounding the pool.

"GOOD GOD." DEAN'S EYES widened as he watched Kendra enter the Starbucks glass door. "What truck ran over you?"

"Mom didn't tell you?" Kendra lifted her hand to her bruised cheek. "It's not as bad as it looks."

"It couldn't be. Coffee?"

"Black."

"Me, too." He told the server behind the counter. "And one of those Danish." He turned back to Kendra. "All your Mom said was that you'd had a fall and that was why you hadn't called me. I thought you'd probably tripped on a rug or something."

"A little more than that. The fall was out of a second-floor window." She took her cup of coffee from the server and moved toward a table by the window. "But it's like Mom to use it as an excuse to gloss over my apparent rudeness so that you wouldn't think badly of me." She made a face as she sat down in a chair. "And to try to hide the fact that I'm not the kind of woman you should be hanging around if you want a calm and happy relationship. Maybe she thought we wouldn't get together until the bruises faded."

"How did it happen?" He sat down opposite her. "It sounds like an unusual accident."

"You might say that." Give it to him straight and see if he could take it. "I actually jumped from the window to get away from a serial killer."

He blinked. "I . . . see." Then he shook his head. "No, I don't see. I heard something on the news about some case you were working on, but no one said anything about your getting close enough to be chased by the bad guys."

"It happens. Not often because I try my best to avoid getting involved. But it does happen."

He gazed at her thoughtfully. Then he smiled. "May I say I'm beginning to understand your mother's fondness for me? If I kept you occupied, you wouldn't be chasing around jumping out windows. Or if you did, I'd be there to catch you."

"Would you?"

"You bet." He took a sip of his coffee. "Did you catch the bad guy yet?"

"Not yet." He'd taken it amazingly well. "But we will. It's only a matter of time. We have to get him. He's a monster."

His smile faded. "I don't believe I like your dealing with monsters all by yourself."

She chuckled. "Wouldn't you say that the San Diego PD and the FBI are capable of giving me a little help? They'd be insulted."

"I'm afraid I don't appreciate the mighty arm of the law. I saw it from the underbelly. It wasn't a pretty view." He paused. "I'd much rather you let me stick close to see if you need me. How about it?"

He meant it. There was no doubt of his sincerity.

She was touched. "Thanks, but no thanks." She reached out and squeezed his hand. "Mom is right, you are a great guy, Dean."

He turned his hand and grasped hers. "And the other half of what she told you is that you'd be a fool not to let me in your life. Believe her." He lifted her hand and kissed her palm. Then he laughed and dropped her hand. "Hey, I'm coming on too strong, aren't I?"

"Yes."

"And it turns you off?"

"A little."

"I'll tone it down, I promise." He looked around the shop. "Besides, this isn't exactly the best place for romantic gestures. You've got to give me a chance to do it right." He picked up his fork and cut the pastry. "This is always great pastry. Would you like a bite?"

She shook her head. "No, thank you."

"No sweet tooth?" He took a bite and sighed blissfully. "I do. Though my favorite sweets are fruit pies. My parents had a farm in Seminole County, Florida, and my mother was a great cook. She'd make the greatest cherry pies for the family and the workers."

"Are your parents still alive?"

"Not my mom. My dad married again and still lives on the farm. Nice woman. But I don't go back and visit often. Too many lingering memories." He finished the pastry and pushed the plate aside. "Besides, I think it's time I made a few memories of my own." He lifted his cup to her. "And you're the most memorable woman I've ever met."

"Yes, but not the kind you're looking for. We have virtually nothing in common." She was experiencing regret even as she said it. It was nice to think of making memories with a sweet guy like Dean. "I'm independent and I can be self-centered and I have trouble with the word compromise. Tell my Mom to fix you up with someone else."

"I like her first choice."

"She's brainwashed you."

"Maybe a little, but I volunteered." He held up his hand as she opened her lips to speak. "From now on, your mother is out of it. We're on our own, Kendra. I'm not going to be overaggressive. I'll just give you a call now and then to keep myself in your mind." He thought about it. "But not before tomorrow morning. How about making these coffee breaks a daily ritual?"

"Dean."

"Okay, I'll drop it for now." He smiled. "And I'll work on being that charming guy I told you I'd be to lure you into my spell. Would you like to hear why I became a teacher? It's kind of amusing."

"You're trying to distract me."

"Right. I've only got an hour before you fly away from me. I've got to make you want to come back tomorrow."

She gazed at him with helpless exasperation. His smile held a hint of mischief, but his determination was clear. She suddenly realized she didn't wish to fight that determination. He was like a ray of sunlight, and she wanted to bask in it for a little while.

"Okay." She smiled as she leaned back in her chair and lifted her cup to her lips. "So distract me. Tell me why it was so funny that you decided to become a teacher."

"NO. NO. NO." ANOTHER SET OF PICTURES flicked in front of Kendra's eyes. "No. No. No. No."

Kendra leaned back in the FBI conference-room chair, watching the projection screen as Saffron Reade clicked through the photos she had compiled from the police-sketch tip line.

She had to laugh out loud at how off base many of the photos were, but some had a passing resemblance to the police sketch she had helped produce.

"No. No. No. No." Kendra glanced over at Reade. "Where did you get all these pictures?"

"Many of the callers had a name and address, so we were able to pull most of them from driver's license photos."

"Yes, I thought I recognized that dazed, thousand-yard, Department of Motor Vehicles stare."

"And it looks like quite a few of them were taken on the sly from the tipsters themselves. You have to watch out for those camera-phone-wielding neighbors . . . They just may be trying to finger you as a serial killer."

"If any of them succeed, more power to 'em." Kendra shook her head "no" as Reade showed her a few more slides. "None of these is hitting even close to the mark. But it's early yet. Maybe if you keep that police sketch in circulation, someone will—" She leaned forward. "Wait. Go back to that last one."

Reade clicked her remote and displayed the previous photo. The picture was somewhat blurry, but it showed a man in a brown United Parcel Service uniform who looked remarkably like the man she had encountered at Corrine Harvey's house.

The photo was obviously taken from a distance, shot through a window screen. The UPS man, seen only in profile, was pushing a dolly down a suburban sidewalk. The hairline, cheekbones, and even the swimmer's physique were all just as she remembered them.

Kendra looked over at Reade. "Holy shit, this could be our guy."

"Are you sure?"

"Sure as I could be without seeing him here in this room in front of me. I had an uneasy feeling he might have changed his appearance to fool me, but this is the man I saw that night. What details do you have?"

Reade glanced down at her laptop screen. "This was sent by a Kensington resident named Tom Keating. He says he thought the police sketch looked like this UPS driver who has been delivering in his neighborhood during the last six months or so. According to the time stamp on the photo, it was taken at 5:46 P.M. yesterday."

"We need to follow up on him."

Reade's fingers flew across her keyboard. "I'm forwarding this to the team right now. I guarantee that a UPS area supervisor will be getting a visit very soon."

"Good." Kendra gazed at the screen as the PowerPoint slideshow automatically resumed. She suddenly stiffened.

What in the hell?

"Stop."

There was another photo of who appeared to be the same man, this time wearing a striped vest and train engineer's hat. He was holding two dozen helium balloons, which he was passing out to children at a park.

Kendra quickly studied his physique and facial features. "This is the same man."

Reade's gaze narrowed on this screen. "It certainly looks like him."

"It is, I'm positive. It's taken from a distance, but look at his forehead and jawline."

"So he's a UPS driver *and* a balloon peddler?"

Kendra stepped closer and examined the blue time stamp imprinted on the photo's lower right corner. "I don't know what he is. But we're meant to believe this picture was taken at the exact same moment as the other one—5:46 P.M. yesterday."

"What?" Reade checked her PowerPoint notes. "This came from a man named Eric Hebborn. No other information."

"Show me some more."

Reade flashed more photos on the screen in front of her until Kendra spotted the man again, this time wearing dirty coveralls at what appeared to be an automotive garage. "Don't tell me—5:46 P.M. yesterday."

Reade checked the photo's digital time stamp. "Bingo."

"He's screwing with us. Screwing with me. He posed for these with his own camera and set the camera clock time himself. He knew I'd be looking at these. Who sent this one in?"

"Someone named Tony Tetro."

Kendra pulled out her phone and furiously thumb-typed her way through the Google search screen. "And the other photos came from Eric Hebborn and Tom Keating?"

"Yes."

After a moment, Kendra raised her phone and showed Reade the search-screen results page. "Look. Those are the names of three of art history's most notorious forgers."

"More forgers . . . So this is all bullshit."

"Except these photos really are of him."

Reade leaned back in her chair and shook her head. "Kinda ballsy, a serial killer sending us photos of himself."

"Except none of these are all that clear and don't approach the level of detail in that police sketch. If the news outlets start running these instead, we'll only be taking a step backward."

"Maybe that's what he wants."

"What he really wants is to show that he's not afraid of us, that everything that we're doing doesn't matter to him."

She could feel a chill as she stared at his face on the screen. It was as if she could *taste* the mockery he was displaying toward her.

"Kendra? Is something wrong?"

She moved her shoulders in an effort to shrug off the uneasiness that was close to fear. She told Reade, "No, it's okay. Go ahead and show me the rest. Right now I just want to be done with him and get the hell out of here."

CHAPTER
7

HOURS LATER, KENDRA WAS STILL staring at the three photos on her dining-room table. She had requested the printouts from Reade, but they hadn't told her anything more than she'd known back at the FBI conference room.

The Bureau, no doubt, was racing to track down the IP addresses from which they had come and had perhaps even identified one or more of the locations in the photos.

Just as Myatt knew they would.

Her cell phone rang. Lynch.

Warmth and eagerness flowed through her. She was tired of staring at these photos of that monster who was sure that he could block her at every pass. She wanted contact with Lynch, who was every bit as dangerous as Myatt, but not to her.

At least, not in the same way.

She answered the call. "Why do you keep phoning me? I told you to tend to your business, and I'd tend to mine. I think you must be bored with all those Washington types. Not that I blame—"

"I'm outside your condo, Kendra," Lynch broke in impatiently. His voice was tense. "One of your neighbors was careless enough to hold open the building's front door for me, but your FBI bodyguard won't let me within ten feet of your condo without an okay from you."

"That's because he's good at his job. Maybe you can learn a thing or two from him."

"I don't have time to convince him that I'm harmless, so I'm left with the option of either taking him out or having you call him off. I don't give a damn which one. Choose."

There was no question he meant it.

"Don't touch him." Kendra walked to her door and opened it wide. She nodded to Agent Nelson. "Thanks for being so efficient. My friend tends to be a little rude."

He smiled. "My job. You're sure he's no threat?"

"It depends on who you ask. But not to me." She stepped aside for Lynch to enter. "I'll call if he proves a problem."

"Do that," Lynch said as he walked into the condo and slammed the door behind him. "I'm feeling edgy, and I'd welcome a confrontation."

"Not with Agent Nelson. Olivia would never forgive you."

"What?" Then he dismissed the subject as unimportant. "I heard about your photo lineup today."

"Unproductive as it was. When did you get back in town?"

"Just now. I came straight from the airport."

Her brows rose. "All finished in D.C.?"

"Not really, but I got some news that made me think that I was needed back here."

"We've discussed that before. I'm handling this—" She stopped. Lynch had mentioned being on edge and she could see that was an understatement. Definitely not his usual self. "What news?"

"I heard from the FBI lab manager. I've guaranteed that he gets in touch with me with any information directly after he tells Griffin."

She stiffened. "I haven't heard anything from Griffin."

"I think they're still trying to figure out what it means."

"Tell me."

"It's about the clothing you recovered from Corrine Harvey's house. They recovered fresh skin cells from the sweater. They were able to extract DNA they thought might be from the killer."

"That's great."

"And what's more, they got a match off the CODIS DNA database."

"Even better. So why do you look like you've just come from a funeral?"

Lynch shook his head, then looked her in the eye. "The DNA is from Eric Colby."

Her eyes widened with shock. "What? Impossible."

"Eric Colby," he repeated. "The first killer you ever put away."

Kendra's brow wrinkled. "That doesn't make sense. How in the hell could—"

"You tell me. He's been on death row in San Quentin State Penitentiary for the past four years." He paused. "He's scheduled to be executed by lethal injection Monday night."

Eric Colby.

Kendra felt a little light-headed. She moved toward the sofa and slowly sat down. "This is a nightmare. I don't believe it."

"Believe it." His gaze narrowed on her face. "You look damn shaky. Can I get you something? Glass of water? Shot of brandy? Handful of barbiturates?"

"I feel as if I could use all three." She looked up at Lynch. "I've spent four years trying to forget Eric Colby. When we were walking through the maze of my old cases at the field office Sunday, I did everything I could to avoid looking at his photo. I've never felt such darkness, such total evil, in anyone before or since."

"That's saying a lot."

"It's true. You know . . . I'm kind of conflicted about the death penalty, but not for him. A lot of people would breathe easier knowing he's no longer on this earth."

Lynch nodded grimly. "Count me among them. I read up on him during the flight. I can't get those crime-scene photos out of my head."

Eric Colby.

"You said those were fresh skin cells on Corrine Harvey's clothing?" she asked.

"Correct. First thing I checked."

"His cells somehow found their way onto her sweater. We were meant to find them."

"*You* were meant to find them. Your reward for finding the sweater."

Eric Colby.

Kendra tried to shake off the chill. "Even though he's sitting in a prison four hundred miles away . . . He's somehow involved. And he wants me to know it. It's his parting shot."

"He'll be dead in five days. That doesn't give us much time to get the answers we need from him."

"I don't need anything from him."

"Kendra . . . Every day that goes by is another day that someone could die. If we know he's somehow connected to this, it's an angle we have to pursue."

"Which is exactly what he wants," she said fiercely. "And it's going to lead nowhere, except where he wants it to lead."

"You outsmarted him once. You can do it again."

She shook her head. "Don't you understand? I don't want to do it again. I want to turn my head and not turn back until they're rolling his corpse out of that prison."

"This isn't like you. What—" The front-door buzzer rang from the wall-mounted intercom unit. Lynch strode over and pressed the talk button. "Hello."

After a moment's hesitation. "Michael Griffin, Roland Metcalf, and Saffron Reade here to see Kendra. Is that you Lynch?"

"Yes, come on up." He pushed the button to buzz them in through the front door.

"Griffin wasn't expecting to hear your voice," Kendra said.

"He thought I was still in Washington. I didn't tell anyone I was coming back here. They obviously came to break the news to you personally."

"No matter how many times I hear it, it's not going to be any easier to believe . . . or to accept."

Lynch walked over and leaned close to her. "Listen, Kendra, I know you have some seriously bad history with this maniac."

She half smiled and tried to joke. "Griffin's not so bad."

"The other maniac. Colby. However you want to play this, I'll back you up. Don't let them talk you into doing anything you don't want to do."

"Just a few seconds ago, you were telling me we needed to follow this lead."

"They do. You don't. Not if you don't think you can. I don't like your reaction to this creep. Just say the word, and I'll build a wall around you so strong that Griffin and friends won't even think about breaking through. Understand?"

That damn protectiveness again.

There was a rap at the door, and Lynch opened it wide for Griffin, Metcalf, and Reade to enter.

Griffin stared at Lynch for a moment before stepping into the condo. "Welcome back. This is an unexpected pleas—" He paused and substituted. "Occurrence."

"The feeling is totally mutual, Griffin. I just got into town."

"Huh. Why do I have feeling that my lab has been in touch with you . . . maybe even before they were in touch with me."

"With the tight ship you run there?"

Griffin muttered a curse and turned toward Kendra. "So you know about the skin cells we pulled off Corrine Harvey's sweater?"

She nodded. "The ones with Eric Colby's DNA? Yeah, old news."

"I've already been in touch with the warden at San Quentin. He's pulling together a visitor's list, mail and call logs, and other information he has on Colby. It seems you're not the only one with a rabid fan base, Kendra. Especially since his execution date was set, he's become quite popular."

"Exactly what he wants, I'm sure."

Reade stepped forward. "The attention will increase exponentially when this gets out, you know."

"Then don't let it get out," Kendra said harshly. "Don't give him the satisfaction. You can keep a secret for five days, can't you?" She took a deep breath in an attempt to calm down. Anger, shock, and frustration were all whirling around within her. "Don't let him play us like this."

Griffin spoke in a slow, measured tone that was probably supposed to be soothing but only served to make her angrier. "Trust me, we're not calling a press conference. But we are flying to San Francisco tomorrow morning. We'll visit San Quentin, inspect the logs, and speak with Colby and the prison personnel who know him best. You're the only one of us who has any previous experience with him, so we would like you to join us."

Kendra had known it was coming, but it still hit her like a swift, wicked, kick. "I already know what it's like to be face-to-face with Colby. It's not an experience I'm anxious to repeat."

"We can certainly understand that," Griffin said in a tone bordering on patronizing. "But this isn't really being done for your benefit. Your presence there might provoke more of a reaction from him. He might be more forthcoming."

"You think the sight of me will make Eric Colby spill his guts?" She smiled bitterly. "Then you really don't know him. Colby is an iceman." Her gaze circled the agents. "So what's the consensus? Do your profilers think we're dealing with a tag team?"

"No, they're very cautious." Griffin dropped down in an easy chair facing her. "Serial-killer tag teams are extremely rare. It's almost always an *extremely* solitary pursuit."

"I've never encountered one," Kendra said.

"Very few investigators have," Metcalf said. "Thank goodness. But it's not unheard of for a killer to draw inspiration and even guidance from an incarcerated murderer."

Kendra looked away from them. "Incarcerated murderer" sounded so sterile, so civilized, compared with the brutal and venomous image she still held of Eric Colby. This time she couldn't shake the image from her mind. "Aren't communications with death-row inmates monitored?"

"Depends," Griffin said. "Mail and telephone are, but in-person visits aren't. And we all know that it's distressingly easy to smuggle almost anything in or out of a prison."

"Like a woman's sweater?" Kendra asked.

"Or maybe a handwritten serial killer how-to manual," Reade said. "Thanks to the Web, some of these guys have a worldwide following."

"That's depressing."

Griffin shrugged. "It's the world we live in. You can sit back and be depressed or do something to change it."

"Back off, Griffin," Lynch said. "She's done a hell of a lot already."

"I agree," Griffin turned toward Kendra. "We'll be on United flight 498 to San Francisco at 7:00 A.M. tomorrow. We'd like you to be with us. A reservation has already been made in your name, and a boarding pass has been e-mailed to you."

"How efficient." Kendra picked up her phone from the couch armrest. She glanced at the screen and clicked on an e-mail. "You're right. It just came in."

"Then will you do this for us?"

She glanced at Lynch. His eyes were narrowed on her, and she knew exactly what he was thinking.

Screw 'em. You don't owe these assholes anything.

Tell 'em to shove this case up their asses.

Kendra stood up and gestured toward the front door. "I need to think about it."

Griffin was definitely not pleased. "When can we expect your answer?"

"At 7:00 A.M. tomorrow. When you're on the plane, look over at seat 4D. If I'm there, take that as a strong indication I'm coming with you."

"Okay." Griffin stood up. "But just remember something, Kendra. This wouldn't be like the last time you saw Eric Colby. This time there would be all of us and a squad of armed guards between you and him."

"She knows all that," Lynch said. "She said she had to think. Let's all get the hell out of here so that she can do it."

"I'm going," Griffin said testily. "I don't need you to tell me what to do." He motioned for Metcalf and Reade to join him and he glanced at Kendra as he turned toward the door. "I hope to see you tomorrow."

Kendra watched Lynch open the door as they exited and exchanged words with the guard outside.

Lynch turned back toward her. "Me, too?"

She nodded. "Thank you," she silently mouthed.

He shrugged and stared at her for a long moment. "If you need me, call." He turned and followed the other agents out of the condo.

She *did* need him. She didn't want to be alone with the memories that were bombarding her. But if he stayed, she would reveal weakness, and she didn't want Lynch to see her like that. She had to be strong. That was another time, another place. She wouldn't let Colby beat her now.

But oh, dear God, those memories . . .

Four Years Earlier

Carlsbad, California

10:40 P.M.

"HOW MUCH FARTHER?" Kendra asked.

FBI Special Agent Jeff Stedler eased off the accelerator as their car hit a dense patch of fog. "Almost there, Kendra."

A thick, soupy marine layer had descended on the coastal town of Carlsbad, thirty-five miles north of San Diego. The town's tourist brochures touted the family-friendly resorts and expansive state park, but there was nothing inviting about this dark, lonely stretch of road in a long-abandoned industrial corridor. Large signs proudly trumpeted the cookie-cutter housing developments that would soon wipe the area clean.

"I don't know why you think I can do this," Kendra said tensely. "You should take me home."

"Please. Just give it a shot."

"I'll be wasting your time."

"I don't think so."

Kendra studied him. Of course he didn't think so. His belief in her and everyone else in his life was unwavering, if a bit naïve. But she couldn't dispute the fact that his confidence in people did seem to bring out their best. And that included her. In the seven months she'd been living with Jeff, he'd helped her finally find her truest, best self that had eluded her in those chaotic years after gaining her sight.

But tonight was still a mistake.

He glanced over at her. "Did you read the file I gave you?"

"Yes."

"And . . ."

"It made me ill."

"I'd be worried if it didn't."

He'd given her excerpts from the case file of a current FBI serial-killer investigation. It consisted mainly of descriptions and photos of nine grisly crime scenes that had one thing in common: each of the victims was decapitated, with no trace of the head left behind.

She shuddered. "Those photos were horrible. All those people . . . Even children."

Jeff nodded. "Two little kids. I talked to the mother of one of them just yesterday. She kept telling me how much she wishes it was her."

"I'm sure she does. I can't imagine how someone goes on from that."

"I can't, either."

She was silent. "Looking at those pictures, at first I just felt sick. Then I was depressed. Then I just got angry. I'm pretty much stuck at angry."

"Good. Hold on to that." Jeff turned on the wipers to clear away the condensation. The fog thinned, then billowed, with each turn of the road.

"Do you really think I can help?" Kendra asked. "I'm not like you, Jeff. This investigating stuff isn't my thing. I don't even like doing it."

"You like helping people. You'll get used to the rest. And I do think there's a good chance that you might be the turning point. Nothing else is working for us. It might help to have a fresh set of eyes. Especially if those eyes are yours."

"Ever since I was a little girl, even when I was blind, people were telling me I should be a detective." She made a face. "I never thought the FBI would one day say it to me."

He glanced at her with a smile. "I don't know that I represent the entire FBI. I'm just one agent you happen to be sleeping with. If my colleagues seem a little skeptical, just ignore them. They don't know you the way I do."

"Meaning they're not sleeping with me."

"Meaning they haven't seen you do the things you do. They've never watched you walk into a room, pick up on a thousand different details, and immediately give an entire rundown of the place. Or meet someone and hand them their entire personal history."

"Parlor tricks."

"They can be more than that." His expression was intense. "And we can be more than that together. Do you realize how much good we can do? Why do you think I've been pushing you? You have a gift, Kendra."

Jeff was an idealist, and he wanted to pull her along on his quest to save the world. Well, maybe she should go along even if that quest wasn't her own. She had cared enough to want to live with him and begin to share his dreams. This was just another step. "I don't know if you're right or wrong, but I'll see if—" She straightened on the seat. "There's something going on ahead."

The fog was pulsing with white, blue, and red strobes of light. Jeff slowed as they saw that the lights were actually flashers from half a dozen police cruisers parked in front of an old shoe factory.

They stopped and climbed out of the car. The factory's small front courtyard was overgrown with brush and tall grass. Weeds sprouted from every crack in the sidewalk and parking lot. The brick archway of the worker entrance was lit only by the headlights and flashers of the squad cars. Beyond the entrance was a vestibule that had obviously once held the time clocks. After that was the factory's main floor, topped by a multipaned skylight ceiling. Kendra could see the beams of high-wattage police flashlights darting against the ceiling and spearing into the foggy night sky.

Jeff handed her a dark blue FBI windbreaker that matched his own. "Here. Put this on."

"I'm not cold."

"I didn't think you were. It's so the local cops know you're working with us. Go ahead."

She slipped on the windbreaker, which was clearly meant for a man Jeff's size. She rolled up the sleeves and followed him through the archway.

"Are you ready for this?" he whispered.

She wanted to tell him no, that she wasn't sure she'd ever be ready for what lay ahead. She nodded jerkily, then was silent as they walked past a pair of cops securing the entrance. "I . . . think so. I've been preparing myself."

"It may not matter. Sometimes no amount of preparing helps. If it gets to be too much, just leave the same way you came in. It'll be okay."

"Got it. And if I—"

That smell.

A sharp, acrid odor flooded her nasal cavities and burned her eyes.

The stench of death.

She hadn't prepared herself for that.

They entered the cavernous factory floor, which was illuminated only by the investigators' flashlights and a stray light from squad-car headlamps against the dusty upper windows. Kendra counted almost two dozen uniformed officers, detectives, and FBI agents pacing around the scene. Some looked busy, but most just looked freaked-out.

Then she saw why.

The remnants of several belted assembly lines could still be seen on the factory's concrete floor, some more complete than others. Every fifteen feet or so, tall metal poles towered overhead, anchoring the conveyor-belt chassis to the slab.

Each pole had a human head impaled upon it.

Every single one of the victims on Jeff's list, Kendra realized. The men, the women, the two children . . .

And their eyes were glued open.

Shock. Horror. Nausea.

"Are you okay, Kendra?" Jeff asked.

"No." How could she be okay in a world that could produce a human being who could do this? She started to shake. "Terrible. It's terrible."

"Take deep breaths."

If she took deep breaths, she'd smell the stench even more clearly. Didn't he realize that?

"You can leave," Jeff said quietly.

"No, I can't." Her gaze was held by those faces, by those staring eyes . . . "They're looking at me. Can't you see? They're all *looking* at me."

"Kendra, it's not that they're—" Jeff stopped. "This is too rough. You should go back to the car."

"Too late." She closed her eyes. But she could still see those faces. Particularly the faces of the two little children. She opened her eyes. "Too late for them. Too late for me." She fought back the nausea and took a step forward. "And they know it. They know someone has to make him pay. *I* have to make him pay."

"Kendra, I didn't think that you would—"

"Get me closer to those heads. Maybe he left something, did something, that will let me find a way to help them."

"Forensics will do that. It's not your—"

"Don't tell me that." Her eyes were blazing as she whirled on him. "You brought me here. You almost made me come. Now you get me the help I need to make sure the monster responsible will never do this again."

Jeff hesitated. "Stay here. I'll talk to Griffin and the local police and get permission. I'll be right back."

She watched him start across the room, then forced herself to turn and look back at those heads.

She was becoming accustomed to the horror now that she had made her decision to not let herself be helpless before it. Sadness, anger, shock were still present, but there was also a burning desire for justice . . . and revenge.

Staring eyes. Broken hearts. Broken lives.

"I'll find him," she whispered to them. "Give me a little time. I'll find him for you."

Staring eyes . . .

STARING EYES.

Block it out, Kendra told herself, as she looked up from her coffee. She had spent the night before being attacked by memories of that fever dream of a night at that factory and had gotten very little sleep. Now that the decision was made, she must not dwell on it any longer.

Easy to say. She had been able to suppress but never forget the eyes of those two little boys, seemingly following her around the factory floor.

Their faces were frozen, forever seven and eight years old, but their eyes were pleading, begging.

Dammit.

She parked herself at the Stone Brewing Co., well away from the Terminal 2 gate of the San Francisco flight. She didn't want to run into any of the FBI agents yet.

In case she changed her mind.

She checked her watch. The plane was already boarding. She imagined Griffin standing on the jetway, neck craned, looking around the gate for her.

"Everyone knows you're here, Kendra."

She whirled around. It was Lynch. He was already at the restaurant, sitting with his back to the concourse.

He swiveled to face her. "Your bodyguard phoned Griffin the second he dropped you off at the curb outside."

"Of course he did." She shrugged. "Which would make it even more awesome if I decided not to go."

"True." He smiled faintly. "Are you okay?"

"Yeah."

"You sure?"

She nodded. "I didn't get much sleep. I was just thinking about my first night on the Eric Colby case. It was hideous, and I wanted to strike out at everyone and everything. I don't know if I could have held it together without Jeff there. He believed in me so much . . . I didn't want to disappoint him."

"You didn't. You made him proud."

"I hope so."

Lynch closed the newspaper app he'd been reading on his tablet computer. "Do you think about him a lot?"

She nodded. Of course she did. She had watched him die only a year before, in the case that had first brought her and Lynch together. Jeff had been abducted during the course of a murder investigation, and Lynch had made her believe she could save him. He was wrong.

"I miss him." She hesitated. "But not in the way you might think. We'd broken up almost a year and a half before he died. We didn't have a future together. But even though I never saw him anymore, I liked living in a world with Jeff Stedler in it. Does that make any sense?"

"It does."

"And the world is somehow sadder without him in it. He was a good person."

"So are you." Lynch motioned toward the concourse. "Are we gonna do this?"

She braced herself and nodded. "Yeah. Let's go."

San Quentin State Penitentiary
Marin County, California

"THERE'S A CROWD UP AHEAD." Kendra was gazing out the window of the rental van she was sharing with Lynch, Griffin, Metcalf, and Reade. Metcalf was driving, and they had just completed the forty-five-minute drive from the airport. As they approached the penitentiary's East Gate, they were greeted by the sight of twenty protestors. "They all have anti-death-penalty signs. Are they here for Colby?"

"They're here for everybody on death row," Lynch said. "But yes, Colby's upcoming execution is what brings them here now. There will be hundreds more this weekend. By Monday night, there will be thousands. On both sides of the issue."

For an instant, those staring eyes were once more with Kendra, haunting her. "Thousands . . ."

"It's their right," Griffin said.

"I know that." She looked straight ahead and away from the protestors. "Just as it was our right to put that bastard here in the first place."

After checking in at the gate, they were escorted to a two-story administration building where they soon found themselves in the office of Warden Howard Salazar, a sixtyish Latino man with wire-rimmed spectacles and close-cropped gray beard.

"When people ask what I do for a living, I say I just take meetings about Eric Colby," Salazar said sourly as he hung up his phone and rose to his feet. "Or answer the phone from journalists about what happened at the last meeting. It's pretty much all I do these days."

"Sorry to make you take this one more meeting, Warden." Griffin shook his hand and introduced him to the team.

"At least you may have a different agenda." Salazar motioned for them to join him in a seating area beneath a large leaded-glass window. "I'm curious about your agency's sudden interest in Colby. When law-enforcement officials come to see me about a prisoner this close to his being executed, it usually means he may be responsible for more killings than those for which he was convicted. Are you trying to close some old cases while you can?"

"No, nothing like that. But it is possible there's some connection between him and a current investigation."

"I see. Well, we've pulled together the information you requested. I hope it will help you."

Reade leaned forward. "Mr. Salazar . . . What kind of prisoner has Colby been?"

Salazar shrugged. "From the moment he arrived, he's been a model prisoner. He keeps to himself, he reads, he writes in his notebooks, and that's about it."

"How can you say that?" Kendra said. "I've been keeping track of him. I know for a fact that he murdered a man within these walls."

"Self-defense. Child murderers aren't treated kindly by the general prison population. Over the years, he's been targeted a few times, but he's always been able to take care of himself. One of those attacks involved a sharpened railroad spike that had been smuggled in from a work detail. It happened at the athletic track. During the confrontation, Colby wrested it away from his attacker and almost decapitated him with it. There were plenty of witnesses, two of whom were guards. They testified that it was a clear matter of kill or be killed. Of course, the media just saw 'Eric Colby' and 'decapitate' in the same sentence, and all those other details receded into the background."

"Does his family visit him?" Lynch asked.

"He won't allow it. His parents, sister, and a few other relatives have submitted applications to be included on his visitor list, but he won't approve them. They tried again just last month. They wanted to see him before the execution. He hasn't laid eyes on anyone in his family since his trial."

"So who visits him?" Griffin asked. "Friends? His legal team?"

"You'd know better than I if he actually has any friends. From what I understand, he sees no one from the life he had before he came here. But one of the products of worldwide notoriety is that he gets mail every day and he has a mile-long visitor's list of people with whom he's exchanged e-mails. Plus, a lot of television and documentary crews come to interview him. He's an unrepentant monster, and they just eat that stuff up. As for attorneys, he dismissed his early on. His case would probably be tied up in appeals for the next ten years if he wanted it that way."

"So he wants to die?" Kendra asked.

"He's never come out and said that. He has agreed to meet legal representatives provided by anti-death-penalty groups. But each time, he's sent them away. He says they're trying to tamper with his legacy."

"Yes," Kendra said. "He's become very philosophical about his crimes. He considers them his life's work. He thinks he'll live on through them. He believes that will mean he'll outlive us all."

"Like an artist and his paintings," Reade said thoughtfully.

"Exactly," Salazar said. "Colby is being interviewed for a British news show right now. But if you'd like to see his cell, I'll walk over with you."

"Good," Griffin said. "I'd appreciate that."

"No problem." Salazar headed for the door. "Come along."

Accompanied by a pair of guards, they followed Salazar out of the administration building and through a tall gate that led to the main detention complex. Two gates later, they entered the East cellblock.

"This is where most of our death-row inmates are housed," Salazar said. "We classify them as either Grade A or Grade B. If they behave themselves, they're Grade A and put here. Our more troublesome death-row inmates are classified Grade B and put over in the Security Center. Colby has spent time over there after some of his altercations, but he usually stays here."

Kendra looked up at the huge, double-sided cellblock. It was five tiers high, with each tier holding about fifty cells on each side. The cell doors were standard-issue prison bars, covered by metal security gates with a diagonal crosshatch pattern.

Salazar pointed to a contraption that looked like a ladder on wheels. A telephone was mounted on its upper surface. "Prisoners have telephone privileges every other day, in the morning and evening. This cart is wheeled in front of their cell, and they can reach through their food port and use the phone."

Kendra heard dozens of television programs wafting down the cellblock. "They have TVs in their cells?"

"They can, if they want to pay for it. It's two hundred and fifty dollars as a onetime fee. I don't believe Colby has ever requested one. Though, as you know, money has never been a problem for him. He was a rich kid who became a rich monster."

They stopped in front of a ground-floor cell. One of the guards spoke into his walkie-talkie, and the door unlocked with a distinct "thunk."

Salazar turned back. "I came here this morning with the cellblock commander after we finished gathering the information you requested, Griffin." He turned to Kendra. "Dr. Michaels, I'd like you to be prepared for what you're going to see in here."

Kendra found herself bracing defensively. "Why?"

Salazar grimaced. "Because Eric Colby appears to be as interested in you as you are in him."

"I'm as ready as I'll ever be."

The guard swung the door open.

Kendra stopped short.

Almost every inch of the cell, from floor to ceiling, was papered with pictures of *her*.

"Holy shit," Metcalf blurted out.

Her own face, thousands of times over, stared at her from every direction. She took a deep breath, but it suddenly seemed impossible to get enough oxygen.

Don't freeze up now. Just move.

Kendra slowly stepped into the cell, which was approximately eight feet by ten feet. There was a bed, a toilet, a small table, and wall-mounted shelves with four open compartments. And the thousands and thousands of Kendra Michaels photos, all of varying sizes and quality.

She was ice-cold, drowning, as she stared at them.

Get a grip.

"These were downloaded from the Web," Kendra said. "Crime-scene shots, courthouse appearances, even some pictures taken at educational symposiums."

Reade turned to the warden. "Do prisoners have Internet access?"

"No. We don't even allow them to receive regular mail that includes printed Web pages. Photos are permitted, as long as they're downloaded and printed by themselves. Colby obviously put the word out that he wanted pictures of you."

"And his followers were only too happy to oblige," Lynch said.

Kendra scanned the room, trying not to let the pictures unnerve her more than they already had.

Focus. Block it out.

"How long has he had the Kendra Michaels photo collage?" Griffin asked.

"I asked the block commander about it this morning. It's a fairly recent phenomenon. The pictures started coming in about eight months ago, and they immediately went up on the walls."

"Is it possible that they're all from the same person?" Griffin asked.

"Doubtful," Kendra cut in before the warden could respond. "Almost all of them are from different printers. Some ink jet, some laser, a few thermal. And they're cut differently, with various types and sizes of scissors, razor blades, and paper cutters."

Warden Salazar nodded. "We open every piece of mail that comes through here, but if it isn't contraband, we don't log individual senders. But apparently these have been coming from all over the country. By the way, Colby has to take them down every few days so that we can inspect the walls."

"In case he's trying to pull a Rita Hayworth/Shawshank Redemption number over on you?" Lynch asked.

The warden smiled. "Or using them to help hide contraband. As soon as the search is complete, he spends the rest of the day putting each picture back up."

"A lot of work," Metcalf said. "Though he doesn't have a lot else to do."

Kendra's eyes narrowed on the wall near the bed, straining to see past the photos of herself.

"Is this cell telling you anything?" Lynch asked.

"Surprisingly little," Kendra said. "Or maybe not so surprising. Prisons are designed to strip inmates of their individuality."

Griffin knelt beside the small table, examining it. "Maybe you're just being distracted by the thousand pictures of yourself."

"Possibly." She glanced up at the ceiling, one of the few spots in the room where her face wasn't staring back at her. Griffin was right. The photos had rattled her.

Close your eyes. Concentrate.

After a moment, she resumed her scan of the cell. "Are smuggled mobile phones a problem in this prison, Warden?"

"They're a problem in every prison. Guards are the biggest offenders. If they're caught, they usually just wind up with probation. Not much of a deterrent, especially since they can get a thousand bucks a pop for passing them along to inmates."

Kendra continued her search. "Well, Colby has used two of them here fairly recently."

The warden's jaw went slack.

Lynch chuckled. "When I'm around her, I get that same look on my face."

"How did—?"

She glanced up. "And did he attack a guard in the last week or so?"

The warden nodded warily. "Yes, there was a slight altercation. May I ask how you—"

"The room smells vaguely of bleach. None of the other cells we passed had the smell. That led me to think there was a special reason.

There are a few drops of blood on the ceiling. I'm guessing there was more."

"There was. The guard was actually trying to take away some of these pictures of you, Dr. Michaels. Colby objected, and there was a bit of a scuffle. Colby took the brunt of it."

"But he obviously got to keep his shrine," Lynch said.

"He . . . bargained."

"With what?" Kendra asked.

"Information. He gave us the name of the guard who had sold him some prescription meds. The guard is now on administrative leave pending an investigation, and Colby got to keep his collection. It's rare for a prisoner to inform on a guard, but I guess he figured he won't be here that much longer." The warden turned toward Kendra. "How did you know about the phones?"

She picked up the envelopes of mail on the table. "A guard apparently slipped them to him with his opened mail envelopes. Look at the creased outlines on this one." She held up a greeting-card envelope. "This is the imprint of an inexpensive flip phone." She held up another envelope. "And this one is exactly the same." She flipped them over and showed that each envelope had a lengthy series of numbers written on it. "And I'm willing to bet that these numbers unlock minutes on the accounts of those phones." She handed the envelopes to Salazar. "Do you recognize the handwriting?"

"Not immediately." He pocketed the envelopes. "But you can bet we'll do everything until we do identify it."

Lynch placed his hand on Kendra's back. Silent support. Comfort. "Anything else, Kendra?"

"No. Nothing."

Nothing except those damned pictures.

Griffin turned toward the warden. "We need to talk to him."

"Of course. I didn't expect anything else. We have an interrogation room you can use in the visitor center." He glanced at his watch.

"He should be done with his media interview by now. I'll have him brought over right away." He looked curiously at Kendra. "Tell me, are you nervous? You haven't seen him in a long time, have you?"

"Not long enough." She followed Griffin out of the cell. "And 'nervous' isn't the term I'd choose." Dread, horror, and a curious sense of inevitability. "And, yes, it's been over four years . . ."

CHAPTER
8

Four Years Earlier
Coachella Valley, California
7:42 P.M.

"THE GAME'S OVER, KENDRA!"

Panic.

Kendra's heart was beating hard as she huddled behind a clump of large boulders protruding from the mountainside. Although darkness had fallen, the rocks were still warm from the late-afternoon sun.

She desperately needed that cover. Eric Colby stood at the top of the hill, staring in her direction.

"You're very clever, Kendra. But not clever enough."

Colby's voice carried down the small ridge. He had manipulated events perfectly, drawing her and the two FBI agents out to this remote desert valley.

Now the agents were dead.

And she was next.

Kendra carefully moved down the hillside, hugging the large boulders as she mentally mapped an escape route.

"You could have saved them, Kendra. I didn't care about those agents. I only cared about you."

Don't listen. Don't let him rattle you. Keep moving.

"It gets cold out here. You can wrap yourself in the skin of those dead agents, if you like. Yes, that would be a great idea. The heavyset one looks like he would be hairy and warm. I can skin him in just a few minutes. Want me to throw it down to you?"

It. Throw it down. Special Agent Steven Byers, the sweet and funny man with a wife at home who was expecting a baby in two months, was now an *it.*

"Don't feel bad," he called down. "Before the night is over, I'll be wearing *your* skin." He paused. "Do you think I'm joking?"

He wasn't joking.

She moved through a deep gully, scrambling to put as much distance between her and that madman as she could. She stumbled, then she stumbled again. What the hell was blocking her way?

Then she caught wind of an awful odor. The same odor as before.

And she knew what was blocking her path.

Her eyes were adjusting to the darkness.

She looked down.

Half a dozen corpses surrounded her on the gully floor, piled like dolls in a toy chest.

She choked back a scream.

No. God, no.

Move. Don't stand here frozen.

She pushed on, trying not to look at the horror around her.

Colby laughed. "Have you found my friends yet? Did you think that those heads in the warehouse belonged to my only kills? Dozens more, Kendra." She heard his footsteps sliding down the embankment.

He was coming for her.

She stopped as the sheer rock side of the mountain loomed before her.

No!

The gully's sides were now over eight feet high, and she was boxed in.

Trapped.

No weapon.

No place to hide.

And he was getting closer.

She dove for the canyon floor and crawled back. Only one chance . . . She hurtled forward and found herself flat on her stomach.

And face-to-face with a young woman's corpse.

Kendra grabbed the corpse's shoulders and rolled over with it, intertwining her arms and legs with those of the decaying bodies on the canyon floor. Kendra fought her gag reflex as the odor flooded her nasal passages.

Must stay still. Perfectly still.

She heard Colby moving faster in her direction. Then he stopped, his gaze searching his macabre graveyard.

He began stepping over the corpses as he called out to the end of the gully. "There's no way out, Kendra!"

Her head was turned away from him, lost—she hoped—in the horrific jumble of his victims. She heard his boots moving through the brush.

Could he see her?

She pictured him still holding his two large knives, overhanded in his right, underhanded in his left. The blades would still be dripping the blood of those two FBI agents.

He moved over her, close enough that she could hear him breathing directly overhead.

He stopped, his head tilted, listening.

Could he hear her breathing? She held her breath.

Keep going, please keep going . . .

He stepped over her . . .

. . . and then past.

In seconds, he'd know she wasn't at the end of the trench.

No time to waste.

Or even think.

Her hand closed on a large rock, its jagged edges cutting into her palm. She slid out from under the corpses.

In one smooth motion, she rolled over and jumped to her feet.

A second later, she was behind Colby.

She struck him on the back of the head.

And again.

And again.

He howled in pain as the jagged edge of the rock cut his head. He tried to spin around with his knives, but she struck him again with all her strength.

He staggered forward and fell to his knees.

"Die, you son of a bitch." She struck him again.

He pitched forward and went limp.

Kendra stood over him, still holding the bloody rock as she waited for any sign that he might rise again. Was he dead?

She hoped he was dead, she thought savagely.

No. He was still breathing.

But three or four more blows would surely do the trick. No jury on earth would convict her. After all, it was the only way to be sure he wouldn't come after her . . .

She was giving herself excuses to kill Eric Colby. He was helpless, down for the count.

And she was not a murderer. She wouldn't let him make her into the same monster he had become. She'd climb the nearest ridge and hope for cell reception there. If that didn't work, she'd take Agent Byers's car to the nearest town.

It would be okay. The evidence against Colby was overwhelming. They'd put him away and send him to death row. Eric Colby would never hurt anyone again.

But she still couldn't let go of that rock. She gripped it tighter.

Just three or four more blows . . .

She craned her neck, trying to breathe air that wasn't infected by that awful stench of death.

She staggered backward and scrambled up the side of the gully.

Three or four more blows . . .

She climbed the ridge and reached for her phone.

And only then did she let the stone fall from her fingers.

San Quentin State Penitentiary
Interrogation Room A
Present Day

KENDRA SAT BEHIND THE INTERROGATION room's one-way glass, still overcome by the sights, sounds, and smells of that horrible night. She had glanced at Colby at his trial only long enough to point him out for the jury. Otherwise, she hadn't seen him since their confrontation in Coachella Valley.

And she didn't want to see him now, especially after seeing the sick shrine he had erected to her in his cell. Even Griffin thought it best that she stay in the closet-sized observation room with Reade and Metcalf while he and Lynch spoke to Colby.

The interrogation room was empty, pending Colby's arrival. It looked remarkably similar to every police interrogation room in every medium-to-large city in the country. Except for the bolted-down prisoner's chair, complete with steel eyeholes for leg and wrist restraints.

Where was he? The warden had said he'd have him here right away.

The rear door finally swung open, and Eric Colby walked into the room.

He looked precisely as Kendra remembered him. Jet-black hair, high cheekbones, pale skin, and the bluest eyes she'd ever seen. His lips were almost always pursed, and only when he spoke did he reveal his straight, tiny, rodentlike teeth. She'd always thought the effect was downright bizarre, almost as if they belonged in someone else's mouth.

He sat down, but the guards didn't secure him to the chair. After a moment, Lynch and Griffin entered the room and sat across from him.

One of the guards held up a pair of handcuffs. "Are you sure you don't want us to use these?"

"That won't be necessary," Griffin said. He raised his eyebrows at Colby. "Will it?"

"Not unless you want to wear them." Colby's tone was bitterly ironic, almost as if he was telling a joke only he understood. "And what brings you here, Mr. Special Agent in Charge Griffin?"

"No need to be so formal," Lynch said. "Just call him Special Agent."

Colby's gaze shifted to Lynch. "And what do I call you?"

"Sir. Mister. Hey you. I answer to pretty much everything."

Colby nodded. "So what brings you here, Special Agent Hey You?"

Griffin leaned toward him. "Your DNA was found at a crime scene in the past week."

Colby raised an eyebrow. "Is that a fact?"

"Yes. We thought maybe you could tell us something about it."

"I'm a little busy right now. Come back and ask me about it next week. You might find the conversation a little one-sided, though."

"We'll ask you about it now."

Colby shrugged. "Ask."

"Your DNA was found at the home of Corrine Harvey in San Diego. She was murdered."

Colby shook his head. "She's not one of mine."

"We know," Lynch said. "She was murdered last week."

"Fascinating."

"Glad you think so," Lynch said. "You've no doubt heard of the copycat serial killer we've been chasing."

"Of course. Someone's been paying tribute to Kendra Michaels's rogues gallery. But so far, he's neglected to include my work. It's very hurtful, you know. I don't appreciate your rubbing my nose in it."

Lynch studied him for a long moment. "Oh, but I think it is your work. At least partially."

"Really? I'm flattered. But in case you haven't noticed, I've been a wee bit . . . indisposed, of late."

"You're the architect. Someone else is working from your designs."

"Now *that* would be interesting." Colby leaned back and clasped his hands behind his head. "Tell me more."

"Interesting?" Griffin tried to hide his disgust. He didn't succeed. "Taking human lives is interesting?"

Colby's lips curled into a sly grin. "Only if you do it right."

"Tell us how your DNA got into that murder scene," Griffin said.

"You're asking the wrong question. The question isn't *how*, it's *why*."

"Okay," Griffin said. "Let's start there. Why?"

Colby slowly stood up. "It wasn't a clue, gentlemen. It was an *invitation*."

"An invitation to what?" Lynch asked.

"Again, you ask the wrong question." Colby moved to stand before the one-way glass.

"Sit down," one of the guards ordered.

"What you should want to know is to whom was the invitation addressed?" Colby stared into the glass. "She *is* here, isn't she?"

Kendra felt a jolt of shock.

He was staring at her.

He was only inches away, and there was no way he could see through that glass. Yet she could swear he could see her.

Colby smiled. "Of course she's here," he said softly. "Hello, Kendra."

Kendra couldn't take her eyes from Colby's icy stare.

"I'd like to say I missed you," he said. "But it wouldn't be true. Because you've always been with me." He paused. "Just as I've always been with you. Do you remember the gully? Do you still wake at night with the stench of death in your nostrils?"

She instinctively shrank back, away from the glass.

"I dream about it, too. But it's a pleasant scent to me because I know what horror it brought you."

"Get him," Lynch told the guards sharply. "Get him away from that glass."

The guards grabbed Colby and literally dragged him back to his chair. He laughed, but his eyes never left the one-way glass.

Lynch leaned forward across the table. "Enough," he said tightly. He struck the table with his fist. "She has nothing to do with this."

"She has everything to do with this, Mr. Lynch." As Colby finally turned to face him, Colby picked up on his surprised expression. "Yes, I know who you are. I know who all of you are. Has it occurred to you that every single thing that has happened these past few weeks . . . just might have been all for one reason and one reason only?"

"What's that?" Griffin asked.

Colby smiled. "To bring me face-to-face with Kendra Michaels once more."

"Yes." Lynch's face was expressionless. "I've been considering it as a distinct possibility since I arrived here."

"My God," Kendra whispered.

Griffin shook his head, as if trying to comprehend what he'd just heard.

Colby smiled. "Think about it. How else could I have ever gotten her here? How else could *you* have gotten her here?"

Griffin finally spoke. "You're positively insane."

"No. If that was the case, I never would have had to stand trial."

Lynch's hands clenched into fists. "So you're taking at least partial responsibility for these new copycat murders?"

"I'm doing nothing of the sort. But what I'm telling you is . . . if you want this conversation to continue, Kendra Michaels must join us."

Lynch shook his head. "That's not going to happen."

"Then we're finished here."

"We'll decide when we're finished," Griffin said.

"Actually, no." Colby tapped his fingertips together. "The moment I accepted my death sentence, I became free. It was incredibly liberating, believe it or not. I simply cannot be compelled to do anything I don't want to do. How many people can say that? There's nothing more you can do to me, nothing more you can take away from me. You should envy me."

"The hell we should," Griffin said.

"Not you." Colby's gaze turned to Lynch. "But I think you'd have the imagination to grasp what I'm saying, Lynch. I believe that you may think outside the box."

"We've seen your cell," Lynch said. "And I don't envy you."

"Not until you have the same sentence pronounced on you." He shrugged. "Those are my last words until Kendra joins us. If she chooses not to come in here, I wish you all a pleasant journey home. And good luck with your investigation."

Colby folded his hands in front of him on the table and gazed straight ahead.

On the other side of the glass, Kendra stared at Colby in helpless fascination. He was wrapped in silent power, shutting them all out.

And he'd meant every word he'd said.

Don't make me do this.

She'd fought against it, told herself that she could dip her toe in the ugliness that was Colby and not be pulled beneath the murky wasteland.

But she'd known in the end that it would come down to Colby and her.

She shut her eyes to close him out.

But she could still see him staring at her.

She opened her eyes. "I have to go in there."

Metcalf shook his head. "He's playing you."

"He's playing all of us."

"He doesn't care about the rest of us," Reade said urgently. "It's you."

"Yes, it's me. And that's why I have to let him take his shot at me." She got to her feet and left the observation room. She walked around to the interrogation-room entrance, where Lynch was already waiting outside the door to meet her.

"No," he said flatly.

"It's not your choice."

"Whose choice is it? That maniac's?"

"Mine. If I don't go in there, this whole trip will be for nothing. And, in case you've forgotten, there's still a killer out there we need to stop. It's not all about Colby."

"Isn't it? I'm not entirely sure."

"That's right, you said that you were seeing possible connections since we got here. Why didn't you mention it to me?"

"It was too far out." He grimaced. "Colby was right, I think out of the box."

"So do I. Next time, tell me. I won't feel so alone." She braced herself. "Open the door."

He didn't move.

"Open it, Lynch."

"I don't like this," he said harshly. "He's going to crucify you. I wish to hell we knew what his angle is."

"There's only one way to find out."

"Let me go in with you."

"No, you can't protect me from Colby. I found out a long time ago that I'm the only one who can do that. Now let me get this over with."

Lynch still didn't move.

"Lynch."

"Griffin is in there. Why not me?"

"I don't mind Griffin's being there. He won't get in my way. You always interfere."

He muttered a curse. Then he rapped on the door, and one of the guards unlocked and opened it.

Kendra entered the room.

Although she had already seen Colby through the glass, she felt the chill return as she breathed the same air as the man she had so long associated with pure evil.

"Hello, Kendra." He smiled mockingly. "I can't tell you how happy I am to see you at last."

She froze for a moment. Could he see how his voice went through her like one of his knives?

"I want a name," she said. "Who's killing these people?"

Colby tilted his head. "You know . . . I still get headaches. All these years later, I still get horrible headaches from the concussion I got when you hit me with that rock."

"I guess a fractured skull will do that to you. I had to force myself not to make the damage permanent."

"That's no surprise. I thought as much later once I delved into your character." His smile faded. "You were very clever, Kendra. You forced me to revise my plans. That's the only reason they all fell apart."

"Give me a name."

He ignored her request. "I was at a disadvantage. It was your first case, and I didn't know you. I didn't know how you worked. But things are different now. I know you better than you know yourself."

She gave him a skeptical look. "You always were an egomaniac, Colby."

"You may think I'm exaggerating, but I'm not," he said. "Most people really don't know themselves very well. It gives me a tremendous advantage."

"Oh, because you're smarter than all of us . . . ?"

"I've had the benefit of a lot of time and a lot of motivation. And I've summoned you here for a very special reason."

"You *summoned* me?"

"You're here, aren't you?" He smiled. "Just last week, if someone had asked you to get on a plane, come here, and stand three feet in front of me, there's no way you would have done it. My, what a difference a few days can make . . ."

"I'm here because innocent people are being massacred."

"And you thought I might somehow be able to help stop the massacre."

"I never thought that. Others did, but I didn't. I know you better than that, Colby."

"And yet here you are."

"You're just an item that needed to be crossed off. We'll catch this psychopath with or without your help."

"Admit it. As you say, you know me and my little quirks. You're aware that I never hide my cleverness and superiority from lesser beings. You thought that, in all my preening, I just might give you something you needed to solve your case."

"You do preen with the best of them."

"I do. I really do."

"Okay, here's your chance. How did you get your DNA on Corrine Harvey's sweater?"

"I knew that would bother you." His smile widened, his tiny teeth reminding her of a serpent's fangs. "It's kind of a wonderful magic trick, isn't it?"

"You're dying to tell us. You want to show the whole world how brilliant you are."

He clicked his tongue. "You know . . . people think they want to know how a magic trick is done, but they don't really. When they find out the secret, the wonder disappears. They're suddenly not impressed.

They respect the magician less, not more, regardless of how brilliant and mystifying his methods may be."

"We're not talking about magicians, Colby. Romanticize it all you want, but in the end we're talking about killers. Thugs." She forced herself to stare him in the eye. "There's only you and your puppet on the outside. There's no magic, there's no wonder. Just a pair of pathetic psychopaths."

If Colby was bothered by her words, he didn't let it show. He nodded to where Griffin was sitting down the table. "Your FBI handler isn't happy with your attitude toward me, Kendra. You're not following the Bureau playbook. Don't you know you're supposed to stroke my ego in order to keep me talking, so that I'll give something away?"

Kendra glanced at Griffin. He did indeed look tense and upset. She shrugged. "I told you, that may be what these agents are here for, but I wouldn't waste my time. It wouldn't work with you."

Colby laughed. "Quite right."

"So if you're not going to answer my questions, why did you 'summon' me?"

"It was important to me that I see you one last time, Kendra. I have an announcement to make."

"Then make it."

He paused. "A drumroll please."

"Say it."

"I've changed our story."

"What story is that?"

"The one where the gifted, formerly blind Kendra Michaels uses her intellect and powers of observation to stop a deranged madman in his tracks."

"That story is over, finished."

"No. To crib a phrase from Shakespeare, what is past is prologue."

He paused. "Because our story will not end until you know how it feels to truly suffer, Kendra. In every way imaginable."

She took a deep breath. Don't react. Don't give this creep one shred of satisfaction.

"You're trying so hard not to show your fear." His voice dropped to almost a whisper. "But that terror is part of the new story. The terror and the pain have already begun and won't leave you until the end. And it won't even be over when the federal government shoots poison into my veins Monday night. Trust me on that."

Kendra felt a chill that went to her very core. She had seen the many horrible ways Colby had backed up his promises.

"Enough." Lynch had opened the door and strode into the room. "Get the hell back to your cell and talk to your paper-doll cutouts." He nodded to guards. "Take him."

Colby raised an eyebrow. "Giving up so easily, Mr. Lynch? That isn't your reputation."

"Like the lady said, you're just another lead to be crossed from the list."

Colby rose to his feet as the guards approached. "We all know that's not true." His gaze shifted from Lynch to Kendra, then back again. "I do believe he's a trifle upset, Kendra. Interesting." He held her gaze. "He'll be more upset the closer we get to the end of the story."

"Bullshit." Kendra was trying to hold it together, but the interrogation room suddenly felt as it were getting smaller, bringing her closer and closer to Colby and his serpent smile. She had to get out of here. As she walked to the door, her throat was closing, and it was getting harder to breathe. "I'm done with you."

"But that's the delightful twist to the story," he called after her. "You'll never be done with me, Kendra."

She practically stumbled into the hallway as the guard unlocked the door for her. Lynch was right behind her. He took her by the arm and half walked, half carried her around the corner. "Stop. There's no one here." He jammed her up against the wall and stepped closer, taking her in his arms, hiding her from view. "Let it go."

"I'm okay." She wasn't okay.

Heads in the warehouse, eyes glued open.

The smell of the dead in the gully.

Lifting the corpse off her to try to get to Colby.

Colby's looking mockingly at her. "You'll never be done with me, Kendra."

She could hear Lynch cursing beneath her ear. "Stop shaking. You'll never have to see the bastard again."

She hadn't realized she was shaking. She tried to control herself. But she wasn't ready to let him go yet. He was pouring strength and warmth into her as he always did. Just a few more minutes . . .

It was more like five when she said, "You can let me go now."

"No, I can't. You're stuck with me. I'm not going to let Griffin see you like this. He'd enjoy it too much."

She didn't want Griffin to see her like this either. She was becoming better by the moment, but she had to be entirely herself before she faced him. "Griffin didn't say one word while I was in that room with Colby."

"He probably thought that he might get what he wanted if he left it up to a confrontation between the two of you. You were holding your own."

"Not toward the end."

"Colby didn't see it." His lips brushed her forehead. "But I couldn't stand any more. So I broke it up."

And she was glad he had. Colby would not have done anything but torment her. He had made it clear why he'd 'summoned' her. "I think . . . he's even more evil than when I knew him before. I didn't think that possible. Yet he's changed somehow."

"Perhaps you blocked him out."

She shook her head. "He's changed. There's something . . . new."

"Well, you don't have to worry about him any longer. He dies Monday, and you don't have to see him again."

She drew a deep breath and shook her head. "You heard him. I'm never going to be done with him." She pushed him away. "And all your promises won't change that." She straightened. "They wouldn't anyway. This is between Colby and me. That's how it's been from the beginning. You have nothing to do with it, Lynch."

"Not true." He paused. "And that was only a threat to intimidate you."

"No, it wasn't. He meant every word. I don't know how he means to follow through, but that's his intention." She moistened her lips. "And it will be soon. He would want to see it happen." She ran a hand through her hair to straighten it. "Now let's go and find Griffin and the others. Colby was pretty much a waste of time except that it's almost a sure thing that Myatt was in contact with him." She moved down the hall toward the interrogation room. "We have to find out how that contact was made."

"Wait." He hurried to catch up with her. "I expected to have at least another ten minutes or so helping to bolster and raise your spirits. What a disappointment."

"You'll recover." She paused, then said, "You did bolster me. I . . . wasn't myself. Thank you, Lynch."

"My pleasure." He smiled. "You're very, very welcome. But I prefer you to be the Kendra I know. That other 'self' scared the hell out of me."

"Me, too." She looked away and her pace quickened. "Me, too, Lynch."

San Quentin State Penitentiary
East Gate

BOBBY CHATSWORTH SHOVED THE MICROPHONE into the protestor's face. "Tell us why you're here. Why this inmate, why this prison?"

The young woman with the poster froze. Dammit, she looked like a deer caught in the headlights.

Lily Holt shook her head. She and Bobby had just taped one of the most riveting interviews in British television history, but Bobby was insisting on grabbing a few more lame sound bites from the crowd outside. Oh, well. It was his show. She was only the producer.

The protestor nervously stumbled through her anti-death-penalty tirade, missing every opportunity to make a cogent point. When she finished, Bobby thanked her and stepped away with his camera operator and soundman.

"That was terrible," Lily said quietly. "Why did you choose her?"

Bobby smiled impishly. "Are you joking? That was brilliant."

"No. Your interview with Colby was brilliant. I still have goose bumps. There was one moment there I might have actually peed myself a little. But that woman was rubbish."

"Could you ask for a better counterpoint? The intelligent articulate condemned man juxtaposed with the all-heart-no-brains do-gooder? See what I'm going for?"

Lily nodded. She didn't like it, but she got it.

Bobby Chatsworth had made a name for himself as an "activist reporter" on a second-tier satellite news network in the UK, and his extreme positions gave him an engaged audience both on his network berth and video-streaming sites. His red beard, bushy eyebrows, and trademark round spectacles made him ripe for parody on comedy shows and political cartoons, but that only served to grow his audience. He'd recently been advocating the return of the death penalty in England, and in Eric Colby, he had found a terrifying poster boy for his cause.

"I get it," Lily said. "Anybody who's against the death penalty must appear to be a total idiot."

Chatsworth smiled. "But on my show, they *are* total idiots. Got it?"

"Of course. No sense in examining issues from more than one perspective."

"It sounds as if you'd prefer to work at a television station back in, oh, 1965."

"If you know of any openings there, let me know. Until then, I'll keep carrying your sorry bum."

He laughed. "That's my girl. I can always count—" He stopped, looking behind her.

Lily turned to see what had grabbed his attention. A van passed a security checkpoint and emerged from the prison, prompting the protestors to wave their signs and shout their positions with renewed vigor.

"Get that van," Bobby shouted to the cameraman. "Hurry!"

The van rolled by just as the cameraman lifted his rig and zoomed in on the passenger compartment.

Chatsworth gave a low whistle. "Would you look at that . . ."

"What am I supposed to be looking at?" the cameraman asked.

Chatsworth watched the van move past the protestors and turn at the intersection. He turned back to Lily. "Believe it or not, Kendra Michaels was in there."

"Are you sure?"

"Positive." He handed the microphone to the soundman. "That guard said we had to cut the interview short because Colby had some important visitors. Apparently, she was one of them."

"Why would Kendra Michaels want to see him?" Lily asked. "To share a pint and relive fond old memories?"

"Hmm. Don't know. But we really need to interview her. It's like a gigantic hole in my show."

"She was on our list, but she didn't even return my e-mails. She never comments on her investigations."

"I've heard that . . ." Chatsworth thought for a moment. "What if we offer something in return? Something that might be of use to her?"

"And what exactly might that be?"

He smiled. "I think we may already have it."

DON'T THINK ABOUT COLBY NOW, Kendra told herself, as she boarded the flight back to San Diego. She had to overcome the emotion and separate it from logic. It was the only way she could come to any reasonable conclusions.

"Want to talk?" Lynch asked as he watched her buckle her seat belt.

She shook her head. "There's been enough talk. Too much. I just want to rest and close everyone away from me."

He nodded. "I'll try to keep Griffin and the rest off you." He made his way down the aisle.

Evidently he succeeded because Kendra spent much of the trip home lost in her thoughts, trying her best not to mentally replay her conversation with Colby. Lynch and the FBI agents spent most of the short plane flight tapping out memos on their laptops and passing around pages from documentation provided by the warden. She knew that there would be a complete copy of the file in her e-mail in-box the next morning, and she'd be better able to focus on it then.

They landed at the San Diego airport at eight thirty. After a few mumbled good-byes between her and the other agents, Griffin pulled her aside.

"Look, I'm sorry about the way things went down at the prison. I shouldn't have asked you to join us."

Her brows rose in surprise. "I'm touched." She paused. "You were right to ask."

He blinked at the response. "Your first reaction was that you didn't want to go."

"Damn right. But I thought about it and realized it had to be done." She looked him in the eye. "So it was my decision. Everything that happened was my responsibility, not yours."

"That's very . . . generous." He started to turn away, then looked back at her. "I can see how a guy like that can get inside your head, especially with your history with him. I know it took a lot for you to go there. Thank you."

She nodded. "Good night, Griffin. See you tomorrow."

Griffin walked away.

"I'm amazed," Lynch said from behind her. "That's not a guy who usually makes apologies."

"Well, it doesn't come easily to him. His teeth were practically clenched for the entire conversation."

"Baby steps, Kendra. Baby steps." Lynch motioned toward the terminal exit. "This way. I'm taking you home."

She frowned. "Since when?"

"Since I remembered that you didn't bring your car here. How did you think you were getting back to your place?"

"Cab."

"Nope. Anyway, there are a few little things I want to go over with the security detail outside your condo. Let's go."

After the quick ride home, Kendra was surprised at what Lynch considered "little things" he wanted to discuss with her security guard.

"Nelson, until you hear otherwise, your services will no longer be needed," Lynch said to Agent Nelson the moment he reached him.

"What?" Nelson and Kendra said in unison.

"Thank you for your service," Lynch said. "You've done a fine job."

Nelson was obviously blindsided. "Uh, I'll need authorization from Griffin for this."

"Then get it. Or don't get it. Whatever. In any case, Kendra won't be here."

"And just what makes you think that?" she asked.

"Colby. You wouldn't let me in the room with the two of you, but that was good. From behind the glass, I was able to watch the two of you as if you were on a movie screen. Every expression, every nuance. His promise of making you suffer was all the inspiration I needed."

"Your inspiration, not mine. I don't recall any discussion about my leaving my home."

"That's because there wasn't any. I just thought of it a little while ago." Lynch opened the door and walked with her into the condo and closed the door on Agent Nelson's troubled face. "Go pack a suitcase. Bring enough for at least a few days."

"Wait. Hold it. Where am I going?"

"The safest place I know."

"Where's that?"

"My house."

"Like hell."

"Trust me, there's no place safer. The house was designed from the ground up to withstand almost any kind of assault. It's the best place for you right now."

She gave him an incredulous look. "Your house is designed to withstand an assault? I knew you had a habit of making enemies, but seriously . . ."

"I'm being very serious. But you'll never know that you're in an impenetrable fortress. You'll be staying in a nice, cozy guest room. It's very comfortable. More to the point, it will throw off any plans that Colby and his psychopathic friend might have for you. It's a contingency they wouldn't have planned for."

"What makes you so sure?"

"Well, you sure didn't plan for it."

Kendra thought for a moment. "I can't argue with that."

"You can't do anything predictable. That means you don't stay with friends or family."

"A hotel?"

"Not safe enough. Too many people coming and going. At my

place, you'll have me *and* the house defending you." He grinned. "You'll be impressed. We're a formidable team."

"I have no doubt." She made a face. "But I value my privacy, dammit."

"More than you value your life?"

She hesitated, and he took the opportunity to nudge her toward the condo's back hallway.

"Start packing. It's safer for you and safer for the people you care about. I'll wait in your living room and take the call from Griffin that's surely on the way."

At that moment, the phone vibrated in his pocket.

Lynch smiled. "Right on cue." He pointed to the hallway. "Pack."

CHAPTER
9

FORTY MINUTES LATER, Kendra found herself in Lynch's car exiting I-5 toward Carmel Valley Road.

She turned toward him. "I thought you lived in Riverside."

"I did. I just moved here about eight months ago. This place took over two years to complete."

"I guess that's what you get when you build a fortress in suburbia."

"Building a fortress is easy. The trick is to make it not *look* like a fortress."

She shook her head. "I can't believe I let you talk me into this."

"I didn't talk you into anything. You can't be talked into doing anything you don't really want to do. Just like Griffin didn't really talk you into traveling to San Quentin. As you said, deep down, you know what needs to be done. You know you'll be safer here than at your place."

"I've seen you work your Puppetmaster routine on a lot of people, Lynch. First you identify their buttons, then you press them. You found my button."

"Which is?"

"Logic. Common sense."

He chuckled. "There are worse weaknesses." He glanced at her. "But that wasn't the button I pushed. I slipped in one sentence that tilted everything my way."

"What?"

"I told you it would be safer for the people you care about."

She stared at him thoughtfully. "Mind and emotion. You're very, very intimidating."

"Why do you think I need a fortress?" He didn't wait for an answer but gestured up ahead. "It's to the right, around that bend."

A few minutes later, they approached a large gated home at the end of a row of luxury estates.

Kendra's eyes widened. "Impressive. You bought this on a government salary?"

"No. When I was with the FBI, my place was considerably more modest. My agent-for-hire income allows for a much grander lifestyle."

"Obviously. This is what, ten thousand square feet?"

"Oh, not that much." He shot her a sideways glance. "Nine."

She shook her head. "Aw, man. You didn't tell me I'd be slumming it."

"You'll just have to suffer." Lynch pressed a remote on his sun visor, and the electronic gate swung open. His house was a classic Tudor, surrounded by an eight-foot wall. Although it was night, artfully placed outdoor lighting showcased the landscaping and intricate stonework on the structure's face.

Kendra pointed up toward the house. "You're not worried about someone's just breaking in through a window?"

"No. At the first sign of a perimeter breach on the property, steel shutters drop down over each and every one. They're built into the walls."

She glanced at his face, then said slowly, "You're not joking."

"No, I promised you a fortress, didn't I? You were right about one thing. I've made a lot of enemies in my time. Everyone from crime bosses to gunrunners and terrorists. Most of them I take care of before the job is done, but there are always a few who linger in the shadows . . . waiting. I can never be sure when they'll strike." He shrugged. "So I like having a place where I can come back and relax. Out there on the street, I may have to be on guard. Not here." He parked the car in the garage, and the door automatically closed behind them. He leaned close to her and spoke softly. "I hope I can give you the same peace of mind."

Heat.

Sexuality.

Intimacy.

She looked away and tried to say carelessly, "You're off to a very good start."

"I'm glad you think so." His face was only inches away from hers, close enough for her to feel the warmth, the vitality. A few minutes before, she had been thinking that Lynch was right, that she could relax here. He knew what she needed almost before she knew it herself. But she was not at all relaxed right now. Every muscle was tense, and her heart was pounding hard.

Don't let him see it.

She gripped the door handle. "Give me a tour?"

He studied her expression for an instant. "Sure."

They pulled Kendra's suitcase from the trunk and moved toward the door. Lynch raised a fob and pressed it to throw the lock.

He showed her the fob. "The code changes every seven seconds. This fob and the door-lock codes stay in perfect synchronization." He gripped the doorknob, then froze. "Oh, shit."

"What is it?"

"Nothing serious," he said, sensing the tension in her voice. "I just remembered something."

"Remembered what?" Adam Lynch was actually looking sheepish, she realized with wonder. She hadn't been aware he was even capable of that expression.

"Look," he said. "You're going to see something kind of unusual in my living room. Promise not to judge, okay?"

She smiled with anticipation. "I'll promise nothing of the sort. What is it?"

"Damn. I can't believe this. Okay." He pushed open the front door.

Kendra entered the house. The place was still dark except for a few accent lights. At first, she was impressed by the modernistic furniture, travertine floor tile, and black galaxy granite countertops.

Then she saw it.

She stopped short, eyes widening. "Oh, my God."

In the large living room, one single windowless wall was covered by a twenty-foot-long enlarged print of his latest girlfriend's bus ad. Beautiful bikini-clad Ashley overwhelmed the room.

"Uh . . . Wow," was all Kendra could say.

"Yeah."

"Why . . . ?"

Lynch was looking more sheepish than ever. "A couple weeks ago, I came back from a trip out of the country and . . . there she was on my doorstep with that poster, several movers, and an interior decorator. She whisked them inside, and an hour later, it was done."

"She had this wall-sized picture of herself made for you?"

"This was actually hanging from the ceiling at the campaign's launch party. She asked for it and had it mounted and framed for me." His expression was baffled as he stared at the poster. "I guess she thought . . . it should occupy an entire wall in my home?"

Kendra started laughing and found she couldn't stop. She pointed to a row of eyeball-recessed light fixtures aimed at the print. "Did she have the spotlights put in, too?"

"No, those were there already. They were installed to showcase a collection of my favorite paintings in all the world. Paintings, by the way, that the movers relegated to a hall closet."

Kendra laughed even harder.

"What can I do?" Lynch said. "She's very proud of this. She took a lot of time planning it. I don't want to hurt her feelings."

"You're so damn tough. Yet you can't say no to a bikini model?"

"I could say no, but I have to work my way around to doing it humanely. She thinks most guys just want to screw her." He frowned ruefully. "Okay, that may be one of my prime objectives. But she's decent and likeable, and I don't want her to think that's all she is to me. We have enough problems understanding each other's point of view. She honestly thought this was a terrific gift."

"I'm sure she did." Kendra struggled to catch her breath. "Hey, if I had a body like that, I'd give out wall-sized pictures of myself, too."

"You have a fantastic body. And no, I don't think you would do that."

"I agree it's not very subtle. But at one time I might have yielded to the temptation." Kendra realized she was laughing so hard that tears were rolling down her cheeks. She wiped them away. "Oh, that felt good. I needed that, especially after the day I've had today."

"Glad I could be of service." He grimaced. "Now, if you're through enjoying your laugh at my expense, I'll show you your room."

"I can hardly wait." She followed him up the stairs. "But nothing could impress me more than beautiful Ashley."

"You're not going to drop it, are you?"

"No way. Unless you can offer me something to make it worth my while."

He slanted a look over his shoulder. "Oh, I could do that. Just give the word."

She lost her breath as she met his gaze. Dammit, being with Lynch was like riding a seesaw that pitched and changed with every second. "Forget it. It's much more amusing to laugh at your vulnerabilities, Lynch."

"Is it? Do you realize that displaying my vulnerability might have been planned? It's a prime tactic to disarm." He opened a door. "Did I disarm you, Kendra?"

Had he planned it? She didn't know, and she wouldn't think about it right now. "What do you think?" She glanced away from him and looked at the guest room. "This is very nice."

True to Lynch's word, the guest room was large and comfortable, centered by a four-poster bed and half a dozen overstuffed pillows.

He handed her a touch-screen remote. "Pretty much every song ever recorded is at your fingertips. You select your tunes here, and the sound comes out of the ceiling speakers. In case you'd like to listen to music as you fall asleep."

Kendra looked at the remote and smiled. He knew how important music was to her. It was medicine not only for her clients, but for herself. Music had helped her through some of the most difficult times of her life, bringing life and color when there was literally only darkness.

"Thanks, but I doubt I will. I get too interested in the music, and it keeps me awake."

He pointed toward a side door. "There's an adjoining bathroom, and you'll probably find any toiletry you didn't bring with you."

"Really?" She smiled mischievously. "Chosen by our Ashley?"

"No. Saks Fifth Avenue." He paused, gazing at her. "I'm doing the best I can, Kendra. This isn't easy for me either. I'm not accustomed to platonic living arrangements."

"You know, I gathered that from the moment I walked into your living room."

"I mean it."

Her smile faded. "I know you do." She moistened her lips. "Look, I'd have to be blind again not to realize that you're very highly sexed. It's natural that you might possibly want to screw me given the intimacy of the circumstances. And, I admit I find you sexually desirable." She shrugged. "But neither of us want to go down that path."

"Don't we?"

"It would confuse things. I don't need that, and neither do you."

He smiled. "So logical. So reasonable."

"You betcha. We just have to remember what's important."

"This is the second time you've seen fit to lecture me on what I want or don't want in our relationship." He tilted his head. "I find it very interesting. You've noticed I haven't commented on your analysis of my needs or desires? When I decide to do so, you may be surprised."

"You often surprise me. But I can usually count on you for clear thinking." She was silent a moment, her gaze meeting Lynch's. Time to bring this encounter to an end. There were too many shadings of emotion and erotic response. She was too *aware* of him, dammit. "But I do thank you. I feel much safer in your fortress. It was a good idea to come here."

"Sure."

She was having trouble looking away from him.

Lynch took a step closer and moved a lock of hair from her face. "You're sure I can't give you anything else?"

A loaded question if there ever was one. She was tingling, her breathing shallow. She shook her head.

Another long moment of silence.

"I guess . . . I should let you get some sleep. Since we're determined to be so logical."

She didn't reply.

Another pause.

"Well . . ." He motioned toward the door.

He was waiting for a sign, any sign.

And she wanted to give it, she realized.

"Good night," he said softly. His hand caressed her cheek, then he turned and left the room.

Kendra let out the breath she hadn't realized she was holding. She was still tingling from the electric charge between them. Her cheek felt warm, sensitive where he'd touched her.

On the plane, all she had wanted was to go to sleep. Right now, that seemed impossible.

Damn him.

"KENDRA? KENDRA, WAKE UP."

She opened her eyes, at first confused about where she was. Then she remembered.

Eric Colby.

The ridiculous and wonderful suburban fortress.

Bikini-model Ashley.

Lynch's amazing, unexpected, yet frustrating restraint.

"Wake up, dammit." Lynch was standing over her. His shirt was unbuttoned, and he was zipping up his pants. His hair was tousled, and he looked intense. She glanced at the window and saw that it was still dark out.

"What time is it?"

"Three thirty. Get up and get moving."

She sat up in bed. "What the hell, Lynch?"

"Griffin just called. There's been another murder."

Go Nuclear Dance Club
University Avenue, San Diego

KENDRA AND LYNCH MADE THEIR WAY toward the club's main entrance, where velvet ropes held back the ejected patrons who had decided to remain behind and see what was going on. As Kendra walked past the crowd, she heard snippets of conversations that confirmed the rumor mill was in high gear. In the space of fifteen seconds, she heard that the cops had closed the place down due to a) a drug bust, b) a brawl upstairs, or c) the discovery that the club was a front for the Russian mafia.

If only.

Lynch flashed his government ID to the cop outside and opened the door for Kendra. "Ever been here before?" he asked.

She shook her head. "Not since they changed the name and went respectable."

"Respectable?"

She glanced around at the mirrored walls and pulsing, rotating lights, which emitted mechanized whirring sounds that were eerily audible now that the club music was turned off. "Yeah, this used to be a real dive. The bartenders would cheat drunk customers on their change, you'd see rats in the corners, and next to the back bar, some woman would always be treating customers to Jell-O shots off her bare stomach."

"Seriously?"

"Absolutely." She shot him a look. "And a couple times, that woman was me."

"I'm finding that hard to imagine."

"Why? I wondered what it would feel like. The world was full of curiosities and wonder for me back then. And most of the time, I didn't hesitate to satisfy it."

Lynch smiled faintly. "If you decide you want a replay, you'll have to let me experience that sometime."

"Dream on. That was another time. Been there, done that." Kendra glanced around. "I have to say, this place was probably a lot more fun in those days."

"Hi, guys." Metcalf was approaching them. "Long time no see."

"What do we have?" Kendra asked.

"The victim was a twenty-seven-year-old woman in a men's bathroom stall."

"The *men's* bathroom?" Lynch asked.

"You know what it's like in places like this. When there's a mile-long line in front of the ladies' bathroom, it's not uncommon for women to slip into the men's room."

"How was she positioned?" Kendra asked.

"On her knees. Classic hugging the porcelain goddess pose."

Kendra chilled as memories flooded back to her. "Like in Phoenix . . ."

"Exactly like Phoenix," Metcalf said.

"The Gregory Hammond case." She swallowed, hard. "He lured clubgoers into bathroom stalls promising drugs and/or sex. He killed them and positioned them just like this. Sometimes, the victims weren't discovered until closing time."

"A couple people looked in on her, and she just appeared to be ill," Metcalf said.

"The last thing most people want to do is tangle with someone who looks like they're puking their guts out," Kendra said. "And I guess she was bleeding out from her slashed throat into the toilet?"

"Yes. No one had any idea. She'd probably been dead an hour before anyone realized."

"San Diego PD realized it was patterned on the Phoenix case?" Lynch asked.

"The homicide detectives knew it right away," Metcalf said. "We briefed them a few days ago, so they're on the lookout for any cases that match."

Lynch glanced around the club, which was empty except for the cops and club employees. "Did anyone see who was in there with her?"

Metcalf shook his head. "Not so far. And the only security cameras are in the offices upstairs." He gestured toward the bathroom. "You want to take a look?"

Kendra stared at the open door, through which she'd seen half a dozen crime-scene investigators come and go since her arrival. She braced herself. "Yeah. Let's get this over with."

They entered the large men's bathroom, where in front of the last of six stalls, the woman's corpse was stretched out on the floor. She was on her back, surrounded by a photographer and two crime-scene investigators.

Griffin was standing near the door. "They'll be done with her in a minute."

"Who did she come to the club with?" Lynch asked.

"No one. She was a regular, and she always came by herself. A couple of the bartenders knew her. She had a disabled kid at home, and she used to come here to blow off steam."

Kendra turned toward him. "Disabled *how?*"

"I don't know. Whatever it was, she was almost never able to leave the house with her, and this was her only release."

Kendra turned back toward the corpse. Don't let it be true. Please, please, please . . .

She pushed past Griffin and moved quickly toward the back of the bathroom.

One of the crime-scene investigators tried to stop her. "Ma'am, if I can ask you to stand clear while we—"

"No! Get out of my way." She stared at the dead woman's face. "No. Oh, shit, no."

"Kendra?" Lynch and the two FBI agents were suddenly beside her.

Kendra felt her legs weaken, and she fell to her knees. She suddenly realized she was crying. "I know this woman . . . I know her."

Lynch knelt beside her, holding her. "Who is she?"

Kendra couldn't take her eyes off the woman's once-vibrant face. "Her name is Danica Beale."

Lynch glanced back at Griffin, who nodded his confirmation.

Kendra wiped the tears from her cheeks. "I've been to her house. Her daughter is a client of mine. They live with Danica's parents. The little girl is agoraphobic, and I was trying to help her. My God . . ." She looked up at Lynch. "You saw her on the embarcadero the other day."

Lynch nodded.

"That poor woman. And that little girl . . ." Kendra felt a sudden surge of panic. "This is because of me."

Lynch turned her to face him and looked her in the eye. "No. I can see how that would be your first reaction. But this atrocity is because there's a psycho out there. No other reason."

Kendra shook her head. "He's upping his game. If it weren't for me, Danica would still be alive and home with her daughter by now."

"Maybe. And we'd still be standing over someone else who didn't deserve to die. This isn't your fault, Kendra. Not in any way, shape, or form."

Griffin shook his head. "Maybe the mother of a disabled little girl shouldn't have been out partying at two in the morning."

Kendra whirled on him. "You don't know what the hell you're talking about," she said fiercely. "She gave her daughter everything she had. And more."

"I'm just saying . . ."

"Just stop, Griffin. The more you talk, the more of an ass you make of yourself."

Griffin motioned toward the door. "Take her outside, Lynch. Let her get some air."

Kendra pulled away from Lynch. "Let me alone. I'm not going any-where."

Griffin frowned. "Under the circumstances I believe—"

"I said I'm not going anywhere." She looked down at Danica's face. "Not until I've done what I can for her."

Lynch asked quietly, "Are you really up for this?"

She drew a deep breath. "Give me a minute."

Kendra closed her eyes for a long moment to clear her head.

Detach. Concentrate.

She crouched next to the corpse and tried to block out all the memories of the warm and loving person Danica Beale had been. Kendra scanned her from head to toe, pausing to examine the wound across her throat. She moved in to make a closer examination of her face and hands.

Finally, she stood up.

"Well?" Lynch asked.

"The killer is left-handed, which is consistent with what I saw with Myatt at Corrine Harvey's house."

"You got that from the neck wound?" Lynch asked.

"The angle of the cut suggests that he grabbed her from behind and sliced from right to left. He was wearing chocolate brown leather gloves when he killed her, so you might ask the employees here if they noticed anybody wearing them."

One of the young crime-scene investigators stepped forward. "I'm Agent Herb Elon, ma'am. Leather gloves? I don't understand. How do you figure that?"

"When he was cutting her throat, he would have had to place the other hand over her mouth to keep her from screaming. A natural response would be to bite him, which is probably why he was wearing heavy gloves. Look at her teeth. There are two tiny slivers of brown leather caught between her incisors."

The crime-scene investigator, Elon, shined his flashlight into her mouth. "Holy shit."

"And you might also check neighborhood security cameras," Kendra said. "Here in Southern California, it's rare to see a man wearing gloves anywhere but on a construction site."

Lynch nodded. "Good idea."

"And the killer may have a scratch on his face or neck."

The other crime-scene investigator spoke up. "We checked her nails. No skin or blood there."

"The fingertips on her right hand have been cleaned with a liquid bacteriological soap. Cuticura."

The investigator wrinkled his brow. "How do you know?"

"I can smell it."

"I've dealt with that soap. Cuticura is a fragrance-free soap."

"That just means it wasn't perfume-scented. It's not the same as odor-free. Myatt may have cleaned the nails on her right hand postmortem because she scratched him. He was hoping to remove any blood or skin cells that might have his DNA on them. But antibacteriological soap doesn't kill human DNA, so the medical examiner might still find some if he looks hard enough." She looked at Griffin. "She may have marked our killer for us."

"Anything else?" Lynch asked.

"Myatt may wear a wristwatch with a metal band." She pointed to a series of abrasions under Danica's chin. "As he was cutting her throat, something was cutting her higher up. My money is on a metallic wristwatch, but it also could have been a bracelet. Either way, there may be blood or skin cells on it that the murderer doesn't even know are there."

"Is somebody getting all this?" Griffin asked.

Metcalf raised his notepad in which he'd been scribbling furiously. "Yes, sir."

Griffin looked back at Kendra. "Anything else?"

"You should also check cameras and potential witnesses at the trolley stations in case she was followed. She probably boarded it at National City and got off just a couple blocks up the street." Before anyone could ask, Kendra pointed to the front pocket of Danica's tight slacks. "She has no purse with her, unless she left it at her table?"

Griffin shook his head. "No purse."

"Then she might have a credit card and maybe a lipstick in those tight pants. But you can see she's probably only carrying her house key, no car keys. They would be too bulky. Danica was much too responsible to drink and drive. She was a woman of limited means, so a taxicab isn't likely. I happen to know that the National City trolley station is only a couple blocks from her house. There's probably a round-trip MTS ticket or maybe a monthly pass in one of her pockets."

Kendra stepped a few feet away from them and took several short breaths. Hard. Dear God, that had been hard.

"You okay?" Lynch asked.

"Yeah. That's all I have."

"Good work," Griffin said. "Listen, Kendra, I'm sorry if I seemed callous about—"

"You have no idea what Danica went through every day of her—Don't judge if you don't know what you're talking about." She turned away. "I think I do need some air. I'll see you all outside."

Kendra pushed her way out of the bathroom and practically ran from the club. When she reached the sidewalk, she bent over and fought the nausea and waves of sheer anxiety coursing through her.

Our story will not end until you know how it feels to truly suffer, Kendra . . .

Colby's words echoed in her mind.

Terror is part of our new story.

Fight it.

Don't let him win.

Was she thinking about Colby or Myatt?

Perhaps both. Myatt seemed to be an extension of Colby, a part of the evil. Colby might have been guiding him, but Myatt was his alter ego.

And that alter ego had killed a woman who was loved and needed by that poor child.

Sweet little Zoey, asleep in her bed, about to wake up to a world without her mother in it. There was no father in the picture, but at least she still had a loving home with two doting grandparents.

She finally stood upright. The cool night air felt good on her face. She took a few deep breaths.

"Better now?"

She turned. Lynch was standing outside the entrance, watching her.

"I'm fine. I just needed to get out of there."

"They had no idea you knew her. I never would have let you go in there if I'd known."

"You couldn't have stopped me."

His lips curved ruefully. "I believe that, but I'd have seen that you had warning."

She pulled her jacket closer around her. "It doesn't matter if I'm safe and secure in your fortress. Myatt can still get to the people in my life."

He nodded. "You can't protect everyone."

"No, I can't. And he knows it. Who would dream Myatt would choose to target a woman on the outskirts of my life just because he thought it might hurt? It's what Colby meant when he said I'd know what it means to truly suffer."

"Do you want off this case?"

"No. It wouldn't make any difference. He'll still come after me and the people I care about. I just wouldn't be able to do anything to stop him." She gazed up at the glowing neon lights above the club entrance. "It's like I told you before. We need to find the link between Colby and this killer, Myatt. That's the key."

"The Bureau has already started going through all the information we got from the prison. They'll dispatch agents to follow up on each and every lead that comes up."

"Well, they can dispatch *me,* dammit."

"We'll see what they come up with. We may have some leads in just a few hours."

"They'd better." She turned to Griffin and Metcalf, who had just emerged from the club. "Griffin, I want my security detail back."

Griffin motioned toward Lynch. "I thought he was your security detail now." He smiled slyly. "Has he proved inadequate?"

"This isn't for me. This is for my mother and my friend, Olivia. Myatt is obviously beginning to target me through the people in my life."

"Why just those two? I'm sure you never would have suspected he'd murder the parent of one of your clients."

"Of course not. But I can't ask for special protection for every single person I know. You'd never give it to me. Olivia and my mother would be at the top of the list of people he might target to hurt me."

"So you want two security details?"

"Just one. I'll send them out of town together until this is over."

"And they've agreed to this?"

"Not yet, but they will. I'll see to it." She made a face. "Though neither one of them is going to be pleased with me. Mom and Olivia care about each other, but they're both too independent to be bosom buddies."

"I don't know, Kendra. We're really not in the personal security business, and there is no proof that—"

"Stop arguing, Griffin. You know you'll do it. If you did it for me, why not them? You just like the idea of wielding a club over my head." Her lips firmed. "If you don't agree, then I'll take them out of town myself. If I'm forced to do that, I won't be able to help you on this case any longer. Do you understand?"

Griffin gave her a sour look. "You've made yourself very clear. Where are you going to send them?"

"I'll tell you once I know. In person. I'm not trusting phone lines right now."

He shrugged. "Okay. I'll work something out."

"Thank you. I'm going to talk to them right now."

Metcalf checked his watch. "It's 4:40 A.M. They *are* going to be displeased with you."

"This can't wait. I need to take care of them before I do anything else. When can we expect some analysis of the prison logs?"

"Agent Reade went straight to the office with them after we landed. She was entering them into the case-file database until the wee hours, which is why I didn't ask her to join us here." Griffin started across the parking lot toward his car. "Meet us at the office after you're through, and we'll see where we stand."

"ARE YOU CRAZY?"

Olivia opened her door for Kendra and Lynch to enter. She tied the belt of her robe and ran her fingers through her tousled hair.

"We just got back from a crime scene. There's been another murder."

"And you felt compelled to tell me about it at this ungodly hour?"

"This one was different. Olivia, it was someone I knew."

"Why didn't you tell me?" The annoyance immediately drained from Olivia's face. "I'm sorry. Who was it?"

"The mother of one of my clients. I'm afraid the killer is trying to get at me through the people in my life. I need you to do something for me."

"Anything that you—"

There was a distinct bump from the next room.

Kendra tensed. "What's that?"

"Nothing. What can I do to help, Kendra?"

"I'm sure I heard—"

"It was nothing," Olivia said quickly.

Lynch pulled the gun from his shoulder holster. "Stay here. I'll check it out."

"No," Olivia said firmly. "Do *not* go back there." After a long moment, she shrugged. "I have company, all right?"

Lynch stopped. "Oh."

"Yeah. So where were we?"

Before Kendra could reply, there was another bump from Olivia's bedroom.

Olivia sighed. "Jeez, it's like there's an elephant tromping in there.

This is ridiculous." Olivia called to the back bedroom. "Don, come on out!"

A few seconds later, a disheveled Donald Nelson emerged from the hallway, tucking his shirt into his pants. "Uh, hi."

"Hi." Kendra was trying not to sound as surprised as she felt. "This is an unexpected pleasure, Agent Nelson."

Lynch holstered his automatic and nodded to the man. "But it could prove convenient, Kendra. Griffin won't have to call him to tell him that he has a new assignment."

"There is that." Kendra was a bit flustered. The situation was clear, but she didn't know quite how to handle it. She tried to affect an air of nonchalance but was finding it impossible. "Okay. Well. Uh . . ."

Olivia nodded intently, but the upturned corners of her mouth gave her away. She was enjoying this way too much. "You were saying something about a favor?"

"A favor. Yes."

Agent Nelson pointed to the front door. "If you'd rather I step outside while you talk . . ."

"That's not necessary," Kendra said.

Lynch nodded. "This actually concerns you, Nelson. Your boss, Griffin, has agreed to keep a security detail on Olivia and Kendra's mother. He didn't say if he'd be assigning you, but since you've already been watching over Kendra . . ."

"I haven't heard anything from him yet."

"We just left him," Kendra said. "And it's not even five yet. He's obviously more respectful of your sleep requirements than we are of Olivia's." She turned to Olivia. "The favor is that I need you to leave here. I want you and my mother to go someplace where Myatt can't get to you."

"You want us to run away?"

"I want you to dodge a bullet."

"You're asking me to leave my home. Leave my *life*."

"Take your laptop. You can run your site from anywhere."

"That isn't the point. If our roles were reversed, there's no way you would let this guy run you out of town. You know you wouldn't."

"I know it's a lot to ask. Believe me, I know what a big deal this is. But I just saw a woman dead on the floor of a club bathroom with her throat sliced open. She left behind a sweet little girl. And you know what? That woman's only crime was knowing me."

Olivia shook her head stubbornly and didn't respond.

She had to get through to her. "There's a monster out there." She reached out and took her hands. "I need to do everything I can to catch him. And I won't be able to do that if I don't think you and Mom are safe. Even if you don't want to do this for yourself, do it for the people who could die if he isn't stopped."

Olivia frowned. "Damn, Kendra. Way to slather on the guilt."

"I can't make you go, but I sure hope you will." She paused, then played another card. "Because I need you to help take care of my mother. You know how stubborn and self-willed she can be."

Olivia groaned. "And you want me to try to stop her? Yes, I do know, and it promises to be one big headache. Does she know what you have in store for us?"

"I called her on the way here, and she turned me down flat. I decided I'd go to her place after I came to you. I need your help talking her into it."

"You'll need all the help you can get." She grimaced. "How long are we talking about?"

Kendra thought for a moment. "At least a few days. If it's any longer than that, we can discuss it then."

"You're damn right we'll discuss it."

"So you'll do it?"

Olivia hesitated for a long moment, then finally nodded. "Yes." She added, "But I wish you'd come with us."

"If it makes you feel any better, I packed up and left my condo earlier this evening. I'm staying with Lynch, and his place couldn't be safer."

"I'm glad to hear that. Don told me you'd left your place."

Kendra cast an amused glance at Agent Nelson, who was trying to be stone-faced. "Of course he did. Come on, I'll help you get your things together."

She followed Olivia to her bedroom and pushed the door closed behind them. The second the door clicked shut, Kendra jumped in front of her, and whispered, "How in the hell did that happen?"

"How did what happen?" Olivia said with a blank expression. "Please hand me the duffel in the corner."

"Oh, don't play dumb with me. You know what I'm talking about." She added teasingly, "You seduced the poor guy?"

Olivia laughed and walked over and grabbed the duffel herself. "I'm kind of surprised, too."

"So what happened?"

"You know what happened."

"Of course. But how did it happen?"

"You want to know the details?" Olivia opened a drawer and felt the Braille codes on her blouse clothing tags. She selected a few articles of clothing and shoved them into the duffel. "He stopped by earlier this evening. He wanted to say good-bye."

"*That's* how he says good-bye?"

Olivia smiled. "No. He told me he wasn't going to be guarding you anymore. He said that he was going to miss seeing me. Sweet, right?"

"Precious."

"Stop it. So I let him in for a few minutes, and I suddenly got sad at the thought of not having him around anymore. I . . . didn't want him to go. One thing led to another, and—"

"—And the guy never had a chance."

"Well, I didn't hear him complaining."

"Oh, I'm sure not. So . . . what is this? A one-night stand? Where's it heading?"

"Hell if I know. I told you I was curious, and he was very good in bed. Maybe it's going nowhere. You're the one who's throwing me out of my home, out of my life."

"He may be going with you."

"Along with your mother." She made a face. "Not exactly a romantic getaway."

"It's not supposed to be. He'll be working. Don't you go distracting him."

"Don't worry." Olivia threw in some jeans, shoes, and a clear gallon-size Ziploc bag of toiletries. "He was good, but not good enough to risk my life or your mother's." She zipped the duffel and slung it over her shoulder.

"All set?"

"Yeah. On the way out, you guys can grab my laptop, my work knapsack, and some of the boxes next to my desk. I'll take the opportunity to get some articles and reviews done." She turned back toward Kendra. "By the way, where are we going?"

"I'm not sure. I need to talk it over with Mom. She'll like having some control. It might make it easier to convince her. It has to be someplace no one could possibly predict."

"No one." Olivia smiled. "Including us?"

"Exactly.

CHAPTER
10

"NO WAY, NO HOW."

Kendra was alone with her mother in the large Ledden Auditorium, an amphitheater-styled lecture facility in the campus Humanities and Social Science Building. It was a few minutes before seven, and, as Kendra had predicted, her mother was there preparing for her early-morning class.

Also as predicted, she was having none of Kendra's plan.

"If I left town every time you took on a case, I'd have to quit my job."

"Mom, this is different. He's zeroed in on me. The people in my life aren't safe."

"Now you know how I feel every time you take one of these cases."

"This is your idea of payback?"

"It's not payback. I have a life."

"And I want you to keep—" She broke off.

The door at the front of the lecture hall swung open. Kendra and Diane turned around as Dean Halley walked into the room.

He smiled. "Kendra . . . I thought I saw you come in here. Did you come to see your mother lecture and show you how it's done?"

"Something like that. Good morning, Dean."

Diane looked at the wall clock. "Good lord, Dean. I didn't think you ever woke up before ten."

"Aaah, I had some work to take care of here in my office." He spread his arms wide in a flamboyant gesture. "I guess it was fate, huh?"

Kendra smiled. "I'm not a big believer in fate."

"Okay, then. I'll settle for a happy accident. In any case, it's nice to see you." He looked from her to Diane. "Am I interrupting something?"

"Just my mother's stubbornness."

"Nothing will ever get in the way of that."

Kendra flipped back the cover of Lynch's tablet computer and raised it to chest level.

"Are you trying to take my picture?" Diane asked.

"No, I have some photos to show you."

"Please, no more Maui vacation photos."

"This isn't Maui." A dismembered corpse appeared on the screen.

"Whoa!" Her mother recoiled and raised her hands. "You could have warned me."

"No one warned this woman before she was hacked to death two weeks ago." Kendra swiped her finger across the tablet, and the screen lit up with another bloody corpse, this one almost decapitated by a long strand of piano wire.

"Kendra!"

Dean looked as if he were going to be sick.

Another finger swipe, and they were looking at the corpse with a Latin phrase carved on his chest.

Her mother frowned. "Kendra, please."

Dean finally turned away. "More dead bodies . . . Is this becoming our thing? Because if you think I'm into that, you've been seriously misinformed."

Kendra moved the tablet closer to her mother's face. "Look. This is the kind of diseased mind I'm dealing with. And just a few hours ago, he killed the mother of one of my clients. That's why I've arranged a security detail for you and Olivia." She said urgently, "Olivia is blind. She's smart and strong, but she needs you to care for her. The way you cared for me all those years. Help me, Mom."

Her mother was silent for a long moment. "When would you want me to leave?"

"Now. Olivia is waiting in Lynch's car outside."

"Impossible. I have a class in twenty minutes."

"I can stick around, answer any questions and give them their reading assignments for next time," Dean said.

"I couldn't ask you to—"

"You didn't ask." Dean shrugged. "I offered."

Kendra nodded. "See? And I know for a fact your teaching assistants are chomping at the bit for some lecture experience."

"Of course they are. That doesn't mean they can do it. I'm too exceptional to replace."

"You wouldn't tolerate a T.A. who was anything less than brilliant. You know they can do it. Perhaps not as well, but adequately."

"Where do you propose we go?"

"Nowhere you'll be expected. I prefer it would be someplace you've never been. Where do you suggest?"

Diane thought about it. "Maybe Mount Laguna. Remember I told you about another professor who offered me her weekend house in Mount Laguna anytime I wanted to use it?"

"Vaguely. There's no guarantee it's free right now, though."

"On a Tuesday? Odds are pretty good. I'll call and ask her." She frowned. "But I don't have her number with me."

"I do," Dean said. He pulled out his phone and scrolled through his contact list. "You're talking about Dr. Richmond, right? I spent a weekend down at her place when I first came here. It was a sort of welcome to the academy family."

Diane nodded.

After a few seconds, Dean looked up. "I just e-mailed you her home, office, and mobile numbers." He grinned. "Now get out of here. I have to have a little time to recover my composure after that deluge of sickening photos Kendra threw at us. I have a class coming here in twenty minutes."

Mount Laguna, California
11:37 A.M.

"BEAUTIFUL PLACE," Lynch said as he pulled in behind Diane's and Agent Nelson's cars in front of the rustic two-story house on a hill overlooking the Cleveland National Forest. "I wouldn't mind spending a few days here."

"Neither would I. It's supposed to be a vacation house deluxe, with balconies and an entire finished rec room in the basement." Kendra got out of the Ferrari. "But I guarantee Mom and Olivia aren't going to feel that way. I'm glad that Agent Nelson is here to report back if there's an insurrection, and one of them takes off."

"If Olivia doesn't persuade him to take her away from here himself," Lynch murmured. "I had no idea she was such a vamp."

"Olivia is many things. She's had to survive and make a good life for herself, and she's done it her way." She looked at him. "But she's smart and honorable. She wouldn't do anything that would hurt Mom. She'd just figure out a way to do what she had to do that wouldn't have dire consequences." She started to walk toward her mother, who was standing by her car and looking up at the sleek, lovely house.

Diane's expression was gloomy. "It looks like a damn gingerbread house."

"It does not, it's lovely," Kendra said. "Maybe not your cup of tea, but it's bearable." She paused. "Anything is bearable if you know you're doing the right thing. And you *are* doing the right thing, Mom."

"Maybe." She whirled to face Kendra. "What are you doing standing around here? You've delivered us. You should get the hell out and get rid of that nasty piece of work who's causing all this ugliness."

Kendra smiled. "Yes, ma'am. May I say good-bye and ask you to take care of yourself?"

"Of course I'll take care of myself."

Kendra's glance went up the path to the front door Agent Nelson was unlocking while Olivia stood waiting. "And ask you to take care of Olivia?"

Diane gave her a glance. "She grew up running in and out of my house. Do you think I'd let anything happen to her?" She frowned. "Though sometimes she forgets that I know better than she does."

"She's an adult, Mom."

"She's blind," Diane said bluntly. She started up the path toward the front door. "And that young FBI person who is hovering around her doesn't know anything. I'll have to get her familiar with the house and choose a bedroom where she can smell the fresh pine breezes. And she has to be able to hear the sound of the wind through the trees."

"And not fall off the damn mountain," Kendra called after her.

"There's always that." She turned and looked back at Kendra. She held out her arms. "Come here, brat."

Kendra ran toward her. She was immediately enveloped in her mother's arms.

Love.

Security.

"Thank you, Mom," she whispered as she held her close. "I know how hard this is for you. I promise it won't be for long."

"The only promise I want from you is that you won't let that monster touch you. Not even a hair on your head."

"I promise." She gave her a final hug and stepped back. "Now go and take care of Olivia." She smiled mistily. "Or that FBI agent, whoever needs it most."

"I don't need you to tell me what to do." Diane's voice was throaty as she moved up the path toward the front door. "Get going. You always did dillydally."

Kendra turned and quickly headed for Lynch and the Ferrari.

"Okay?" His gaze was studying her expression as he opened the passenger door for her.

She nodded jerkily. "I don't want to leave them. I want to stay and take care of them."

"Nelson is a good agent. I checked on him." He got into the driver's seat. "And I just made a call to an ex–Special Forces buddy who lives in LA and hired him to come up tonight and guard the perimeter. He's hell on wheels."

"You did?" She swallowed. "That was very kind."

"Yeah. That's me, brimming with the milk of human kindness." He shrugged. "And I didn't want to have you worrying and gnawing your fingernails if I could prevent it. It would be counterproductive to the investigation."

"Heaven forbid." She smiled. "Still, it was thoughtful even though you don't want to admit it."

"Of course I want to admit it. It makes you believe I'm a sterling character." He tilted his head as she laughed. "No, you're too intelligent to fall into that trap. But it can't help but soften you a little."

Soften . . . Yes, she did feel an undeniable softening toward Lynch. But she would have felt a softening toward anyone who was trying to protect Mom and Olivia, she told herself. She looked back over her shoulder at the lovely house on the mountain. It looked very solitary from this distance.

"You're scared," Lynch said.

She nodded. "I've been scared since I saw that poor woman on the floor of the bathroom." She straightened in the seat and looked straight ahead. "But I've done all I can for the time being. Now the only solution is to get Myatt before he reaches out and destroys anyone else."

*   *   *

SHE THOUGHT SHE WAS SO CLEVER, Myatt thought scornfully as he watched Kendra get back into Adam Lynch's Ferrari after leaving her mother. Not that she wasn't clever, or she would never have been able to trap Colby and throw him into that prison. But she hadn't been able to touch Myatt yet, and he'd see that she never did. He'd learned so much from Colby during these last months that he felt as if he was invulnerable. Sometimes he wondered if he had risen to be even greater than Colby.

No, he scurried away from the thought as disloyal.

Colby was the master. Myatt worshipped him and had been lucky to have him for a teacher.

But Colby was lucky to have him here on the outside, too. Myatt had been able to do his bidding and yet still give himself the satisfaction of displaying a razzle-dazzle talent that even Colby had praised. They were two of a kind that formed a magnificent whole.

Kendra and Adam Lynch had now passed the tree-shrouded byway where Myatt had pulled in when he'd seen that the three vehicles had reached their destination on the forest's edge.

Follow her? Or stay and stalk her mother and the blind woman?

He would stay here and scope out all the details on the setup for when he wanted to make a move here. He'd plant a GPS bug on the mother's car similar to the one he'd placed on Lynch's when he'd realized that Lynch would be constantly with Kendra. Then he would go back to the city and keep Kendra in his sights.

But first he had a few other things to do.

Time was flying, and he had to make certain nothing could go wrong at the last minute. He took his notebook out of his pocket and flipped it open. Colby disapproved of notebooks. He thought Myatt should memorize everything. But what Colby didn't know wouldn't hurt him. Colby had rattled off these details so quickly that Myatt had barely had time to absorb them. He wanted to get this right, and his memory wasn't as keen as the master's. He could always destroy the notebook after the plan was in place.

For instance, he had to be accurate about all these difficult names that Colby seemed to have at his fingertips. That tetrodotoxin and Vecuronium Bromide that he'd used on that cop at the Harvey house had been Colby's idea.

So he had to be sure that nothing got in the way of Myatt's fulfilling every aspect of Colby's plan for Kendra Michaels.

He looked back at the house on the hill. Two people Kendra cared about were within his reach.

So very tempting . . .

FBI Field Office
San Diego

THE DOORS OF THE ELEVATOR SLID OPEN at the still-unfinished floor of the FBI field office, and Kendra and Lynch stepped off. The bulletin boards detailing Kendra's previous cases were now surrounding two long folding tables pushed end to end. There were even more freestanding bulletin boards and whiteboards than before, now adorned with crime-scene photos and note cards detailing the latest rash of killings.

She gazed straight ahead and tried not to look at the photo of the bathroom at the nightclub. She stared instead at Griffin, Metcalf, Reade, and several additional agents and support staff who were there.

"Everyone safe and sound?" Griffin asked her.

"I just left my mother and Olivia. They're not happy, but they're safe." She added, "I hope."

"Since I assigned an agent to protect them, at some point I'll need to know where they are."

"I have an address. I'll give it to you before I leave."

"Good. You know that Agent Nelson was most anxious to hold on to this assignment. I told him it was for your friend and mother, not you, but he was still insistent."

Kendra hurriedly looked away from him at one of the bulletin boards. "Oh?"

Lynch nodded solemnly. "You have to admire an agent who throws himself into his work like that. Good man."

Griffin looked as if he might have picked up on the sudden awkward vibe, but he didn't pursue it. "Yeah, Nelson's coming along."

While Kendra had been pretending to look at the bulletin board, something really did catch her eye. "What's this?" She pointed to a whiteboard labeled 'Myatt.'

Griffin walked toward the board and angled it toward her and Lynch. "This is the profile we're building. If he has been somehow working with Colby, it puts him in a unique category of serial killer."

"The tag team."

"Yes. Most serial killers are loners who feel powerless in their everyday lives. Carrying out these types of specific, meticulously planned murders is their means of exerting control and gaining a sense of power that's missing in everything else they do. The tag team is a different animal, especially when the partner is someone as notorious as Colby." Griffin gazed at the list of characteristics that had been written on the board. "Assuming Colby is the dominant partner, Myatt is most likely someone who's comfortable taking orders, perhaps ex-military. He's extremely detail-oriented. These people tend to be obsessively focused on a very narrow range of interests."

Kendra turned toward the agents behind her. "Kind of like you and your comic books, Metcalf."

He shrugged. "Or you and your music therapy."

"Point taken." She studied the whiteboard. "I can imagine there could be an element of hero worship in Myatt, but he may also enjoy one-upping the serial killers he copies."

Lynch nodded. "If he's really working with Colby, what do you make of the fact that Myatt hasn't reproduced *his* murders?"

"Respect," Reade said. "He doesn't want to insult the master."

"Or he's been saving it," Kendra said. "As much as I hate the thought, what if he's planning something even bigger?"

"We're up against a ticking clock," Lynch said. "The only man who might know his identity will be executed in three days."

"Could we reach out to the governor?" Metcalf asked. "Maybe he'd agree to stay his execution until our investigation concludes."

Griffin shook his head. "The problem is that Colby was damn cagey in his responses to us. He never came out and said he was in communication with the killer or even admitted he knew who he was. Anything he said could fall under the category of screwing with the heads of the people who brought him down."

"Plus, the governor wants this execution to happen," Lynch said. "His constituents have been demanding it ever since Colby put those kids' heads on a pike. That kind of thing has a way of whipping up strong emotions. Anything we want from Eric Colby, we'd better get in the next seventy-two hours."

Kendra felt that familiar chill. "I want nothing from him." She nodded toward the stacks of files. "Are those the logs that the warden gave you?"

Griffin nodded.

"Anything there?"

"Nothing yet, but we're still going through them." He glanced at Metcalf. "We had a strange phone call a little while ago. It actually concerned you."

"Me?"

"Yes. Have you ever heard of Bobby Chatsworth?"

"No, should I have?"

"Probably not. He works in England. He's a minor broadcast personality. I was going to say reporter, but that's giving him too much credit. He's been on a tear pushing to get the death penalty reinstated in the UK."

"Really?"

"It'll never happen, but he's made quite a name for himself. Which was obviously the point. Anyway, he's been doing his show from northern California to capitalize on the Colby execution. He and his team were actually at San Quentin yesterday the same time we were." He paused. "They want to interview you."

"Why me?" Kendra asked.

"You're the one who captured him."

"I beat his brains out with a rock."

"Even better. We told them you never spoke to the press about your cases, but they claim that their investigative reporting has uncovered some information that might be helpful to us. *If* you consent to an interview."

"I hope you hung up on them."

Griffin checked his watch. "Actually . . . Chatsworth's producer is in the conference room upstairs."

"What?"

"I made no promises. I only said if they gave us what they have, I'd let them meet you and pitch you on the idea of an interview."

Kendra glared at him. "Are you rolling out the red carpet for every nutjob who claims to have a tip? Or just the ones who want to impose themselves on me?"

"Hear her out, politely decline, and we'll see what they have."

Kendra looked over at Lynch.

He shrugged. "We could subpoena their materials, but I have a hunch they would refuse anyway. If this guy likes to showboat the way his reputation suggests, he'd love nothing better than to see himself as a crusading reporter caught in a U.S. First Amendment case. It would be quicker to just hear them out."

Kendra muttered a curse. "Fine. But if I see a camera, it's going right out the window."

A FEW MINUTES LATER, Kendra joined the FBI team in the conference room where Lily Holt was seated at the table's head with a thin binder in front of her. The woman's choice of seating and regal posture immediately annoyed Kendra. It seemed as if she was positioning herself as the CEO, and they were her underlings.

She didn't stand as they came into room. "Dr. Michaels, nice to meet you."

"Please make this fast, Ms. Holt." Kendra sat in the chair closest to her. "As you can imagine, we're all very busy."

"As am I," she said.

"I have one question for you," Kendra said. "Why on earth do you want to give Eric Colby any more attention than he's already been given? Don't you realize that's exactly what he wants?"

"What Eric Colby wants has no bearing on what we do. It's what our viewers want."

"They want to see a diseased maniac ranting and raving with an inflated sense of self-worth?"

"No." Lily gave her a tight-lipped smile. "They want to see him die."

The producer's icy demeanor left Kendra momentarily speechless.

"Trust me," Lily continued. "We're not putting him on a pedestal. It's clear he's a vile human being, and this world will be an infinitely better place once he's not in it."

"I heard that your show advocates the return of the death penalty in England."

"Yes, it's been half a century since Great Britain has executed a prisoner, yet over two-thirds of the population now favors capital punishment. Bobby Chatsworth and his show just reflect the frustration that society has with the justice system."

"Are you sure that he's not helping to shape it?"

"I'll let sociologists be the judge of that. What I can say is that we've devoted a lot of airtime lately to people whose lives have been touched by violent crime. Citizens are outraged. They feel that the perpetrators of these horrible crimes have forfeited their right to share the planet with the rest of us."

"Enter Eric Colby."

"As soon as the execution date was set, we knew this was a story our viewers would have interest in. This is a system that works. Not often enough, perhaps, but the families of Eric Colby's victims will see justice done in a way that victims in the UK never could. We've interviewed police officers, a retired FBI agent, and several close relatives of Colby's victims, all in an effort to paint a portrait of the man. A portrait of a monster."

"Then what do you want with me?"

"You witnessed the horror in the way no one else did. You saw Eric Colby murder two FBI agents. Then you survived an attack from him, the only person to do so. Not only did you survive, you were the one to finally bring him down. Your story will always be intertwined with his, Dr. Michaels."

"*You'll never be done with me, Kendra . . .*"

Colby's words. Colby's voice echoing in her head.

Again.

Shake it off. He would soon be a memory, no more than a bad dream.

"I have no interest in helping you perpetuate his memory."

"Don't think of it that way. Think of it as having the last word on Eric Colby."

"His actions speak for themselves. And nothing will speak louder than his dying in front of a roomful of witnesses."

"Bobby Chatsworth begs to differ. We saw you leaving the prison yesterday. What did you and Colby say to each other?"

"I'm not going to discuss it. Not now, not ever."

"Dr. Michaels, if you'll just sit down with us for ten minutes . . ."

"It's not going to happen."

"I came here in good faith—"

"You're here because I agreed to meet with you, which is a courtesy I never extend to people in your profession. Ask around."

"I have."

"Then you know I've already given you something that I never expected to give. Now, what do you have for us?"

Lily's lips tightened. "I do hope you'll change your mind."

"I won't."

"I'm sorry to hear that." She folded her hands in front of her. "Okay, a deal is a deal." She was silent, trying to decide where to begin. "In addition to victims' families and law-enforcement officers, we've also conducted several interviews with people who have corresponded with Colby and even visited him in prison. Over the weekend, we interviewed an attractive young woman who actually proposed marriage to him."

Kendra didn't even try to hide her revulsion. "What's most disgusting is that she's probably not the only one."

"She isn't. The ironic thing is, even Colby thinks these people are nuts. We've spoken to several journalists, a movie producer, and a true-crime author who seem quite captivated by him."

"So?" Griffen said impatiently.

"It's no secret you're investigating the serial murders here in San Diego, and suddenly you all have cause to visit Eric Colby just days before he is to be executed. You obviously believe there is some link between Colby and this killer. We don't know if you've received a credible tip or found some evidence, but it's clearly a path you're exploring."

"We can't comment on an ongoing investigation," Griffin said.

"Of course not. But it occurred to us that we still may be able to help each other. We've spoken to many of the people who represent Colby's most likely allies in the outside world."

"We already have all of his visitor's logs," Griffin said.

"I'm sure you do. But what you don't have"—Lily pulled three DVDs from her binder and placed them on the table—"are these."

Kendra picked up a DVD. "And these are?"

"Raw interview footage of the people I was just talking about. I'm sure you may have already begun interviewing them yourselves, but this could prove helpful to you. They're an odd bunch."

"I don't doubt it." Kendra dropped the DVD back onto the table. "So this is what you wanted to give us in exchange for an interview with me?"

"That was my boss's idea. He'll be angry that I didn't hold out for that on-camera interview with you, Dr. Michaels. Somehow, I think this is more important than that interview. But this actually isn't all. Contrary to our reputation, we actually take our research very seriously. We check our sources very carefully."

Lynch's eyes narrowed, his interest piqued. "What did you find out?"

"It's more like what we didn't find out. There's a crime author named Lance Kagan. He's written a few articles for the pulp true-crime magazines. He wrote Colby and said he wanted to write a book about him. Colby agreed to see him a few times."

"And?"

"The man who came to see Colby, the man we later interviewed . . . *wasn't* Lance Kagan."

Kendra tensed. "What do you mean?"

"I mean that true-crime writer Lance Kagan exists, but he has no special interest in Eric Colby. He lives in New Mexico, and he had no idea someone was using his identity to visit a death-row prisoner."

Kendra looked back at Griffin. "You have to undergo an application process before you're allowed to visit a prisoner. Don't they verify the identity?"

"Yes." Lily answered for him. "They do, but evidently he had some excellent fake credentials. Plus, on his first visit, they would have fingerprinted him. Whoever he is, a complete set of his fingerprints are on file at San Quentin State Penitentiary. I'm assuming that if they run them at all, it's just to see that they don't match a convicted felon's."

"Exciting." Reade suddenly entered the conversation, her expression eager. "Did Colby know he wasn't really talking to Kagan?"

"We brought up the subject at yesterday's interview with Colby. He acted as if he had no idea what we were talking about."

"That means nothing," Kendra said. "He's a stone-cold psychopath."

"We're of the same opinion," Lily said. "So the answer to your question is that we have no idea if he knew. But you can look at Colby's interview footage yourself. It's on the third disk, the same one as the phony Lance Kagan."

Kendra glanced at Lynch, then at Griffin. She knew they were all thinking the same thing that she was: Was Kagan their Myatt? But there was no way they'd put that thought into words before a tabloid TV journalist.

Lily looked at the projector on the other side of the room. "Go ahead and pop in the DVD. I'll go through it with you."

"That won't be necessary," Griffin said. "We'll call you if we have any questions."

"I really think it would be best if I'm here when you—"

"We'll watch it later," Lynch said. "But thank you for coming in. This could be very helpful."

Lily glanced hopefully at Kendra. "Worth at least a ten-minute interview, don't you think?"

As annoying as Lily was, Kendra had to admire her persistence. And she had kept her word when she could have backpedaled on that promise. "I'll consider it."

"I can have a crew here tomorrow, anywhere you choose."

Kendra stood up in dismissal. "Give me your card. I'll let you know."

LILY HAD NO SOONER BEEN ESCORTED from the conference room when Reade grabbed the third DVD, popped it into the player, and fired up the projector.

Metcalf picked up the remote and smiled. "I don't think I've been this excited about a show since the last episode of *Breaking Bad*. Who wants to make the popcorn?"

Griffin crossed his arms. "Just get this guy on-screen. I want Kendra to take a good long look at him."

Metcalf scanned through the interview footage, playing a few seconds each time a new subject appeared on screen. Each segment featured a header card that gave the name and a brief description of each interviewee.

It opened with a long shot of Bobby Chatsworth himself, walking and talking among the dozens of protestors they had just seen at the San Quentin East Gate the day before. After a few seconds, Metcalf scanned to the first interviewee. He appeared to be transfixed by the demure prospective bride discussing the simple yet tasteful wedding she envisioned in the prison chapel.

"Man," Metcalf said. "If we don't arrest her as a serial killer, she's just nutty enough to be a reality-TV star."

"Skip it," Griffin snapped. "Get to Kagan."

"Sorry." Metcalf advanced to the next interviewee. "Here we go," he said, reading the header card. "Lance Kagan, true-crime author. Okay, Kendra, you're on."

She eagerly stepped front and center. The on-screen image faded in, and—

Her hopes plummeted. "It's not him."

"Are you sure?" Lynch asked.

"Positive. Damn. I've never seen him before in my life."

Griffin frowned. "Well, he still goes to the top of our list of Colby's suspicious prison visitors. I'll get in touch with the warden and have them transmit those fingerprints to us. We need to find out who this guy really is."

Reade stood up with her laptop. "Well, I have another one we should look at."

"What do you have?" Kendra asked.

"I finally got all of Colby's prison visitor logs in my database. I just now cross-referenced them with the names we gathered from online discussions about you, Kendra. I got a hit. He's a local."

"What's his name?"

She glanced at her laptop screen. "David Warren. He has a Little Italy address, probably one of those funky lofts. On his visitor application, he listed his occupation as 'artist and dreamer.'"

Lynch rolled his eyes. "Great."

"He's obviously a big admirer of Kendra's, which would fit the profile of our copycat. He commented on many of her cases in the online forums. But he also visited Colby for some reason."

"You're right," Lynch said. "We should talk to him." He turned to Kendra. "Shall we take this one?"

Kendra nodded emphatically. The disappointment she had suffered about the identity of Kagan was still with her. She did not want this morning's work to be a complete waste.

"Let's do it."

"WARREN'S BUILDING *IS* BEING marketed as a collection of artist lofts," Kendra said as she walked with Lynch toward the Ash Street address. The building was nestled in the heart of Little Italy, which had recently emerged as a trendy neighborhood of restaurants, coffee shops, and art galleries.

Kendra glanced down the street. "I like this neighborhood. I come here most Saturday mornings for the farmer's market."

"That's interesting. I stay away from here most Saturday mornings for the exact same reason. Street closures aren't my thing."

"Huh. You might think it was worth it if you used veggies for something other than a garnish for those strong alcoholic drinks you pound back."

"You may have a point there." Lynch found David Warren's name on the building directory and pressed the buzzer.

After a moment, a young man's voice came from the intercom. "Yeah?"

"David Warren?"

Long pause.

"Yeah?"

"My name is Adam Lynch. I'm here with Kendra Michaels. We wondered if we might—"

The buzzer sounded, and the front door unlocked.

Lynch grabbed the door and swung it open. "Looks like I found the magic words: 'Kendra Michaels.'"

"Somehow, that isn't very comforting."

They entered the lobby and climbed the open stairway to the third floor. Except for the light hardwood floors, the building interior was entirely white, with a minimalist aesthetic that bordered on antiseptic.

Hard-driving metal music pounded their ears as they approached Warren's door, which was open a few inches.

Lynch grimaced. "Can't stand that stuff."

"It's Queensryche. You should try opening your mind a little."

"I know who it is. It's just that as far as their lead singers go, Todd La Torre doesn't hold a candle to Jeff Tate."

Kendra's eyes widened. "Wow."

"Impressed?"

"In shock. This conversation isn't over."

Lynch leaned into the open doorway. "Hello?"

No answer.

Lynch and Kendra exchanged a glance.

"It could be Myatt in there." Kendra tensed. "I hope to hell I recognize him in some way. That damn disguise he used at the Harvey house . . ."

Lynch nodded and moved his jacket just enough to put his holstered automatic within easy reach. He pressed on the door with his fingertips.

"Hello?"

They walked into the apartment, which, like most so-called artist lofts, featured high ceilings, exposed ductwork, and ample natural light. In keeping with the minimalist design, there was almost no furniture. In-progress artwork leaned against almost every available inch of wall space and several of the large windows.

"Just one minute!" At the far end of the room, a thin young man in an untucked pink flannel shirt held a paint-spray gun in each hand. He moved back and forth in front of a tall canvas, firing off bursts of red and pink paint. His face was covered by a twin-filtered mask that reminded Kendra of a robotic sci-fi villain.

She didn't have to see his features. "It's not Myatt," she murmured to Lynch. "Warren is almost a foot shorter than the man I saw at Corrine Harvey's."

"I'm at a crucial point," Warren shouted over the music. His voice was muffled by the mask in a way that only bolstered the sci-fi-villain vibe.

Kendra stared at the canvas as he paced back and forth and sprayed more paint from every conceivable angle. It was chaotic and abstract in a way that gave modern art a bad name, with no form or meaning.

But then, with a few deft bursts from the spray gun, that all changed. What had appeared to be random suddenly became nuanced and complex; what had appeared unsightly was now beautiful.

Kendra gasped.

The painting was of *her*.

The artist yanked off his mask to reveal a pair of dark eyes, a beak-like nose, and a reddish brown goatee. "You weren't sure about it at first, were you?"

Kendra studied the painting, which was a larger-than-life representation of her profile. Her head was tilted down slightly, and her eyes were closed. "It's beautiful."

"It's shit. But I'll keep working at it." He looked between her and Lynch. "I'm David Warren. What do you want?"

"We're investigating a series of murders, and we'd like to ask you some questions," Lynch said.

"Why me?"

Lynch shrugged. "We're looking for a twisted son of a bitch with a fascination for serial killers *and* Kendra Michaels. Sound like anybody you know?"

"I'm fascinated with purity." Warren walked over to the portable stereo, where his iPhone was docked. He punched a button and turned off the music. "There's nothing more to it than that."

Kendra shook her head. "Pure? No one could describe me as pure."

"Not you. I'm talking about Eric Colby."

Lynch raised his eyebrows. "You think Colby is pure?"

"Of course. Evil is often pure. There's no good, no light, to be found in someone like him. Just darkness. But in the so-called good people, there's always a bit of darkness mixed in with the light."

"You sound like Colby talking," Kendra said.

Warren flashed them a thin-lipped smile. "You say that like it's not a compliment."

"Is this something you and he have discussed?" Lynch asked.

"I don't remember. Our time together was very limited. I only visited him once, but, of course, you know that. That's why you're here, isn't it?"

Kendra noticed that Warren wasn't looking at them when he spoke. His eyes were focused on the painting, and she and Lynch appeared to be just minor distractions, like flies buzzing around while he tried to work.

"What possessed you to visit Colby?" Lynch asked.

"I have a show coming up at a gallery down the street. One of the main theses is the nature of evil. I corresponded with him a bit, then I asked if I could see him. He agreed."

"What did you talk about?"

"His murders. What he was thinking and feeling during each one."

"Pleasant."

"It wasn't supposed to be pleasant. I was trying to understand him and others like him. I'm not interested in just painting what people look like. I need to work from the inside out, what they think and feel. Otherwise, I might as well be a portrait photographer at Sears."

"Did Colby ask you to do any favors for him?" Lynch asked.

"Like what? Commit murder? Uh, no." Warren glanced over at Kendra. "But I did send him a few pictures I found of you online. It's all he ever asked of me."

"How many pictures?" Lynch asked.

"Thirty or forty. I got the impression he had already gathered quite a collection from his other pen pals."

Lynch took a step closer to Warren and his voice lowered to soft menace. "Dr. Michaels here has been the focus of a lot of your online time, hasn't she? You've written about her at great length in a few different true-crime forums."

"You have done your homework, haven't you?" For the first time, Warren was studying Lynch with something approaching respect. "Just more information-gathering. She's squared off against some of the darkest souls imaginable. What does it take to defeat and outsmart people like this again and again? How do they affect you? Do you become more like them, or does it make you run even further from that side of yourself?"

"We're here to ask questions, not answer them," Lynch said. "Where were you between midnight and 3 A.M. this morning?"

"Ah, now we're getting down to business."

"It was a direct question," Kendra said. "Care to give us a direct answer."

"Sure. I was here."

"And is there anyone that could confirm that?"

"Like an alibi? Hell no. The woman I usually live with left me three weeks ago. She can't stand my guts right now."

"Can't imagine why," Lynch said.

"Is that attitude really necessary, man? Just so you know, I haven't left this place in two-and-a-half days. I've been on a major creative roll and haven't wanted to disrupt the flow. Which is exactly what the two of you are doing to me right now."

"What about last Friday night?" Kendra asked.

"Same story. Like I said, I have a show coming up. These canvases don't paint themselves." He thought for a moment. "The last time I was anyplace where people could speak up for me was a week ago Wednesday. My friend's band was playing at The Casbah. Otherwise, I can't help you."

"Maybe you should think about helping yourself," Lynch said.

Kendra leaned forward toward him. "And here's a thought . . . You can also stop lying to us."

Deer in the headlights time. "Lying? About what?"

"You were on the other side of town late Friday night. Around La Mesa. What were you doing over there?"

His face flushed with anger. "Have I been under surveillance?"

"Please answer the question."

"Yeah, I went there for a little while . . . to see somebody."

"You bought some weed."

"Shit," he said under his breath.

"And two women joined you here last night. At least for a couple hours. Friends of yours?"

He nodded.

"What time were they here?"

"Ask those snoop cops you had staking out my building," he said bitterly.

"She's asking *you*," Lynch's voice was steely. "And I suggest you tell her."

Kendra tried to hide her smile. It was always nice to have a sledgehammer handy.

"Fine," Warren spit out. "The girls were here maybe between eleven and one last night."

Kendra nodded. "Too bad. If it was a little later, they could have helped you."

"That's why I didn't think it was worth mentioning."

"Don't lie to us anymore," Kendra said wearily. "You aren't good enough at it."

He glared at her. "Do I need a lawyer?"

"We're almost done here. Have you ever spoken to Colby by phone?" Kendra asked.

Warren considered the question, then admitted reluctantly, "Yeah. Twice. The first time was to remind me to send the Kendra Michaels pictures. The second time was just a couple weeks ago. Believe it or not, he offered me one of the family seats to witness his execution."

"He did?" Kendra couldn't hide her surprise.

"Yeah. He didn't want his own family there, so he asked if I wanted to go. He thought it might give me something to paint."

"Are you going?" Lynch asked.

"I thought about it. I've never seen a man die before, especially like that. An artist needs to open himself up to new experiences, you know?"

Warren shook his head. "But in the end, I said no. I'd already gotten what I needed from him. Why in the hell would I put myself through that?"

Lynch handed him a card. "Just so you know, we may be following up with your friends and associates. If you have anything you'd like to tell us, now is the time to speak up."

He shook his head. "No, nothing. Do what you have to do. I don't give a damn."

"That's my number on the card, along with the number of the FBI field office. If you think of anything, just call."

"I hear you." Warren turned toward Kendra, who was looking at his still-drying painting of her. "Pretty sweet, huh?"

She nodded. "I have to admit it's amazing. Especially since I know how quickly you did it."

"I tried painting you a few other times, but they never came out right. But this is the first time I painted you with your eyes closed. For some reason, that makes the whole picture work." He shrugged. "If I decide to do anything with it, I'll let you know."

CHAPTER
11

"INTERESTING TECHNIQUE," Lynch said, as they exited the building and walked down the sidewalk to his car. "Bust him on some little stuff, create anxiety, then move in for the kill."

"Spoken like the true puppetmaster you are."

"So how did you know about his Friday evening drive to La Mesa?"

"The pizza box on the counter. The box itself was generic, but the laser-printed label on the side told me it was D'Agostino's Italian restaurant. The label also had David Warren's name and phone number and showed that it was a pickup order phoned in at 10:37 P.M. Friday. D'Agostino's is just a few blocks from one of the most notorious drug neighborhoods in the city. Since I had already smelled three distinct types of weed in that apartment, it wasn't a stretch to think that he had gone over there for a late-night fortification run. It would also explain why he hadn't wanted to tell us about it."

"And what about his guests last night?"

She shrugged. "There were two drinking glasses in the sink, and they each had slightly different shades of lipstick on their rims. The glass top of the coffee table showed fresh rings that matched the size and contours of those two drinking glasses, but no others I could see. Clearly, the women sat on the couch, and Warren sat in the chair facing the two of them."

Lynch smiled. "Clearly."

"The couch reeked of weed, enough that I figured they were there drinking and smoking for a couple hours."

"Even I could smell that. But how do you know it was last night and not today?"

"Because the stench wasn't on Warren. Not on his clothes or hair, meaning he had changed and showered between then and now. That tipped the odds in favor of last night. Also, the lipstick on the drinking-glass rims was dry and cracking. It probably wouldn't look that way after only a couple of hours."

"Dazzling as usual."

"Are you being sarcastic?"

"No, I wouldn't presume. I've always known exactly what your capabilities are. However, you still manage to occasionally surprise me. But all this still doesn't place him at or away from the murder scenes."

"You're right, but it did allow me to exert pressure and get more from him than we might have otherwise. All I know for sure is that he's not the man I saw at Corrine Harvey's house. That still doesn't eliminate him as having played a part. Griffin should have his people flash Warren's picture around at the club."

"I'll make sure he does."

Lynch's phone vibrated, and a second later the text chime sounded on Kendra's. She glanced at her screen.

CONTACT GRIFFIN ASAP.

She showed it to Lynch. "You too?"

Lynch showed her his phone with the identical message. He punched Griffin's number, and it was answered immediately. "Lynch, is Kendra there?"

"Yes, right next to me. I'm on speaker."

"Good. Kendra, we just hit the jackpot on those numbers you picked up from the envelope in Colby's cell."

"It was a usage account?"

"Yes. It was a five-hundred-minute talk time refill from Lightwire Communication, a regional mobile carrier that sells disposable mobile phones and pay-as-you-go account cards. You usually see them at discount stores, price clubs, and gas stations. The card was activated in a mobile phone about three weeks ago."

"We need to subpoena those records," Lynch said. "I have a contact in the Justice Department who can help push that through in a hurry. If you give me the—"

"It's already done, Lynch." Griffin sounded annoyed. "I don't need your contacts. Believe it or not, my position comes with a fair amount of influence."

"Of course. Just trying to help."

"Anyway, within the hour, we should have information on everyone who was called by this phone."

Kendra's hand tightened on the phone as excitement gripped her. "And there's a good chance one of them is Myatt."

"That's the way we see it," Griffin said. "We'll immediately pull photographs on them, and we'll send agents out to round up as many as we can. You two should probably be here for this."

"Do you think we'd miss it?" Lynch took Kendra's elbow and nudged her toward the car. "We're on our way."

THE MOMENT KENDRA STEPPED off the FBI office elevator and entered the second floor "war room," she immediately sensed a different energy than on her other visits. There were more agents and support staff, now numbering approximately thirty, and they moved with greater purpose and barely contained excitement. They spoke louder and more quickly, and even the clicking of computer keyboards seemed to be supercharged.

"Can you feel it?" Lynch squeezed her arm. "It's called optimism. You did this."

"I just hope it pays off."

Across the room, Griffin motioned for them to join him. Reade and a few other agents were at the long tables at the front of the room.

"The reports came in from the phone-service carrier," Griffin said. "Every call originated from the tower that covers the prison."

Kendra looked over his shoulder at one of the report copies. "What about the call recipients?"

"He called nine different numbers. We already have six identified. Three are here in Southern California, two in New York, one in Chicago. Most appear to be journalists. We'll try bringing them in for questioning and see what they discussed. I've already alerted offices in NYC and Chicago."

"What about the other three numbers?"

Reade waved a printout. "As far as we can tell, they're throwaway phones with no names registered to them. Two of them are registered with the same mobile network as the prison phone, and our warrant was broad enough that the company also gave us information on those. The only time those two phones were ever used was to receive calls from the prison. We're still tracking down the carrier for the third throwaway phone."

Lynch nodded. "That's *it*. One or all three of those has to be Myatt's."

Kendra was quickly studying the report that Griffin was still holding. "Where were those two phones? Does the report tell you that?"

"Yes," Reade said. "Both here in San Diego County. One pinged a tower north of the city, another one due east."

Kendra nodded. "What about the timing of the calls? Do they line up with the homicides?"

Reade shook her head. "I was just working that out when you came in, but it doesn't look like it. The calls almost always came a day or two later."

"Assuming that the local-call recipients don't lawyer up or otherwise refuse to come in, we'll conduct their questioning in the interview rooms upstairs," Griffin said. "The two of you will be able to observe and send in questions, if you have any."

"Good," Lynch said. "You can bet there will be questions."

"Welcome back, Kendra." Metcalf had emerged from a crowd of agents with a small stack of color printouts. He smiled and gestured toward the busy war room behind him. "Look at all the overtime your observations are costing the U.S. taxpayer. I hope you're happy with yourself."

"I'll be happy when we catch this guy."

"Speaking of which . . ." Metcalf spread the photo printouts on the table. "Here are photos of the six people we've identified as having received calls from Colby's prison phone. Five men and one woman. Are any of the men a match for the guy you saw at Corrine Harvey's house the other night?" He watched as she grabbed the printouts and scanned them at lightning speed. "Take your time and—"

"No." Disappointment sharpened her voice. "It's none of them."

"Okay, I'm glad you took your time."

She shrugged. "No sense in wasting your time or mine. These aren't him." She turned to Griffin. "I was hoping . . . but evidently it's not going to be that easy. But we'll get there. And I'm very interested in seeing their interviews. When do we start?"

MUCH OF THE INITIAL enthusiasm—and staffing level—had evaporated by the time the last local interview was completed at 10:16 P.M. All of the local-call recipients were indeed journalists of some sort, with whom Colby had shared disgusting details of his crimes that he presumably didn't want recorded by the prison on their internal phone system. Kendra joined the other agents in listening to the interviews conducted in Chicago and New York. Two of those were also journalists, and the third was a woman in Manhattan who had actually pitched Colby on the idea of a Broadway stage musical based on his life and crimes. Kendra sat in horrified amazement as they listened to excerpts of several songs the woman had written for the endeavor.

Griffin nodded to the assistant, who cut the connection with the New York FBI office.

"My God," Metcalf said. "We really have to find a reason to arrest that woman. Agreed?"

Kendra nodded, sick. "Absolutely terrifying."

"Obviously, we'll check out all of them," Griffin said. "But right now our focus should move to those disposable phones."

Reade looked down at her printout. "Assuming at least one of these belongs to Myatt, he may have already tossed it and moved on to another one."

"It's possible," Griffin said. "And if it hasn't happened yet, it could happen at any time. We need to work fast."

Lynch leaned forward. "A coordinated ping?"

Griffin nodded. "Tomorrow morning. 10:30 A.M."

"Good idea."

Kendra frowned as she looked first at Lynch, then at Griffin. "What the hell are you talking about?"

Lynch turned toward her. "A coordinated ping. One way or another, we're going to force those phones to ping their local towers. Sometimes, the wireless carrier can do it with a remote command, but these burner phones are often so simple that we may have to do it the old-fashioned way: picking up the phone and calling them. If the phones have power, we can narrow them down to a limited area."

"I'll have response teams standing by," Griffin said. "Once we get a fix on the signal, they'll swarm over the area and put up roadblocks, go door-to-door and do whatever we need to try and find whoever's using that phone."

"Can you really narrow down the area that much?" Kendra asked.

"It depends," Griffin said. "But if it's hitting two or even three towers, we can get very close. If Myatt is using one of those phones to stay in touch with Colby, we'll find him. If he's discarded it, we may still have a place of contact to start searching."

"Don't say that." Kendra got to her feet. "I'm going to believe that we'll find him. We're coming so near to getting him." She could feel a flush heat her cheeks as she stared fiercely at the agents at the table. "Your coordinated ping is going to pay dividends. I know it." She turned toward the door. "Come on, Lynch. Let's get out of here. We can't do anything until tomorrow, and Griffin is beginning to depress me."

"Heaven forbid," he murmured as he followed her from the room. "And this case is so bright and cheery."

"WE'RE CLOSE," KENDRA SAID as she preceded Lynch into the living room. "For the first time, I feel as if I'm not up against a blank wall. We're getting close to that bastard, Lynch. I feel it."

"There's hope, at least." Lynch shut the door. "But I'm surprised you're so optimistic. You're usually so pragmatic."

"Pragmatic is boring. I want to be giddy. I want to believe that everything will come up roses. I want to catch Myatt and put him away for the rest of his life. I want Olivia and Mom to be able to come home." She came forward to stare up at the giant photo of Ashley. "I bet you understand, Ashley. You look like a woman who looks on the bright side. Of course, it could be that bikini you're wearing. But you need to talk to Lynch about his attitude."

"I usually keep her too busy to discuss my character flaws. Of course, I don't have that many." He went to the mahogany bar against the wall. "Would you like a drink?"

She nodded. "Red wine."

"Right." A few minutes later, he crossed the room and handed her the glass. "Enjoy."

"I will." She sipped the wine. "It's excellent. I believe I'm beginning to appreciate your good taste."

"Don't. I'm only a peasant who likes his beer and hard liquor. So I have an expert keep an eye out for good vintages and send them to me." He glanced down at his glass of beer. "For the pleasure of my guests."

"Ashley?"

"She likes vodka on the rocks." He looked up at the photo. "Why do you keep talking about her?"

"She's hard to ignore." She lifted her glass in a toast to the woman in the poster. "To Ashley."

His gaze never left Kendra's face. "To Kendra. I like you giddy. I just wish it was for some reason other than Myatt."

"Take what you get." She took another sip of wine. "And you probably only want me giddy because you think I'll be easier to manipulate. You have that—"

Her cell phone rang. She pulled it out of her pocket.

She stiffened. "Griffin."

"So much for giddy," he murmured. "Crashing down to earth."

"Maybe he's found out something more about—" She punched the access button and turned up volume. "Griffin? What's happening?"

"I'm sorry to disturb you," he said hesitantly. "Believe me, I'm not insensitive to what you went through at the prison. You may think that I've been—"

"Stop stuttering." She tensed. She didn't like this. "Just tell me why you're calling."

"I just received a call from Warden Salazar at San Quentin. He had a request and decided to go through me." He paused. "Colby wants to talk to you one more time before the execution."

"No!"

"I told Salazar that would be your answer. He said it was his duty to make the request from a condemned prisoner. Colby dies tomorrow night, you know."

"I could hardly forget."

"Salazar said he refuses to see any family members but he's been spending a lot of time with the chaplain during the last few days. A couple times he's even requested to be taken to the chapel for prayer."

"What?"

"Well, you know the old saying about there not being any atheists in a foxhole. Colby may be running scared."

"Or he may be playing games."

"Possibly." He hesitated. "But what if he's had a true change of heart? This might be an opportunity."

"Or it might be a chance for him to rip me to pieces one last time."

"That could be true." He lowered his voice. "But do you want to refuse, then later wonder if you'd done the right thing? There's a lot in the balance."

"Leave her alone, Griffin," Lynch said roughly. "You saw what he did to her before."

"Hello, Lynch," Griffin said. "It's her choice, after all. Stay out of it. Kendra?"

"I'm not going to fly up there and let him—"

"That wouldn't be necessary," Griffin said. "Salazar has arranged a Skype with your computer. Colby is waiting for the connection. Just a few minutes of conversation, then you can hang up. You'll be in total control."

"No one is ever in total control with Colby. He only waits until you turn your back, and he springs." She was starting to shake at the thought. She made an effort at control. "He wants to see if he can make me afraid." Oh God, and she *was* afraid. "It's all a big con game."

"Then the answer is no?"

"Of course it's—" She closed her eyes. Don't give in to him. Stand your ground.

"Don't do it," Lynch said.

"Shut up." She opened her eyes. "Dammit, I have to do it. Because there's a million-to-one chance Griffin might be right. I have to let Colby take one more shot at me to make sure." She spoke into the phone. "Set it up. Give me five minutes." She hung up.

"You'll regret this," Lynch said.

"Probably." She drank the rest of her wine in two swallows. She wished she had another one. She was probably going to need it. No, she had to have a clear mind. "But it has to be done." She sat down on the couch and took her computer out of her bag and set it up on the coffee table. "So either be quiet or sit down in that chair across the room and commune with your humongous poster of Ashley while I get this over with."

He stood looking at her for a moment, then went across the room and sat down.

She sat there, taking deep breaths, waiting.

The computer sounded. She accessed the call.

Salazar's face filled the computer screen. "I appreciate your consideration in doing this, Dr. Michaels. I know how difficult it is for you."

"No, you don't. But that's okay, I agreed to do it." She shook her head wearily. "God knows why. Hope springs eternal. Griffin asked if I might regret saying no, and I couldn't answer him. I know that you're only doing your job, Warden. But do you honestly think Colby has seen the light?"

"I have no idea," Salazar said. "He's certainly been displaying the signs of a man seeking salvation. I've seen other condemned men who have searched desperately for forgiveness during these last few days. It's not my place to judge."

"And whose place is it?"

"It seems it's yours, Dr. Michaels. Are you ready to speak to him?"

"No. Yes. Go ahead."

The next moment, Colby's face replaced Salazar's on her screen. "Hello, Kendra. It's kind of you to take the time to speak to me. I know you must be very busy." His small, pointed teeth showed in a smile. "While I'm not busy at all. I'm taking the time to look back and inward."

"Either way, you're seeing nothing but a horrible festering."

"Is that any way to talk to a man who is seeking forgiveness for his sins?"

"Bullshit." She drew a deep breath. "Why did you ask to speak to me?"

"Why, you were the one who stopped me from committing even more sins. I wanted to thank you." He leaned forward, and said softly, "We've been together on a great journey. I somehow feel that even after the good warden shoots me with his poison that we'll still be together. Our story will continue into the afterlife."

"You're crazy."

"I think about you all the time. Do you know what I remember most? That gully and your hitting me with that stone." He chuckled. "I want you to remember the gully, too, Kendra. It's important."

"It's the past, and I'll forget it as soon as they put you to death."

"No, don't do that. As I said, it's important."

"The only thing that's important is that you tell me where I can find that bastard you sent out to do your murders. If you're repentant, give me his name."

"I don't know what you're talking about." He smiled. "I can hardly be blamed for some copycat trying to best my record. If you find out who he is, have him call me, and I'll tell him the error of his ways."

"I might do that." She stared him in the eye. "Because we're very close to getting him, Colby. It might even be before they execute you.

I'd like you to know that your pupil will be following you to the grave. Your legacy will be over."

"Are you bluffing?" His face was without expression, but she could sense a minute change in his demeanor. "It doesn't matter if you are or not. After all, tomorrow night this talk of legacies will be settled one way or the other. I'll have gone on to that other place."

"Hell."

"It's possible, if hell exists."

"If it didn't, God would create one for you."

"But what about forgiveness?"

His tone was solemn, but she knew he was mocking her. "I'm done with talking to you, Colby. I'm hanging up."

He nodded. "I'm ready for you to do that now. I just had to see you one more time and speak to you. It was important to me. Important to both of us."

"The only thing important is that after tomorrow, I'll be able to erase you from my life." She hung up.

She was shaking. She turned off the computer and shoved it across the coffee table, rejecting it. She wanted a total disconnect. She felt somehow that he was still there, waiting for her to open the laptop so he could pounce.

"A total waste." Lynch was suddenly beside her on the couch, pulling her into his arms. "Salazar should have told him to go screw himself."

"He couldn't do that." Her voice was muffled against his shoulder. "Don't you know we have a merciful justice system even to those who don't know the meaning of mercy?" She should push him away, but she wasn't going to do it. She needed his strength right now. "Salazar had to go by the rules. I'm the only one who could say no to Colby. I didn't do it."

"I hate to say I told you so. But if I don't, you might ignore my sage advice again."

"Bastard."

"All Colby wanted to do was taunt you, to get his final jab before he bowed out."

"Maybe. I don't know. I guess that was what he wanted. He's crazy, and he's obsessed with me. He kept talking about the gully . . . But he didn't really do anything but reminisce and—you heard him."

"Yes, I heard him." His arms tightened around her. "I wanted to kill him. I didn't want him to have even twenty-four hours more of life."

"Neither did I," she whispered. "I know that I couldn't be safer with him shut away in that prison, but he frightens me. He's always frightened me. Do you know, it's said everyone has a nemesis. If that's true, Colby is mine."

"Not true. A nemesis is unconquerable. You've conquered Colby."

"Have I? He doesn't think so."

Lynch cursed low and fluently. "That's because he's trying to use Myatt against you in some way. It won't do him any good. We'll get Myatt soon, and Colby will die tomorrow night. No more nemesis."

"I can almost believe you."

"Dammit, don't give me that almost bullshit. *Believe* me."

"Yes, sir." She laughed and pushed him away. "And you're right, I'm being an idiot. Colby seems to have that effect on me. Thanks for the comforting shoulder to lean on. I seem to be using it ad nauseum. I'll watch it from now on."

"How disappointing." He grinned. "I'm beginning to look on it as a fringe benefit of working with you."

She could feel her pulse begin to pound, and she hurriedly looked away from him. "That would be exceptionally humiliating for me. I'd hate for anyone to think I was that weak." She got to her feet. "And now it's time for me to get to bed."

His brows rose. "Is it?"

She felt the heat sting her cheeks at the subtle sexual intimation. Ridiculous . . . and immature. "Yes, it's going to take me a long time to get to sleep after that damn Skype call. Tomorrow, we've got to hit the ground running."

"You're sure you wouldn't like me to come and—" He shook his head as he saw her expression. "Just offering comfort, nothing else. I've officially appointed myself guardian against all nemeses attacking you."

"Yeah, sure. You could be a pretty rough nemesis yourself. Thanks anyway." She looked up at the poster of Ashley. "And I'm sure she wouldn't approve. Good-night, Lynch."

"Good-night, Kendra." He got to his feet as she left the room. He glanced up at the Ashley poster, and murmured, "And good-night, Ashley. I'm beginning to think I may have to do something about you . . ."

SHE COULDN'T SLEEP, DAMMIT.

As Kendra had told Lynch, she had known that it would be a lost cause.

After two hours, she gave it up and went out on the balcony for air.

It was only eleven thirty, she realized with surprise. It was going to be a long night. She supposed she could work on her files. It was better than sitting around thinking about Colby.

Or Myatt. He was the threat.

Which reminded her that she hadn't heard from her mother since early this morning.

Call her? Why not? She was a night owl and never got to sleep before one or two.

Besides she wanted to hear her voice. She wanted to hear sanity and intelligence and goodness. She wouldn't dump on her, but she just wanted to know that those qualities survived because Diane was in the world.

Diane answered the phone in two rings. "What's wrong?"

Oh, shit. "Nothing. I just wanted to talk to you. How is every-thing there?"

"Boring. Olivia has been working on her computer all day and that FBI person, Nelson, has been drifting around being solemn. He tries not to be obvious, but I think he has a thing for Olivia."

"Very observant."

"But I'm not sure about Olivia. I've never really been able to read her. Even as a child, she was something of an enigma."

"Not to me."

"She was your best friend. She kept me at a distance."

"But you liked her."

"That doesn't mean I understood her."

Kendra changed the subject. "Is everything quiet up there?"

"As far as I know. Tad Martlin, that Special Forces friend of Lynch's, came by today and introduced himself and gave me his cell-phone number. Very polite. Cold eyes. I wouldn't want to be on his bad side. Lynch chose well. But then he knows about things like that, doesn't he?"

"In spades. He knows about a lot of things."

Her mother was silent. "But evidently he doesn't know how to keep you from worrying and feeling bad." She repeated, "What's wrong?"

So much for trying not to dump her troubles on her mother. Diane wasn't about to give up. She sighed. "Colby. I had to talk to him today, and I'm having trouble shaking it off."

"I can imagine. He dies tomorrow, right?"

"Yes."

"Good." She said grimly, "I'm tempted to go up to San Quentin and watch it happen. I remember when you had to deal with that mon-ster. It nearly killed you."

"It was a pretty terrible time."

"But you fought your way through, like you always do. You wouldn't talk about it, but you were strong, and I was proud of you."

She paused. "As I'm proud of you now. Maybe I don't tell you that enough. I couldn't have a daughter I respect more or that is more deserving of love."

"Hey." Kendra had to swallow to clear her tight throat. "I didn't call you to hear that, but I'll take it."

"You called me because you knew that I'd fight the battles that you'd never think of asking me to fight. You called me because I always understand you even though I don't always approve." She added, "And you called me because you know I'm here to heal your wounds. It's my job and my privilege." She went on brusquely, "Now that we've got that settled, do you want to hang up and try to go to sleep, or shall we talk?"

"Talk, please."

"Okay, but nothing to do with that son of a bitch at San Quentin or why I'm stuck up here on this mountaintop. Instead, I'll tell you about my weird ultraliberal class at the university and some of the stories that Dean told me about his time in the service. He really has a unique sense of humor and I enjoy . . ."

IT WAS MORE THAN FORTY MINUTES LATER that Diane hung up the phone after talking to Kendra.

It had been good to hear her voice, she thought, but she didn't like the fact that Colby had been able to put Kendra on edge. She'd be glad when the bastard was dead and permanently out of all their lives.

She stared out at the moonlight shimmering on the forest below. But even with Colby dead, there would always be another killer, another case, putting Kendra at risk. Like this Myatt who had thrown her and Olivia together on the top of this damn cliff. No matter how much she tried to persuade Kendra it was going to be a—

"Was that Kendra?"

She glanced at the French doors and saw Olivia standing there. Dressed in a high-fashion striped-silk turquoise caftan, she looked like an exotic Asian princess. "Yes. Nothing was wrong. Just chitchat. Come and sit down. The chair is six feet forward and two feet to your left."

"I know." She glided forward. "It was kind of you to show me where everything was located, but I have it now. As long as you leave everything in place, I'll be fine." She dropped down in the rattan chair. "I may not be as good as Kendra was before she had her operation, but I'm very, very good. And I've had more time than Kendra to practice. She had a miracle that interfered."

"And does that bother you?" Diane asked quietly.

"Am I jealous? Of course I am. I'm not perfect. But I love Kendra, and I'm happy for her." She inhaled deeply. "It's wonderful out here. The pines and the fresh breezes . . ." She turned to Diane. "I know you're impatient being here. So am I. But there are a few good things about it."

"Tell me about them."

Olivia was silent, then smiled. "I get to have Kendra's mom to myself for a little while."

She hadn't been expecting that answer. "What?"

"Another thing I was jealous about. I always envied Kendra her relationship with you. It's pretty wonderful, you know. Oh, I had my father, and he loved me, but it was different. Dad's a high-powered businessman and he has a new wife every few years. Most of the time, he left my care to qualified schools and nannies. Then I met Kendra at school, and everything changed. She became my good friend and invited me home with her. I saw how different it could be to have someone not only in your corner but on hand to back you. You never stopped Kendra from doing anything that she thought she could do, but you were always there for her. And when you did step in for her, everything turned out all right." She chuckled. "I desperately wanted a Diane of my own."

"I'm . . . surprised. You never showed me. You seemed to be so absorbed with Kendra. She was your friend, and sometimes I felt in the way. Around me, you were always very reserved." She paused. "I tried to be friends with you. Should I have tried harder?"

"No, you were wonderful to me. It wasn't your fault that I couldn't be at ease around you."

"It *was* my fault. I was the mother of a blind child, and I should have looked beyond her to try to solve the problems of her best friend, who was also blind. I was just so involved with Kendra that everything revolved around her."

"I know that," Olivia said. "I'm not giving you a guilt trip, Diane. We worked our way through it, and we're friends now." She added softly, "But there's no true friendship without honesty. I want that for us. I couldn't be honest with you when I was growing up. I had too many hang-ups." She made a face. "Not that I don't now, but my problems and hang-ups don't have anything to do with you."

Diane gazed at her for a long moment. "You need some help dealing with them? I'm damn good at solving problems. Even you have to admit that, Olivia."

"Hell, yes." Olivia smiled. "But you know that wouldn't work. We're both too independent these days."

"I could be tactful . . . maybe." She nodded, thinking. "Sure. Why not? Kendra obviously won't let me run her life and keep her happy and safe. I have plenty of time and energy to spend on you. Yes, it's an excellent idea. I'll take you under my wing, and it will be good for both of us. Think about it, Olivia."

"I am thinking about it," Olivia said warily. "And it's scaring me."

"Coward. You wanted someone in your corner, here I am." She smiled. "I may be a little late, but look at all I've learned in that time that can benefit you. I'm a treasure trove of knowledge and experience. For instance, I don't believe you've been pursuing medical ways to cure your blindness with enough dedication. I've been doing a good bit on my own, but I left it up to you. Maybe I shouldn't have done—"

"You've been searching for a cure for me? I didn't realize that, Diane."

"You should have. You're my daughter's best friend, aren't you?"

"Yes. No. I think you're her best friend, but I come pretty close."

"The relationship is completely different. She thinks I'm obsessive and possessive."

"Are you?"

"Of course, but I make every effort to control it. And the love makes it palatable for her. I wouldn't be that way with you."

"Good. I'm relieved. Because I've no intention of being adopted by you in any shape or form."

"Don't be absurd, it wouldn't be like that. Think about it. I'd be very good for you." She hesitated. "Besides, I'd enjoy it. I like you."

"I like you, too," Olivia said. "But you could smother me."

"Take the challenge. You're stronger than that."

Olivia lifted her chin. "Yes, I am." She got to her feet and took the three steps to the balcony railing. "I'll consider it. But don't be surprised if I don't agree to be your next pet project."

"I *will* be surprised. We have issues to resolve, and this is one way to do it. In the end, we might shape a relationship that will be something extraordinary."

"Diane, you're impossible." Olivia ruefully shook her head. "I took one innocent step, and you're pulling me willy-nilly down the course to the finish line."

"And what's wrong with that? There's always a prize waiting at the finish line."

"True." Olivia was laughing as she turned back to the forest. "But sometimes it's a booby prize. Did you ever—" She stopped, her head suddenly lifting.

"Olivia?"

"Shh." Olivia was silent a moment. "Diane, you said that this balcony faces straight out to the forest? That the hillside curves around on either side of us?"

"Right."

"Then no one could be looking at us unless they're in the middle of that forest down there. But that's not likely at this hour."

Diane straightened in her chair. "No. Why?"

Olivia didn't speak for another instant. "Someone's out there. Maybe in the woods. He may not be looking at us but he's *there*."

"Agent Nelson?"

"No, he's guarding the front of the house."

"It could be that Tad Martlin, the Special Forces person we met today."

"Maybe." She shook her head. "But I don't think so."

"You heard something?"

"No. Or maybe I did. I can't be sure." She tilted her head, listening. "I have very good hearing. Not as good as Kendra, and I can't put things together like she can." She looked out into the darkness. "I don't think I heard him. I *feel* him." She moistened her lips. "And it's not a good feeling. Bad . . . it's bad."

Diane jumped to her feet. "Then let's do something about it." She grabbed Olivia's arm and pulled her toward the French doors. "I doubt if anyone could get on this balcony, but we won't take a chance." She whisked her inside and locked the doors. "Call Agent Nelson and have him come inside. I'll phone Tad Martlin and tell him to scour the woods on either side of the house." She reached for her phone. "We'll take care of it."

Olivia was looking at her. "It's only a feeling. I have no proof, Diane."

"There's always a theory before there's proof. And some theories are based on feelings. As a blind woman, your instincts are finely tuned," she said as she checked the number and started to dial. "So we won't discount them. I'm in your corner, and we're fighting this together. Now go call Agent Nelson and we'll check it all out."

CHAPTER
12

San Diego
9:05 A.M.

LYNCH FELT THE TENSION GRIP him as he saw the ID on his phone. Tad Martlin.

Not good.

He punched the access. "What's the problem?"

"Nothing that I can tell. Diane Michaels called both of us late last night and told us to scour through the woods around the house."

"She heard something?"

"No, she said Olivia sensed something."

"Sensed?"

"That's what she said." Martlin paused. "And I'm not ridiculing her. You and I both know that instinct is a valuable tool. But no one can testify to accuracy."

"What did you find?"

"Nothing last night. I went out this morning when it got light, and I still saw no footprints or marks of passing. If someone was out there, they were very woods-savvy."

"What did you tell Kendra's mother?"

"The same thing I'm telling you. She's sharp, and she deserves the truth. What's more, she can handle it. She accepted my report and asked only two things. One, that I keep alert and assume there was someone out there last night. Two, that I not tell her daughter that there was a possible problem. Since it didn't pan out, she didn't want her worried."

"Neither surprises me."

"She shut down that FBI agent that's parked inside guarding them, too. However, I didn't promise I wouldn't report to you. What do you want me to do?"

He thought about it. He didn't like even a hint of a threat to Kendra's mother and Olivia, but this was too vague to be a legitimate concern.

And God knows, Kendra had enough to worry about right now.

But Kendra would kill him if she found out there was danger to the people she loved, and he hadn't told her.

However, no real threat had been demonstrated.

So accept the responsibility and do what Kendra's mother was doing. Keep a close eye out for potential peril and protect Kendra from frantic worry for no reason.

"Lynch?"

"You've got a pretty good commander in chief out there. Do what she tells you. But keep me informed. I want to know if there's even the slightest inkling of anything wrong."

"You've got it." He hung up.

Lynch stared thoughtfully at the phone as he pressed the disconnect. He was definitely uneasy.

Forget it. Nothing he could do now.

He had to concentrate on getting Kendra to that FBI meeting and zeroing in on Myatt.

FBI San Diego Field Office
10:25 A.M.

"FIVE MINUTES UNTIL SHOWTIME," Griffin said into the P.A. microphone at the front of the war room. "Unit leaders, verify that your teams are in place and ready to move."

Now it did seem like a war room, Kendra thought as she and Lynch moved through the crowd of agents and support personnel. A high-wattage projector was throwing a map of greater San Diego onto a twelve-foot-wide screen high on the front wall, augmented by two flat-screen monitors. Pulsing blue dots indicated the GPS tracking beacons of the response teams, located at strategic locations around the city.

A systems chief from the wireless telephone provider, Lightwire Communications, stood at the front of the room wearing a headset, linked to the company headquarters in nearby Escondido.

One by one, the response teams checked in. They were ready.

The room's roar of voices abruptly subsided, dropping in volume as the clock inched closer to ten thirty.

Metcalf stepped closer to Kendra, watching the countdown displayed on the big screen. "With a little luck, this could be over by lunchtime," he whispered.

"I sure hope so."

The digital countdown clock neared zero.

10 . . . 9 . . . 8 . . . 7 . . . 6 . . .

Please let this work, Kendra prayed. Let this nightmare come to an end.

5 . . . 4 . . . 3 . . . 2 . . . 1.

Griffin nodded to the systems chief, and he spoke into his headset. After a moment, the technician looked up and spoke to the assembled agents and support staff. "They've initiated the ping test."

He punched a button and patched his headset audio through the P.A. system.

"Account one is a no-go," said the voice on the line. "I repeat, it is a no-go. We have no connection."

Groans erupted in the room.

Griffin raised his hands to silence the staff.

Kendra looked around the room. Metcalf no longer had the same confidence he'd shown only moments before.

"Account two is also a no-go," said the voice on the P.A. "Same story with account three. No connections with the towers on any of them. Sorry, guys."

More groans from the staffers.

"Shit." Kendra's shoulders slumped. She had hoped against hope. All that soaring optimism she had tried to keep alive was ebbing away. "I guess there's a reason they call them disposable phones."

"It's not over," Griffin said. "We know that third phone has made contact with the prison less than twenty-four hours ago. He probably just leaves it powered down until he's ready to use it. We'll continue to live-monitor, and the teams will stay in place. I'm telling you this could still work."

Kendra leaned against a table. "I want to believe that. Damn, I want to believe it."

"It's our best shot," Lynch said. "In the meantime, we'll just keep following every lead. You know how it works . . . keep chiseling until the dam breaks."

"Chisel? I wanted a sledgehammer, remember?"

He smiled. "Just point me in the right direction."

"Maybe I can point you there." Agent Reade called from the other side of the room. "Come look at this."

Reade was immediately surrounded by Kendra, Lynch, Griffin, and several other agents. She pointed to the screen of her laptop. "San Quentin sent over the fingerprints they had on file from that visitor who was posing as a crime writer. I ran them, and we got a match."

Kendra inhaled sharply. Hope was again beginning to stir.

Lynch bent down and squinted at the readout. "And who is it?"

"His name is Norman Wallach."

Kendra froze. "And where does he live?"

"Right here in San Diego. I haven't had a chance to do a full search on him yet, but his record is fairly clean. He had a DWI about a year ago, and he was arrested for drunk and disorderly conduct earlier this month. It looks like he's lived at several different addresses in the past few years."

Kendra studied the record. "I want to talk to him. I *have* to talk to him."

Reade looked at Griffin. "I don't mean any disrespect, sir. But I thought since I ran this down, I should be the one to—"

"I know. I know," Kendra said. "I understand. And I'm not trying to run roughshod over you, Reade." She moistened her lips. "But I have to be the one. You see . . . I know who this man is."

Mission Heights
San Diego
2:15 P.M.

LYNCH PULLED UP TO THE CURB in front of the dilapidated Mission Heights apartment building. He nodded toward the chipped stucco and dozens of missing vertical blinds. "It looks condemned."

Kendra sadly nodded. "He used to live in such a beautiful house."

Lynch gazed at her. "You talk as if you've been there."

"I have."

He was silent a moment. "You notice how tactful I'm being not to bombard you with questions? I figure you'll tell me eventually."

"I appreciate the restraint. Being tactful must be extremely painful for you."

"Exceptionally." He smiled faintly. "But you're worth it."

They climbed out of the car and walked up the sidewalk to the front entrance. Although it had obviously once been a security door, it now opened freely without being buzzed by a tenant. They climbed the stairs to the second floor and made their way to an apartment at the end of the hall.

Kendra knocked on the door, and after thirty seconds with no answer, she tried again. Finally, she heard footsteps. The door opened a crack, just enough to see that it was indeed the man from the interview footage."

"Norman Wallach?"

"Yeah." He looked as if he'd been sleeping. He was a slender man, midforties, with longish gray hair.

"I'm Kendra Michaels and this is Adam Lynch. We're working with the FBI on an investigation. May we come in?"

He stared at her for a long moment. "Kendra Michaels. You know . . . actually meant to write you a note or something. I just . . . couldn't."

"I understand."

"Do you?" He opened the door wide for them to enter.

Kendra and Lynch stepped inside the virtually empty studio apartment. The furnishings consisted of a single lawn chair, a sleeping bag, and a small television set.

Wallach ran his hand through his hair. "So what can I do for you?"

She said gently, "I believe you might guess. Mr. Wallach . . . why were you visiting Eric Colby in prison?"

After a long moment, he finally spoke. "I guess I've been waiting for somebody to call me on that." He looked away from her as he dropped down in the lawn chair. "It should have happened before."

"A man murders your little boy, and four years later you pretend to be someone else in order to visit him?"

Eyes glued open staring . . .

Wallach still didn't look at her. "Yeah. Pretty messed up, huh?"

"Pretty messed up."

"Nothing's been the same since he took Stevie from us. Nothing."

"I know it's been hard."

"No. Life is hard. This is something else entirely. This is hell. That . . . creature, he took all the love from our lives, he robbed us of whatever happiness we could have had."

"Where's your wife?"

He finally looked back to her. "We didn't make it very long, not after . . . She had such a good heart."

Kendra nodded. "I met Sheila right after I joined the case. She was a strong woman."

"Stronger than me. She ended up leaving town and living with her sister in Mississippi for a while. She couldn't stand it here anymore. Now I think she's just moving around a lot. It's hard for her to settle anywhere." His tears welled over. "You know, before they found what was left of Stevie, the cops actually thought I might have had something to do with it. I was going out of my mind with worry, and I had to deal with that shit."

"The police had to look at every angle," Lynch said quietly. "They were just doing their job."

"I know that. But then Sheila even started doubting me for a while. I never got over that."

"You were both under an incredible amount of stress."

"You think?" he said sarcastically.

She leaned forward. "Norman . . . Why did you visit Eric Colby?"

He shrugged. "Would you believe I just wanted to see him for myself and try to understand how that kind of evil could exist in the world?"

"No. I wouldn't believe that."

Wallach smiled. "Smart woman."

"So tell me."

"I went to see Eric Colby . . . so I could kill him."

She nodded.

Wallach stood up and walked over to the window. He stared out through the opening left by a missing vertical blind. "For years, I thought it would be enough to see him executed. But after his date was set, I knew it wasn't enough. I wanted to do it myself, and I wanted it to be painful."

"This whole point of yours, masquerading as that writer, that's what this was all about?" Lynch asked.

"I knew they'd never let me near Colby, so I had to come up with another way. I found this true-crime writer who I thought had done enough to interest him, yet wasn't so famous that there would be pictures on the Web, just in case someone at the prison wanted to check me out. I got some good fake IDs and gave it a shot. There's a whole application process. I was sure I'd get tripped up somewhere along the way, but it never happened. I got in to see him three times."

"How did you think you were going to do it?" Lynch asked. "There's no way you could have gotten a weapon in there."

"But I did. Three times."

"How?"

Wallach reached down to the windowsill, picked up a thin white blade about six inches long. He displayed it to them. "It's made of carved animal bone."

Lynch's gaze narrowed on the thin blade. "Very deadly. But I know from personal experience that the guards pat you down extremely, even obscenely, thoroughly."

"Yes, they do." Wallach used the tip of the blade to fold back an almost imperceptible flap of skin on the underside of his upper left arm. He pushed the blade until it entirely disappeared beneath his skin.

Kendra's eyes widened. "How in the hell . . . ?"

"It's a skin pocket. I cut and cauterized it myself." He showed her his scarred right arm. "I tried doing it on this one first, but I made a mess of it. It got infected, and I was afraid I was going to lose my arm for a while. But that didn't stop me from trying it on the other one. This time it worked. Unfortunately, I probably won't ever be able to completely straighten my arms."

"So you got it inside the prison," Lynch said. "What good did it do you? You never used it on Colby."

"I practiced my move for weeks. I knew I was only going to have one chance before the guards jumped me. One jab straight to the heart, maybe a second or third if I could work 'em in." He swallowed. "But each time, I lost my nerve. He looked at me with those ugly eyes, and I'd cave. I was a coward. Sheila was right to leave me. Toward the end, I was afraid he'd get suspicious and not let me come back anymore. He asked me to talk to that TV crew, and I did it just so that he'd let me come back. I figured by the time anybody found out I wasn't that crime-writer guy, it'd be over." Wallach used his thumb and forefinger to slide out the blade from the cauterized slot in his arm. "And each time I lost my nerve, I was so disgusted with myself that I decided to come home and stab myself in the heart with this." His mouth twisted with disgust. "But I didn't have the nerve for that either."

"Nerve has nothing to do with it," Kendra said. "Deep down, you don't want to die. And you know Eric Colby isn't worth rotting for the rest of your life in prison. I know your son wouldn't have wanted that."

Wallach wiped the tears from his face. "I'm just hanging on for tonight. It's going to happen, isn't it? After all this time they're going to kill the bastard. It'll be such a relief to see that shit stain wiped from the face of the earth."

"Yes, it will."

Wallach was silent, then asked, "May I ask you a question?"

She nodded.

"Why didn't you kill him when you got the chance? Then it would have all been over a long time ago."

She flinched.

Lynch immediately stepped in, "That's not fair, Wallach."

"Yes, it is," Kendra said. "No one has a better right to ask." She stared Wallach in the eye. "I've asked myself the same question. I was tempted and resisted the temptation. I thought I was being virtuous and doing the right thing. I didn't realize that the lingering ramifications of not doing it would be this terrible. Not only for you, but for others." She reached out and grasped his arm. "I'm sorry that you went through all this. I hope God brings you peace after tonight."

"I do, too." He looked down at her hand on his arm. "I hope we all have peace." He glanced at Lynch. "He was right. I don't have any right to blame you. You're the one who caught the bastard. I've just been thinking it would have been so much easier for Sheila and me not to have had to go through that court case or the rest of it."

"Yes," she said unevenly. "I can see how you would think that. But we have to look forward now. After Colby is dead, it's not the end for you. As I said, your Stevie wouldn't have wanted that. What are you going to do?"

"I don't know."

She glanced at Lynch, then back at Wallach. "Look, Norman. Let us take you someplace where you can get some help. I know people who can make you feel a whole lot better."

He frowned. "Do I have to go?"

"No. We're not arresting you or anything. This is just for you."

"I don't want to go anywhere."

"Fine. But can I have someone come and see you? They can help you here."

He finally nodded. "Okay."

"How about you let me hold on to that blade? Would you do that?"

He slowly, gingerly extended the carved blade.

She took it and slipped it into her jacket pocket. The thin blade felt light as air. She couldn't even tell it was in her pocket. "Thank you, Norman."

"You're welcome." He sat down in front of the television set. "Would you go now? I have to watch the news programs and make sure that Colby isn't going to slip through the cracks because of those nutty people who want him to live because they never had a son like my Stevie." He switched on the set. "I feel better that someone knows why I went to see Colby. It was kinda hanging over me."

"I'm glad we know about you, too, Norman. Remember, you said that I can send someone to talk to you." She stopped at the door. "That's a promise, right?"

He nodded, his gaze on the TV screen.

Kendra turned to go.

"Kendra."

She looked back at him.

"You may need peace even more than the rest of us," Wallach said quietly. "I'm sorry I made it harder for you."

"No problem." She tried to smile as she left the apartment and hurried down the stairs.

"The hell it's no problem." Lynch was right behind her. He opened the front door for her. "He nearly tore you apart."

"No, Colby tore me apart. Like Wallach said, life is hard. This is hell. None of it was Wallach's fault. We've just got to keep him from killing himself after Colby is dead, and he has no purpose." She got into the Ferrari. "As for blaming me, if he'd known about Myatt, he would have had a right to blame me even more. The chain never really stopped once Colby got his hands on Myatt to influence." She held up her hand as he started to protest. "I know. You don't have to tell me. That's all under the bridge, and we have to move forward. Call Griffin and see if we have any more news on those disposable cell phones. He said that pinging business wasn't a complete wash." She took a deep breath to release the tension. "I hope *someone* can tell us *something*."

"You're a bit on edge."

"Now why would I be on edge? Just because Colby is going to die, and I'm afraid Myatt will do something horrible to someone when he does?"

"That would do it." He started the car. "You need this day to be over. But since you're not like Wallach, who can park himself in front of a TV and zone out until the deed is done, I think we've got to keep you busy." He smiled. "So that's what we'll do. I'll keep you so busy that you won't have time or mind to worry about Colby or Myatt. We'll concentrate on details and pings and anything else that comes along. Deal?"

"Deal." She looked at him with a surge of gratitude. He was solid and sledgehammer tough, and she could trust him to do anything he said he would do. How many people could you say that about? "So what's first?"

"I guess we should report in to Griffin and see what progress he's made." Lynch routed the call through his car's speakerphone. After briefly discussing their encounter with Norman Wallach, he said, "So what info do you have for us?"

"Not anything that's very promising." Griffin paused. "We need time, Lynch. And we haven't got it."

"That doesn't sound good. You were more optimistic this morning."

Griffin was silent. Then he said, "This isn't easy for me, Lynch. I have a favor to ask."

Lynch chuckled and glanced over at Kendra. "A favor. From me?"

"It's not that big a deal," Griffin said sourly.

"By all means, let's hear it. I can't tell you how I'll enjoy having you in my debt."

Griffin unfurled a string of curse words. "That will never happen, you smug son of a bitch."

Lynch clicked his tongue. "And this is how you ask for a favor?"

"It's not as if this wouldn't benefit all of us. I've already asked the FBI deputy director to intervene with the governor." He paused. "I've decided that we have no choice but to try to stay Colby's execution while this investigation is active."

Kendra felt as if she'd been socked in the stomach. The breath was knocked out of her.

No. No. No.

Lynch was no longer smiling as he glanced at Kendra's expression. "Really? I thought that wasn't on the table."

"I don't have a choice but to try. As we've already discussed, it's going to be a tough sell. The governor's office wants this execution to happen, and the longer it's postponed, the greater the chance that Colby might decide to start the appeals process. We know what that means."

"Dammit, it means his death sentence might never be carried out," Lynch said. "Especially if California voters get another whack at capital punishment. The last time it came up at the polls, we came within 250,000 votes of doing away with the death penalty altogether." He paused. "Which begs the question, do you really want to do this?"

"It's a devil's bargain, I know. But we have a serial killer on the loose, and we're all sure Colby knows who it is."

Kendra stared at Lynch in disbelief. So cool, so calm. How could he even discuss the possibility of letting that monster live even one more day?

"You may have a difficult time making the governor feel as sure," Lynch said.

"That's why I'm forced to ask you for help. I know you have some fairly powerful connections in Washington. People who owe you favors, perhaps."

"Like you do, Griffin."

Griffin ignored the comment. "The governor's office is now evaluating our case-file brief, and we'll hear by the end of the day. But I would appreciate any influence you can bring to bear."

"I'll think about it." Lynch cut the connection.

"You'll think about it?" Kendra repeated, amazed. "How can you even consider helping Griffin keep Colby alive?"

"I said I'd think about it, Kendra. I'm not as emotionally involved as you are. I have to weigh the pros and cons."

"You're damn right I'm emotionally involved, but I still see right and wrong."

"Even if I threw in my influence, it would still be an uphill fight. Our governor ran on a state's rights platform. He's not going to be receptive to a lot of Washington power brokers telling him what to do."

"Then let him do what's right. I can't understand why you would even contemplate helping Griffin."

"Because I don't want any more murders if I can help it." They were approaching the FBI field office, and he pulled over to the curb. "I'm not you, Kendra. I'll do what I think is right, not according to Kendra Michaels."

She looked at him in anger and frustration. Only a short time before she had felt so close to him, and now they couldn't be further apart. She suddenly couldn't bear either Griffin's move or that separation with Lynch. She had to escape.

"Fine." She jumped out of the car. "But I don't believe I can stand Griffin and all his people buzzing around trying to commit a crime of their own. I'll see you all later."

She heard Lynch curse behind her. The next moment, he was standing beside her. "You know it's not safe for you to be strolling the streets."

She kept walking.

He grasped her arm and whirled her to face him. He took her

hand and dropped the keys to his Ferrari in her palm. "Take my car. But if you get so pissed you wreck it, you'll have me to deal with. I'll call you when we hear something." He turned and walked away.

She looked down at the keys. He loved that stupid, ego-building car. It would serve him right if she—

But that would make her actions totally immature, and she wouldn't do anything that lacked dignity. Her anger and viewpoint were just.

And Lynch should know that, dammit.

She turned and walked toward the Ferrari.

San Quentin Penitentiary

Chapel

8:40 P.M.

"THIS IS VERY GOOD OF YOU, WARDEN." Colby smiled gently. "I'm grateful that you gave me this last opportunity. I didn't want my final prayers to be in that cell." He looked around the chapel. "This seems more . . . fitting."

"It was a last request. You're entitled to it as long as there's no threat, and it doesn't interfere." Salazar gestured to the four guards. "Follow him to the altar but allow him space and privacy for his last prayers." He turned to Colby. "Do you wish to see the chaplain?"

"Why? I've seen him before, but it's too late now. I die in four hours. He can't give me absolution. I don't need a middleman." He looked at the glowing candles and the crucifix above the altar. "How long before I have to go back to my cell?"

"I can give you thirty minutes."

"That should be enough time." He glanced at the guards. "I'll try not to keep them waiting." His lips twisted. "Nor you, Warden Salazar. I know this is going to be a big night for you. Is it going to be a full house to watch me die?"

Salazar said without expression, "I understand many people are interested."

"I can see how they would be. I'm something of a superstar." He started down the aisle, his gaze fixed on the flickering candles below the crucifix. "Let's hope I won't disappoint them with my performance."

Salazar didn't answer, and Colby closed him out of his mind. He was nothing. Colby had used him, but he was no longer important. He had to concentrate on the task at hand.

He moved into the second pew back from the altar. It was the same pew he'd occupied every time he'd come to the chapel for the last few days. He'd made sure that everything was exactly the same.

Even the guards were in their same positions in the aisle six pews to the rear.

He knelt and looked up at the crucifix. His lips moved as if in silent prayer.

His hand moved down beneath the pew in front of him.

He closed his eyes.

Let it be there.

He could control almost everything but the guard whom Myatt had bribed to do this job. It annoyed him that he'd had to leave details like this to Myatt. He could make Myatt do anything he wanted him to do, but he couldn't control his choices when he wasn't in contact with him.

But this time, evidently, Myatt had chosen well, and the guard was not quite a fool.

The cell phone was here.

He punched the access button, his gaze still on the flickering candles on the altar. "Bless you, my son," he said mockingly. "You did well."

"I told you I'd get it done," Myatt whispered. "I had to do it. I haven't been in contact with you lately. I had to make sure you knew that I was out here doing everything you told me to do."

"And have you?"

"Of course. I've done practically everything we discussed and agreed is necessary. I've not been able to take care of Kendra Michaels yet. But I'll do it within the next couple days. I may have to use her mother and maybe Michaels's friend to draw her into the trap." He added quickly, "But you don't have to think it won't happen. I made you a promise."

"I trust you. Why wouldn't I after all you've done for me?" He trusted no one, but Myatt needed to think they were close in every sense, so that he'd continue with his tasks. "I just had to make sure everything is in place." He folded his hands in prayer, his head bowed. "I need you to move quickly. I Skyped Kendra Michaels yesterday, and she seemed to think that she'd gather you into her net soon. I told her she was bluffing, but you mustn't take the chance. Not after all we've done to bring her down."

"All *I've* done," Myatt said.

"I beg your pardon," Colby said softly. "Did I hear you correctly?"

"A slip of the tongue," Myatt said quickly. "You're brilliant and guided me all along the way. But you have to admit I've handled everything cleverly and inserted my own bits to the big picture. One of the kills I committed a few days ago you didn't even know about. You wouldn't let me get in touch with you."

Arrogant bastard, Colby thought with annoyance. "Yes, you're clever. I wouldn't have chosen you if I didn't believe you could do what I wished. But I told you to concentrate on Michaels."

"And I will. I just had to prove to her who was running this show."

"Concentrate on doing what I told you to do," he said through set teeth.

"I didn't mean to make you angry. You know I only want to please you."

Keep it cool and calm. "You always please me." He paused. "I just have to be sure everything is clear. I don't have much time." He added sardonically, "In a few minutes, they're going to take me back to my cell and perform the usual rituals for my meeting with the executioner."

Myatt was silent for a long moment. "Are you frightened, Colby?"

"You insult me," he said sharply. "Fear is for lesser men. Not for me. Not for you, Myatt."

"I'm sorry. I didn't mean to—"

"I'll forgive you if you do your duty to me. I have to go now. Good-bye, Myatt."

"I won't disappoint you."

"I know." Colby broke the connection and pushed the phone once more beneath the pew in front of him. He remained kneeling there for another few minutes, his lips moving as if in prayer.

Then he lowered his head on his arms on the pew in front of him as if in despair. Two more minutes, and he lifted his head. He gave a deep sigh and rose to his feet.

The next moment, he was moving down the aisle toward the back of the chapel, where Salazar waited.

The guards in the aisle parted for him like the Red Sea did for Moses. A very apt comparison, he thought bitterly. His power and intelligence against their stupidity and brawn.

Salazar straightened as he saw Colby coming toward him. "Did it help? Did you make your peace?"

"You could say that." Colby didn't look at him as he headed for the door of the chapel. "At least I made sure that I wouldn't be forgotten."

CHAPTER
13

MORE THAN TWO THOUSAND PROTESTORS lined the roadway outside the prison gate, almost matched in numbers by the TV news crews, print journalists, and online bloggers with video cameras.

Lily Holt had just finished an interview with the particularly bloodthirsty female president of a victims' rights group when Bobby Chatsworth walked up and joined her behind the barricade.

"Any luck?" she asked.

"No. I wasted an entire day trying to buy our way into that witness room. A reporter from the *Los Angeles Times* almost sold me his for five thousand dollars, but he got cold feet. He was afraid of losing his job."

"They don't allow cameras in there anyway."

Chatsworth smiled as he fluffed his full red beard. "Cameras they can detect, you mean."

Her gaze narrowed on his face. "What are you saying?"

"My day wasn't entirely wasted. I found out there's going to be a very special auction tomorrow morning. One of the 'reputable citizen' witnesses is smuggling in a miniature HD video camera, possibly in a pen or a brooch. Video of the entire execution will be sold to the highest bidder."

"That's grotesque, even for you."

"Thank you, my dear."

"The network will never air it."

"Certainly they will. I'll promote the hell out of it, and it will be the ratings event of the season. And when we put it online, millions more all over the world will watch for years to come."

"My friends and family are already asking me how I can work with you. What will I say then?"

Chatsworth laughed. "I'm leaving immediately after the execution. The auction will take place in San Francisco tomorrow morning."

"Please understand if I don't wish you good luck."

"Understood. Any progress on the Kendra Michaels interview?"

"None yet."

He shrugged. "No worries. If this execution footage comes through, we'll have everything we need."

THE SUN WAS GOING DOWN when Kendra drove the Ferrari back to FBI headquarters.

Lynch was standing on the street, waiting.

She got out of the car and went to meet him. She gave him the keys. "You didn't call me. The governor hasn't made a decision?"

"We just heard five minutes ago. Griffin just got off the phone with the governor. They didn't believe our grounds were strong enough to delay the execution."

"What about your Washington friends? No influence?"

"It didn't come into question. I didn't call them." He looked her in the eye. "But it had nothing to do with you. If the death penalty hadn't been in jeopardy, I would have done it. I would have pulled every string I could. I just couldn't stand the thought of Colby's not getting his full punishment."

"So I guess Griffin doesn't owe you after all."

"What a disappointment."

"Is he angry?"

"I don't give a damn." He looked at his Ferrari. "It's in pretty good shape. You must have resisted temptation."

"I didn't drive it very much," she said. "I just went to the park and sat and tried to make sense of everything."

"And did you do it?"

"Not very well. But it's looking better right now." She moved toward the door. "And now that the governor did the right thing, we can get back to the business of finding Myatt. Where's Griffin?"

"In the war room. Breathing fire."

She could see what he meant when the elevator doors opened, and she saw Griffin.

"I guess you're happy," he spat out bitterly when he saw her.

"Not happy. But a little more . . . satisfied."

Griffin cursed and walked over to the uncovered windows where there had once been a row of offices. The sun had just set, and the lights of the city twinkled in the distance. He called over his shoulder to Metcalf. "Anything in those prison files?"

Metcalf stepped forward. "A few things to follow up on. We won't know until we—"

A high-pitched beep sounded from the phone-company technician's laptop.

Kendra's eyes flew up to the large projected map, which had remained unchanged all day long. But as the beeping continued, she noticed that a pulsing red dot now appeared on the map.

"What does that mean?" she yelled over the noise.

"I'll check." The technician, who had passed much of the day hovering near the desk of Griffin's attractive assistant, snapped to attention and ran back to his laptop. "This is *it*." His voice was filled with wonder. "One of the phones has made contact with the network."

Griffin ran back from the windows. "Where?"

"Northeast of the city." He picked up his phone. "I'll see how far we can narrow the location."

San Quentin State Penitentiary
Death-Watch Cell

COLBY STARED AT THE NEW JEANS and denim work shirt that one of his death-watch guards, Tom Lester, handed him. "What's this?"

"Put them on, please."

Colby raised his eyebrows. "*Please?* That's the first time I've heard that word in all the years I've been here. Dead Man Walking evidently has its privileges."

The guard pointed to the crisp new clothing. "It's routine. It's almost time. Do it."

"Funny. A costume for an execution. May I have some privacy while I change?"

"Not a chance."

Colby nodded to Lester and his fellow guard, Patrick Nevis. "Of course. The death watch. Can't have me killing myself before the big show." He pointed to his left. "The execution chamber is just on the other side of this wall, isn't it?"

"Just put on the clothes."

Colby turned his back on the guards, stripped out of his prison uniform, and pulled on the jeans and shirt. He turned back around and adjusted the collar. "Blue really isn't my color, you know."

"Sit down, Colby."

He smiled and sat on the edge of the bunk. "Be nice. You'll miss me when I'm gone."

FBI Field Office
San Diego

"GROUP LEADERS, PREPARE TO MOBILIZE your response teams. We have an active target." Griffin whirled away from the gathered agents and leaned toward the telephone-company technician, who was still on the phone and scribbling furiously on a Post-it note. "Got it?"

The technician tore off the note and handed it to Griffin. "That phone is most likely within thirty yards of this address. They just confirmed it at the office."

"It's 26613 Breaker Drive," Griffin said. "Get the response teams rolling. I want the names of every resident on the street. Reade, let's see if there's a match with anyone on the suspect database you've been compiling."

Reade was already pounding her keyboard. "I have the resident list up. Cross-referencing now."

Kendra stepped closer and looked over Reade's shoulder at the dozens of names displayed on the laptop screen.

She went rigid with shock. "No," she whispered.

Lynch quickly moved closer to her. "What is it?"

She shook her head dazedly. "It's crazy." She moistened her lips. "It has to be a coincidence. The third name on the list. Dean Halley. A history professor. He works with my mother. He was with me on the bridge that night. But I can't believe that he's the . . ." Her voice trailed off as she tried to comprehend and connect the dots. "But he does have a prison record, and it might not be for the reason he told me. But he was so damn . . . plausible."

Lynch snapped at Griffin. "It's 26613 Breaker. That's the target." He turned toward Reade. "Pull up a photo of Dean Halley and make sure all teams have it. If you can't immediately pull up a driver's license or passport photo for him, check the UC San Diego Web site."

Kendra barely heard him, her eyes were still locked on that screen. Dean Halley.

San Quentin Penitentiary

"COZY." COLBY SMILED AS HE STEPPED through an oval door and was escorted by his three guards into the octagonal execution chamber. It was approximately seven-and-a-half feet in diameter and centered around a single table. Five large windows separated the chamber from the witness area, which was populated by forty-five journalists, politicians, and so-called reputable citizens, some of whom included victims' family members.

Colby didn't attempt to make eye contact with any of the witnesses as he was led to the table and strapped down with nylon restraints.

He looked up at the execution leader, Ron Hoyle, a stocky man with a thick moustache. "I have a final statement to make."

"You waived that right, Mr. Colby."

"I've changed my mind."

Hoyle glanced at the warden, who was standing next to the state attorney general in the back of the witness room. Salazar slowly nodded.

"Okay," Hoyle said. "Go ahead. Make your statement from there. The witnesses can hear you."

"I really don't care whether they can hear me or not. It's on my chest."

"What?"

"My final statement is on my chest. Please unbutton my shirt."

Hoyle hesitated.

"Or tear it open. Makes no difference to me. I won't be using this shirt much longer."

Clearly thrown by this break with protocol, Hoyle froze for a few seconds. He then leaned over and unbuttoned the top two buttons of Colby's denim shirt. He pulled apart the fabric, glanced at Colby's chest, then quickly let go of him in disgust.

Colby laughed.

Hoyle angrily turned toward the physician, who was standing with the cardiac sensors. "Proceed."

Breaker Drive
San Diego

THE FBI AND THE SAN DIEGO PD had already barricaded off the 26600 block of Breaker Drive by the time Kendra and Lynch arrived. Agents had quietly surrounded Dean's house, while uniformed officers escorted perplexed neighbors from their homes to barricades at the end of the block.

Kendra and Lynch got out of his car and ran for the other side of an FBI armored van parked in the cul-de-sac four houses away from Dean's.

Griffin's gaze was trained on the one-story, Spanish-style house through his binoculars. "That's Dean Halley's car in the driveway, but there are no other signs that he's home."

"He also has a motorcycle," Kendra said. "He keeps it in the garage. You can see the skid marks he leaves at the top of the driveway."

Griffin nodded. "We'll wait for SDPD to finish securing the street behind his house before we make any kind of move. Anything else you can tell us about him?"

She shook her head. "Nothing. Except that I can't freaking believe this."

"Believe it. According to his record, Halley was in the Special Forces in Afghanistan during his military stint and damn good at removing the Taliban from his path."

A tech officer handed Griffin a tablet computer in a reinforced plastic case. It offered a greenish night-vision live view of Dean's house.

Griffin turned to Kendra. "If you're up for it, I want you to try to call his home number."

She stared at him. "You want me to call and talk to him?"

"Only when I give the word. He knows you, and he hasn't already seen us. Your caller ID won't raise any red flags. If he answers, keep him talking until our team can break in and rush him." He gave her a cool glance. "You appear reluctant. After all, it's for his safety as well as that of the personnel on the scene."

Lynch nodded. "Good idea."

She didn't know if it was a good idea or not. She was bewildered and uncertain of everything that was going on. But the plan appeared to offer the best chance for nonviolence. "Okay." Kendra pulled out her phone. "Just give the word."

San Quentin State Penitentiary
Execution Chamber

THE SUPERVISING PHYSICIAN, Dr. Edward Pralgo, stepped back from Colby and checked the IV lines he'd placed into two veins of the condemned man's left arm. Each line was running a slow drip of saline, primed for the three medications that would soon course through his system.

The doctor realized that his own hands were shaking. Hopefully not enough for anyone else to see. Any sign of psychological weakness would put him in front of a review board in spite of all his experience. Executioners were supposed to be above emotion. But executioners were also human beings, and he'd defy anyone not to have an emotional reaction toward Colby.

He exited the chamber and checked the printer outside, which was unspooling a long roll of graph paper. Sharp, jagged lines indicated Colby's heartbeat.

In the tiny adjacent anteroom, Dr. Pralgo picked up the tray with the three labeled syringes. He checked his watch—11:01 P.M.

The phone rang, and the execution supervisor picked it up. "Yes, sir." He hung up the phone and addressed the physician, as always, in the clearest and most direct language possible. "The order has been given by the warden. Please proceed."

Dr. Pralgo took a deep breath and stepped back into the execution chamber, where Colby was staring at the ceiling with his cold, dark eyes.

Dead eyes, the doctor thought, even though the man was still very much alive.

He administered the medications one syringe at a time: the first syringe, labeled sodium pentothal, was administered first to anaesthetize the condemned. Indeed, Colby quickly lost consciousness as it flowed from the IV though his eyes closed only slightly.

After a quick saline flush, the syringe labeled Pancuronioum bromide was injected to paralyze his system. After another saline flush, the syringe labeled potassium chloride was injected to place Colby in full cardiac arrest.

After a minute, Dr. Pralgo stepped over to the still-printing cardiac monitor.

Flatline.

He moved back to Colby's body and administered the simple tests that would indicate death had occurred. The pupil check, brushing the cornea for a blink reflex, and listening for any sign of breathing.

Pralgo had done this check hundreds of times in his career, but this was different. This was no ordinary human being, capable of love and being loved.

This was pure evil.

He turned toward the execution supervisor.

"Time of death—12:09 A.M."

Breaker Drive
San Diego

KENDRA LOWERED HER PHONE. "Nothing. Dean's not answering."

Griffin nodded and tapped his earpiece. "A couple of the officers just caught some kind of flashing in the living-room windows. They think it could have been his mobile phone lighting up when you called it." He ducked low and looked around the back corner of the armored van. "Move in when you're ready," he said into his headset.

Lynch pulled Kendra closer to the protective plates of the van, and they huddled closer to Griffin's tablet and its night-vision view of the house.

The night suddenly exploded with action!

Within seconds, the front yard was swarming with tactical teams, and she heard the front door splinter open even before she saw it happen.

Silence.

She saw the flashlights playing against the interior windows as the teams checked out the entire house.

No shots fired.

No shouts.

What the hell was happening?

After another two minutes, some of the officers emerged from the front door. The swagger and bold athleticism was now gone from their strides; their faces were drawn, and something was definitely different now."

"Clear!"

She heard the word several more times down the street. She turned to Griffin. "What's happened?"

He yanked off his headset. "There's a body inside."

"What? Whose?"

"We haven't made a positive ID yet. Give our guys a couple minutes, and we'll—"

"Screw that." She took off running for the house.

"Kendra!" Griffin shouted. He started after her, but Lynch grabbed his arm.

"It's too late. You'd have to knock her out to keep her out of that house," Lynch said. "What did they tell you on that headset?"

"Nothing good."

Kendra ran across the front yard toward the front door.

The cops and response-team members looked somewhat dazed and made no serious effort to stop her.

But as she reached the door a young officer stepped toward her. "Ma'am, you really shouldn't—"

Kendra pushed past him and ran through the splintered doorway. She stood in the foyer for a long moment, allowing her eyes to adjust to the dark living room. One of the officers helpfully, or perhaps cruelly, swung his flashlight to the middle of the room to show her what they had already seen:

Dean Halley's decapitated head.

It was impaled on a tall pole in the center of the room. The pole was held upright by a small light stand.

She couldn't breathe. Memories of that factory so long ago were there before her.

Heads on poles. Eyes glued open. Heads on poles.

"Oh, God . . ." She staggered backward, nauseous and dizzy. "No . . . No . . ."

"Kendra." Lynch was behind her. His strong hands gripped her arms, propping her up.

"It's Dean."

"I know."

"God in heaven. I can't believe it . . ."

Lynch wiped away the tears she hadn't realized were on her cheeks.

Only then did she look down at the oversized chair on the other side of the room, where Dean's headless corpse was seated. It was positioned comfortably, with hands on the end of each armrest.

As police flashlights played across the corpse, Kendra could see that Dean's shirt was unbuttoned.

Letters had been carved into his chest. A Latin phrase, she realized.

One of the cops crouched next to the corpse and tried to read it. "Meteor?"

"No," Kendra said numbly. "It says '*Mereor.*"

"*Mereor?*"

"It means . . . 'I win.' "

San Quentin State Penitentiary
Execution Chamber

WARDEN SALAZAR LOOKED DOWN AT COLBY'S FACE. Just as icy and cruel in death as in life, he thought.

The last of the witnesses had just left, and the execution team was prepping the body for transport to a waiting hearse.

"I want to see it," he told Hoyle.

Hoyle shrugged. "Whatever you say, sir." He stepped closer to Colby's body and moved aside his open shirt to reveal Colby's final message to the world.

There, scabbed and bloody, was scratched a single Latin phrase: *Mereor.*

San Diego
1:33 A.M.

"COME ON." LYNCH OPENED KENDRA'S passenger door. "I need to get you inside and give you a strong cup of coffee. I don't like the way you're looking right now."

"I'm okay." It was a lie. She felt frozen. The last hour she had spent at Dean Halley's house had been a nightmare. She had not been able to concentrate enough to find any way to help with the investigation. All she could do was to keep trying to connect that grotesque headless corpse to the sweet, humorous man she had begun to care about. Memories kept flooding back to her of Dean at that Starbucks telling her about his family and offering her some of his pastry. Dean whisking her mother out of that classroom and taking over himself. "But I can use the coffee. I'm . . . cold." She followed him to the door and watched him unlock it. "Though God knows I don't want the caffeine to keep me awake tonight."

"No, you want to block it all out." He headed for the kitchen. "And that's what I want for you, too. Just one night of rest and freedom before you dive into this horror again." He gestured to the chair at the granite bar in the kitchen. "Sit down. I'll have your coffee in just a minute." He set the K-cup in the automatic coffeemaker. He didn't look at her as he got down a cup from the cabinet. "You really liked him, didn't you?"

"He was a good guy. Kind of funny and sweet . . ." She swallowed. "Mom thought he was the perfect match for me. Nice, solid, and steady. She was hoping he'd be able to persuade me to—" She stopped and drew a shaky breath. "How am I going to tell Mom about this? She thought the world of him, and now he's—"

Head on a pole.

Headless corpse in a chair.

Mereor.

"You don't have to tell her yet." Lynch set the coffee in front of her. "Griffin is trying to keep the details of what happened from the media. You'll have a few hours at least."

"No more than that. I can't risk her hearing it from someone else." She took a sip of the coffee. It was hot and strong, and she needed it. "I just . . . don't know how yet. How can I tell her that Dean Halley died because she arranged a blind date for me with him? Because that's what happened, isn't it? Myatt saw him with me at some time or other and decided that he'd be a perfect chess piece in this game he and Colby were playing with me."

Head on a pole.

Back away. Don't think of that unspeakable sight.

"Myatt thinks he's won. He thinks he's hurt me."

"And has he?" Lynch asked quietly.

"Yes, he's hurt me. No, he's not won." She took another sip of coffee. "I just have to be able to think again. It may take a while." Her lips twisted. "But I may not be able to afford that time. He's closing in on me, isn't he?"

"Yes." He took his own cup from the coffeemaker. "But I won't let him get any closer. I have your back."

"Do you?" She looked at him over the rim of her cup. "That can be dangerous. Dean wanted to protect me, too."

"I have your back," he repeated. "There's no comparison between Halley and me." He added bluntly, "If anyone's going to end up on a pole, it's not going to be me. Or you."

Sledgehammer. But she welcomed that roughness at this moment. It soothed the rawness and shock and brought her back to what they were together.

"No, that's not going to happen again. I'll be sure—" Her phone rang.

San Quentin. Salazar.

She tensed. "It's Warden Salazar." On some layer of consciousness she had been expecting the call, but the night had been so full of horror that she had not been able to process it. Yet she knew that what was going on at San Quentin had been there, hanging over her through everything that had happened tonight. She punched the access button. "Kendra Michaels. Is it over?"

"Yes, Colby was pronounced dead at 12:09 A.M. I'd have called you sooner, but I had to make arrangements to get his body off the prison grounds as soon as possible." He added sourly, "Those anti-death-penalty demonstrators at the gates were having too much fun mugging for the cameras and burning me in effigy because I obeyed the law."

"Dead." She felt weak with relief. "Thank God. I knew it was going to happen, but I was afraid the governor would change his mind and give him life instead."

"That wasn't an option he would have chosen," Salazar said. "The voters would have sent him a clear message of disapproval at the next election." He paused. "And I admit I'm glad to be done with Colby myself. My duty is not to judge but to enforce the law. But I stared down at that ugly face twisted by evil and death when they were putting him in the bag and I felt that justice truly had been done."

"Not entirely. He should have died years ago. That's what the father of one of his victims told me very recently. That I should have killed him instead of just wounding him in that gully where we captured him."

"That's between you and your conscience."

"Yes, it is. But my conscience is screaming that I was wrong. If I'd killed him then, he wouldn't have been able to influence Myatt, and we wouldn't have had a whole string of new murders to deal with." And Dean Halley wouldn't have been one of them. He'd be riding his motorcycle and joking and living the good life.

"I was hoping your time with Colby would lead you to Myatt. I was sorry to have to ask you to Skype with him yesterday. I know it upset you."

"You had to do what you had to do. It was my choice. Thank you for phoning and telling me about Colby. I appreciate it."

"I wanted to bring you closure." He paused. "I was considering not telling you about Colby's last statement, but I decided you should know."

"Statement?"

"Not a verbal statement. He carved it on his chest. Just one word."

A chill went through her. One word.

"*Mereor*," she whispered.

He was silent. "Yes. It seems I made the right decision. Good night, Dr. Michaels."

She hung up the phone and turned to Lynch. "Colby died at 12:09 A.M."

"Hallelujah," he said softly.

She nodded jerkily. "Salazar said he wanted to bring me closure. Nice thought, but there's no way. Not while Myatt's out there acting like a Colby Wannabe."

"We've cut off the head of the snake with Colby's death."

"Some freaky snakes have two heads. Haven't you heard?"

"I've run into a few." He reached out and touched her cheek. "One victory at a time. We'll get Myatt, then I'll mount that two-headed snake on our living-room wall."

She smiled shakily. "But then we'd have to displace Ashley. All I want is to have him as dead as Colby." She added, "But we have to get him soon. He concocted this horrible bloody plan tonight to give his hero a glorious send-off. Or maybe Colby concocted it. The same word was carved on Colby's chest." She was feeling a panicky urgency begin to ice through her. "We have to stop Myatt in his tracks. We don't know who else is being targeted. Maybe I should go back to Dean's house and go over the forensic evidence. I should probably have done it tonight before I—"

"No," he said firmly. "Go to bed and get a few hours' sleep."

He was right. She was not much better mentally than she had been before.

And she still had to phone her mother and tell her that her good friend, Dean, was dead.

"I'll be in touch with Griffin," Lynch said. "If there's anything new, I'll wake you."

She put her cup down on the bar and stood up. "I'll see you in a few hours." She moved toward the door. Her smile was bittersweet as she glanced over her shoulder. "Too bad Dean didn't have an ironclad fortress like this one to keep that bastard out."

"Yeah, he was probably taken by surprise." Lynch stood looking at her. "I'm here for you if you need me. You know that, don't you?"

"I know it," she said wearily. "Thanks." She moved down the hall. Rest for a while, then call Mom. It was going to be a terrible conversation. But she wouldn't tell her right away about that horrible word that kept echoing in her mind.

Mereor.

"DEAR GOD," DIANE WHISPERED. "I can't believe it. Dean?"

"I can't believe it either," Kendra said. "I'm sick about it. I can imagine how you're feeling."

"I don't know how I'm feeling. I think I'm numb." She was silent. "No, I'm angry. I'm furious. That son of a bitch."

"Yes."

"I want to cut his throat," Diane said. "Dean was . . . special."

Kendra was silent.

"And you're feeling guilty. I can feel it," Diane said. "Don't be stupid. It wasn't your fault." She was silent for an instant. "You expect me to ask you to bow out because I'm afraid for you. I'm tempted to do it. But that won't help Dean, and it won't help you. Myatt is going to keep going after you because that's the nature of the vicious bastard.

Anyone who would go after a nice guy like Dean just to punish you will just keep on until someone stops him." Her voice was steel hard. "*You* stop him, Kendra. And if you can find a way, let me help. I'd like that, and I think Dean would like it, too."

"You can help by staying safe and far away from Myatt," she said unsteadily. "Is everything okay up there?"

Diane didn't answer for a moment. "We're protected and there have been no signs of Myatt. It appears he's been busy in other areas." She paused. "I'm going to hang up now. I'm going to have a good cry, then I'll call Dean's father and break the news to him."

"Good night, Mom. I'll call you tomorrow." She hung up the phone.

The call had been as difficult as she had thought it would be. Her mother had not responded how she had thought she would, but she was always unpredictable.

But her basic instincts were infallible.

She had realized that the first order of business was to mourn the dead. Dean Halley deserved that Kendra as well as her mother think of him and his life first. His murderer who had taken that life should be second on the list.

She lay down, her cheek on the pillow.

Good-bye, Dean. We'll miss you.

And she let the tears come.

CHAPTER
14

"WHAT IN HELL ARE YOU DOING HERE?" Griffin stood up from the desk at the front of the war room and strode toward Kendra, who had just stepped off the elevator with Lynch. "She was almost in shock last night, Lynch. Couldn't you keep her away from here for a while?"

"You should know better." Lynch put his hand on Kendra's shoulder. "She insisted. Even at my place, she spent the entire day poring through the prison logs you e-mailed her." He added dryly, "And here I thought my natural charisma and charm would be enough of a distraction."

"Yeah?" Griffin said. "No wonder she couldn't stop working the case."

Kendra turned toward Metcalf, who was trying to discreetly roll away the bulletin board with Dean Halley's grisly murder-case photos. "You don't need to do that," she said. "Believe me, those eight-by-tens are nowhere near as upsetting as it was to actually be there." She paused. "Or the memory that kept replaying in my mind all night."

Metcalf stopped. "I just thought—"

"Let him take it," Lynch murmured. "It's okay for you to be human, Kendra."

Kendra glanced at the board, but, in spite of her words, she found herself quickly looking away.

Dean.

Eyes glued open. Staring.

"You're right, Metcalf. Thank you." Kendra struggled to maintain her composure. Damn. This was even harder than she'd thought it would be. It was her duty to be here trying to do everything possible to stop that murderer, but Dean's death was too fresh in her mind. "Maybe you should move it to another part of the room."

Metcalf looked as if he wanted to offer some words of comfort, but he finally just turned and awkwardly moved the bulletin board away.

"You shouldn't be here." Griffin was frowning. "At least take another day or so. We have agents in the field following up on Colby's visitors and call logs. I haven't even received the preliminary forensics report on the Dean Halley crime scene. Go home, Kendra."

"I can't. I'd just go crazy. What are you and the team doing?"

"Not anything that's promising." Griffin checked his watch. "We're about to go into a teleconference with a profiler from Washington. You're welcome to join us, but you may find it as pointless as I will. I doubt he'll tell us anything our own profilers haven't already come up with."

He was right, not very promising, Kendra thought. She had hoped for more. But she turned and followed Griffin toward the desk. "If it's the only game in town, you can bet I'll sit in."

TRUE TO GRIFFIN'S WORDS, the meeting was a fairly pointless exercise, with few new insights. They were just wrapping up when a shrill, high-pitched beeping sound pierced the relative quiet of the war room.

A terribly familiar sound.

Lynch looked over at the large projection screen. "Is that what I think it is?"

Again, Kendra thought. The nightmare was beginning all over again.

"Shit!" Griffin abruptly cut the teleconference link. The agents around the long table bolted toward the front of the room.

As it had the night before, the beeping was coming from the phone-company technician's laptop. Once again, a red dot now appeared on the map.

Kendra's eyes widened as she jumped to her feet. She gazed up at the large projected map, which had remained unchanged since yesterday. Excitement was gripping her, taking her breath.

Excitement . . . and dread.

Have we got you this time, Myatt?

The technician was already looking at his laptop screen. "This is another one of the three phones we've been tracking, Agent Griffin. It just connected with the network."

Griffin shook his head. "Myatt used the other phone on a timer to draw us out to Dean Halley's house. He may be using this one the same way."

Lynch studied the map. "He's east of Descanso. It almost looks like—"

"Oh, my God." Kendra felt a sickening jolt, her gaze fastened on the map. It couldn't be true.

Don't let it be true.

Lynch nodded slowly as he saw her face.

"What's happening?" Griffin asked.

The worst thing that could possibly happen.

"He's found my mother and Olivia."

"MOM, YOU HAVE TO GET OUT OF THERE. Do you hear me? Immediately. Don't argue, just *move*."

"Hold on, you keep fading out. I'm out on the balcony, and I get lousy reception here." Diane moved through the house with her mobile phone, trying to find the spot with the best reception. She finally found herself in the living room. It was dark outside, and Nelson was turning off lights in the living room as he talked into his phone. He was standing straight and speaking in the clipped, efficient tone he adopted whenever he spoke to the Bureau higher-ups. Not a good sign, Diane thought.

"Now, what's happened?" Diane said into the phone. "Nelson is looking very . . . professional."

"Good. That's what we want from him. Myatt's found you. He's somewhere in your vicinity. Griffin's explaining it to Nelson right now. You're going to leave the house immediately and go to the Sheriff's Department in Julian."

"Wouldn't it be better for us to stay here and let the police and FBI come here? This could be your chance to catch this psychopath."

"No. We will *not* use you as bait. Do exactly as Nelson tells you to do. Okay?"

"I still think—"

"No. Mom, don't think. Please don't think. Just get the hell out of there. Where's Olivia?"

"In the kitchen. She's on her laptop."

"Good. Stay together. Do exactly as Nelson tells you."

"You already said that."

"Because I know you." She paused. "I love you, Mom."

"Oh, Lord. You're being sentimental. Now I *am* scared."

"You'll be fine. I'll see you in less than an hour."

Kendra cut the connection. Diane looked up to see that Nelson had pulled his automatic from the holster and was checking the cartridge.

"It'll be okay," he said.

"You sound as if you're trying to convince yourself." Olivia entered from the kitchen with her work knapsack slung over her shoulder.

"We have a bit of a situation," he said. "But nothing to worry about."

"Nothing except for the killer lurking outside. Excuse me for eavesdropping on your phone conversations, but since no one bothered to call me, I had nothing better to do."

Still holding the gun, Nelson picked up his phone and punched a number. He listened, then hung up. "No answer from Tad Martlin."

"That doesn't necessarily mean anything," Diane said. "The cell reception is spotty up here."

"True, but it's been a while since he checked in." Nelson walked to a front window and looked through a parting in the curtains. "The two of you wait here by the front door. I'll bring the car from the road and pull as close to the house as I can."

"You don't want us to go together?" Olivia asked.

"No. And don't bother with your luggage. We'll get it later. Right now, I just want to put some distance between us and this house."

Diane nodded. "Okay. The second you pull up in your car, we'll be ready to jump inside." She turned to Olivia. "When we go out the door, take my arm and I'll lead you to—"

"You know me better than that," she said. "I'll hear the car engine, it'll be no problem. Just worry about yourself."

"For some weird reason, that's scarier than worrying about you."

Olivia chuckled and reached out and squeezed Diane's hand. "Hey, I'll take care of you."

"How humiliating."

Nelson moved toward the door. "Sixty seconds, ladies. Be ready."

"Be careful," Olivia said.

Nelson was gone. They listened as his footsteps pounded the pavement outside.

"Come closer to the door," Diane said seconds later. "He said for us to be—"

Rat-tat-tat-tat.

The booming, staccato crack of gunfire outside.

"Don!" Olivia shouted.

A window shattered. Then another.

"Down," Diane shouted as she pulled Olivia to the floor.

Rat-tat-tat-tat.

The door flew open, and Nelson barreled through and hit the floor.

Rat-tat-tat-tat.

A lamp broke in the living room. Nelson swung his leg around and pushed the door closed.

He gritted his teeth in pain. "I'm hit."

"What happened?" Olivia ran over and knelt beside him.

"Somebody's firing from the bushes across the road. I couldn't even see him." Nelson gingerly touched the bloody wound at his side. "Shit."

Diane grabbed a throw blanket from the couch and wrapped it tightly around Nelson's midsection.

Rat-tat-tat-tat. A fresh burst of gunfire destroyed another window.

Olivia pulled Nelson's arm over her shoulders. "Can you stand?"

"Yes." He gasped in pain as she lifted him to his feet.

Olivia pulled him toward the back of the house. "We'll go downstairs to the basement. Diane, you told me when you took me around the house that there are no windows in a couple of the rooms down there on the lower level, right?"

"Right," Diane said. "One side of the house faces the road, the other the forest."

"We'll barricade ourselves in one of those rooms and wait for the cavalry to arrive. Sound like a plan?"

"Yes." Diane moved cautiously and threw the lock on the front door.

"Good." Olivia started for the door leading to the basement. "Now help me get Don down the stairs."

Together, they carefully helped Nelson down, one step at a time. More gunfire rained behind them.

Chase/Wyndham Heliport
San Diego, California

LESS THAN A MILE FROM THE FBI field office, Kendra, Lynch, Griffin, and Metcalf emerged from the elevator atop the forty-four-story Chase Wyndham Building. A six-seat helicopter was warmed and waiting on the helipad.

"Our response teams are on the way," Griffin yelled over the sound of the rotors. "We have ground units and another helicopter tactical team en route."

Lynch frowned absently, as he stared at his phone, but he said nothing until after they climbed into the 'copter and closed the door behind them. "I can't get through to Tad Martlin," he said. "I tried to call and send a text, but there's been no answer." He looked grimly at Kendra. "I don't like it."

"We'll be there in fifteen minutes," Griffin said. "The helicopter response team may be there even sooner. Don't worry."

Don't worry?

Kendra gazed at him incredulously as the 'copter lifted off and made a wide arc over the city of San Diego. Fifteen minutes could be an eternity. Fifteen minutes could be life or death. Her mother's life, Olivia's life. There wasn't any way she could do anything else but worry.

OLIVIA STOPPED TO ADJUST Nelson's weight on her shoulder as they finally reached the lower floor. He was weaker now, and she could hear his breathing becoming more labored. "Don, how are you doing?"

"It hurts like hell."

"I know. Hold it together for me, okay?" Olivia suddenly turned, her head lifting. "What's that smell?"

Diane sniffed. "Gunpowder?"

"No." Olivia shook her head. "That was my first thought but it's . . ."

"Smoke's billowing through a doorway in front of us," Diane said. "There has to be a fire up ahead." She looked behind her at the stairs. More pungent smoke was curling from that direction. "And behind us."

It suddenly hit Olivia. "This is too much like another one of Kendra's cases . . . I remember the killer burned people alive in their homes, sometimes after sealing them inside."

"Myatt's set the house on fire," Diane said. "My lungs are burning from the smoke. Get down. Close to the floor . . ."

She and Olivia dropped to their knees beside Nelson and scrambled across the floor. They coughed and breathed through their sleeves in a vain attempt to filter the smoke.

"We can't barricade ourselves down here. Scratch that plan. But there's a way to get out of here," Diane said. "I think I saw an exit that led to the woods when we were touring the house."

"Then let's find it," Olivia gasped, her lungs searing. "I hear the flames. Do you see them yet?"

"Can't see—" Diane barely managed to choke out her words. "Too much smoke. I can't tell which way to go. It's like a maze down here."

But they couldn't just stay here, Olivia thought. They had to find a way out, or they'd be unconscious in minutes. Think. Find a way.

She suddenly stiffened as a thought came to her.

"Maybe . . ." She unzipped her knapsack. "Pray for American ingenuity and just plain luck, Diane."

"American ingenuity?"

Olivia was no longer listening. She could do this.

God, she hoped she could do it.

She felt around in her knapsack until she located her plastic sample pack. She opened it and felt inside, trying to touch each product and identify.

There it was. She'd located the object she'd been looking for. Finally, she pulled a contraption that resembled aviator sunglasses with attached earbuds. She put the glasses on her face and inserted the foam earbuds.

"What are you doing?" Diane coughed.

"It's a gadget I'm reviewing. I hadn't gotten around to testing it. It appears I'm going to do it now. I'm sure the inventor didn't mean it to be used for a situation like this. It uses sonar . . ." She started crawling. "Follow me."

With Olivia as their guide, they pushed on through the black smoke, navigating the twists and turns past the laundry room, spare bedrooms, and recreation room.

Even as visibility dropped close to zero, Olivia could hear the glasses emitting a series of beeps that distinguished between walls and passageways every time she turned her head. She stopped as she was about to take a right turn. She placed her hand against the wall. "This one's warm. Quick, the other way."

They retraced their steps through the poisonous fog until Olivia found another hallway that would take them into the TV room.

"There's no outside door here, but I remember a window across the room." Diane quickly closed the hall door behind them.

Diane turned on her phone, and the illumination was just enough for them to see to make their way to the room's single window, some six feet over the floor. Diane dragged a stool over, climbed onto it, and slid open the window.

Fresh air blew into the smoky room.

"Careful," Nelson said. "He may be out there. We have no idea which side of the property he's at right now."

Diane crouched lower and coughed again as more smoke poured

into the room from the hall, smothering the fresh air from the window. "Well, we can't stay in here."

Nelson pulled out his gun. "I'll go first. Then I can cover you if I need to."

Olivia looked at him skeptically. "Can you make it?"

"Yes." He sounded indignant, but he winced as he climbed on the stool. "It will be painful, but I can do it. It's my job. And the two of you have had to treat me like a basket case." He peered through the window, then hoisted himself up and through it. He rolled onto the ground just a foot below the outside of the window. He took cover behind a bush outside, then motioned for Diane to join him.

"Olivia, he just gave us the sign," Diane said. "You first."

"No."

"This isn't the time to argue, dammit."

"No arguments. You're not as young as I am. I'll help steady you. Then you guys can pull me out if I need it."

"Okay." Diane pulled herself through the window. "But I'm insulted that you think I'm decrepit. I'll get you for that." She started to turn around but heard a coughing behind her that told her that Olivia had already climbed out the window.

"So much for pulling you out," Diane whispered to her, as they crouched next to Nelson.

"Anything, Don?" Olivia asked Nelson.

"Looks clear." He turned back and looked up at the house, which was rapidly becoming engulfed by flames. "But we need to get the hell away from here. You and Olivia run for the woods." His hand tightened on his automatic. "I'll be ready to cover you if he's still out there."

"OH, MY GOD."

Kendra looked out of the helicopter window at the burning vacation house, a flaming torch on the dark hillside.

"I'm sure they got out," Lynch said quietly.

"How do you know?" Kendra snapped. "How can anyone know?" She was dialing her phone. "I can't get through to Mom."

"I don't know. But your mother is smart, and so is Olivia," Lynch said. "And Nelson is a good agent. They'd find a way to get out of that inferno."

"Myatt is down there," Kendra said. "Even if they're out of the house, they might be running straight toward him."

"You're right." Griffin lowered the microphone on his telephone headset. "But I've just had word that the response team is down there. They've called the paramedics. The paramedics are four minutes out."

Kendra felt as if she were going to jump out of her skin. "Paramedics? What the hell happened? Have they reached them? How are they?"

"We'll find out soon." Griffin held up a finger as he listened. He leaned toward the pilot. "Did you get that?"

"Got it," he said. "We'll be on the ground in sixty seconds."

The helicopter was banking around the burning house and hovered over an empty field down the road. Kendra looked down and saw that the response team's helicopter had already landed there. Its searchlights illuminated the field.

What was she going to find down there?

In less than a minute, Kendra unbuckled herself and jumped out of the helicopter. She bolted across the small field, which was lit up by crisscrossing searchlights from the landed copter, which also provided fierce wind and noise from their rotors.

There they were! At the edge of the field nearest the road. They were being treated by personnel of the response team.

And they didn't look good.

"Mom?"

Kendra dropped to her knees in front of the spot where her mother, Olivia, and Agent Nelson were being treated. Blackened faces, torn and rumpled clothes. And they were each wearing oxygen masks.

Kendra took Diane's hands in her own. "Are you okay?"

Diane pulled off her mask. "Agent Nelson needs help. Immediately. I've been telling them to fly him to a hospital. They're not listening to me."

Kendra looked over to see Nelson on his back, his shirt off and bandaged around his torso. He was being tended by two agents, one of whom leaned over and replaced the mask over Diane's nose and mouth.

"Ma'am, the paramedics will be here any minute. They'll help him." From his steely tone, it was obvious Diane had been getting on his every last nerve.

An encouraging sign, Kendra decided with relief.

Diane said something that caused her mask to fog. Kendra figured it was a good thing they couldn't understand her.

She turned to Olivia. "How are you feeling?"

Olivia just nodded. She was staring down at Nelson and holding his hand. Then she looked at Kendra. "He took a bullet for us. Myatt was out there waiting."

"Can you tell me what happened in there?"

"It's better if they don't talk." The response-team agent leaned toward Kendra. "They've already discussed it with the commander when we first found them. He'll fill you in."

Kendra looked over and saw that Griffin and Lynch were already on it, intently discussing the situation with the response-team commander.

She saw red flashers, strobing over the hillside. Relief. Two paramedic units rounded the bend and stopped on the side of the road.

As the paramedics jumped out and started to work, Kendra joined Lynch and Griffin. "Will somebody please tell me what happened?"

As they brought her up to speed, she could see that Lynch was clearly troubled. "Still no sign of Tad Martlin?" she asked.

She'd clearly hit a nerve. "Not yet."

"I'm sure the paramedics will take Olivia and my mother to the hospital, along with Agent Nelson. I need to go with them."

"Of course."

"So what are you going to do?"

"I'll stay here a while and join the search for Martlin." Lynch shook his head. "I'm the one who brought him into this."

"He had to know what he was doing when he took this job."

"Did he?"

"As much as any of us did."

Lynch nodded. "Keep in touch. I'll let you know what we find out here. The local police have already put up roadblocks on the highway. No one's driving off this mountain without our knowing about it."

"If he's still on the mountain." Kendra turned toward Nelson, who was on a gurney being placed into one of the paramedic units. "Well, that's my cue. You know the expression, 'Doctors make the worst patients?' Whoever said that never met my mother." She glanced back at Lynch. "Be careful."

"You too."

She looked out into the darkness of the woods as she moved toward the paramedic unit. Was Myatt there, watching, planning? Surely not. This area was crawling with agents and response teams now.

But who knew what Myatt was thinking or planning. His move in attacking her mother and Olivia had been very bold, and it had almost been successful.

When this had started, she had never dreamed that it would lead her down this twisted road. Now the only thing of which she could be certain was that Myatt would take any chance, go any distance.

And take down anyone who got in his way.

"YOU'RE JOKING." Diane stared incredulously at the young female emergency-room doctor. "I am not staying the night here. Cut this bracelet off me right now."

"Ma'am, it's for your own safety and wellness . . ."

"I'm quite safe and well, thank you. I'll make that decision."

Kendra rolled her eyes. "Give my mother a sedative and a plausible horror story. Those are the only things that will work, trust me."

The doctor, who appeared to be in her midtwenties, frowned in puzzlement. "A sedative and a . . ."

". . . horror story. Tell her what can happen if she goes home right now."

"We try not to unnecessarily frighten our patients."

"Frighten her," Kendra said. "It's absolutely necessary."

"Don't listen to her," Diane said to the doctor. "My daughter is just—"

"You could die," the doctor said bluntly.

"That isn't funny," Diane said.

"I assure you it's not. But you and your friends breathed poison, plain and simple. It's unavoidable in a house fire. We have no idea what toxins are only now entering your bloodstream. We need to observe you for the next four to six hours. During that time, you can help yourself by keeping your mask on and breathing oxygen."

"But I already feel better."

"That's good. But I served my residency with a physician who treated a fire victim who unknowingly breathed toxic levels of chorine and hydrogen. Apparently, the house's molding and baseboards were made of a plastic material that released those elements at high temperature. The patient had only a minor cough, but he went home and several hours later his respiratory system shut down, and he died."

"That's a horror story, all right," Diane said sourly. "Now I think I really need that sedative."

On a gurney a few feet away, Olivia pulled off her mask. "For the record, I really didn't need to hear that."

"I'm sure you'll both be fine," the doctor said. "It's just a precaution."

Olivia sat up and leaned toward Kendra. "What about Don?"

"I'll check on him again. They told me he'd be in surgery at least another hour and a half."

Olivia frowned. "That sounds like big-time surgery. Can you check now? Please?"

"Sure." Kendra shrugged. Her current duties here at the hospital appeared to be everything from trying to keep her mother in line to aid and comfort to the lovelorn. "I'll be back in a few minutes."

"It's not what you're thinking," Olivia said. "After all, Don could have been killed protecting us."

"I'm not arguing." Kendra smiled as she moved toward the exit. "I'm grateful to him, too. You'll have your report."

FBI San Diego Field Office

"MR. DILLINGHAM . . ." SPECIAL AGENT Saffron Reade stepped off the elevator and smiled as she greeted Bill Dillingham in the lobby. "I'm Agent Reade. I've heard so much about you. I'm very happy to meet you."

Dillingham struggled to stand up from the long wooden bench near the reception desk. He wore high-waisted knit slacks and a short-sleeve white dress shirt and carried a large sketch pad.

Reade had heard that the freelance sketch artist was in his mid-eighties, but he appeared to be an even older man.

"Hello, young lady." He frowned. "I was hoping to see Kendra Michaels. I know it's late, but I thought she might still be around."

Reade smiled. "She and the rest of the team are out in the field tonight. I got stuck heading up things here. Good thing, or I would have missed you."

"Yeah."

Her brows rose. "Won't I do?"

"I guess so. It's just that Kendra and me sort of . . . bonded. We're kinda on the same wavelength."

"Try me. Can't hurt, can it?"

"No." He shrugged. "But don't be too sure it was a good thing that you stayed around to see me. I might be just wasting your time." Dillingham held up his large sketch pad. "Kendra asked me to draw up some alternate sketches of that psychopath she saw last week. She wanted me to research all the different ways someone might disguise themselves without its looking like a disguise, you know? Fake teeth, nostril inserts, cheek and jaw liners . . . Based on what she gave me, I made up a few dozen alternates."

Reade took the pad and flipped through the pages. "Amazing. You do great work, Mr. Dillingham. I've seen some of your sketches before, but it's wonderful to finally meet the man behind—"

She froze.

This had to be some kind of sick joke.

Dillingham touched her arm. "Agent Reade?"

"I don't believe it," she whispered. She stared at the sketch for a good fifteen seconds longer before looking up.

This was no joke. Dillingham seemed completely mystified by her reaction.

"I need you to come upstairs with me. I want you to tell me exactly how you came to draw this."

"Uh, sure."

She looked at the sketch again. A sickening sense of dread was rising within her. "But first I have some phone calls to make."

Sharp Grossmont Hospital
La Mesa

KENDRA STEPPED OUTSIDE THE HOSPITAL with her phone pressed against her ear after passing two nurses who had testily pointed to the NO CELL PHONES signs in the corridors. She had been trying without success to connect with Lynch when a call came for her. She hit the talk switch.

"Dr. Michaels?" It was a British-accented voice that she didn't recognize.

"Yes?"

"We haven't met yet, but my name is Bobby Chatsworth. How are you this evening?"

Ugh. "Mr. Chatsworth, this really isn't a good time."

"Please don't hang up, Dr. Michaels. I know what's happened. We're in San Diego, and we've been monitoring the police bands."

"Why would you be doing that?"

"Frankly, to get some footage of you in action. In lieu of an actual interview with you. There's the very real possibility your killer may strike again, and if you arrive on the scene, we'd like very much to be here on the spot."

"My mother and friend are in the hospital, Mr. Chatsworth. Your show is the furthest thing from my mind right now."

"Naturally. But I wonder if you might grant us just a few minutes of your time. A few quick sound bites, and we'll be off to England and out of your hair forever."

"Mr. Chatsworth, I don't—"

"You have to admit, it's tempting." His voice now came not from the phone, but behind her.

She whirled around. Bobby Chatsworth, all beard and glasses, smiled as he walked across the nearly empty parking lot. He lowered the phone from his ear. "What do you say, Dr. Michaels?"

Kendra put down her phone. "Unbelievable. You're persistent, I'll say that for you. Did you bring your crew here, too?"

"They're five minutes away, getting rooms at the Old Country Lodge down the highway. You can join me down there, or I can bring them here. Either way, after the next half hour, you'll never have to see any of us ever again."

She didn't need this, Kendra thought impatiently. She opened her lips to refuse him once again.

She suddenly went still.

Oh, God. Of course.

She felt icy fingers run up her spine to her neck.

Don't let it show. Don't let it show.

Stay cool.

"Have your crew here in twenty minutes, Mr. Chatsworth. I'll give you five minutes in front of the camera." Kendra turned and headed up the walkway to the hospital side entrance.

"Very gracious of you," Chatsworth said. "But before we do that . . ."

A cloth snapped in front of her nose and mouth.

She tried to wrestle free.

But Chatsworth was strong. Too strong.

Not Chatsworth, she thought, panicked.

Myatt.

He whispered into her ear. "Nice try, Kendra. But you have a terrible poker face."

Darkness.

PAIN. HORRIBLE, skull-shattering pain.

Kendra snapped awake. She couldn't breathe.

She'd just vomited, she realized, and she was helpless to move and clear her air passages with anything but her throat muscles. She coughed and gasped until she could finally suck back some oxygen.

Darkness. Darkness everywhere. Where in the hell was she?

There was movement beneath her body. Then it hit her. She was spread out in the back of what must be Chatsworth's SUV. The backseats were folded down, and a tarp covered her entire body. Her feet were tied together, and her arms were tied behind her back. The vehicle was moving, and its tires met the road with an airy two-tone hum that she identified as highway blacktop. Was he taking her into the desert?

"I would have been so disappointed if you'd choked to death, Kendra." Chatsworth said from the driver's seat. "Vomiting is an unfortunate side effect of the anesthetic."

Kendra tried to speak, which caused her to gag for a few moments. Finally, she got the words out. "Where . . . are we going?"

"I'm surprised. After all we've been together . . . After all the questions I must have provoked in your mind and imagination during these past few days, that's what you ask me?"

"Sorry . . . to disappoint you."

"For instance, I took a real risk letting you see me the other night. But I wanted to see you, talk to you, touch you. You should be flattered. It was only because I had the highest respect for you, Kendra."

"What . . . a lucky woman I am."

"It was worth the risk. I was thrilled that my disguise was able to fool Kendra Michaels."

"How did you—do it?"

"I had to shave the beard. This particular woolly beard is a fake, but only for the past few weeks. I had to perfect it. I figured if my broadcast audience couldn't detect it through the magic of high definition, you couldn't. And you had no way of knowing that Bobby Chatsworth uses dermal tape to pull back the skin above the temple hairline to remove the forehead lines. And my erstwhile police-officer image wore a set of dental appliances and cheek fillers that further altered the face. Of course, Chatsworth's glasses also helped. You know . . . I don't even wear glasses. It's all part of Bobby Chatsworth's costume. He's a character I created. But I guess we all create characters for ourselves as we move through life."

"So you're a philosopher. How very . . . deep."

He laughed. "Perhaps I've been getting carried away. It's just that I've been looking forward to talking to you about this."

"You wanted to brag, gloat. I've met men like you before. And one woman."

"No you haven't," he snapped, suddenly angry. "There are no others like me."

"Funny thing for a copycat killer to say."

"Copycat? No such thing. I bested them all and showed how it should be done."

Drop it. She might be pushing him toward the edge. She shifted uncomfortably in the rear compartment. "I can't feel my arms."

"Those ropes around your wrists have been soaked in water for days. And I learned to tie my knots from the Bristol University Royal Naval Unit. I know you have no weapons because I searched you before I tossed you back there. So by all means, try your best to get free. It's not going to happen."

"What an efficient serial killer you are. Colby taught you well."

"Yes. And no." He drove in silence for a moment. "I'm not new to the game. I've done this before. But it was Colby who made me an artist. He showed me that it takes more than just skill. It takes imagination. Why do you think people still remember Jack the Ripper? It wasn't just because it was so shocking for the time . . . Throughout history, there have been many more gruesome and prolific killers. The real reason was his letters to the media. Once you capture the public's imagination, you will live forever."

Kendra tugged at the ropes. Chatsworth was right. She wasn't going to slip out of his knots. So she had to go another route. Think. He had said something about weapons and searching her . . .

"Forever? That's a funny thing to say less than twenty-four hours after your buddy Colby dies," she said. "He's already on his way to obscurity."

"Not likely. Long after everyone has forgotten those Scotland Yard detectives, people still remember Jack the Ripper. And soon, everyone will forget you ever existed, Kendra Michaels."

Weapons. He'd said she'd had no weapons. But what about that strange blade she'd taken from Wallach and tucked in her jacket pocket. She'd completely forgotten it in all the action that had followed. Was it so slender he'd missed it? She started to try to manipulate her tied hands toward her pocket. Keep him busy and talking.

"Why did you try so hard to interview me?" she asked. "Was that part of your thrill sport? To go face-to-face with me in front of a national viewing audience, gambling that I wouldn't recognize you?"

"Not at all. Actually, I was never willing to take that chance. I knew you wouldn't consent to that interview. You've turned down every request over the years, many from journalists much more respectable than I. But I knew you and the FBI were checking out all the journalists and others who had visited Colby. I decided to put myself in front of you on my own terms. I chose the video footage you saw of me, and I made bloody sure it was from a distance and angle that couldn't relate to the dashing, fake, police officer you saw. So although my name would inevitably come up on the list of Colby's visitors, they would know you had seen Bobby Chatsworth on the DVD my producer sent. I was sure they'd think it would be unlikely I'd push for a face-to-face interview if I had anything to hide. That's why I sent my producer to try to woo you."

"She has no idea she's working for a monster."

"Oh, she knows I'm a monster. Just a different kind. It became necessary for me to frequently disappear, of course, following story leads that would never quite pan out, so that I could pop back and forth to San Diego and play my game with you. But it was worth the effort." He paused. "It's interesting you could tell I was suppressing an accent during our brief conversation the other night . . . But it wasn't a Southern drawl, it was my distinct West Country British accent I was trying to hide. A few more words, and a few more minutes of conversation, you might have pinned it down. Still, I chalk that up as a victory."

Kendra tried to clear her head. She was still woozy from the anesthetic, but she needed desperately to focus on checking for that needle knife.

And also focus on unsettling him, knocking him slightly off balance. Undercut that sense of control serial killers craved. She had an idea that Chatsworth had an intense desire for both control and self-aggrandizement.

"You didn't do too shabbily that night. But lately, you've been getting sloppy. My mother and my friend, Olivia, are still alive and doing fine."

He chuckled. "Of course they are. I never intended to kill them."

"Seriously? 'I meant to do that' went out in the fourth grade."

The knife was still in the pocket! She could feel the outline half-in, half-out of the lining. Now to get it out and work on those ropes.

"Oh, Kendra. I had every confidence at least one of them would find their way out of that house. You see, I had a small problem. Adam Lynch had you squirreled away in that magnificent bunker of his, and when you're not there, you've been almost constantly under his watchful eye. I needed to do two things, draw you out and draw him away from you. The attack on their mountain retreat was enough to draw you and the entire San Diego FBI field office out here. I knew you would feel compelled to accompany your dear, sweet mother to the hospital, but I knew that the disappearance of Lynch's mercenary compatriot would also leave your protector in the woods for the next few hours."

"You killed Martlin."

"Oh, he was very tough. But the thing about tough guys is that it's harder to be tougher than a bullet. Especially if it's aimed by someone of superior skill and intellect. No one will find him until at least daybreak."

Kendra felt as if she were going to be sick again. Another life lost.

"So you see, with a bit of planning, problem solved. I was waiting for you near the hospital before you even left San Diego. I have to credit Colby. He taught me the value of planning several steps ahead."

"Colby only used you."

"It was a mutually beneficial relationship. I did some things for him on the outside, but he had funds he could tap to help things along, and he was incredibly resourceful. We were able to move things back and forth through the prison's food service vendor, a contact Colby cultivated himself. Those items included the blouse you found at that young woman's house. There were things with his DNA at each of the crime scenes, but Colby insisted that they be difficult to find. I think he was hoping you'd be the one to find them. Which you did on the first crime scene after you joined the case. Well done."

"I don't want your praise."

"But I feel that I have to pat you on the head. You've made the game so enjoyable. However, you should really praise me, too. I've explained how brilliant I've been. Is there anything else you'd like to know?"

"Just one question. Now what?"

"Can't you guess? Why, Kendra, of course you've made the logical deduction." He was silent a moment, then he whispered, "Now I finish Colby's work for him."

CHAPTER
15

Mount Laguna

"GET OVER HERE, LYNCH," GRIFFIN SAID. "I'm at the helicopter. I have something you've got to see."

"Ten minutes. I'm waiting for a report on the searchers in the west quadrant."

"Now," Griffin said. "We may not have ten minutes." He hung up the phone.

Shit.

Lynch didn't hesitate. He didn't like the sound of Griffin's tone. In four minutes, he'd left the woods and was striding toward the helicopter, where Griffin was standing with Metcalf. "So what's so urgent?"

"Reade sent me a sketch by Dillingham that he told her he'd been working on for Kendra. Did you know about it?"

"Yeah, she told me she'd asked him to try to do a mock-up of Myatt without disguise."

"He did it." Griffin handed him his laptop computer. "Take a look."

"Holy shit." Lynch's hands tightened on the computer. "This is Bobby Chatsworth."

"Clearly," Griffin said.

"Incredible," Lynch said.

Metcalf took another look at the sketch. "According to Reade, the sketch artist has never seen Chatsworth before. This was just a concept sketch based on disguises Myatt might have used."

"Brilliant," Lynch murmured.

"Reade got hold of Chatsworth's producer. The team left for England this morning. Everyone except Chatsworth. He's still here."

Lynch tensed. "Have you called Kendra?"

Griffin and Metcalf exchanged glances. "That's why I wanted you to drop everything and get over here. She's not answering her phone."

"What?"

"And she's not at the hospital, either," Metcalf said.

Lynch asked slowly and carefully, "Then where the hell is she?"

"No one knows."

"Don't tell me that. Chatsworth has her. You know it and I know it." Saying the words made that truth more stark and terrible. "Now tell me how we're going to get her back. Chatsworth has to have his own phone. He won't get rid of it if he doesn't know that we've zeroed in on him. Have you started the trace?"

"Reade started that trace before she sent me the sketch. We'll have it very soon."

"Soon?" Lynch started cursing as he started walking toward the burning embers of the house.

"Where are you going?" Griffin called after him.

"I'm taking Nelson's car."

"Where?"

"I'll start with the hospital, unless you can find me a more productive place to go." He stared at him over his shoulder, and said with icy softness, "And you'd better find me that phone location in a damn big hurry. Or I just might be more angry with you than I am with Chatsworth. You don't want that, Griffin."

Jurupa Mountain
Riverside County, California

STILL, DEATHLY SILENCE.

There was nothing else to hear after Chatsworth cut the engine. They had left the paved roads fifteen minutes before, and Kendra had been aware of a slight incline ever since. A slight odor of pines had found its way into the passenger compartment, destroying her previous belief that they were heading for the desert.

Chatsworth climbed out of the vehicle and opened the rear door. He yanked the tarp off and dragged her out of the car by her jacket collar. It was still nighttime, but the full moon bathed the area in a bluish glow.

Chatsworth cut the ropes around her ankles. "Do you know where you are?"

Kendra looked around while she tried to steady herself. They were on a hilltop, at the end of a forest. "Should I?"

"I believe it will come back to you. It's one of your best efforts." He motioned with a long knife. "But it didn't happen quite here. It's up ahead. Come along. I can't wait to show you."

"BAD NEWS," GRIFFIN SAID when Lynch answered. "Chatsworth has dropped off the network."

Keep cool. "Entirely?"

"He hasn't pinged a cell tower in over thirty minutes. Either his phone died, or he decided to yank the battery. Maybe he doesn't want to leave tracks."

Lynch pulled off the road and stared at the map on his tablet computer. "It looks like he was heading toward Riverside County, or maybe San Bernadino."

"That's a lot of territory."

"Unless . . ." Lynch's mind was racing. "Think about your bulletin boards of Kendra's old cases."

"What are you getting at?"

Lynch stared at the map for another long moment. "I have an idea where he's taking her. Griffin, get your helicopter in the air. Quick." He muttered a curse. "I'm close, but I may not be close enough."

"YOU'RE NOT MOVING FAST ENOUGH." Chatsworth pushed her down the path. Kendra stumbled, her hands still bound behind her. She'd managed to whittle at the ropes while in the SUV, but it had been slow going, and she'd only managed a partial cut. She was tempted to try to break the ropes now and make a move, but the timing had to be right, or it could be disaster. If the ropes didn't break, she might not have a second chance.

"Tell me something, Kendra. Back there at the hospital . . . Something tipped you off to me. It was like a light went on. You suddenly knew with whom you were dealing. What was it?"

"Your fingers."

Chatsworth held up his hand. "My fingers?"

"Yes. You have small, dark bruises on the fingers of your right hand. I knew that your victim at the club, Danica Beale, bit her attacker on his right, gloved hand. There were brown leather slivers between some of her front teeth. Not many men wear any kind of gloves around here, nor have them readily available if needed. Much less brown leather ones. But I guess they're more common where you're from. I saw part of a brown leather glove poking up from your jacket pocket."

He smiled. "Very good."

"Also, there were only four cars in the hospital lot. Three had condensation on the windows, meaning they had been there for a while. The one that didn't was obviously yours. It was an Infiniti SUV. That's the engine I heard starting and driving away the other night at Corrine Harvey's house."

"You never disappoint, Kendra." He stopped and grabbed her arm. "Here we are." He gestured to the bottom of the hill at an abandoned, water-filled quarry, its sides cut in straight, vertical sheaths. "Now do you remember?"

She inhaled sharply. "Jurupa Quarry. Mary Delgado." She turned. "And those trees . . ."

"It's where Burton McNair tried to hang his final victim. He murdered and hung three others in the forests around here: equidistant north, south, and east of the spot where the sheriff's deputies killed his father a year before. Here, due west, you kept him from completing his work and killing Mary Delgado." He smiled. "Tonight, you're going to help me complete it for him in a much more satisfying way."

"You're going to kill me and hang me from one of those trees."

"By George, I believe she's got it."

"Oh, yes, I've definitely got it." Keep him talking; she had the ropes frayed and was pulling gently on them.

"As you saw each of your cases re-created, you had to know this was how it would end. My final re-creation must feature you as the victim. It's the final movement of my symphony."

And he was getting ready for that symphony to end with a giant crescendo.

Time was running out for her. She had to make her move.

He took a step closer, his knife ready. "I'm almost sorry, Kendra. I know there will be others, but none I'll enjoy as much as you. You are unique."

She looked down, and her shoulders tensed as she prepared to jerk with all her strength on the ropes.

He nodded. "Unfortunately for you, sometimes history can be rewritten."

"And sometimes it can be repeated."

The ropes flew from her wrists!

She leaped forward and jabbed her carved-bone blade into Chatsworth's stomach.

He swung with his own knife. Kendra ducked, and jammed her blade into the middle of his back. But he was moving, and it was a glancing blow.

Not deep enough. Not deep enough.

But it was deep enough for agony. He howled in pain and tried in vain to reach the protruding blade.

Kendra ran a few yards away before turning. "Not a large blade but sufficiently lethal."

Chatsworth felt his stomach and stared incredulously at his bloody hand in the moonlight. He glared at Kendra. "You think you've won?"

She backed away. "It's not a game."

He reached into his jacket and pulled out a handgun.

Shit.

She dashed into the forest as he fired two shots at her.

She ran deep into the dense foliage, trying to avoid anything that resembled an actual path. His footsteps pounded behind her, crunching leaves and snapping branches.

Another gunshot. A tree branch exploded near her head. She turned sharply, threw herself to the ground, and rolled a few yards down a gentle slope. Hell, that blade in his back had barely slowed him down.

She froze, holding her breath.

He'd stopped somewhere behind her, she realized. Waiting for her to make another move, to reveal her position.

Waiting for her to do something stupid.

A full minute passed. Then another.

A brisk wind kicked up, rustling the trees and giving her an opportunity to move down the hillside undetected.

But also offering him an opportunity to sneak toward her.

She crept farther down the hill, using the shadows as a cloak against the stark moonlight.

There was a clearing ahead. No good. She'd be a sitting duck out there, even more limited in this direction. She was at the quarry's rim, some forty feet above its granite bottom. There was water, but she had no way of knowing if it was twenty feet deep or ten inches.

An indefensible position if ever there was one.

She looked back up the slope.

Was he still waiting for her?

She slowly, quietly made her way back, timing her movements to the gusts of wind.

"Kendra!"

Pounding footsteps. Crunching brush.

Coming her way.

She broke into a run.

But something caught her ankles and sent her flying. She hit the ground hard.

She rolled over and saw what had tripped her.

A length of rope, twenty feet or more, had been pulled taut between the trees.

Chatsworth's rope. It had to be Chatsworth's rope.

She jumped to her feet, but in that same moment, another rope snapped over her neck.

She couldn't breathe.

Chatsworth whispered in her ear. "You can't ruin my symphony, love. I've worked too hard." He applied even more pressure.

She felt her eyes bulge and her tongue swell as he choked the life from her. She could see their shadows in a death dance on the forest floor. Then her vision clouded, but she could see the shadow of the blade still sticking from his back . . .

Not deep enough. Not deep enough.

She bared her teeth, and with every ounce of energy left, hurled herself backward. They both tumbled to the ground.

The ground met the blade and drove it deep into Chatworth's back.

He grunted, and his grip loosened.

Kendra rolled away and jumped to her feet. She stood over him, her breath coming in gasps. She watched as blood bubbled from his wounds. He writhed in agony as the carved blade protruded from his chest. "Take it . . . out."

"No way. That blade is a gift from Stevie Wallach's father. It was meant for your hero, Colby, but you'll do as well. It's incredibly thin and weighs only a few ounces. I guess it was easy to miss with a quick frisk." She added fiercely, "Or maybe I had a little help from Stevie. What do you think?"

Chatsworth's eyes were wide, glittering, and full of hatred as he gazed up at her. "You *bitch*. Do you still think you've won? I'm too smart for you. *We're* too smart for you. This is only the first battle."

"You're a dead man, Chatsworth." She stared coldly down at him. "There will be no other battles. Smart? You're just a two-bit killer who decided to ride the coattails of a scumbag who was only a little more intelligent than you. He used you to amuse himself during those last months of his life. He pulled your strings, and you jumped."

"No!" His cheeks were flushed. "You don't know anything. I was important to him. We were like brothers. He said that I was his eyes, his hands, his sword." He coughed, and a thin rivulet of blood flowed from the corner of his mouth. "I gave him everything he asked of me. Well, almost. He kept talking about you and the gully. Always . . . the gully. It wasn't my fault that I couldn't give him you. But that's okay, sometimes I thought he didn't really . . . want me to be the one to deal with you anyway. Moriarty. He called himself . . . your . . . Moriarty."

"Sherlock's greatest enemy? That's ridiculous. He flattered both himself and our relationship. I'm no Sherlock, and he certainly didn't have the brains of a Moriarty. He was only a butcher who ended up on that execution table at San Quentin." She added fiercely, "As for you, you'd have ended up the same way if you hadn't decided to give Colby one last gift. You shouldn't have come after the people I love, and you shouldn't have come after me, Chatsworth."

"Almost . . . made it." His eyes were closing. "Do you think I'm afraid? I'm not afraid. Colby said that we're above fear. The two of us are . . . different. I'll get . . . over this. Just like him."

"You can't get over death. You're dying, Chatsworth."

"No, you're wrong. You think you're so smart, but you're wrong about me . . . wrong about . . . Colby."

"Open your eyes and look at me," Kendra said. "You'll see that I'm not wrong. I want you to know this is the end. I want you to know that you're on your way to hell, and nothing can stop it. Open your eyes, dammit."

He slowly opened his eyes.

"That's right, look at me," Kendra said harshly. "And think about all those poor people you killed at Colby's bidding. Think about how you're going to burn for all eternity because of them."

She'd gotten through to him at last. For an instant, she saw realization and fear in his eyes. Then they were once more filled with a wild hatred. "The end? Never . . . you'll never be . . ." He coughed, struggling for breath. "Closer . . . come closer, bitch. You've got to hear . . . Listen . . ."

She leaned closer, until they were only inches apart. "I can hear you, Chatsworth. What are you trying to say to me?"

"Only . . . this." His eyes were burning into hers as he whispered, "Tetro . . . dotoxin." Then his lids were closing. "Mereor . . ."

He was dead.

And Kendra was transfixed, frozen, as she stared down at him.

Tetrodotoxin?

She slowly sat back on her heels.

"Kendra?" She was barely aware of Lynch kneeling beside her. "Thank God. I heard the shots when I was down the road. Are you hurt?"

"No." She moistened her lips. "I killed him, Lynch. But I don't know . . ."

"You're in shock." He put his arm around her. "You're shivering . . ."

"You're right, I'm cold. I'm cold to my soul . . ."

"Because you killed that bastard? You know he deserved it."

"Yes."

"Look, you don't have to stay here with him. Let's go back to the car. I've called Griffin, and his team is on the way by helicopter. It's over, Kendra."

"Is it?" She was still looking down at Chatsworth's face. "He didn't think so." Her mind was in high gear, thinking, searching, discarding, searching again. "And I'm not sure that I'm—" She broke off and leaned forward, her hands moving over Chatsworth's body, searching his pockets.

"What are you doing?" Lynch asked. "What are you looking for?"

"I don't know. It could be nothing." She'd found a wallet. Nothing in it but a driver's license and some cash. She dropped the wallet and jumped to her feet. "Maybe in his car . . ."

She was running back to Chatsworth's SUV, where it was parked on the hill.

"What the hell?" Lynch was running after her.

She was already in the front seat of Chatsworth's SUV when he reached her. She'd grabbed the iPad from the front seat and was going through the menu. "I'll check the memos. You check the glove box."

"And what am I'm looking for?"

"Information."

"What kind of information?"

"I'm not sure."

"Great." He opened the glove box and started to go through it.

"Nothing in here but some receipts, gloves . . ." He reached back. "And maybe . . ." He pulled out a small, ringed notepad. "This?"

She gazed at it for a moment and then slowly took the notebook. "Maybe . . ." She flipped open the cover. "Addresses . . ." She felt suddenly sick. "One of them is Dean Halley's." She flipped more pages. More names, more places. The Go Nuclear Club, her own address . . .

She flipped more pages.

Tetrodotoxin.

The word jumped out at her.

And beneath it another name and address.

She frantically flipped other pages. Nothing. No other writing for the rest of the notebook.

"You found what you were looking for?" Lynch asked.

"I think so. Maybe not enough. Give me a minute. I have to think about it." She closed her eyes. Connect all the dots. Put it together.

Impossible. It was impossible.

But impossible was only a word.

And she was terrified that word had become reality.

"You'll notice I'm being very patient," Lynch said mildly.

She opened her eyes. "Come on." She jumped out of the car. "Or give me your car keys. I don't care which."

"I'm coming. And it's Nelson's car." He beat her to the car. "Where are we going?"

"I know the way. It'll be quicker if I drive." She held out her hand. "Please, don't argue, Lynch. Not now."

His gaze narrowed on her face, and he dropped the keys in her palm. "Though it's against my better judgment. I'm not sure you're in any shape to drive."

"That makes two of us." She got into the driver's seat. "Get in, Lynch. We've got to get going."

"Why the hurry?"

"Get in." The car roared as she turned on the ignition. "I have to *know . . .*"

Coachella Valley, California

KENDRA PUT ON THE BRAKES, and the car skidded to a stop. She stared out into the darkness, her hands clenched on the steering wheel.

Fear.

Death.

It was here again, taking her breath, assaulting her.

"May I ask where we are?" Lynch asked. "What is this place?"

"Hell," Kendra said unsteadily. "It's hell."

"Hell?" Lynch gazed thoughtfully at the cliffs and the rutted landscape. "Everyone has their own hell. I should have guessed this would be yours." He gazed down into the deep gully a few yards away. "That's the place where they discovered all those bodies. The place where you captured Colby."

"Yes." She couldn't take her gaze from the gully. "The bodies have been gone a long time. Why do I still smell the stench?" She had to move. She couldn't just sit here. She grabbed her computer and got out of the car. She knelt in the sand and flipped it open. She stayed there, staring blindly at the screen.

Do it.

Her shaking hands flew over the keys. She pulled up the site and scrolled down.

Find the name.

Find the name.

Find the name.

Halfway down the page she found the name.

She couldn't breathe. She felt sick.

"Okay. Tell me. Let me do something besides worry, dammit." Lynch was a shadow standing over her.

She nodded jerkily. "I was looking for a name. The name that was in Chatsworth's notebook. I . . . found it."

"Where?"

"San Quentin personnel." She was dialing her phone. "But I have to be—it doesn't have to be true. I have to call Warden Salazar."

Salazar answered in three rings. He sounded drowsy. "I wasn't expecting to hear from you this soon, Dr. Michaels. And certainly not at this hour of the night. Is there something I can do to help you?"

"Yes. I need information about someone on your staff. Edward Pralgo. Does he have a wife or daughter named Maria?"

"Yes, Maria Pralgo is his wife." Salazar answered, puzzled. "Do you need to talk to her? I can give you Pralgo's phone number, but he may be difficult to reach. He and Maria left on vacation this morning. Hawaii, I think. He said he needed it." He added grimly. "I can't blame him. We all need a spot of paradise after the ugliness we've gone through."

"Give me the number." She quickly took it down. "Thanks."

"Do you need their address?"

"No, I have the address." She hung up. The next moment, she was dialing the number she'd been given.

No answer.

No voice mail.

"The phone's been turned off," she told Lynch as she hung up. "And I'd bet that so have Pralgo and his wife, Maria."

"Pralgo?"

"Dr. Edward Pralgo, the physician who was in attendance at Colby's execution. It wasn't coincidence that name was in Chatsworth's notebook. He had a duty to perform."

"Colby ordered him to kill the physician who was scheduled to perform his execution? Some kind of weird revenge?"

Kendra didn't answer. She was once more delving into information on her laptop. She had to be sure she wasn't mistaken.

Tetrodotoxin.

There it was, in as much detail as was available.

She carefully scanned the info, then slowly closed the computer. "No revenge. Not on Pralgo. He was just a means to an end."

"What end?"

Her head lifted, and she gazed down at the gully. "Colby is still alive, Lynch."

He was silent, his body stiffening with shock.

"No way," he finally said. "It couldn't happen. There are too many checks and balances. Even Salazar examined his dead body."

"He's *alive*. Chatsworth whispered two words to me before he died. One was *Mereor*. The other was tetrodotoxin."

"*Mereor* means I win. The other?"

"The explanation of why he thought he and Colby had won. Tetrodotoxin is a substance sometimes called the Romeo drug because in the death scene Romeo used a drug that faked his death. It's also known as the poison in pufferfish and has been used by voodoo shamans to induce zombification. It lowers your pulse and body temperature while also creating an artificial coma. Unless screened for, it can easily be mistaken for death. But it has to be properly administered, or it can cause the paralysis of the diaphragm and can actually cause death." She swallowed hard. "Colby had no intention of dying in that execution chamber. He set Myatt to seeing that he had an out."

"Pralgo?"

"The physician was in charge of administrating the fatal dose and declaring the criminal dead. He'd be the one to switch the doses. The tetrodotoxin would do the rest."

"This is all supposition."

"Until we find Pralgo. That may be difficult. My guess is that Maria Pralgo was kidnapped by Chatsworth and held captive to force

Pralgo to do what Colby wanted. After the fake execution, Pralgo would have cleaned up any evidence of what he'd done and gone to a meeting place where he'd been promised that his wife would be released." She shook her head. "Pralgo must have been desperate to believe that anything he could do could keep his wife from being killed."

"You think they're both dead?"

She nodded. "Chatsworth killed Dean, then had time to fly up to San Quentin and take care of Pralgo and his wife. I doubt if we'll ever find them. Colby would have told Chatsworth that no one could know that he wasn't dead." She smiled bitterly. "And Chatsworth was always very efficient obeying Colby."

"Colby's body?"

"Probably cremated. Why don't you check with Salazar?"

"I will." He moved a few feet away and dialed his phone.

Kendra didn't bother listening to him. She was only aware of the whistle of the wind through the canyons and the yawning cavity of the gully only yards away.

Are you out there, Colby?

"Immediate cremation." Lynch was back. "And the remains tossed in the Pacific Ocean off the Oregon coast early this morning."

"Chatsworth probably substituted bodies. And the funeral director will also have an unfortunate accident."

"But Chatsworth is dead now."

"That only means Colby will have to take care of his own dirty work." She shuddered. "And he's much better at it than Chatsworth."

"You can't be sure of any of this. No proof. Griffin would say that it's your imagination brought on by stress."

"And what do you say?"

"I say that you're the smartest woman I know, but I hope to hell you're wrong."

"So do I." She slowly got to her feet. "But I don't believe that I'm that lucky." She moved closer to the gully. There were rocks along the edge. She half expected to see one stained with blood, Colby's blood. Crazy. She bent over and picked up a good-sized black rock and looked down at it. No blood, of course.

Not yet. That was in the next act, the next story.

She closed her eyes and listened. Was that the wind . . . or something else?

"Kendra." Lynch's hand was on her shoulder. "Why are we here? Why were you determined to come to this godforsaken place?"

"Not because I wanted to be here." Her eyes opened. "But Chatsworth said that Colby was always talking about me . . . and the gully. Always the gully. And I remembered when I was Skyping with Colby he mentioned the gully and said it was important."

"And you thought that Colby might be here?"

"I didn't know. It might have been some kind of twisted message to me. It's not really reasonable. Colby wouldn't have had time to be running all over the state. And tetrodotoxin has a lingering effect in most cases. He probably wouldn't have the strength to even get out of bed for a little while. If I'd reasoned clearly, I wouldn't have panicked and come here."

"But you did panic."

"Because he's not like anyone else." She moved still closer to the rim of the gully. "He's Satan Incarnate. And he might force himself to get out of a sick bed and come down here to torment me."

That sound . . .

It was the wind. It had to be the wind.

But that wind breathed of Colby and carried the scent of death and those kills that had been here in this foul gully.

"He's not here," Lynch said. "You've gone through hell for the last few days, and I don't want to see you hurting like this. Let's go home, Kendra."

She nodded. "In a minute."

"Now." His hands fell on her shoulders, and he turned her to face him. "If Colby wanted you to come here, we're not going to satisfy the bastard by staying and brooding." He cupped her face in his two hands and looked her in the eyes. "We're going to ignore him until we're ready to go after him, then we're going to skin him alive. Okay?"

"How . . . violent." Yet his harshness was sending a surge of warmth and comfort through her. She was not alone. If Colby was out there, she would not have to face him by herself. She dropped the rock on the ground. "But then it's natural that you would be ready to confront anyone who—"

"Hush." He kissed her, hard. "No more analyzing my motives or telling me what I want or don't want. Accept or walk away." He kissed her again and drew her back from the gully. "But I'd probably follow you. Now can we go home?"

"It's your home, not mine."

"Correction. Until Colby is no longer a factor in either of our lives, you don't get more than a few yards away from me. Look what happens when you do. I told you once that I had your back. I can't do that long-distance."

And she didn't want to leave Lynch. Not yet. She wanted his touch, his humor, his strength. She didn't know where they were going after tonight, but he was her anchor in this storm. "I . . . guess I could stay at your place a little longer. After all, it won't be forever."

"No?" He smiled faintly. "We'll have to see, won't we?" He stepped back and picked up the stone from where she'd dropped it. "You won't need this." He reared back and threw the stone as far as he could. She heard the stone hit the canyon wall. "When the time comes, I'll find you another weapon that will be much more efficient."

"I'll find my own weapons." Once more, she moved away from him to the gully's edge.

The wind was still moaning.

Death was still here.

Together with memories of horror that would never leave her.

And the fear that the monster was hovering close.

All of those sensations and emotions were still as alive as they had been moments before.

Yet everything was different now. *She* was different. She had let Colby and the shock intimidate her, and it had taken Lynch to jar her back to sanity.

The memory of the term Colby had carved on his chest returned to her.

Mereor?

Screw you, Colby.

I'm the one who is going to win.

She turned and moved back toward Lynch.

"Finished?"

"No. Not finished." She impulsively stood up on her toes and gave him a quick kiss. Why not? She wanted to do it, and Lynch had been entirely too much in control of their situation. She might not be sure where their relationship was going, but she had no intention of having a passive role. Then she strode toward his car. "Watch me. I'm just beginning."